SPARROWHAWK

Book Three
CAXTON

A novel by

EDWARD CLINE

MacAdam/Cage Publishing
155 Sansome Street, Suite 550
San Francisco, CA 94104
www.macadamcage.com

Library of Congress Cataloging-in-Publication Data

Cline, Edward
    Sparrowhawk book three : Caxton / by Edward Cline.
      p. cm. -- (Sparrowhawk series ; bk. 3)
    ISBN: 1-931561-53-2 (Hardcover : alk. paper)
      1. Virginia—History—Colonial period, ca. 1600-1775—Fiction.
I. Title: Caxton. II. Title.
PS3553.L544S626 2003
813'.54—dc22
    2003019403

Manufactured in the United States of America.

10 9 8 7 6 5 4 3 2 1

Book and jacket design by Dorothy Carico Smith.

SPARROWHAWK

Book Three
CAXTON

A novel by
EDWARD CLINE

MacAdam/Cage

The special province of drama *"is to create…action…which springs from the past but is directed toward the future and is always great with things to come."*
— Aristotle, *On Drama*

CONTENTS

Foreword ix

Chapter 1: The Visitors 1

Chapter 2: The Town 12

Chapter 3: The Plantation 25

Chapter 4: The Ball 33

Chapter 5: The Encounter 43

Chapter 6: The Empty Houses 58

Chapter 7: The Empty Houses 68

Chapter 8: The Newcomer 81

Chapter 9: The Master 87

Chapter 10: The Host 99

Chapter 11: The Olympians 108

Chapter 12: The Governor 114

Chapter 13: The Freeman 125

Chapter 14: The Rivals 135

Chapter 15: The Conduit 142

Chapter 16: The Riddle 155

Chapter 17: The Hiatus 162

Chapter 18: The Journey Home 171

Chapter 19: The Homecoming 174

Chapter 20: The Member for Swansditch 184

Chapter 21: The Voyage Home 195

Chapter 22: The Bellwether 203

Chapter 23: The Autumn 207

Chapter 24: The News 212

Chapter 25: The Words 217

Foreword

The complaint most often lodged against a certain genre of fiction is that, "Things like that don't happen in real life!" or, "Life isn't like that!"

But, they do. And, it can be like that.

Case in point: The American Revolution — a heroic and successful revolt against tyranny, resulting in the establishment of a republic (if we can keep it, to paraphrase Benjamin Franklin) whose government was charged with protecting and upholding life, liberty, and the pursuit of happiness — and property, which facilitates and is integrally linked to the first three political ends. If judged by the criteria of Romantic literature — it being, in novelist/philosopher Ayn Rand's words, a "category of art based on the recognition of the principle that man possesses the faculty of volition" — then the founding of the United States was the most glorious and dramatic political event in human history, unimaginable in fiction before then, and virtually unprecedented since, whether in "real life" or in fiction.

Most nations can claim a literature, in the form of novels, plays, or epic sagas or poetry, that dramatizes the early histories of those countries. Britain, France, and Spain come to mind. But, except for a handful of novels that dramatize, usually in superficial costume dramas or in sheer action at various levels of literary worth, specific periods or events in American colonial history, America has no such literature. A large body of novels exists for the Civil War, the Indian Wars, even World War II. The colonial period's list is pitifully, almost scandalously short. Representative of this specific subgenre is James Fenimore Cooper's *The Last of the Mohicans*. The *Sparrowhawk* series of novels represents, in part, an ambitious attempt to help correct that deficiency.

I say "in part," because my overall end is to write a story that interests me as a writer, and not specifically to contribute to this country's literature. That could well be a consequence, but it is not my motive. However, I am not unmindful of that consequence, and so this series will also attempt to do justice to the founding of the United States. And doing justice to it has meant understanding, in fundamentals, what moved the Founders to speak, write, and act as they did. Those fundamentals were *ideas*.

Except for some "cameos" by the Founders, such as Patrick Henry and Thomas Jefferson, this series does not dramatize the characters and actions of real historical persons. Instead, it focuses on the intellectual and moral development of two men, Jack Frake and Hugh Kenrick, Englishmen who come to the colonies and who reflect the moral and intellectual stature of the men who made this country possible.

Jack Frake, a boy who was brought here as an indentured felon, and Hugh Kenrick, an aristocrat who was sent here to complete his education, are two variations on the same theme: the inviolate, rational, self-made individual. As a former smuggler, Jack is a veteran of harsh conflict, social ostracism, and criminal defiance. As a critic of the customs and conventions of his time, Hugh is a literate rebel against hypocrisy and venality. Jack receives his education in a Cornwall cave, tutored by a colorful outlaw; Hugh, his in the safety of his Dorset home and in the best schools in London. Yet, although a social chasm separates their origins, both men meet at the same point of independence and self-reliance, and make decisions that affect the course of their lives.

This third volume opens in colonial Virginia. Jack and Hugh, however, are introduced in the first two titles of the *Sparrowhawk* series, which are set entirely in the England of the 18th century, in the decades immediately preceding the beginning of serious conflict between the mother country and her colonies. England was the proper setting for the outset of this series, for it was chiefly British political ideas and philosophy, espoused by 17th century thinker John Locke and his contemporaries and predecessors, that animated the colonials throughout the 18th. *Book Three: Caxton* moves from the stark cliffs of Cornwall and the roiling streets of midcentury London to the deceptively placid rivers, hills and towns of colonial Virginia.

Alarmed by a stealthy, and later blatantly aggressive encroachment on their constitutionally guaranteed rights by Parliament and King George the Third, American political intellectuals advocated and applied these ideas to their own lives to a degree unimaginable to the British political establishment. Unimaginable, and inimical to it, for while that establishment paid lip service to life, liberty, and property, in fact it largely rested on a corrupt and corrupting system of unquestioning servitude, arbitrary expropriation, and a resigned tolerance of that servitude, expropriation, and corruption.

The taking of such ideas so seriously by men that they would pledge their lives, fortunes, and sacred honor to fight for them was both inimical to that establishment, and nearly a personal affront to 18th-century

Britain, which prided itself for being the freest country on earth, which many patriots and persecuted individuals from other countries looked to as a beacon of hope or chose as a place of resident exile.

However, American political intellectuals were steeped in Roman and Greek history, as well as British and Continental political philosophy, and learned from it, drawing from it important lessons of cause and effect, of means and ends. As British legislators grew more arrogant and implacable in their demands on the colonies, the well-read American "activist" would have been knowledgeable enough to remark: "When Tiberius asked Cato why the Dalmatians revolted from Rome, he replied that it was 'because the Romans sent not dogs or shepherds, but wolves to guard their flocks.'" And, he would have subsequently concluded that he was not a member of anyone's flock, needing neither trained dog, nor gentle shepherd, nor predatory wolf to live his own life for his own reasons.

If conflict is the driving force of plot, then *Sparrowhawk* is a plotted saga. Jack and Hugh may meet at the same point of independence, and even become friends, but is their relationship smooth and frictionless? If it isn't, why isn't it? As one character in this present volume remarks: "One of you is the needle, and one of you the north." Who is the ideal, and who is the aspirant to that ideal? That is for readers to find out. And, having found out, to read on to learn why.

Historical fiction differs from "contemporary" fiction only in the amount of research required to re-create a period's culture and society. Other than that, plot, characterization and action should be its chief attributes. Difficulties may be imagined in that one's characters are moving and thinking in a period defined by its recorded events, and so the element of volition surely must be compromised. Not necessarily. In the *Sparrowhawk* series, history is always in the background, and its characters are the story's movers.

Also, accuracy in re-creating a period is of paramount importance, but should not govern the course or content of a story. License may be taken and accepted, so long as it captures the essentials of a period's customs, practices, and institutions. If this were not true, historical fiction would be impossible to write. Victor Hugo could not have had Quasimodo pour molten lead onto a 15th-century mob from the gallery of a cathedral in *Notre Dame de Paris*, and Hemingway could not have had Robert Jordan blow up bridges in *For Whom the Bell Tolls* in 1930s Spain. Edmond Rostand's *Cyrano de Bergerac* could never have flashed his sword in 17th-century France, and Robert Bolt's (or Terence Rattigan's) T. E. Lawrence could never have taken Aquaba in *Lawrence of Arabia* (or in *Ross*) during World War I. The events depicted in these and other works of historical fiction didn't happen in "real life," and often their authors "fudged" on insignificant historical details to make a point. In fiction, and especially in historical fiction, what might or ought to have been is more important than what actually happened.

This is the crucial difference between historical fact and historical fiction. Aristotle emphasized the distinction over 2,000 years ago in his *Poetics*. He and John Locke, though they never set foot in America, were this country's chief philosophical founders. And *Sparrowhawk* will be judged, I hope, a worthy testament to their continued role in men's lives and minds.

Long live Lady Liberty!

Chapter 1: The Visitors

In early October, 1759, the sloop *Amelia* dropped anchor at Caxton on the York River. From Philadelphia she carried cargo, visitors, and news. The cargo was expected, as were some of the visitors. The news was not.

It was good news, and important news, and it brought elation to the Virginia town, prompting some men to propose endless rounds of toasts in the taverns, and some women to kneel in prayer in thanks and gratitude. Others thought that the news deserved a regular celebration by firing the old cannon that stood on the sheriff's property and holding a dance. One small planter was so excited that he put his twelve-year-old son on a horse and sent him off to Williamsburg with the news. Reverend Albert Acland, pastor of Stepney Parish Church, was pressed by a number of citizens to ring the church bell, but he advised waiting until the news was confirmed.

The news curtailed curiosity and speculation about two of the visitors who stepped off the sloop. They were strangers. One was a man of about forty, the other a young gentleman of nineteen or twenty. Both were finely dressed in clothes of the very best quality. They were the last passengers to step off the *Amelia*, once it was secured to the finger pier and the gangway lowered. The older man was courtly but amiable, the younger grave in the set of his face, almost forbidding. In the older man, there was a slight hint of deference to the younger. Once ashore, he made enquiries at the customs house, and paid a pair of idle boys to carry his and his companion's traveling bags and follow him and his companion up the dirt road to the town above the bluff.

Three men were expecting the strangers, who had come on business, but did not meet them, for the sailing time from Philadelphia to the York River could have lasted between two and four days, depending on the winds and the water. These three men were Arthur Stannard, Ian McRae, and Amos Swart. Stannard was the consignment agent for the London tobacco merchants Weddle, Umphlett and Company. McRae was the York River's sole Scottish factor, representing the Glasgow tobacco merchants Sutherland and Bain. Together, they were the principal creditors of Amos Swart, whose plantation was ordered into receivership by a county court in lieu of large and long-standing debts. Swart was persuaded to liquidate his debts in a single stroke by selling his property, which consisted of nearly one thousand acres of arable land, a great brick house and its outbuildings, livestock, wagons, tools and other implements, the indentures of five servants, and thirty slaves. He agreed to accept whatever price and terms a buyer might reach with Stannard and McRae, and to vacate the property once the sale was registered with the Queen Anne County court.

Swart had tried, in the summer, to placate his creditors by holding a lottery, offering as a prize the unconditional, ten-year lease of three hundred acres of his best land for a penny a year, and the free use of some of his slaves to clear and cultivate it. The proceeds from the ticket sales would have erased some of his debt. But few men purchased the tickets. Swart was not liked. He had married into his property — Brougham Hall — and out of his class. To the gentry, he was crude, obnoxious, unread; little better than a fur trapper from the mountains. To other, smaller planters, he was a cheat, a liar, and a thief. To all he was a rogue who had come from nowhere and ingratiated himself with the late, respected Covington Brougham, and had married his daughter, Felise. The daughter died mysteriously one night four months after their marriage. Title to Brougham Hall reverted automatically to Swart.

That had been six years ago. The townsmen, planters, and sheriff all suspected murder. The charge could not be proved. Brougham Hall went into decline. Swart owned smaller properties to the west, in other counties, and it was said that these were as badly managed by him as was now Brougham Hall. Residents of Caxton regarded Swart as a blot on their town's reputation as a loyal and prosperous community; he was as repellent as a pirate; he was a seducer of virtuous women and wives; a corrupter of youth; and certainly not a crop master.

When the lottery failed, Stannard and McRae formed an alliance and sued Swart. The nine-man bench of the county court, composed mostly of planter gentry, examined the case and with ill-concealed alacrity ordered Brougham Hall into receivership. Advertisements were placed by the creditors in the *Virginia Gazette* and the Caxton *Courier*, which appeared twice a month. A stray copy of the *Courier* found its way to Tun Tavern in Philadelphia. The older stranger and his companion patronized that establishment, had seen the advertisement, and an exchange of letters between them and the creditors had led to the visit today.

The older gentleman's name was Otis Talbot, of Talbot and Spicer, Philadelphia merchants. He was acting by proxy for Baron Garnet Kenrick of Dorset, England, having been granted the power and means to purchase any property that the baron's son expressed an interest in. By written agreement, once the son reached his majority at the age of twenty-one, title to such property would automatically revert to him.

Talbot's companion was Hugh Kenrick, recently graduated from the Philadelphia Academy. He was nearly twenty.

They made their way to the house of Arthur Stannard on Queen Anne Street, the town's only thoroughfare. The news spreading through Caxton was old news to them. They understood its significance as well as any Virginian.

France had lost Canada — and, as a consequence, North America.

*   *   *

Quebec had fallen, and the French had lost their ablest general there, Louis Joseph de Montcalm de Saint-Veran. His error — and it was not so much an error as an only choice — was to fight the British on their terms, in the first Continental style battle in North America. He and his army of regulars and Canadians awoke on the morning of September 13th to find 4,500 British regulars arrayed against them, ready for battle or siege, on a plateau called the Plains of Abraham. In an unusual and daring maneuver — unusual and daring at least for a British general — Brigadier General James Wolfe had overnight slipped his army up the cliffs from the river so quietly, completely, and successfully that not even Montcalm's sharp-eared Indian allies detected the move. When dawn came, it revealed the scarlet menace. Montcalm, desperate to remove both the British army and the Royal Navy from the St. Lawrence River, so that supplies for his garrison could arrive for the winter without impediment, had no choice but to face Wolfe. Wolfe, too, was desperate, because winter was coming and he needed to capture Quebec before the river froze and he and the Navy were penned in.

Montcalm met the challenge, and marched out his army. It advanced *en masse*, in straight lines, to within fifty yards of the enemy to trade fire. The two lines of scarlet fired a pair of devastating volleys into the French, then followed with a bayonet charge. The Canadian militia broke first and ran, then the regulars. Montcalm, wounded in the stomach, died before Quebec was abandoned by the French Governor-general and forced to surrender. Wolfe, wounded three times, died on the field, a happier man than Montcalm.

France was fated to lose North America, no matter how long that theater of war lasted. Its imperial policy differed radically from Britain's. It was not conceived to encourage colonization and the development of agriculture or industry. The French were there to literally skin the continent for as much as they could get — in the fur trade. Their military presence was wholly dependent on a corrupt civil government in Montreal, parsimonious largesse from a French king and his advisors, whatever it could wring in taxes and obedience from a handful of local French farmers, and what little it could buy or steal from New Englanders. On the other hand, Britain's military presence was sustained by the British-nurtured civilization on the Eastern seaboard, together with a colonial animus for French policies. Wolfe could have met disaster on the Plains of Abraham, and it would not have mattered. In time, Canada would have become British.

To the colonists, the surrender of Quebec, and a year later of Montreal, meant the elimination of the French threat from the north, and also easier settlement of the west. It meant the end of "Papist" designs on the colonies and the preservation of English liberties they enjoyed. It meant a British Canada. It meant a secure northern frontier.

A British Canada. To Parliament, to Secretary of State Pitt, to the Privy Council, that meant quite different things, but this was something that would not become apparent for a long time.

For Virginians, the war with France in North America was almost as distant a conflict as the war in Europe, fought as it was on the far frontiers of the colonies. The past disasters of the British army, balanced by its more recent victories, did not immediately affect the citizens of Caxton. Britain was out of the European part of the Seven Years' War, fighting it by proxy with subsidies to Frederick the Second of Prussia. His changing fortunes, and those of his enemies the French, Austrians, and Russians, were of only passing interest to most colonials. George the Second may have gasped in horror, and grown livid with outrage, when the French occupied his electoral domain of Hanover, and when his son, the Duke of Cumberland, threw away a victory by assuming that he had been bested at Hastenbeck by another third-rate general, and signed the humiliating treaty of Kloster-Zeven two years ago. Virginians, however, merely shrugged their shoulders. The war in Europe was being fought over issues, claims and lands that they and their forbears had disowned long ago.

Neither did the war affect Virginians much in the purse. The colony's chief export, and the basis of its prosperity, was tobacco. While French and British navies and privateers preyed on each other's sea commerce, British merchantmen were able to sail regularly, under a flag of truce, to French ports with cargoes of tobacco bought by the Farmers-General of the Revenue, the French state tobacco monopoly, and the largest single buyer on the world market. Both Crowns needed the revenue generated by that trade in order to prosecute the war. The same *concordia discors* had been in effect during King George's war, or the War of the Austrian Succession. If the arrangement seemed paradoxical, or suicidal, or venal, the observation was noted by only a very few minds. The era abounded with such contradictions: If the French were gracious, civil, and cultured to a fault, but employed Indian allies specifically for their reputation for unmitigated savagery and the terror they could instill in English settlers and soldiers, then the British were stubbornly arrogant, presumptuous and hard-nosed, but basked in the demonstrable superiority of English common and commercial law.

* * *

"Do you trade in the leaf, Mr. Talbot?"

"Only occasionally, Mr. Stannard. My goods are decidedly *inflammable.*"

This remark caused the parties gathered in Mr. Stannard's parlor to chuckle in amusement. Talbot added, "Mr. Spicer and I correspond almost exclusively with the firm of Worley and Sons, of London, and we trade mostly in dry goods, perishable only through an act of arson or nature."

"I see," said Mr. Stannard. "Worley and Sons? I've heard of them."

"They are Mr. Kenrick's family's principal agents there." Talbot nodded to his companion. "Mr. Kenrick has recently divided his time between his education and our office."

Hugh Kenrick said, "I have spent some years handling made goods, Mr. Stannard. I wish now to try my hand at producing them, in order to more fully appreciate their value."

Mr. Stannard grinned a little at this confession of ambition, then frowned. "Have you any experience in raising tobacco, Mr. Kenrick?"

"None, sir."

"With all due respect, sir, it is not merely a matter of planting a seed and watching it grow."

"I am aware of the constant attention required by tobacco, Mr. Stannard."

Talbot said, "My companion has taken an especial interest in the planters west of Philadelphia, and has invested some time in observing their practices and methods."

"Their art does not differ greatly from that practiced here," Hugh said. "This region, however, has the advantage of a longer growing and curing season."

"Yes, that is very true," conceded Mr. Stannard.

"Undoubtedly, Mr. Swart has retained a staff who manage his business and crops," suggested Talbot.

"Oh, yes. Of course. But they are a very unhappy lot, at the moment."

A floor clock in the parlor struck three o'clock. Stannard gestured to the tea service that sat on a small table between the seated men. They had already had the beverage. The guests shook their heads. "Well," Stannard said, "it would be unfair to Mr. McRae if I continued our interview in his absence. I shall send word to him and to Mr. Swart that you gentlemen are here. And, you must find lodging for the night. I recommend Mrs. Rittles's boarding house, and if she has nothing that you approve, then Mr. Gramatan's inn may oblige you. You must have passed those establishments on your way here. Perhaps you would like to attend to that now, sirs, while I arrange for us to meet again at Mr. Gramatan's inn. He has the best fare in Caxton, and we can engage a private room there to discuss our business."

Hugh and Talbot rose. "That sounds agreeable, sir," Talbot said.

The agent walked the pair to his front door. "Supper at seven, then, at the Gramatan Inn." He paused. "Oh! Forgive me for asking this, sirs. But if the property is attractive to you, how would you propose to pay for it?"

"With a private draft drawn on Swire's Bank in London, sir," Hugh said.

"Swire's Bank, you say? Well, I've heard good things about that enterprise. Yes, very good things, indeed."

Talbot asked, "Who are the prominent planters here, Mr. Stannard?"

"Reece Vishonn, of Enderly — that is the name of his place — to the east of town. Ira Granby, of Granby Hall, which neighbors Enderly. Ralph Cullis, Henry Otway, and some others. All the original families, you know. To the west, Brougham Hall, and Morland Hall, once the late Captain Massie's, now owned by Mr. Frake."

Hugh's face lit up for the first time. "Is it *Jack* Frake you mean?" he asked.

"Why, yes, sir. Jack Frake," said Stannard. "Are you acquainted with him?"

"I only know of him," remarked Hugh, not volunteering more.

Mr. Stannard grinned, but uneasily. "Perhaps you do. He saved Captain Massie's life in that awful affair with Braddock on the Monongahela, and also that of one of his sons. Another perished there. Captain Massie led one of the Virginia companies, you see, from this very county. Unfortunately, the son Mr. Frake saved died of wounds en route home. The last son, the oldest, was left at home to look after Morland, but later got himself run through in some drunken altercation in a Williamsburg tavern. Mr. Frake had by that time completed his indenture and married Captain Massie's only daughter, Jane, and with her came three hundred acres of Morland. Sweet girl, she was. But — she died during childbirth. Mrs. Rittles was her midwife, and the child, a boy, survived his mother by only a month. Captain Massie had taken a French ball that passed through one hip and out the other. The wound flared up again and he died of it. Mrs. Rittles ascribes a more sentimental cause, that he died of a broken heart; his whole family had gone.

"Well, anyway, Mr. Frake was like a son to him, and his will left that gentleman all of Morland, or another six hundred acres. If there were any remote relatives who could have challenged the will, none came forward. Now, Mr. Frake is a gentleman, but he's a solitary fellow, and keeps mostly to himself. He is regarded as a crop master, and produces between thirteen and fourteen hogsheads of sweet-scented every season. His staff are loyal to him, and he treats his tenants with generous fairness. He manages with but six slaves. Stood for burgess two years ago and promised to work for a bill in Williamsburg that would allow citizens to free their slaves without the House's or Governor's consent." Stannard chuckled. "Of course, he was not elected. He has a fine library, perhaps the finest in Queen Anne County, after Mr. Reisdale's. Morland runs parallel almost the whole length of Brougham Hall, from the river to Hove Creek."

The men were standing on the brick steps of the front door of Stannard's modest house. Talbot asked, "Has he or any of the other planters expressed interest in Brougham Hall, Mr. Stannard?"

The agent nodded. "Some have. But my and Mr. McRae's terms are not negotiable. We are asking for cash, or in-kind — or a draft note — to settle Mr. Swart's affairs and to clear our own books. Regrettably, few of the others are in better positions to extend themselves so much without aggravating their own debts. Mr. McRae and I have resisted all attempts by them to beat down the value of the property, and we are determined to absorb no loss ourselves on Mr. Swart's balances."

"What are you asking for the property, sir?" asked Talbot.

"Eleven hundred sterling, sir," said Stannard without hesitation.

Talbot glanced at Hugh, who nodded acceptance. Talbot said, "Well, sir, that is agreeable, depending, of course, on what we see on the morrow."

"I am certain that you and Mr. Kenrick will not be displeased."

"Where may we engage mounts?"

"I shall arrange that for you, sir, and pay the rate myself — "

A loud report startled the three men and caused them to turn in its direction. Pedestrians in the street also paused to look toward the river. The noise touched off a chorus of barking dogs.

"Why, that was the old cannon that sits in front of Sheriff Tippet's place," Stannard said. "It's fired only on the King's birthday and Christmas day. What the devil…?"

"I must apologize to you, Mr. Stannard," Talbot said. "Perhaps we should have conveyed the news to you first before discussing our business."

"News, sir? What news?"

"Quebec has fallen to General Wolfe. That was on the thirteenth of last month. The general opinion is that the rest of Canada cannot help but follow. Unfortunately, it will not be to General Wolfe, who died on the field, as did his opponent, General Montcalm, if the reports are precise."

"Oh!" exclaimed Stannard, clapping his hands once. "That *is* wonderful news! Thank God and General Wolfe!" The agent beamed. "Yes, yes! Astoundingly good news! There will be some form of celebration here to mark the occasion, I can assure you! Why, I hope your stay permits you to partake of it!"

"We shall see, sir," Talbot said. He touched his hat. "We take our leave now, sir, and look forward to supping with you and Mr. McRae this evening." The visitors picked up their bags and walked up Queen Anne Street.

Mr. Stannard immediately sent his son, Joseph, who clerked for him, to inform the Scottish factor of the arrival of the prospective buyers, and then to ride to Brougham Hall to warn Amos Swart to prepare for a visit the next morning. He then found his cane and walked briskly down the street to the parish house of the church, a trim little pine-board place that sat near the red brick, cruciform church and its wooden steeple. He found Reverend Acland in his garden, picking beans from his corn stalks.

The minister paused to wipe his hands on his apron. "If you are here about the news from Quebec, sir, I'm afraid other heralds have preceded you, including Sheriff Tippet. But, I will not have the bell rung until the post-rider brings some form of written, official confirmation."

"Still, it's wonderful news, is it not?"

"If it is true, yes — in which case I shall deliver a sermon on Sunday on the subject, and call for a moment of silence to pray for General Wolfe's soul."

Mr. Stannard's excitement propelled him to make an injudicious remark. "I imagine it may be too late for that, Reverend," he laughed, "for his soul must have already journeyed to wherever it was ordained to go!"

Reverend Acland frowned. "If, indeed, he died, sir. The glory of his late career cannot but have helped compensate for his reputedly dissolute life." He paused. "Surely, this is not the only reason you have paid a call, Mr. Stannard?"

"True. Here's more recent news I wish you to hear and appraise." The agent told the minister about his visitors, and described Hugh Kenrick.

Reverend Albert Acland came to Caxton fifteen years ago upon graduating from Oxford and taking orders. He came from an old family of Anglican ministers, but found no assignments to his liking in England. He prevailed upon his established clerical friends to persuade the Bishop of London to post him to a colonial parish; the colonies were chronically short of Anglican ministers. He sent twice-yearly reports on his parish and the religious turmoil in Virginia to the Bishop, who had jurisdiction over Anglican churches in the colonies. He was also in regular correspondence with former classmates who had also taken orders and maintained parishes in the British Isles and in other colonies. With church and political news, Acland exchanged gossip with his distant colleagues about the fortunes of other men of the cloth, about the fulminations of certain members of government and Parliament, and about the eccentricities and scandals of many members of the aristocracy. Much of this gossip found its way into the Caxton *Courier*, in items written by Acland under a carefully guarded pen name.

By the time Stannard finished speaking, the minister stood open-mouthed. "Dear me!" he exclaimed. "That *must* be the son of the Baron of Danvers, who is brother to the Earl!"

The agent said, "He has that air about him, sir, though I could not put my finger on it." He frowned. "How could you be certain of his antecedents, good sir?"

"I have a colleague in Devon who writes me about the Kenricks and other worthy families there — about Danvers, and Dorset all in all — that is the Earl's seat, and.... My word! To think of a scion of nobility settling *here*!" Reverend Acland straightened up and discarded his apron. "Come in for tea, Mr. Stannard, if you can spare the time, so that we may discuss this intelligence!"

In Reverend Acland's parlor, half an hour later, Mr. Stannard put down his cup and saucer and said, "Mr. Talbot did most of the talking." He paused. "And the lad knew of Mr. Frake!"

"Did he?" the minister said. "How on earth could he know?"

"He did not say, Reverend."

"Mr. Frake is noted in these parts, but I can hardly believe that his repute could extend to the metropolis of Philadelphia!" The minister made this remark with a condescending smirk.

Mr. Stannard frowned in thought. "The lad strikes me as being a forth-right gentleman, sir. There is an easy way to clear any doubts about his identity. I will simply ask him, this very evening, and apologize for my igno-rance."

The minister waived a hand. "No, no, sir. Not that! If he does not wish to advertise his rank — if neither he nor Mr. Talbot volunteered the infor-mation — we should not presume to impinge on his privacy. He might take offense and flee, regardless of his appraisal of Brougham Hall."

"If that is your advice, sir, I shall heed it."

"Oh, Mr. Stannard!" mused Acland. "We would be blessed if he pur-chases Brougham Hall! A scion of nobility residing here would have many benefits! Why, he could be appointed to the Governor's Council, and check certain sentiments there among the gentry here, and benefit the county in so many ways!" He lowered his voice. "Perhaps he could contribute to improvements in the parish, and perhaps help repair our superannuated steeple! A new bell, perhaps! I cannot begin to count the possibilities!"

"*I* would get back much of Brougham Hall's tobacco crop!" remarked Mr. Stannard, more to himself than to the minister, "for such a gentleman could not but raise the best sweet-scented, instead of the near-trash Swart now sells to Mr. McRae." He frowned again. "This has occurred to me just now, sir: If he purchases the property, we can be sure of friction between him and Mr. Frake, who is not friendly to nobility. They would watch each other like rival panthers stalking a doe in the Piedmont."

"Perhaps," the minister said. "My memory is foggy, and I must find the letters from my correspondent in Devon, but I believe there is some evil feeling between Mr. Kenrick and his uncle the Earl. And, I vaguely recall some other scandal attached to his name."

Mr. Stannard shrugged. "Perhaps these matters have little to do with why he would be interested in the property, sir. Sons of merchants or nobility do not usually come here for their education and experience. The gentlemen here often send their sons to London. It is a most curious phenomenon, do you not think, sir?"

Chapter 2: The Town

The five major rivers flowing into Chesapeake Bay formed penin-sulas that together roughly resembled, on a map, the fingers of a greedy hand reaching into the Bay for the Eastern Shore. Of these rivers — the James, the York, the Rappahannock, the Potomac, and the Patuxent — the least troublesome to navigators was the York. Its mouth lay between Mobjack Bay off of Gloucester and the Marshes to the south off of York County. Its source, some twenty-five miles northwest, was the near confluence of the smaller, serpentine, and almost parallel Pamunkey and Mattaponi Rivers, whose peculiarities screened much of the silt that would otherwise have been deposited in the York. Thus the York was able to scour its own bed. Its shoals and sand bars were known and static, while its slowly shifting tidal flats rarely caught watermen, pilots and sea captains by surprise. Sea-draft vessels were almost as common on the river as water-fowl and planters' tobacco barges. Its channels ranged between thirty to eighty feet deep, often plunging to those depths only a few yards from either bank.

On the north side of the "thumb" of the greedy hand, midway up the York River, sat the town of Caxton, a few dozen houses and structures atop a rolling bluff that was enclosed by plantations and farms. Caxton had grown rapidly after the county's founders' petition was granted in 1711 by the House of Burgesses and the Governor's Council to "secede" from the parent county. By 1750 the town's population and commerce began to rival Yorktown's some ten miles down the river. Caxton's fortunes were in the ascendant.

Before it was known as Caxton, it was called Caxton's Forge, a stop in the wilderness on the way across the river or to Williamsburg. In the late seventeenth century John Caxton and his wife operated a barge ferry at the riverbank on what was now Morland property, and at the top of a gentle slope a smithy that could repair travelers' carriage wheels and harnesses and replace horseshoes. Mrs. Caxton also served refreshments, drawn largely from an apple and pear tree orchard her husband's father had planted years before Bacon's Rebellion in 1676. The Caxtons' one-room dwelling and smithy were in ruins now, overgrown with weeds, bamboo, scrub pine, and poplars. The Caxtons had sold their small patent of land to

Captain John Massie's father shortly after Queen Anne County came into existence, citing the noisy influx of people as a reason to move on, and left with their few belongings for the interior of the colony. They were never heard from again. The neglected orchard was reclaimed by Jack Frake, whose small press supplied Caxton's three taverns with much of their cider.

"Which establishment do you think is patronized exclusively by the gentry here, Mr. Talbot?" asked Hugh Kenrick.

The pair had found a room at Mrs. Rittles's boarding house, had unpacked their bags, and after an exchange of money and talk with the intrigued Mrs. Rittles, decided to explore the town. Louise Rittles ran neither a tavern nor an ordinary, but a rooming house for "excursioning" travelers for ready money or tobacco notes. For an extra two pence she served a breakfast and supper. Her husband Lucas owned a store that carried sundry necessities and novelties — most of them imported — and also a farm that supplied Mrs. Rittles's famous table with most of its fare. Mrs. Rittles had deemed Mr. Talbot a gracious gentleman, but the younger gentleman was someone extraordinary, she was certain of it. She could not pry from them their business in Caxton, though they said they would be here for two or three days. When she invited them to supper, they regretted that they had a previous engagement. And when they had left for their walk, she rushed across the street and spoke excitedly with her husband, whom she found in the back of the store supervising a servant in candle pouring. "They're a plumb pair, let me tell you, Lucas!" she said. "From Philadelphia, no less! I've a good mind to nose through their kit while they're out! Won't do no harm!"

"Don't you think of it!" said Mr. Rittles. "If they notice anything amiss they'll think we're sharpers. No, you keep your nose out of their things. We'll learn soon enough why they're here."

Hugh Kenrick and Otis Talbot stood in the middle of Queen Anne Street. The Gramatan Inn, a large, rambling, two-story place of white-painted wood, stood near the courthouse, across from the church. Its signboard read "Gramatan's Inn." Nearer to them was the King's Arms tavern; its signboard displayed a newly painted coat of arms. Closer to the waterfront, at the top of the road leading from it, was a tavern whose signboard bore a racing horse, stretched in midstride in an unlikely and physically impossible gallop.

Mr. Talbot shrugged. "Gramatan's Inn, no doubt," he answered. "There is no picture on the board over the porch. It's a rare gentleman who can't read."

Hugh smiled, and they walked on in the direction of the waterfront. "The King's Arms there," he gestured with his cane, "is very likely a patriotic place where one can pick up all sorts of information about the county. The racing horse there suggests a low kind of place, an overblown gin shop."

"Patronized by laborers and ships' crews," added Talbot, "but no less creditable a place for intelligence on all sorts of matters."

"True," Hugh said.

As they passed the place, a man came out and scrutinized the pair. He wore a filthy apron, dirty hose, and a shirt stained with brown and green smears. "Can I get you sirs something?" he asked. "Grenada rum? Barbados spirits? Madeira? There's a chill in the air and come evening your blood may want some stoking."

"No, thank you, sir," said Talbot with a nod. "What is the name of your establishment? The Arabian Racer, perhaps?"

The man looked offended. "No, sir! Saracen's Wind!" He smiled. "Though you was damned close. No, sir," he went on, nodding to the sign-board. "That's Saracen's Wind. Used to own him. Won me a few trophies and prizes some years back. Had to enter him under Mr. Granby's name, of course, as I aren't a gentleman, and split the spoils with him, too. Then Saracen goes and breaks a leg while he's out to pasture, and we had to put him down. Sad matter. Couldn't even stud him, could've made some extra money studding him, you know. Oh, well...." The man paused and studied the pair again. "My name is Joshua Fern, and my establishment is better known here as Fern's Tavern."

Talbot nodded again. "Otis Talbot, of Philadelphia," he said. "And my companion, Mr. Kenrick."

"What brings you to Caxton, sirs?"

"Business," Talbot said.

When he realized that neither of the strangers was going to state their business, Mr. Fern said, "Hope you enjoy your stay, sirs, and find the time to give me some custom. Mine's an interesting kind of place. The county was born here, you might say, right in my Jamaica Room, when my father, Samuel, owned it. All the old gentry met here and plotted their petition. The Broughams, the Massies, the Granbys, the Vishonns, the Otways, the Cullises. The town's grown since then, of course. Got us a regular church and a courthouse and even a jail back of it. Some of the finest houses in Virginia is to be found right here."

"We hope to view some of them on the morrow," Hugh Kenrick said. "Thank you for the invitation and your information." He and Talbot continued their stroll to the waterfront.

Water Street, as it was informally called, ran for almost a quarter of a mile. On it was packed a collection of tobacco warehouses, warehouses for other crops and exports, cheap, crude hostelries for laborers and seamen, barracks-like structures for slaves and servants, the homes and shops of chandlers, shipwrights, and merchantmen's stores and equipment. The visitors made the acquaintance of Richard Ivy, the county court-nominated and Governor-appointed tobacco inspector, at his office, in back of which was his home. Mr. Ivy was the third inspector to hold the post in Caxton since passage of the Tobacco Inspection Act in 1730 to ensure the quality of tobacco exported from the colony. He had the power to pass judgment on any hogshead and to destroy its contents if he judged them trash. Some yards from his office was a black patch of ground on which stirred in the wind the ashen remains of many tons of burned leaf. Mr. Ivy shrewdly guessed the purpose of his visitors' questions.

"I've been condemning more and more of Mr. Swart's 'heads," he volunteered. "Thinks he can blackleg me by packing trash beneath good leaf. Deposits ten 'heads here and I cut 'em down to six or even five, usually. He's probably busy right now with another scheme. Won't do him no good. I'll open every lid. It's a shame, what he's done to Brougham Hall. Used to turn out top grade. We'll all be glad to be rid of him."

His visitors neither confirmed nor denied any interest in Brougham Hall. Hugh Kenrick asked, pointing to three small, round-bottomed vessels farther down the riverbank, "Whose are those, sir?" Two lay on their sides, the third was encased in scaffolding. Men were busy on all three of them.

"The one in stocks is Mr. Vishonn's, for his river trade," said Mr. Ivy. "The other two belong to Mr. Cullis and Mr. Granby. They're having their hulls scraped of worms and barnacles and such. Mr. Vishonn is replacing his hull. Those three gentlemen carry a lot of wheat and grain to Fredericksburg, and even to Maryland."

The visitors thanked Mr. Ivy for the chat and took their leave. The buildings on Water Street all sat on an elevated line of the riverbank, far away from the water and tide lines. The river, Mr. Ivy informed them, could become as wild and violent in a storm as the surf on an ocean beach.

Queen Anne Street ran for half a mile from just above the riverfront, through the town, to a wide wooden bridge that crossed Hove Creek. Paralleling it were two shorter streets on either side of it, Prince George and Caroline. The first was named after George the First's son — who was now king — and the second after George the Second's late wife. Caroline Street was originally called Sophia, after George the First's wife, but a secretary to the Lieutenant-Governor pointed out to the mayor and the parish vestrymen that George the First had divorced her for having committed adultery and locked her in a castle in Hanover for thirty-two years.

Scattered along these three oak- and poplar-lined avenues and their nameless cross-streets were the homes of the town's permanent residents, the "town" houses of the major planters, and various tradesmen's establishments, each with its own garden or tobacco patch. An apothecary and a grocer's shop shared the same wooden house, across Queen Anne from a cobbler's, a leathersmith's, and a dressmaker's. The sun was beginning to set when the visitors stopped beneath the signboard of the Caxton *Courier*, which depicted several tomes between the jaws of a press.

Hugh smiled up at the sign, and peered through the shop's window. Inside he saw an apprentice arranging quarto pages on a length of twine that was suspended over him from wall to wall. A short, stocky older man and another apprentice were busy printing pages on a two-pull press. On another side of the shop were shelves laden with books, stationery, writing articles, blank ledgers, and copies of the *Courier*. Hugh nodded to the press that was producing the quarto pages. "See that, Mr. Talbot?" he said. "I cleared that very press in London in Mr. Worley's office, some years ago."

"Do you wish to go in and introduce yourself, sir?" asked the merchant.

"No. The older fellow is probably the publisher, and he would ask us questions."

The pair began walking back to Mrs. Rittles's house. Mr. Talbot waved at the town in general. "If the property suits you, Mr. Kenrick," he said, "are you certain you could endure living here? I myself would regard a stay here of only a month as a kind of criminal sentence, and would need to fight with myself not to succumb to the malaise of boredom."

"If the property suits me, Mr. Talbot, I would not have time to grow bored." Hugh Kenrick paused. "I would be making something my own."

"Who *is* Jack Frake?" asked Talbot.

"Perhaps a kindred spirit," answered his companion, "if he is still anything like the man Captain Ramshaw once described to me. It was a pleasant surprise to hear Mr. Stannard pronounce his name."

"Judging by Mr. Stannard's manner, he is not much more liked here than is Mr. Swart."

Hugh Kenrick did not reply.

"There is the matter of the slaves," said Talbot. "I know very well your views on the institution. How would you propose to handle that — if the property suits you?"

"It would be a challenge, and I would resolve it."

They walked together in silence again, nodding in greeting to the occasional passerby. Otis Talbot had grown fond of his charge over the last two years, and with the fondness had naturally come sensitivity to the young man's moods. He decided that the best course was to change the subject. He said, "Had you not once a tutor by the name of Rittles, Mr. Kenrick? I seem to recall a story you told me about him."

Hugh Kenrick smiled. "That is true, sir. I had forgotten him. I shall ask our hostess — discreetly, of course."

He asked Mrs. Rittles that evening if she had relations in England. She had not, nor had her husband, or, at least, none that she knew of or had been told about. Mrs. Rittles appeared to be nervous during the cordial chat with her guests. She had disobeyed her husband and poked through their belongings. She discovered nothing telling in them, except that the articles were of the very best quality.

*   *   *

Later that evening, Hugh Kenrick asked, "Why was this property not auctioned, as is the usual practice in these circumstances?"

Arthur Stannard gestured to Ian McRae, who answered, "Because Mr. Stannard and I knew we would not raise enough in an auction to cover Mr. Swart's debts and also recover our own costs of handling the matter. Mr. Stannard more so than myself."

Mr. Stannard added, "And, we would have likely been obliged to extend credit again to the purchasers of the meanest parts of the property." He paused. "We are both under strict instructions from our respective firms in London and Glasgow to clear our books of the Brougham Hall accounts. They are quite as tired of Mr. Swart as we are."

"Instructions?" scoffed Mr. McRae. "Nay — say, iron orders!"

Five men sat at a round table in the Cumberland Room of the Gramatan Inn. Supper was finished, and Mr. Stannard ordered a fresh round of port over which to discuss business. He, Mr. McRae, and Mr. Talbot lit pipes and rekindled them occasionally from pouches of tobacco. The room was spacious, large enough to accommodate twenty patrons, and insulated from the noise in the rest of the inn by plastered walls and walnut wainscoting. Two candelabra on the table and a dozen triple-mirrored sconces on the walls brightened the room with near-daylight.

Adorning one of the walls was a crude reproduction of a painting depicting Cumberland's rout of the Jacobite Scots at Cullenden Moor, the Duke astride a rearing, fierce-looking stallion, brandishing a sword, his background a confused rendering of the battle. Hugh was amused by the painting, for the Duke he remembered did not look anything like the person in the picture. He remarked privately to Mr. Talbot, "Cullenden, say wags in London, compensated for Fontenoy."

The fifth gentleman at the table was Mr. Thomas Reisdale, an older man who sat on the county court, maintained a private law practice in

Caxton, and was the only justice in Queen Anne County versed in law. Born in Fredericksburg, he was sent to London for his education by his planter father, attended Cambridge University, and studied at the Inns of Court, where he obtained a law degree before returning to Virginia. He owned ten thousand acres of land in the Piedmont and a profitable plantation in Queen Anne. Having been edged out of inheriting his father's vaster holdings by an elder brother, he settled in Queen Anne and assembled his own little empire. He corresponded frequently with Richard Bland, burgess for Prince George County and a recognized authority on English and Continental law. Mr. Reisdale was the attorney representing Stannard and McRae, and the one who had persuaded his fellow justices to declare Amos Swart bankrupt. He did not say much during the meal, or after it.

Hugh Kenrick was also amused by the British and Scottish agents' behavior. They had both greeted him effusively, but there was an element of hesitation in the courtesies they paid him, as though they were not certain they were being courteous enough. He suspected that they had discovered his true identity, but he did not care enough about the matter to inquire how.

Arthur Stannard had been visited hours before the supper by Reverend Acland, who informed him in hushed whispers that, to judge by what he could glean from his correspondents' letters, Hugh Kenrick was indeed the son of a baron and the nephew of an earl. "It seems he once snubbed the Duke of Cumberland, and got into some trouble in London, and even spent time in the Tower for his association with some Leveller rascals!" the minister said, who was beside himself with excitement and disapproval. "Why, it is suspected even that he slew a marquis in a nocturnal duel!"

"Well! What do you think of that!" exclaimed Mr. Stannard. "It's no wonder to me at all that he was sent away!"

"I shall write my friends in Devon and London and ask for more particular information," confided the minister.

"But I beg you not to speak to anyone else of this," said Mr. Stannard. "Not until my business is concluded one way or another."

Mr. Stannard in turn informed Mr. McRae, but cautioned, "He seems to prefer the address of a commoner, and so I strongly advise that we humor him in that respect, and not let on that we *know*."

"Iron orders, indeed," remarked Mr. Talbot. He smiled. "I am fully sympathetic to your dilemma, sirs. Mr. Spicer and I are no strangers to the need to dun a spendthrift and recalcitrant patron. We have resorted to the courts a number of times to recover our due."

Hugh Kenrick leaned forward and said, "We would have expected the sterling value of such a considerable property to be much higher, sirs, than the eleven hundred quoted by you, which must reflect a drastically reduced appraisal of Brougham Hall." He paused. "The property must be in a very sorry state."

"That is true, sir," acknowledged Stannard. "Although it is not the largest plantation in these parts, under Mr. Swart's management it has lost more than twice the value of a property three times its size. The late Covington Brougham was a crop master, and the envy and mentor of even the bashaws here."

Mr. Talbot asked, "Have you the particulars of the property, sirs?"

Mr. Stannard opened a portfolio and took out a sheet of paper, from which he read: "The property known as Brougham Hall consists of one thousand and six acres, of which fewer than half have been cleared for cultivation. Of the cultivated acres, between one hundred and one hundred and fifty are devoted to tobacco, although," added the agent parenthetically, "that number has steadily risen over the years as the quality of Mr. Swart's leaf has declined and attempts were made by him to make up with bulk. The balance of the acreage is set aside for wheat, corn, and other staples. There are some orchards on the property — peach, apple, pippin, and others — but Mr. Swart has neglected these and allowed them to be overcome by scrub pine, elms, and hackberries."

Mr. Stannard paused to sip his port, then continued. "I might add that one of the most egregious expenses incurred by Mr. Swart was that associated with his experiment with growing orange trees, a few hundred saplings of which he purchased from a ship's captain who had to delay his departure from Caxton to have his hull treated for worm. Mr. Swart, unmindful that our climate does not favor the cultivation of that admirable fruit, planted the trees in a field he had only recently decided to let lie fallow. What folly! When they succumbed to an early frost and their leaves rotted, Mr. Swart accosted the captain and was prevented from doing him bodily harm only by the strenuous intervention of others. The whole incident merely contributed to the contempt in which he was already held."

The agent cleared his throat and read from his paper. "The buildings? The main house has a vista of the York over a landscaped lawn that has seen only desultory care. From bank to house, the lawn is some two hundred feet. The brick house itself is seventy by forty feet, of two stories, the first twelve feet in height, the second, nine. Inside and out, the architecture is of simple, formal lines — what I would call 'modest Grecian,' if I may take the liberty. In it are five fireplaces, four in the corners, and one in the center. There are several cellars for the various beverages, cheeses, meats, and cook's necessities, plus a vault for claret, wine and such. On the first floor are the supper room, a parlor, a ballroom, a library or study, and a

breakfast room with a view of the river, in addition to a game room with a
billiard table fashioned of Cornish slate. The second floor, reached by a fine
oak staircase, consists of three bedchambers, two children's chambers, and
a parlor or busy room for the ladies of the house. Of course, there are
numerous closets on both floors, and on the first an unobtrusive accom-
modation for the house's major domo and cook." Mr. Stannard chuckled
and looked up from his paper. "Gentlemen, the place is nearly half as grand
as the Governor's residence in Williamsburg. Have you ever visited our
capital?"

"No," answered Mr. Talbot.

Before Stannard could continue, the Scottish factor held up his pipe.
"May I interrupt for a moment, sir?"

The British agent nodded and took the opportunity to finish his glass
of port.

McRae said, "Mr. Stannard's son, Joseph, was informed by Mr.
Beecroft, the business agent at Brougham Hall, that Mr. Swart left two days
ago to see to one of his Henrico properties, and is not expected to return for
a week or so. This fact needn't concern us, if there is a happy ending to
these matters. By the terms of the court order, Mr. Swart's signature is not
required to either endorse or conclude the sale of the whole property or any
part of it. He is, for all practical matters, a tenant at Brougham Hall."

"This is true," volunteered Mr. Reisdale.

Stannard said, "Forgive me for not informing you gentlemen of that
important fact, and of Mr. Swart's absence."

Talbot chuckled. "I suppose, then, we shall be denied the chance to
meet this gentleman when we visit the property tomorrow."

McRae smiled. "You will be spared the pleasure of meeting an apish,
unkempt man, who is usually reeking of rum."

"Should he not, as master of the place, at this time be supervising the
stemming and prizing of his leaf?" asked Hugh Kenrick.

"He should," said Stannard, waving his document. "But, there you are.
It is so characteristic of the man." He squinted his eyes and continued to
read. "The outbuildings consist of a laundry, a kitchen — close by a door
to one of the cellars, I should add, which also happen to be connected themselves by doors — a baking house, a dairy, a storehouse for provisions, a
stable, and a coach house — which contains a riding chair and a landau,
neither of which I have seen in use in years — all very prettily situated
around the main house in a courtyard laid with brick fashioned in a kiln
elsewhere on the property, but which Mr. Swart has allowed to fall into dis-
repair. There is a smaller house, of two stories, twenty-five by twenty-five,
the quarters of the business agent, the overseer, and the clerk, just beyond

the courtyard....There are two tobacco barns, each thirty-two feet by twenty...." The agent droned on about the livestock, the cooper's and carpenter's sheds, the smithy, and other facilities, finally touching on the servants, the slaves, and their quarters.

When his colleague was finished, Mr. McRae cleared some space on the table and unrolled a surveyor's map of Brougham Hall and neighboring freeholds. The next half hour was spent discussing the property and its natural assets.

At one point, Hugh Kenrick looked up from the map and asked, "Have there been any conflicts or differences between Mr. Frake and Mr. Swart?"

"None that we know of, sir," said Stannard with a shrug. "Mr. Frake seems to have less esteem for Mr. Swart than what decent Christian tolerance would allow, while Mr. Swart appears to have made an effort to avoid Mr. Frake's company and temper."

McRae chuckled. "One would never see those two standing on the same side of a room," he remarked.

Later, as the Scottish agent rolled up his map, Stannard called for some bottles of French brandy to be sent in. When each man's glass was filled, he said, "Now, good sirs, on to an important matter. Naturally, we are curious about the arrangement between you, Mr. Talbot, and you, Mr. Kenrick, should a purchase be decided on. Your *bonafides* are undoubtedly impeccable and beyond reproach, but still, Mr. McRae and I are anxious to grasp your situations."

Otis Talbot, who repacked his pipe during this address, paused to light it with a match lit from the candelabrum near him. He spoke. "Should a purchase be decided on, sirs, the deed to the property would be registered in my own name as a private person. However, I would be the owner in name only, having no power over the property itself. Mr. Kenrick here would in fact occupy and manage the property, and be answerable to the man in whose place I would sign any document concerning Brougham Hall. When Mr. Kenrick has reached his majority, title to the property would instantly revert to him, and neither I nor the third party could claim any part of it."

Mr. Reisdale leaned forward and asked, "Are you his guardian, Mr. Talbot?"

Talbot shook his head. "No, sir. For two years now, Mr. Kenrick has been acting, in effect, as an apprentice in my and Mr. Spicer's business, in accordance with the wishes of his father." He paused. "It is Mr. Kenrick's father's funds that would make any purchase possible."

Stannard turned and addressed Hugh Kenrick with the hesitant, circumspect delicacy of a man asking a marriageable young woman about the state of her chastity. "Well, sir…who *is* your father?"

Hugh Kenrick said, without any stress in his words, "Garnet Kenrick, Baron of Danvers, and brother of the Earl of same. In addition to managing the family's property in Dorset, my father has conducted a lucrative commerce with the colonies and the Continent through Worley and Sons, with whom I have also served in an apprenticeship. Much of the family's commerce is carried on that firm's merchantmen, the *Busy* and the *Nimble*, in addition to the family's own schooner, the *Ariadne*, devoted almost exclusively to trade between these colonies and Britain. My father is also an unnamed principal in the banking firm of Formby, Pursehouse and Swire, in London."

Stannard and McRae were more pleased than they could permit themselves to say. Had they been alone at that moment, they would have risen from their seats, called for a fiddler, and linked arms to perform a lively jig. Instead, both men merely blushed. Mr. Reisdale stared at Hugh Kenrick in open-mouthed disbelief.

Stannard said, "Yes…well…I believe the *Busy* and the *Ariadne* have both called on Caxton in the past…."

McRae said to his colleague, "The *Ariadne* has carried quite a lot of tobacco to Glasgow and Liverpool…and other goods as well…." To stop himself from whooping with joy, he took a sip of his brandy and added, "Why, a goodly portion of my store's stock was brought in on the *Ariadne*…nails, and claw hammers, and broadaxes…and such…."

Otis Talbot and Hugh Kenrick waited for the agents to collect themselves.

Mr. Reisdale sat back in his chair. "May I inquire, milord, what is your father's — not to mention your own — interest in this property?"

"Purely proprietary, sir," Hugh Kenrick said, "as any man's would be had he the means. This is also my own motive. I can assure you all that there is no governmental or political scheme behind our interest." He paused. "In future, gentlemen, I would be grateful if you continued to address me as 'Mr. Kenrick' or 'sir,' and to treat me with the same courtesies and civilities with which you would treat each other."

"As you wish…sir," Reisdale said. He frowned. "And your uncle, the Earl of Danvers: May I ask what is *his* interest?"

"None, sir. I will speak frankly and say that he is mere ballast, and has been an undeserving beneficiary of my father's efforts and accomplishments — and often an obstruction to them. He is an active peer in Lords, and fortunately does not meddle much in my father's affairs. My father limits his service to occasional turns as justice of the peace in our part of Dorset."

With the exception of Talbot, none of the other men had ever heard such sentiments expressed vocally by a sober man about a peer of the realm. Again, they were more surprised — indeed, aghast — than they thought they could permit themselves to show. At the same time, however, the young man's speech convinced them of the sincerity of his intentions concerning Brougham Hall.

For some reason he could not identify, Reisdale was prompted to remark thoughtfully, "Covington Brougham's older brother, Cerdic, on the day that the petition for the founding of this county was drawn up, proposed that the county be named in honor of a commoner, the noted John Locke. It was thought a preposterous notion at the time, but it very nearly won him election as one of our first burgesses." The attorney paused. "It is no shameful thing to be a commoner, I suppose."

Hugh Kenrick smiled amiably. "No, it is not. The petition was debated and drawn up in Fern's Tavern, was it not?"

Reisdale nodded. "Yes, sir. In the Jamaica Room." He shook his head. "A disreputable place now."

Hugh said, "Perhaps it was not as preposterous as that man's contemporaries thought. I fully expect that, at the conclusion of this war with the French, Secretary Pitt will be similarly honored, in numerous instances and without objection."

The other men nodded in agreement. "This is true," Stannard said. "Why, the site of that French fort on the Ohio is already called Pittsburg, and I imagine that once the new fort is completed, it will be called Fort Pitt."

Before anything more could be said on the subject, there was a knock on the door, and one of the inn's maids came in. "Begging your pardons for the intrusions, sirs," she said, "but Mr. Stannard's servant just came with a note he said it was urgent for Mr. Stannard to see." She approached the agent, handed him the note, and left.

Mr. Stannard scowled and opened the note. Then he looked up with a broad grin. "I was *certain* of it, sirs!" he exclaimed. "Mr. Vishonn has called for a ball to be held at Enderly tomorrow evening to celebrate General Wolfe's triumph at Quebec! My wife writes that a post-rider arrived at dusk at Mr. Barret's shop with copies of the *Gazette* from Williamsburg that contain full accounts of the battle!" He tossed the note onto the table. "Gentlemen, we will have ample time to see the property tomorrow and return to prepare for the ball!" He looked hopefully at Talbot and Hugh Kenrick. "Of course, you are both invited to attend, as my and Mr. McRae's guests."

Hugh Kenrick glanced at his companion, who nodded assent. "Thank you, Mr. Stannard," he said. "We would be happy to attend, on the condition that you, Mr. McRae, and Mr. Reisdale agree to make no fuss about my identity, and introduce me as just another gentleman. I do not wish to be paid special or undue deference, in business matters or in social circumstances."

"As you wish, sir," mumbled the three men in unison. Stannard sighed. "It is a novel request, to be sure, and we will honor it." He paused with an expression that was half-frown, half-smile. "But, you must own that it leaves us not a little curious about the...reason for it."

Hugh Kenrick shrugged. "I have spent enough time in the colonies now that I have acquired an appreciation for the notion of equality. It is a better foundation for honest relations between men than airy titles and artificial respect. There is no place for those customs here, and I find them tiresome." After a brief pause, he added, "What I seek, gentlemen — and what I may find in the responsibilities and labor demanded of me by a place like Brougham Hall — is the solitude and satisfaction of a private man who is not bedeviled by a deference he has not earned."

Although they smiled in sympathetic concession to and agreement with the young man's statement, it left Stannard and McRae nonplussed and too dumbfounded to reply. Only Otis Talbot, who had heard his companion express similar sentiments in Philadelphia, understood it, while Mr. Reisdale, who was widely read in the political tracts of the age, recognized in the statement something he could not decide he liked or disliked.

Chapter 3: The Plantation

West of Queen Anne Street and its adjacent streets were several freehold farms, and west of these, separated by a line of woods, was Brougham Hall. This broad rectangle of fields and forest, about one and a quarter mile square, was similar in size and topography to Morland, which neighbored it in the west, and Henry Otway's plantation, whose western-most boundary was also the county line. East of Queen Anne Street were more freeholds, and then the vast and regal plantations of Enderly, Granby Hall, and Cullis Hall, the eastern-most holding in the county. To the south, across Hove Creek, were some large farms and plantations owned by "middling" freeholders, none of them nearly as large as those that lined the riverbank. On the surveyor's map, the county was a neat assemblage of rectangles that was almost square, with Queen Anne Street acting as a narrow stem beginning at the river and ending at Hove Creek.

Mr. Stannard arrived at the boarding house with saddled horses rented from the Gramatan Inn's stables. Mr. McRae was not with him. "He sends his regrets, sirs," he said to Hugh Kenrick and Otis Talbot, "but pressing business at his store detains him. He will perhaps join us for dinner at Brougham Hall."

It was a cool morning. In the night, some passing clouds had sprinkled the town with a light rain. As the day progressed, the air grew warmer. Hugh rode with a blank ledger book and a pencil, and made copious notes of his own observations and his host's factual statements. The British agent was struck by the new differences in the young man and the older. Talbot seemed to be in a more congenial, conversational mood, while Hugh Kenrick kept his remarks to business. Mr. Beecroft, the business agent, had met the party halfway between the main house and the two brick stanchions that marked the formal entrance to Brougham Hall, prepared to escort the visitors around the property. But the agent preferred to show the property alone and instructed Beecroft to have a light dinner ready for them at two o'clock.

While they watered their mounts at Hove Creek a few hours later, Hugh Kenrick asked, "What is the source of this brook, Mr. Stannard?"

"A spring that emanates somewhere beyond the Morland place, sir. It has never been known to dry up."

"Where does it end?"

"Somewhere past the Cullis place, sir."

Working their way north through the property, they ambled along a path that cut through the corn and wheat fields. Some slaves were busy picking corn from the stalks and carrying them in cloth bags to put into an enclosed cart across the field. Near it an overseer on his own mount eyed the visitors with suspicion.

Hugh remarked, "This corn ought to have been gathered in June, or July, Mr. Stannard." He reached down and plucked an ear from a stalk, then tossed it to the ground. "It is half eaten by worms."

Mr. Stannard looked apologetic. "In all fairness, Mr. Kenrick, we cannot hold Mr. Swart entirely responsible for the conditions you see here. The crops of all the planters got off to a late start. These last few years have been oppressed by drought, and everyone has been obliged to struggle beyond their usual exertions."

"About how many hills would you say are here?" asked Hugh.

The agent glanced around. "About fifty thousand, sir."

Hugh rode forward and inspected a few more stalks. He turned to the agent with a frown. "Of which, perhaps only a quarter is fit for anyone's table. The rest may be fodder for livestock. Are there so many cattle in the county?"

The agent smiled in irony. "I purchase most of Mr. Swart's corn, sir, for my firm's account, for the West Indies trade. Also, much of his wheat. These particular crops have prevented him from increasing his indebtedness."

Later, when the party reached the tobacco fields, Hugh paused long enough to dismount and pick up a forgotten pile of leaves left on the ground to wilt before being taken to a barn to dry. He slapped the leaves flat against his other open hand, and a shower of fragments fell to his feet. He dropped the bundle and remounted. "Why is Mr. Swart growing sweet-scented, and not oronoco, Mr. Stannard?"

"There is a considerable market for it in England, Scotland, and Ire-land."

Hugh scoffed. "I believe that his troubles might have been mitigated had he planted oronoco, which, as you know, fetches a better price on the Continent."

The agent shrugged. "The war has upset that market, sir," he remarked. "And, the Broughams raised sweet-scented, and Mr. Swart will not be turned away from it. He has an almost child-like attachment to it."

"Nevertheless, the market for it has been reduced, and there is no allowance in this business for child-like fancies." Hugh glanced at Otis Talbot, and in this glance was the suggestion that since Mr. Stannard was attempting to defend Swart on the matter, he must have an interest in ensuring that Swart continued to grow such an unprofitable crop. Hugh reined his mount around and walked it in a wide circuit through the bare stalks, then rode back to his companions. "He puts his hills too close together," he said. "Neighboring hills must starve each other for the same soil and water." He pointed vaguely to a spot. "Some over there are no more than two feet apart from any side. Most seem to be three. It is no wonder to me that his leaf is mediocre, as you say, Mr. Stannard. You were correct in your remark that he is attempting to compensate with bulk. How many hills would you say are here, sir?"

"About one hundred thousand, sir." Stannard paused. "That's as Mr. Swart told me."

Hugh waved a hand at the field. "He could not have had more than four good leaves per stalk, when he ought to have had eight. Allowing for spoilage and negligence, this season should produce for him some ten hogsheads — of which Mr. Ivy would likely condemn three or four." He shook his head. "Altogether, a rather pitiful reward for so vast an enterprise."

The agent sighed in concession. "I could not agree with you more, sir."

"Well, let us see what condition his barns are in." Hugh turned around and rode on.

Stannard looked at Talbot, who wore a faint grin. The Philadelphia merchant remarked, "My friend labored for a while in the field of a customer of mine, in Pennsylvania," he said.

"I see," said the agent. "But — why?"

"He called it catharsis." Talbot said nothing more, and urged his mount to follow his companion. Stannard sat for a moment, not knowing what to think. On one hand, he was pleased that the young man was as critical of the property as he himself was; on the other, he was worried that Mr. Kenrick might conclude that the property was in too abominable a condition to purchase.

Hugh had few kind things to say about the rest of the plantation. He ventured no appraisal of the staff, servants, or slaves. He inspected the yard that contained the smithy, cooperage, and woodworks, and watched with apparent admiration two slaves in the smithy repair a plow.

When they passed through the slave quarter, Hugh asked, "How many slaves did you say there were, Mr. Stannard?"

"Thirty, Mr. Kenrick," answered the agent. "Twenty-one hardy males, five females, four children, and three superannuated females who mostly tend the slaves' gardens and perform minor chores in the kitchen. Those three are counted as one."

Without looking at the agent, Hugh remarked, "Do not speak of them as though they were sows, sir."

Stannard frowned in genuine perplexity. "It is the custom, sir," he said. "They are property, and how else ought one to speak of them?"

Hugh, in reply, merely gave him a brief, withering glance, and rode on.

Stannard followed, and hastily added, in an attempt to allay the young man's displeasure, "That fellow in the smithy, sir, is likely the best iron-master in these parts. And the cooper's apprentice owns the distinction that none of his hogsheads has ever broken, even for the most brutish handling. Even Mr. Ivy has expressed his admiration. The fellow is on occasion sent to other plantations to instruct other apprentices." He paused, unsure that Hugh was listening. "Some of these fellows are paid a shilling or two a month, in addition to being allowed some discretion in the tending of their own gardens. They are permitted to keep whatever they are paid for the things they raise in them and sell — though more often than not what they sell is mixed with edibles taken from Mr. Swart's and other planters' gardens. They are allowed time to stand at crossroads and at the bridge over Hove Creek, and accost travelers."

Hugh said nothing more until they reached the main house. There they were taken on a tour of it and its outbuildings by Mr. Beecroft, a stocky, nervous, abrupt man who wore bifocals.

The party was served a light dinner and ale in the supper room. When the servant left the room, Hugh remarked, "The staff look competent — and hopeful, Mr. Stannard. It is curious, though, that they have remained in Mr. Swart's service. They did not say so, but it is my impression that Mr. Swart commands little affection from them."

Stannard said, "That is because they are, strictly speaking, no longer in his employ, but his creditors'. No doubt," he added in a lower voice, "they have stayed on to avail themselves of what they may and because there are no opportunities elsewhere. Mr. Beecroft is answerable for their conduct."

"Of course." Hugh said, "The books in the library have not been touched in years. There is an inch coating of dust on their tops."

Talbot chuckled. "Obviously, Mr. Swart limits his reading to tobacco notes and legal papers."

"True," said Stannard. "Why, I seem to recollect there being more books on the shelves in that room. Mr. Beecroft some time ago informed me that Mr. Swart will occasionally use the leaves of books to kindle his fires. I did not credit the information then, but now...." The agent shook his head.

"This house, too, is in disgraceful condition," Hugh said, "though it is in sound enough shape."

"But a few more years of Mr. Swart's management," added Talbot, "and the property would look abandoned and invaded by rummagers."

"It can be salvaged, but at some cost," said Hugh. He finished his ale, then put down the glass and sat back in his chair. "I am aware of the rivalry between you factors, Mr. Stannard. That is, between you and Mr. McRae. It is unusual to see you two as allies in this business."

"If the truth be known, sir," said the agent, "Mr. Swart's delinquent accounts are near to breaking both our firms. But, once this business has been settled, we will be in good stead again and will resume our friendly animosity."

"You are quite candid, sir. Presumably you also have a store in town."

"Yes," said Stannard. "Right on Queen Anne, nearly across from Mr. McRae's." The agent paused. "We serve different clientele. Mr. McRae's is the larger, for he has a sitting stock of necessities and toys that the middling planters require. I, too, maintain a stock, but it is somewhat smaller. Some time ago I decided to reduce the cost of keeping such an inventory, and introduced the novel idea of putting together catalogues for things people here seem to favor. My catalogues contain fine drawings of most of these items, together with their manufacturers' names and their costs. The drawings are borrowed from pattern books or are supplied by the manufacturers themselves. This method allows me to offer the same goods to my patrons as those carried by Mr. McRae, but at a lower bill to me."

"I commend you for the innovation," Hugh said. "Do your patrons receive what they see in your books?"

"Invariably," answered Stannard with a smile. "Allowing for breakage and misfortunes at sea, of course." Encouraged by the compliment, he went on. "You know, once my firm got all the Brougham leaf. But it is now Mr. McRae who purchases most of that crop. His company in Glasgow disposes of it somehow. It was the practice of the growers here to merely consign their tobacco to one or another firm in London, or Liverpool. But then the Scots entered the trade, and my firm sent me out about nine years ago to win back what we were losing from this county to Mr. McRae's firm. This object I have accomplished, while Mr. McRae has retained most of the smaller planters. He is welcome to them."

Hugh looked thoughtful. "You imply that you purchase these crops, Mr. Stannard," he said, "when in fact the hogsheads remain the property of the planter until they are sold in London. Your firm, Umphlett and Weddle, warehouses them there, but pays neither that cost, nor the freight, nor the demurrage, nor other extraordinary costs. All that is charged to the planter's account, and deducted from the amount of sale. Of course, there is your firm's commission on the sale, also deducted from the sale price. The only advantage to the planter is the drawback arrangement, when the duties imposed on imported tobacco are charged to the planter's account, but nullified if the tobacco is re-exported to the Continent. On none but British vessels, of course."

Stannard imagined he detected a note of hostility in the young man's words, and did not understand it. "In many instances, sir," he said, "that is true. But, more and more, firms such as my own are purchasing tobacco directly from the planters, instead of merely agreeing to have it conveyed to London. Often, the firms assume many of the costs you have just cited. The trade has grown very sharp in recent years." He smiled. "As you must know, most of the tobacco entering London or any of the outports such as Glasgow or Liverpool, whatever its destination, is kept in Customs warehouses. Umphlett and Weddle, I am proud to say, is among a group of firms now campaigning in Parliament for a law that would allow our firm to billet their purchased and custodial tobacco in their own warehouses."

Hugh hummed noncommittally. "They might also campaign to resolve the stoppage in the Pool of London, Mr. Stannard. I spent enough time there with my father's agent to observe that if there is any profit to be made on the goods stowed in all the idle merchantmen there, an unconscionable portion of it is consumed by demurrage and pilferage."

Stannard could only concede this point. He essayed a change of subject to describe some of the vast plantations in the region, such as Nomini Hall and Westover, then proposed that they continue the inspection. The three men strode out to the lawn with its river view. The agent pointed down-river to the pier of Brougham Hall, where they could see several slaves and servants struggling in the water to load a hogshead onto one of three barges tied to the pier. Three more hogsheads sat on the sandy bank, and as they watched a fourth suddenly appeared, deftly guided by two slaves. Stannard explained that the one-ton barrels were brought from the storage barn a quarter mile away to a "rolling road" that led down the wooded slope to the riverbank and pier. "Some of these Negroes handle those 'heads as though they were mere dice," he remarked.

The party remounted and inspected the western side of the plantation. Here, in fallow fields, grazed sheep and the brown long-horned cattle Hugh knew so well in Danvers. Beyond and south of the fields was forest, and to the west a thick line of trees behind a worm fence that ran for almost the entire length of the property. The agent said, "When the Broughams and Massies were neighbors, there was no fence. The fence is of Mr. Frake's construction. It was one of the first things he put up when he inherited the place." Stannard spoke with a faint tone of disapproval.

"Perhaps this fence is a reflection on Mr. Swart, sir, not on Mr. Frake," Hugh said. "In what condition is Morland?"

"Most enviable, sir. It is not a large holding, compared with some. But it is most rationally managed and seems to be prosperous. Mr. Frake employs some novel methods of cultivation." The agent added, with a resentment that verged on peevishness, "He does not give me his custom."

"Perhaps he has found other, more agreeable arrangements," remarked Hugh.

"I don't doubt that, sir," Stannard said. "They are not with Mr. McRae, either. Mr. Ivy tells me that all of his leaf is carried out by a single merchantman, the *Sparrowhawk*, or by one of its owner's acquaintance. I have not been able to determine what firm back home takes custody of it, nor who is the ultimate purchaser of it."

Hugh turned in his saddle and blessed Stannard with one of his rare smiles, and did not comment. Stannard, for his part, tentatively smiled in return, but was not certain why. It occurred to him later, when he was no longer in the young man's company, that Mr. Kenrick was up to some kind of mischief, and that his smile was a point of secret knowledge.

When the party returned to the ground on the eastern side of the plantation, Hugh took out his pocket watch. "It is nigh four of the clock, Mr. Stannard. Have we seen all that needs to be seen?"

"Yes, sir. Shall we return to town, or would you like to see the house again?"

"That won't be necessary, sir," Talbot said. "If we are to attend a ball this evening, Mr. Kenrick and I would like to return to our room to talk among ourselves, freshen up, and prepare for the festivities."

"Yes, of course," said Stannard. He leaned forward in his saddle hopefully. "Well...what do you think?" His glance moved between his two guests.

Hugh said, "We will have a decision for you and Mr. McRae in the morning." He waved his ledger book once and dropped it into a saddlebag. "There is much that Mr. Talbot and I must discuss."

The road to the eastern flank of Brougham Hall led through some freehold farms. As they rode by, Stannard nodded or doffed his hat to men he knew who were working in the fields.

Hugh asked, "What requirements must a man meet to be appointed a tobacco inspector by the government here, Mr. Stannard?"

The agent shrugged. "That he be an honest man, and able to judge good leaf from bad."

"How does a man acquire such knowledge, except by staining his hands in the care and worming of his own leaf?"

"By having been a good planter, sir, though the victim of some misfortune."

"Is Mr. Ivy such a person?"

"No. Mr. Ivy is a distant relation of Mr. Cullis's wife. Her cousin, I believe. He was overseer for one of Mr. Cullis's places on the James. When Mr. Cullis sold that place some years ago, he nominated Mr. Ivy to succeed old Mr. St. John, who was ailing at the time."

"I see."

Twenty-five minutes later the party was back on Queen Anne Street. When his guests dismounted and stood on the porch of the boarding house, Stannard took the reins of their mounts. "I shall ask Mr. Gramatan's stable to reserve these mounts for you, sirs," he said, "and I will call on you here with my wife and son near six-thirty."

"We will be ready, Mr. Stannard," Talbot said. "Thank you for your time. We look forward to the celebration this evening."

"The *Amelia* will depart on her return voyage tomorrow afternoon, Mr. Stannard," Hugh said. "If we decide in your favor, Mr. Talbot and I would like to be on it, but only after some business has been settled."

"Of course," said the agent. "It will be a bit parky out of doors this evening, but I believe the company will keep us warm. Until later, sirs." Stannard tipped his hat, then rode back up the street with the two mounts in tow.

A while later, in their room, while Talbot shaved himself, Hugh reviewed his notes in the ledger book. He frowned briefly, and remarked, "It is something of a paradox, Mr. Talbot, but I had the impression that Mr. Stannard is quite content to be a creditor, though that status jeopardizes his business." He turned to face his friend and mentor. "Had you that impression, too?"

"Yes," answered the man, wiping his face off with a towel. "But it is no paradox at all. His status as a creditor gives him a dollop of power."

Hugh turned this reply over in his mind for a moment, then resumed his studies.

Talbot studied the back of his protégé. "What would you call the place, Mr. Kenrick?" he asked. "New Danvers, perhaps? Or, Effney Hall — in honor of your mother? She would be so pleased. Or, simply Kenrick?"

Hugh looked up again. "I had not given the matter thought, Mr. Talbot," he said. "No, none of those," he added, shaking his head. "I am certain, though, that I should not continue to call it Brougham Hall. It must be a name of my own choosing…something that would distinguish it from anything in my past…."

Chapter 4: The Ball

The seat of Enderly was a residence not quite twice the size of Brougham Hall, but large enough that its enclosing wings, connected to the main house by roofed colonnades, formed a spacious brick courtyard. In the center of the courtyard stood a mature red cedar encircled by crocuses, hollyhocks, and lilacs. Instead of a wall and an arched gate to complete the square, there were two stands of tulip trees, through which ran a neatly set road of flagstones salvaged from the York River and the plantation's fields. This road, laboriously "paved" and extended by two generations of the Vishonn family to the common road that led out of Caxton, was lined with boxwoods, willow oaks, and several varieties of holly. It was by this road, in the cool October evening, that most of Reece Vishonn's guests came by carriage, cart, riding chair, horseback, and on foot, guided in the growing dusk by cressets placed every one hundred or so feet. Others arrived by boat on the river, stopping at the plantation wharf that sat beyond a vast landscaped lawn on the north side of the house.

The cressets were appreciated by the arriving guests. Sitting in iron baskets atop iron poles, the fires of fatwood hissed and sputtered, and emanated a welcoming warmth as well as light. The fires would eventually die out, and not be relit. Except on nights when there was a full, unobstructed moon, occasions such as the guests were attending were as a rule all-night affairs, for there was no means for people to easily find their way home in the total darkness that enveloped the countryside. At dawn, the guests, exhausted, sated, and perhaps a little woozy from too much tippling of sherry and punch, would thank their host and drift back down the road to their widely spread homes.

Hugh Kenrick and Otis Talbot rode on either side of the two-wheeled riding chair occupied by Arthur and Winifred Stannard. The couple's sixteen-year-old son, Joseph, sat mounted on the horse that pulled the vehicle. Mr. Stannard, throughout the journey to Enderly, chatted on about the place, proudly pointing out landmarks and citing facts as though he owned the plantation. "Mr. Vishonn has a man whose only job is to keep up this road," he was saying. "If he finds a broken flagstone, he must replace it, and regularly sweep the road of dirt, leaves and stones that might lodge in a horse's hooves. These cressets were fashioned in Mr. Vishonn's own smithy here, from pig brought down from a mine he owns above the Falls. He's made a business of selling them around the colony. Why, he has even sold some in New York, and Boston, and Charleston. I'd even wager, Mr. Talbot, that some of his cressets light your way home in Philadelphia."

"Undoubtedly," Talbot said. "And no doubt he knows that if the Board of Trade and Plantations heard of his business, he could be sent to jail, or be fined beyond his means to pay the penalty."

"Stuff and nonsense!" exclaimed Stannard. "Those fellows couldn't prove that his cressets were *not* made in England! The ironmongers there have already got a secure market. Why would they begrudge a loyal Briton a handful of iron? They've enough work now, supplying the army and navy!"

"True, sir," Talbot said. "But, when the war is finished — what then?"

The agent gave the Philadelphian an incredulous glance, then dismissed the question with a scoff. "You worry the matter over much, sir," he said. "The Board and Parliament wink at trade irregularities, as you must well know. They'll go on winking. Besides, when the war is finished, the mother country will have her hands full keeping the peace at home. She's not going to much mind or take notice of a few pounds earned behind her back."

Talbot grinned. "I sincerely hope that our cousins are so benignly distracted, Mr. Stannard."

"We will hear some fine music tonight," ventured Mrs. Stannard, who was bored with politics and wished to change the subject. "Mr. Vishonn owns a pianoforte, which his son James will play. He is most accomplished. A pair of fiddlers, Jude and Will Kenny, will also provide us with the means to dance. They are brothers, my husband may have told you, who own the first freehold across Hove Creek."

"But, topping the bill, sirs," added her husband, "will be 'Angel' McRae."

Hugh Kenrick asked, "Is Mr. McRae musically endowed?"

The agent laughed. "Not by a note, sir! No, it's his daughter, Etáin. She plays the harp."

Hugh remarked, "A harp? I did not think the instrument was known in the colonies."

Mr. Stannard said, "It's known here, sir. Some years ago, a relation of Mr. McRae's who kept a shop of instruments in Edinburgh, died, and Mr. McRae sailed there to settle his affairs. He brought back a harp, and a dulcimer. His daughter is adept on both."

"His wife's brother," said Mrs. Stannard, "Paul Levesque, is a copy clerk employed by Mr. William Boyce, the composer, in London. He sends his sister all sorts of music for his niece to play."

"And," added her husband, "he plays the harpsichord, and often performs with other musicians at Vauxhall Gardens. Occasionally, he tutors children of the best families." Mr. Stannard paused. "He and Mrs. McRae are Huguenots."

"Or were," corrected his wife. "Mrs. McRae frequently accompanies her husband to the church here. Her brother himself owned a large instrument-making shop in Paris, once. It was smashed during a Papist riot. Mrs. McRae's fiancé was killed by a mob that same day. She and her brother went to London, and found a place next door to Mr. McRae's lodgings. He, too, was new to the city. That is how they met."

"Mr. McRae and his family have been at Enderly most of the afternoon, sirs," volunteered the agent. "That is one reason why he could not accompany us to Brougham Hall. They have brought Etáin's harp, at Mr. Vishonn's request, so that she could rehearse some songs with James."

"Who is also an admirable baritone," remarked Mrs. Stannard. "Those two may be a match," she added, "though Mrs. McRae does not encourage the rumor."

"Nor does Etáin," said her husband. "Her heart is set on Mr. Frake."

"Her mother encourages *that* match with her resounding silence on the possibility, every time the subject is raised."

Hugh Kenrick asked, "Do you think Mr. Frake will attend tonight?"

Stannard sighed. "Very likely, sir. And, he may bring his own fireworks."

                              *   *   *

By London standards, it was a small assembly; by rural colonial, a large. Some forty adults arrived at Enderly to celebrate Wolfe's victory at Quebec, mostly neighboring planters and their wives, together with some children and a smattering of adolescents. All were dressed in their best finery: the men in velvet or wool frock coats, waistcoats, and perukes, the women in hooped taffeta or silk gowns, and coiffed hair adorned with pearls, plumes and ribbons. Reece Vishonn had, as usual, arranged to allow his guests to leave their mounts and conveyances beyond the courtyard, where a liveried slave watched them and tended them with water and oats. The guests then walked through the cresset-lit courtyard to the house, where they were greeted in the breezeway by one or another of the Vishonn family. Reece Vishonn, a large, florid-faced man in green silks and an immaculate pig-tailed wig, welcomed Mr. Stannard's party with an almost garrulous flourish. He gave Arthur Stannard barely enough time to introduce his visitors. "Mr. Talbot…Mr. Kenrick, it is such a pleasure to meet you! Mr. McRae told me you were looking over the Swart place. Well, it is my earnest hope that there is a change of ownership! How long will you stay in our fair town?"

Otis Talbot said, "We take the *Amelia* back to Philadelphia tomorrow afternoon, sir."

"What a pity! I should like to have had you both over for a private supper. Has Mr. Stannard told you everything about the property?"

Hugh Kenrick smiled. "What little he may have neglected to tell us, sir, we have deduced for ourselves. No decision has been made yet concerning a purchase."

"Well…," said Mr. Vishonn, wanting to frown in disappointment. "Perhaps this evening's jollities will help you to decide! Because so many are expected, my lady has elected to forgo a formal table and lay out a buffet, which has already been removed from the kitchen. We will have a bonfire down by the water, and some fireworks about midnight. And, of course, there will be dancing aplenty, all night, for as long as the company and musicians can stand!"

More guests appeared at the door, and the host was obliged to break off to greet them. Mr. Stannard took his guests on a round of introductions, and before half an hour had passed, everyone knew who the strangers were and their business in Caxton. And to every query concerning their plans to purchase Brougham Hall, Hugh and his companion demurred an answer.

Hugh easily fit into the company. Colonial society, though mindful to observe contemporary rules of polite decorum, was made more enjoyable by the relaxation of many of those rules. Thus, Hugh was able to converse with married women without arousing anyone's suspicions or offending social protocol. Unattached women, however, remained unapproachable, even for the most innocuous conversation, except in the company of their parents, guardians, or elders, or during a dance. A modest and well-bred young lady could not look a man directly in the eye and not expect to be taken for a libertine extending an invitation to license. It was a supposition impervious to reason.

The three most brilliantly lit rooms were the ballroom, the supper room, and the gaming room. Each boasted a score and a half of double sconces, while from the ballroom and super room ceilings were suspended lustres, or crystal chandeliers, such as Hugh had seen only in London and Danvers. These, however, each had the added feature of a silver cupola, filigreed with gold, fixed above the lustre's chain to absorb the candles' heat and soot. And both the ballroom and the supper room were furnished with Dutch "warming machines," great, black, ornamented iron stoves connected to their own chimneys with sealed tin pipes. The gaming room was warmed by a standard fireplace, and contained a billiard table, a bar, and several round tables for card and dice games.

Hugh and Otis Talbot toured the rooms with Barbara Vishonn, the host's wife, and then, by mutual agreement, separated to find their own company. Hugh returned to the ballroom and studied the lustre overhead. Ian McRae approached him. They shook hands again, and the Scotsman apologized for his absence earlier in the day. Hugh said, gazing up at the crystal, "What a novel idea! I have not seen its like elsewhere."

"It was Mr. Vishonn's innovation," remarked McRae. "I believe he grew tired of seeing the ceiling blackened by the smoke."

"Not only does the crystal magnify the light, but the device above it reflects and distributes it. Further, the cupola reduces the risk of fire."

Mr. McRae laughed. "I'm certain that Mr. Vishonn would like to hear it so complimented, Mr. Kenrick." He put a hand on Hugh's shoulder. "Come, you've not met my wife and daughter. They're in the far corner there."

As they crossed the room, they passed the space where the musicians would play. On the light blue-papered wall behind the pianoforte, harp, music stands, and chairs, was a large Great Union, suspended from the bases of two sconces. Hugh nodded to it and remarked, "And *that* is a decoration I've not seen elsewhere — at least, not in anyone's residence."

"It once flew atop the Capitol here," McRae said, "until it was in tatters. Mr. Granby's son, William, who is one of the county's burgesses, procured it from the keeper and presented it to Mr. Vishonn, whose wife prettily repaired it." In a lower voice, McRae added, "It is said of Mr. Vishonn that he is more patriotic than Mr. Pitt." He paused. "Have you met our two burgesses, Granby and Edgar Cullis?"

"I've not yet had the pleasure, sir."

"A word of advice, then, sir, whether you elect to purchase Brougham Hall or not: Steer clear of politics with them, unless you agree with them."

Madeline McRae was an elegant, captivating woman whose dark eyes seemed to sum up Hugh with approval. Etáin, fifteen years old, was a younger version of her mother. The woman wore a lavender satin gown and a lace-frilled cap over her jet-black hair, the girl a green wool riding suit and no cap over her reddish hair, which Hugh noted, was the only feature she seemed to have inherited from her father.

"If you move to Brougham Hall," inquired Mrs. McRae, "won't you miss all the distractions afforded you in Philadelphia?"

"Yes, madam," Hugh said, "but that town only causes me to miss London. For the time being, I have resigned myself to nostalgia."

"How many people reside there, Mr. Kenrick?" asked Etáin. She spoke with an odd but charming amalgam of Scots, French, and English accents.

"They say some forty thousand souls, Miss McRae."

Ian McRae glanced around and saw Arthur Stannard. He made his excuses and left Hugh with his wife and daughter.

Madeline McRae asked Hugh more questions, about him and about London. Their conversation was cordial, but Hugh felt that there was an ulterior motive behind the woman's questions. Just when he thought that he had succeeded in concealing his origins, the woman turned to Etáin. "Do not stare at the gentleman as though he was a talking statue, dear. It is uncouth."

The daughter blushed and looked at the floor with a grin. Her mother suddenly leaned forward to Hugh and brought up her fan to muffle her words: "Your secret is safe with me, milord Kenrick of Danvers. Have no fear that I will expose you. But — you are a curiosity. You must call on us some day and tell me more about yourself." Before Hugh could reply, the woman folded her fan and drew back again.

Hugh could only nod in acknowledgment.

"There are only a few thousand souls in all of Queen Anne, Mr. Kenrick," said the woman.

"It is a small county, compared with some."

"What do you miss most about London, Mr. Kenrick?"

"The music…the concerts…the orchestras…the theaters…the galleries… the enterprises…the shops…the busyness of the city, where almost everything one could want, is at one's fingertips, where so much is possible…."

Madeline McRae smiled. "I, too, miss all those things — and Paris." She frowned in mock admonishment. "Now you are making me feel…melancholy."

"That was not my intention, madam," said Hugh. He hurried to say, "The Moravians, in Pennsylvania, near Bethlehem, have an orchestra. They play music by Bach, and Vivaldi, and Boyce, and even by this newcomer, Haydn. I rode there twice from Philadelphia to hear them. And Charleston, I have read, is a town greatly enamored of music."

"I shall play a new tune by Mr. Boyce this evening, Mr. Kenrick," Etáin said. "One that no one had ever heard yet, not even in London! And James Vishonn shall sing the words to it, which were written by David Garrick."

"What is its name?" asked Hugh.

"'Hearts of Oak.' It is a patriotic song, about the navy."

"Mr. Garrick puts on so much foolishness on the stage," remarked Mrs. McRae. "And Mr. Boyce composes so much that is forgettable."

"I look forward to hearing you play the tune, Miss McRae," said Hugh.

"I shall also play some pieces Mr. Bach wrote for the harp," said the girl.

"Oh? Which Bach?"

Etáin laughed. "I can't remember, just now! There seem to be as many Bachs as the fingers of one's hand!"

"This is true," smiled Hugh.

"Excuse me, Mr. Kenrick," said Madeline McRae, "but our hostess is waving to me. I must leave my daughter in your charge." Without further word, the woman swept away across the ballroom.

Hugh realized that he had just been paid a compliment by the girl's mother, that she trusted him to be alone with her daughter. By the look on the girl's face, he knew that she understood this, too. He indicated her attire, and asked, "You will not dance tonight, Miss McRae?"

"No. I would not be permitted to. My gown and my harp are not compatible, and so I wear my riding clothes." In a lower voice, Etáin added, "Many of the ladies here opine that it is not lady-like to pose as I must to play the instrument. But my harp will not accommodate my hoops. I shall even be seated behind the pianoforte, for modesty's sake."

"Then those same ladies must not think Britannia lady-like."

"Britannia?"

"The goddess-like symbol of our country. Here." Hugh drew a bronze penny from his coat and showed the girl the relief of the seated figure, whose one arm was raised to hold a spear, while the other rested on the top of her shield that was planted upright on the ground.

"Yes!" exclaimed Etáin, studying the figure. "Of course! What a pretty thought!"

Hugh pressed the coin into her palm. "Please, Miss McRae, keep this, as a token of my esteem, and as a reminder to yourself, the next time you hear someone complain about your musical pose."

Etáin beamed with delight. "Thank you, Mr. Kenrick. You are too kind."

Hugh shook his head. "I am not a kind man, Miss McRae."

Etáin frowned. "Why do you say that, Mr. Kenrick?"

"Kindness is a sort of forgiveness, or an intentional oversight — or the cowardly waiver of a wrong. It is — a tolerance for the intolerable, and very often that is akin to the commission of a heinous crime."

The girl looked down at the floor. "I meant…that you were generous, Mr. Kenrick."

"Then, please, forgive me for having misconstrued your meaning, Miss McRae," said Hugh with some concern. "I am wiling to be called 'generous.'"

"Would you think me a coward, if I forgave you?"

"No. I would think you honest," Hugh said with a smile. "Honesty is nearly an antonym of kindness."

"And generosity: What is that nearly the antonym of?"

"Profligacy," Hugh said, enjoying the exchange. "However, generosity is very nearly a synonym for justice."

"You are oddly persuasive, Mr. Kenrick, though I have not heard such notions before." Etáin's glance wandered for a moment, and she noticed that some guests were staring at them. She bowed her head. "There I go again, staring at you as though you were a talking statue!"

Hugh turned and scrutinized the curious guests, who averted their glances and moved to another part of the crowded room. He said to Etáin, "Ancient lore has it that a dying Amazon would hold her slayer's eyes, and cause him to fall in love with her, so that after she was gone, he would pine away in regret. Love of her was her cruel retribution."

Etáin looked up at him with curiosity.

Hugh said, "I am merely trying to embellish your lapse from a silly custom, Miss McRae. Or to attach to it a better justification."

"It is a strange courtesy you pay me, Mr. Kenrick." The girl paused. "Has an Amazon gazed into your eyes?"

After a moment, Hugh said, "I no longer think so. She is not slain, and has married a Boeotian." He paused. "It is the stuff of one of Mr. Garrick's plays."

"One of his tragedies," remarked Etáin, saying it before she meant to. "I have read some of them."

"For my role in it, yes," Hugh said, who seemed to have forgotten the girl's presence. "For hers, a farce that was not so amusing." He smiled with bitterness. "You see, she wrote me a *kind* letter." Then he remembered where he was and to whom he was speaking. "My apologies, Miss McRae," he said, bowing slightly. "I did not intend to raise tragedy on such a festive occasion."

"I am sorry to have caused you to have such a sad memory."

Hugh shook his head. "No, no. Do not feel sorry. The fault was all mine."

The girl was uncertain whether he was speaking of the present or of the past.

*　*　*

There was a rustle of movement in the ballroom and an ebbing of the hubbub. Madeline McRae appeared again and said to her daughter, "Dear, Mr. Vishonn is about to open the ball. You should take your place. Here are your fingers." She reached into her little purse and handed Etáin a pair of calfskin gloves. The girl smiled at Hugh. "They protect my fingers from the strings. A tanner in Williamsburg makes me several pair every year." She quickly put the gloves on, performed a small curtsy, and joined Reece Vishonn and his son in front of the Great Union flag.

Hugh frowned, and gave Mrs. McRae an inquiring look.

The woman shook her head once. "She has not been told, *Baron* Kenrick," she said in a hushed voice. "She must have noted something about you that deserved the courtesy."

Reece Vishonn waited until the last whisper in the room had died away. Then he spoke. "My honorable guests! We are gathered this fair evening to mark the victory of General Wolfe in Canada, and the glorious triumph of British arms there and the world over! General Wolfe was, to judge by reports, no tent-bound general, but a brave man who died leading his forces at the very moment of victory. And let us also mark a cornucopia of victories — at Louisbourg, at Frontonac, at Duquesne, and in far away India, at Plassey! Yet — I received but today by post a letter from friends in London which contains the details of yet another great victory this last August by His Majesty's naval forces, which, under the superb direction of Admiral Edward Hawke, dealt the French fleet a mortal blow off the coast of Portugal, and in so doing foiled a design to invade England through Scotland!"

James Vishonn, a tall, handsome youth of twenty, raised his hat in the air and led the assembly in a trio of huzzahs. The cheer was followed by the guests' applause.

"I despise my countrymen," murmured Madeline McRae to her husband, "but I am sad for them nonetheless."

Reece Vishonn smiled. "It would be entirely fitting to pay tribute to our multitude of heroes — those living and those dead — by inaugurating our celebration of thanks with a fresh tune by our noted composer, Mr. William Boyce, for which Mr. David Garrick has written some rousing words." He turned and addressed Etáin McRae. "Miss McRae, if you would be so kind," he said, gesturing to the harp. Then he stepped away.

Etáin acknowledged the new applause with a short bow, then sat down at the harp. It was an old instrument, a little over half her height, its frame missing patches of gold paint. The girl leaned forward, raised her arms, and her gloved hands began moving smoothly and confidently over the strings.

It was a memorable tune she played. It had the character of a drinking song, but in her hands it assumed the aura of a hymn, or an anthem. The guests stood enthralled, by the melody, by the sight of an "angel" playing her harp. When she finished the tune, she glanced up at James Vishonn and

cued him to sing. The young man faced his listeners, gave a small bow, and
sang in a faultless baritone voice, accompanied by Etáin:

Come, cheer up, my lads! 'Tis to glory we steer!
To add something more to this wonderful year!
To honor we call you, not press you like slaves.
For who are so free, as the sons of the waves?

Hearts of oak are our ships, hearts of oak are our men!
We are always ready!
Steady — boys — steady!
We'll fight and we'll conquer, again and again!

He sang two more stanzas. One of the Kenny brothers raised his fiddle
and joined in the last one. When they were finished, the guests shouted
approval and loudly applauded both the song and the performance.

Reece Vishonn stepped forward and warmly shook his son's hand,
then bowed to the girl. A servant handed him a stemmed glass of red liquid.
He turned, raised the glass, and boomed to his guests, "God save the king!"

"God save the king!" answered the assembly.

"Long live William Pitt!"

"Long live William Pitt!"

"God bless General Wolfe!"

"God bless General Wolfe!"

On a somber, more subdued note, Reece Vishonn proposed, "And, with
God's help, may British arms soon conclude this unfortunate conflict!"

"Hear, hear!" answered the guests.

Reece Vishonn waited for the commotion to cease. "Now, my friends,
please enjoy yourselves! The table is ready, as is the floor. We are most fortunate to have such able musicians on hand to keep us busy and amused.
Jude Kenny, I have been informed, has also mastered the flute. Milady and
I will take the first dance."

James Vishonn sat down at the pianoforte, the guests parted to two
sides of the ballroom, and the host and hostess bowed and curtsied in the
beginning of a perfectly executed minuet.

Chapter 5: The Encounter

That evening, and into the night, in a whirl of cordial but circumspect encounters with the leading men of Caxton and their families, Hugh became acquainted with those who might be his friends, should he decide to purchase Brougham Hall, and those who might become his enemies. These were Reece Vishonn, and his wife, Barbara, his son James, and daughter, Annyce; Ira Granby and his wife, Damaris, his son the burgess, William, and daughter, Selina; Ralph Cullis and his wife, Hetty, and his burgess son, Edgar, and daughter, Eleanor; and Henry Otway and his wife, Maura, and his son, Morris. Hugh was certain that he was likewise being scrutinized and appraised. Only Madeline McRae, however, had alluded to his origins, but kept the knowledge to herself. For this, he was grateful.

He took Ian McRae and Arthur Stannard aside at one point in the supper room, and said, "Thank you, sirs, for respecting my confidence. No one has bowed to me, or suggested that I present myself to Governor Fauquier."

Mr. Stannard asked hopefully, "Have you…er…made a decision yet, Mr. Kenrick?"

"Not yet, gentlemen. I suggest that we meet for breakfast in town on the morrow. What do you say?"

Ian McRae shrugged. "That is agreeable to me, sir. Mr. Stannard?"

"We will have the papers with us, should they be needed, Mr. Kenrick."

"Good," Hugh said. He picked up a Chinese plate from the buffet table and smiled. "Mr. Vishonn is a very gracious and discriminating host."

At midnight, standing with other guests at the edge of Enderly's riverfront lawn to watch servants feed a great victory bonfire on the bank below, Otis Talbot said to Hugh, "You have been a constant subject of speculation, sir. They are all mystified by you. I cannot discuss commerce or trade with the bashaws here without having to parry questions about you and your intentions. They suspect that you are more than a mere gentleman." He paused. "You will, sooner or later, be obliged to declare your family."

Hugh sighed. "Better later, than sooner, Mr. Talbot." He nodded. "Look! There are fires all up and down the river! It reminds me of home!"

Bonfires could be seen on the opposite bank of the York, and along the bends on their own side, spaced miles apart. "I wonder," remarked Hugh, "if there are celebrations in Williamsburg and Norfolk."

"No doubt," said his companion. "They seem to attach a special importance to Quebec in this colony."

"Well, Virginians were the ones who were in the first frays of this
war."

"On Pennsylvania land," chuckled Talbot. "If the French had not been
so forward in their claims, I imagine the Crown would have had to adjudi-
cate a serious boundary dispute between Mr. Penn's land and Virginia,
instead of bringing the two realms together in common cause."

"You are very likely right," Hugh said. "The colonies here regard themselves almost as separate nations. Especially Virginia."

Some men farther down the bank from the bonfire were busy setting
up a wooden contraption. It contained Reece Vishonn's Italian fireworks.

Though he had tried to avoid it, Hugh danced twice this night: once, in
a country-dance with Madeline McRae as his partner and seven other couples — "My husband does not dance, Mr. Kenrick," she said, "his feet
become two left thumbs, and he has all the grace of an infant taking its first
steps" — and once in a minuet with Selina Granby, a charming, attractive
girl his own age, whose eyes, when they met his during the stately dance,
seemed to extend a special invitation. He was not certain whether this was
her own inclination, or the consequence of a private urging by her parents.
It did not matter to him which it was.

                              *   *   *

"You appear only a little more frequently than does Mr. Halley's comet,
sir," said Ian McRae to the latecomer.

"Morland is a greedy, jealous mistress, Mr. McRae," said the man. "She
does not leave me much time for other society."

"Is such a mistress worth so much time?"

"I cannot project the point at which I would abandon her." The man
turned to Madeline McRae and smiled. "I come mainly from affection,
madam, and because I enjoy your family's society."

"And not to celebrate?" asked the woman.

"If at all, only because General Wolfe has obviated the likelihood that
we should have to swear false fealty to the Roman church. For that, he has
my sincere gratitude."

"Thank God, if only for that," remarked Mr. McRae. He frowned. "But,
sir — why the reservation? This continent may be entirely the Crown's,
unless the diplomats again relinquish their advantage, as they did in the last
peace."

The McRaes stood with their companion at a small distance from the milling guests on the lawn. The light of nearby cressets flickered over the thoughtful face of the tall man. It was a thin, almost aesthetic face, browned by constant exposure to the sun. The broad furrow of a scar ran over the right side of his forehead. His own flaxen hair was tied back into a tail with a black ribbon; he was one of the few men at the ball who eschewed a wig. He wore gray breeches, a gray frock coat of past fashion, a dark gray waistcoat, and a silvery ruffle beneath his neck. In one hand he held a black tricorn. He sported no sword.

Jack Frake, after a moment, guardedly said, "I don't believe the Crown will repeat that mistake. We will no longer be subjected to the depredations of the French. Mr. Pitt seems to have a broader view of what is good for England."

Ian McRae's brow wrinkled in question, but he did not pursue the subject. He knew, as well as did the planter, that they would discuss politics with their host and other guests in the gaming room later in the evening. That was what usually happened at these affairs, when the men sought a respite from the dancing and music and polite chitchat of the ballroom.

"When Mr. Halley's comet appeared earlier this year," ventured Jack Frake, "I would often at night sit on the roof of my house and watch it in the sky. You know that I am not superstitious, but I could not help but think that its appearance was a portent. Whether of a harbinger, or of an omen, I could not decide."

"I've read," said Madeline McRae, "that when he saw it, William the Norman regarded that same comet as a blessing of his conquest of England."

"An omen of what, sir?" asked her husband.

"Perhaps of the Crown's own interpretation of that hurried star."

"Why is it called Mr. Halley's comet?" asked Etáin, who, until now, had remained in deferential silence. "He could not have discovered it, if William the Norman saw it."

"Because he calculated all the times it would appear in our skies," Jack Frake said, "and all the times it ever did."

Ian McRae sighed. "I wish I could predict a certain gentleman's wishes," he commented. "He is a new star, but is in no hurry to make up his mind."

Madeline McRae laughed. "My husband refers to a portentous person in our midst this evening, Mr. Frake. He has kept the company abuzz with speculation about whether or not he will become your new neighbor."

"Oh, yes," Jack Frake said, "him. I arrived only at the beginning of the first dance, but not too late to have him pointed out to me, and to have some of that speculation thrust quite brutally into my ear." He laughed. "The number of guests who were eager to speak with me, for once, was surprising and not a little startling."

Madeline McRae brought up her fan and thoughtfully touched her cheek with it. Another man, she knew, might have spoken the last sentence with resentment, or contempt, or dark irony. Or even with feigned indifference. But Jack Frake had spoken with a gay, genuine carelessness. She smiled and said, "It is your own fault if people find you unapproachable, my dear friend. You say shocking things to them, and your manner does not invite society."

Jack Frake shrugged and smiled again. "If it is a fault, madam, perhaps it is because I expect too much of people."

"What do you expect of them?"

Jack Frake shook his head. "Had I the leisure, I would write a book on the subject of what I expect of society, and what society may not expect of me."

Etáin McRae studied him with special interest now. But she always studied Jack Frake with special interest.

Her father said, "Well, if you two are going to engage in more *salon* talk, I shall join the others to watch the bonfire. My wife and daughter may accompany me if they can find the courtesy to end this courtly chatter." With a friendly pat on Jack Frake's back, Ian McRae turned and strode in the direction of the crowd at the edge of the lawn.

His wife leaned closer to Jack Frake and said, "He is fond of you, too, sir. That is why he runs. He is a sentimental man, beneath all that tartan bluster."

"An endearing cowardice, to be sure," Jack Frake said. He knew how the man felt about him. After a pause, he said, "But — you may be forgetting, madam, that your husband was one of the few passengers who took up a musket on the *Sparrowhawk* to help fight that privateer. There was no bluster in that action."

"I have not forgotten," said the woman. "When it was over, as I sponged the powder and other men's blood off him, I cursed him and praised him in the same breath."

"And I have not forgotten the kindness you showed me before that fight."

"You have shown us more than one, over the years since."

"I still have the crown you gave me," Jack Frake said, "when we first met. It is locked away in a special box in my library, with other memories."

Madeline McRae touched Jack Frake's arm in acknowledgment, then turned to her daughter. "Here is a rare man, Etáin," she said. "He exhibits a valor not common in Englishmen. He is not afraid to confess that he keeps a *trousseau de l'âme*. And, he confesses more than he knows. I envy you."

"Yes, Maman," answered the girl.

The woman sensed that her daughter wished to speak, and that what she wished to say was to the young man before them. "I follow your father, dear one," she said. "You will follow shortly." Mrs. McRae turned and left the pair alone.

Jack Frake grinned. "Your mother is quite shameless in her intimations, Miss McRae."

"She is quite fortunate that my own would not conflict with hers, Mr. Frake. For otherwise we should both be very sad, or very angry."

"That took courage to confess."

"Thank you." She smiled up at the man who was ten years her senior. "I remember when Mother gave you that crown on the ship, when you were wearing that awful iron collar. The wind on the deck was cold, and my father was angry at the winds that would not come. For a while, you remember, there were none."

Jack Frake chuckled. "And I remember a little brat, staring at me with a most disapproving face from beneath a bonnet about half her size."

"On the coach to London, with Miss Morley...." Etáin shook her head, not wanting to dwell on her governess's fate. She glanced at the ground, then said brightly, "I was given a coin, too! Just tonight!"

"Oh?" Jack Frake said with interest, grateful that the girl had changed the subject. She had lost a favorite governess, while he had lost Redmagne, who had become that woman's lover.

"Yes. A penny." The girl took a coin from inside her glove and held it up to the light. "He said that my pose at the harp was the attitude of a goddess. See? It is Britannia."

Jack Frake took the coin from her, and frowned for a reason he did not immediately understand. The sight of the seated figure triggered an indistinct memory. Then he vividly remembered Parson Parmley, and the map, the globe, and the things that minister had said about another penny just like the one in Etáin's hand. Other memories followed these, unpleasant memories. He shook his head to rid his mind of them. He asked, handing back the coin, "Who gave this to you? Mr. Vishonn, or his son?" He frowned in mock anger. "If they believe this pittance is commensurate with your musical skills, I shall challenge one or the other to a duel."

"No," answered the girl. "Mr. Kenrick gave it to me. The gentleman who might purchase Brougham Hall from Mr. Stannard and my father." She glanced around. "That's him, over there." She nodded in the direction of a young man who stood with an older man at the edge of the lawn, apart from the other guests.

Jack Frake glanced at the stranger, then asked, "Why did he pay you such a compliment?"

Etáin explained the circumstances, then asked in turn, "Would you like to meet him? I am certain that you would acquire a friend. You are very much like him."

It did not escape Jack Frake's notice the order in which she had referred to him and the stranger. He felt a pang of jealousy. He was in love with the girl and with the innocent intelligence she emanated. It was understood by her and her parents that they would be married in two or three years. There were no other rivals for his affection. Until now, he had not thought there were any rivals for hers. "No," he said, shaking his head. "Not now. There will be time." He smiled down at her, and hoped that he sounded sincere. "It was very kind of him to give you that penny."

"No!" exclaimed the girl. "Not kind at all! He refuses to be called *kind*." Etáin's was a young mind, and fragments of conversation about kindness, faults, and what society should not expect of her companion, flashed through her thoughts in search of connections she could not yet make. There were similarities between the two men. She could only sense them. She was certain that her companion and the visitor were more alike than unalike. She felt disappointment that Jack Frake did not wish to meet the stranger. She glanced at her penny. "I shall keep this to remind me of all the things he said about it." She slipped it back inside her glove. She smiled. "I, too, keep a *trousseau de l'âme*."

Two men and their wives approached them then, Sheriff Cabal Tippet and his wife, Muriel, and Mayor Moses Corbin and his wife, Jewel. Jack Frake and Etáin were drawn into mundane conversation about the celebration, and the party drifted in the direction of the McRaes at the edge of the lawn.

*   *   *

The Kenny brothers played "Lady Hope's Reel" on their fiddles as the fireworks — expensive Italian rockets which only Reece Vishonn, among all the planters, could afford to import from England — rose into the night sky one after another in a bursting choir of sparkling but short-lived stars. Two or three of them were bright enough to light up the opposite bank of the York a mile away. The guests uttered exclamations of delight and surprise.

Rockets rose elsewhere over the river, their explosions audible seconds after their multicolored stars had died. Otis Talbot said, "Look, sir. It seems that Caxton is not alone in this celebration."

But Hugh Kenrick did not hear. He was, emotionally, back in Green Park, London, many years ago, where he had witnessed a display more spectacular than this, while a great orchestra played an overture that matched the brilliance of that display. The memory of that night was as fleeting as one of the rockets' stars, and was not what caused him to stand with his head uplifted, insensible to his companion's words and to the cheers of the other guests. The sight of the fireworks acted as a catalyst that allowed him now, as it did those many years ago, to reach an evaluation, a conclusion, and a decision.

"*Meum Atrium*," he said out loud.

"Excuse me, sir?" said Otis Talbot.

Hugh glanced at his companion, as though noticing him for the first time. "That is what I shall call the place," he said, as though explaining the obvious. "*Meum Atrium*...my hall.... *Meus*...mine...."

Talbot sighed with relief. "I see. Then...you have decided?"

"Yes. *Meum Atrium. Meum Hall.*"

The agent smiled. "It will be a rather confounding name for persons not well-read in Latin, sir."

Hugh shrugged. "They have only to ask, when the time comes."

"Shall I inform Mr. Stannard and Mr. McRae?"

"No, Mr. Talbot. Not now. I doubt that they would be able to contain their joy at the news. The confidence they have thus far kept would be overtested. No. We will let them know tomorrow morning, at the breakfast. I want no scenes here tonight." He paused. "This is a private matter." Hugh smiled at his companion. It was a happy, proud, and contented smile — a smile of finality.

"As you wish, Mr. Kenrick," said Talbot.

The last salvo of rockets whooshed into the sky, and in a rapid succession of deafening bursts painted a dazzling galaxy of man-made stars.

*   *   *

"I invite you gentlemen to reflect on all the troubles that have festered between the Crown and the colonies since the beginning of this war: the innumerable outrages of impressments of seamen by the Navy in our ports and on our own ships at sea; the embargoes on our trade by that Navy; the quartering of troops in private homes; the interminable quarrels between regular and colonial officers in the field; the coercive methods of recruitment of American men for the regular army, and the abusive treatment of our militia by its officers." The speaker paused, then said, "I ask you to reflect on those matters, and then ask yourselves why you find reason to celebrate."

It was two o'clock in the morning. The air in Reece Vishonn's gaming room was pungent with the smoke of several pipes. The muted notes of a galliard seeped through the room's thick double doors. About a dozen men were present. One guest was sound asleep on a couch. Four other men were playing a brisk game of faro at one of the tables. Two more were engrossed in a round of billiards. Six were stretched comfortably in armchairs around the fireplace. Most of the men, weighed down by food, drink, the exercise of dance, and the late hour, were only hazily conscious of their surroundings and company.

Until they heard these words, spoken in answer to an innocuous question asked in expectation of an innocuous answer. Then half-shut eyes opened, heads jerked up, and cards stopped slapping on the table. The billiards players broke their study of the lay of the balls on the green baize to stare at the speaker.

Jack Frake, pipe in hand, stood casually in a corner near the fireplace and glanced at each of the faces now turned to him, waiting for a reply. Tonight he had joined in a country-dance, something no one in Caxton could remember him ever having done before. Tonight he was uncharacteristically sociable, and listened to other guests' small talk and gossip. Tonight he requested that Etáin McRae play "Westering," and her rendition of it melted the reserve of even those women who disapproved of her pose. Tonight he watched the fireworks with the other guests, and complimented the host on the lavishness of his hospitality. Tonight, Jack Frake had not been the gruff, distant, self-absorbed man they all knew so well.

Reece Vishonn, seated in a chair across the fireplace from him, narrowed his eyes in thought as he scrutinized Jack Frake's austere face. Then he said, "I concede the animosities, sir. What man here wouldn't? But I — and I'm certain that many of us here think as I do — I ascribe them to the careful efforts of a generous parent attempting to perform a kindness for an ungrateful child. Soon the rebuffed parent resorts to impatience and arrogance, and the child to peevishness and parsimonious feeling." He shook his head once. "When peace returns, sir, we'll have no more of those problems."

"It is a stressful time," remarked Ralph Cullis. "Tempers have flared. Obligations have been shirked. People say things they don't mean, and commit actions they later regret."

Reverend Albert Acland said, "Yes, sir. There have been animosities, and altercations, and ill-feeling between His Majesty's forces and our own. But, for all that, it is a time to be thankful, and to celebrate."

Most of the other men grunted or nodded in agreement.

Jack Frake took a draught from his pipe, then said, "I see that the past will not guide you, gentlemen, as it should. Consider these questions, then: What will a Crown victory mean for the colonies? If it no longer has a rival on this continent, what might the Crown, or Parliament, plan with greater ease for *our* futures? Would it need to placate us to secure our support, something it has done with only the greatest reluctance? Or will it feel free to dictate to us in order to secure our slavery? What are the Crown's ends, and what might be its means? Why has the Crown fought so mightily for this continent? Will it ask us to pay for our liberties? Are we represented in Parliament, where at least a man might rise for us and accost the ministry's and membership's policies? Are we as 'libertied' as we believe?"

When he saw nothing but closed, almost condescendingly tolerant faces before him, Jack Frake exclaimed, "For God's sake, gentlemen, our own House" — here he paused to glance at Edgar Cullis and William Granby, the burgesses — "our own House sets the prices the taverns and ordinaries may charge their patrons, and regulates the production of our tobacco!" He paused again. "Governor Fauquier may assent to any bill or law passed by the Council and House in Williamsburg, but you and I know that for such a law to have full force, it must have the King's assent, signature and seal as well — after first being approved by his Privy Council. Years can pass before we learn that a law has been disallowed, and when it has been disallowed, the courts become choked with suits for recovery of damages and costs for having obeyed a disallowed law. His Excellency the Governor may be the most reasonable and benevolent man, but his first allegiance would be neither to his reason, nor to his good will, but to the Crown."

Edgar Cullis shot from his chair. "That is a dastardly thing to say about the man!" he exclaimed.

Jack Frake looked incredulous, but smiled. He leaned closer to Cullis and said, "I heard you express that exact sentiment a week ago, sir. You meant approval of it. I do not."

"You asperse the Crown!" accused the father, Ralph Cullis, pointing a finger. His son resumed his seat next to him.

"A contemptible sentiment!" said Ira Granby.

"Near treason!" grumbled Reverend Acland.

"Near treason, sir?" asked Jack Frake. "Or near the truth?" He faced a dozen sets of hostile eyes and smiled. "Mr. Cullis," he said, addressing the young burgess, "the next time you are engaged in cards with His Excellency at the Palace in the coming session, ask him where is the true home of his loyalties."

Edgar Cullis gasped, then sniffed. "I would not dare, sir. That would be…offensive to his person and station."

"I contest the false conflict you present, Mr. Frake," said Ira Granby. "It would be treason if the Governor heeded his reason, and disobeyed the Crown. Reason must necessarily defer in fealty to Crown imperatives."

"Just as it must defer in faith to God's will," Acland said. He cast a sly glance at Jack Frake. He seemed to be the only man present who was neither surprised nor disappointed by Jack Frake's change in manner.

Jack Frake said with frosty courtesy, "If you gentlemen are correct, then his reason is as superfluous an appendage to his good character, as his peruke is to his head, and cannot be relied upon to defend you in any grave matter concerning the Crown."

Reverend Acland set down his teacup and saucer on the table at his elbow. "I do believe, sir, that the Indian war club that gave you that scar, also addled your brains."

All the men stared in disbelief at the minister. Jack Frake smiled again. "I will say this much for that Ottawa, sir: That he met me in combat, knowing the risks, and died like a man. He did not hide behind holy orders and hurl insults at me, knowing that he did not risk being challenged to a duel."

The minister's face grew livid and he rose from his chair.

Reece Vishonn also stood up. "Now, now, gentlemen!" he blurted. "This…raillery is improper…on such an occasion." He turned to Acland. "Sir, will you please apologize to Mr. Frake?"

Reverend Acland clenched his fists and stood stiffly. "I will not, sir! I have always known that this man is not of my flock! If he had not declined to join it, I would have cut him from it myself with a fowling piece! There is a disease about him, like the cattle that pass through here from Carolina and infect our own herds!" Without a further word, he turned and stalked from the room, slamming the door behind him.

For a moment, no one said anything. In time, Henry Otway remarked, "Well, what do you think of that, gentlemen?"

Ira Granby suggested, "One too many journeys to the punch bowl."

Reece Vishonn sighed and turned to Jack Frake. "Sir, please accept *my* apologies for the reverend's…behavior. I cannot explain what prompted him to say so…rascally a thing."

Jack Frake shook his head. "I can, Mr. Vishonn. But, what he and I think of each other, is not the subject I wish to discuss. Your apology is not necessary."

Vishonn nodded, and took his seat again. Not a word was spoken for the next few minutes.

Then Edgar Cullis ventured, "You are wrong about the fate of our laws,

Mr. Frake."

"Am I?" Jack Frake said. "Is not Reverend Camm expected to return from London with the news that the Privy Council has disallowed last year's Act, the Two-Penny Act, which governs the churchmen's salaries here? Depend on it, Mr. Camm and his colleagues will waste little time lodging suits against their parishes in the General Court on the basis of that likely ruling."

"He may have already lodged it," remarked Mr. Stannard. "I heard some captain remark on his having landed at Hampton a day or so ago."

"Now," Jack Frake continued, "if he loses his suit in the General Court here, what guarantee have we that he will not again plead to the Council, and succeed in having our own court's decision overruled and voided? By all accounts, he is as determined to be paid by his parish as the Council is determined to prescribe our laws."

Thomas Reisdale stirred in his chair. "You know, gentlemen," he said after a moment, "I must admit that Mr. Frake is right. The first disallowance has the effect of placing all Virginia law in a state of limbo. You see, it does not merely concern ministers' salaries. The Crown will uphold our laws, if they please it, and void them, if they please not. The king's protection, so often cited by our few champions, is illusory."

Reece Vishonn shook his head. "No, sir," he protested. "I won't hear of it! Our excellent constitution will not allow that to come about." He glanced at Jack Frake. "And, please excuse it, sir, but I don't believe either that it would allow any of your dark imaginings to come about."

Jack shrugged. "For myself, sirs, I have stopped counting on the sundog of our excellent constitution."

"But are we not Englishmen?" asked Henry Otway. "Do we not, as Crown subjects, inherit the protection of the constitution and the king?"

"The full protection of the constitution is not afforded the colonies," Jack Frake said. "We are, it is true, Crown subjects, but, in the eyes of Parliament and the king's ministers, and the king himself, not wholly Englishmen. We either left England's shores, or were born beyond them. We are, in the scheme of things, but glorified factotums." He paused. "The laws and liberties enjoyed by the inhabitants of Cornwall are more sacrosanct than any enjoyed in the colonies here. We exist, in the Crown's view, not for ourselves, but on sufferance, for the pleasure and convenience of the Crown. Mr. Reisdale has caught my point. The king's protection is illusory. If we enjoy any latitude in liberty, it is only because we have the advantage of distance and time."

"Well put, sir," Reisdale said. "Our remove from the mother country is a pitiful protection of our liberties. Reverend Camm has proven that."

One of the billiard players groaned with impatience. "Why do you belabor these speculative matters, sir?" he asked Jack Frake. "We are here to enjoy the company and a modicum of diversion."

"Yes," chimed one of the card game players. "Damn it all, we'll get politics and speechifying enough, once the new session convenes next month!"

Some of the men laughed. Henry Otway gestured to William Granby and Edgar Cullis. "Here, Mr. Frake, are the men who will apprise us of any evil-doings cooked by the Crown. They are the Roman geese we have elected to so warn us."

Jack shrugged again. "I have merely pointed out an oversight, gentlemen. I am certain that times lie ahead when you will be moved to think ahead, and not be content with the prosaic concerns of the present. You will wonder then why the obvious was not so clear to you in the past, and, if you are honest with yourselves, you will conclude that you did not choose to see it."

He spoke the words in a dry, almost impersonal manner, not intending any offense. But most of the men looked away from him. A few stared at him with a hostility that matched Reverend Acland's. He realized that he had delivered a personal wound to each of them, and that none of the affronted men would continue the conversation. The billiards players turned and resumed their game; the dealer in the faro game reshuffled his cards. A few men rose, walked to the table that held bottles of liquor, and stood with their backs to him.

Only Mr. Reisdale regarded him with sympathy and understanding. Reece Vishonn managed to appear embarrassed with his guests' behavior.

Jack Frake nodded acknowledgment to Mr. Reisdale, then went to the fireplace, emptied the embers of his pipe into the flames, and walked to the double doors. He turned and addressed the men once more. "Good evening, sirs. I leave you with your peevishness and parsimonious feelings."

There was no answer. As he turned and touched the handles of the door, someone in a darkened corner rose from a chair and approached him. It was Hugh Kenrick. "My compliments, Mr. Frake," he said. "Only in Parliament have I seen such resolve cause so acrimonious a division."

Jack Frake smiled, opened the doors, and stepped into the breezeway that separated the gaming room from the ballroom. Hugh Kenrick followed him. Jack Frake closed the doors and turned to the younger man. "You are Hugh Kenrick. You were pointed out to me earlier."

Hugh offered his hand. "As were you to me, sir."

Jack took the proffered hand and shook it. He said, "It is unfortunate, Mr. Kenrick, that no colonial member of that body will ever have a chance to participate in such a division."

"Not as a colonial," answered Hugh. "I know of no factotum who has a voice in the disposal of his master's budget or in the propriety of his diversions." He paused. "You are right to concern yourself with the future. I have seen and heard it myself, in London. I am better acquainted with Mr. Pitt than I am with the Lieutenant-Governor here. He, too, as you remarked, must be a man of divided sympathies and loyalties."

"Divided," asked Jack, "or divisive?"

Hugh smiled. "I stand corrected, sir."

Jack laughed. "Why did you not speak up a few moments ago, Mr. Kenrick?"

"I am a guest here, and an outsider. And, to speak frankly, I enjoyed listening to you address the matter." Hugh grinned. "I came in with Mr. McRae to rest from the ball. Mr. McRae stretched out on one of the divans. You came in afterward. He missed a clash of Titans." After a short pause, he corrected himself. "Well, at least the triumph of one, and the flight of a gnome."

"You have seen Brougham Hall, Mr. Kenrick," Jack said. "Will you purchase it?"

"Yes," Hugh said. "But, please keep that a secret. I want no fuss made about it." He frowned. "Why does that minister hate you?"

Jack shrugged. "I would say that it is because I refuse to waste my time sitting in his church listening to his indifferent sermons. But, that cannot be the whole reason. I can neither fathom his hatred of me, nor much concern myself with it."

"I shall make a point of causing him to hate me, as well, once I have settled in."

Jack shook his head. "I do not think he will need your assistance, sir."

Hugh nodded in acknowledgment of the compliment. He was bursting with the desire to question the man about *Hyperborea*, and about the Skelly gang, and how he came by the scar on his forehead. But he knew that this was neither the time nor the place to ask such questions. Instead, he said, "I sailed with Captain Ramshaw in the *Sparrowhawk* to Philadelphia, Mr. Frake. He told me much about you."

Jack frowned. "Why would he have told you about me?"

"Because I have read *Hyperborea*."

Jack blinked in surprise. After a moment, he said, "We seem to have so many things in common, Mr. Kenrick. Perhaps we will be good neighbors."

"You must tell me the story of your association with that book, some day," Hugh said. He paused, then added, "As you are the last of the Skelly gang, I am the last of the Society of the Pippin."

"Was that a gang, too?"

"The Crown viewed it as such," Hugh said. "No, it was not a gang. It was a club of freethinkers."

Jack smiled tentatively. "I see. Well, when you have settled into Brougham Hall, we will have many stories to tell each other."

The ballroom door opened then, and Etáin McRae came into the hall. She stopped when she saw Jack Frake and Hugh Kenrick standing together. She smiled and said, "You have met."

Jack's welcoming smile vanished. He remembered her words from earlier in the evening. "Were you expecting us to, Miss McRae?"

"In *time*, Mr. Frake," the girl answered, placing a special stress on *time*. "I knew that you must." She paused. "Excuse me for interrupting, sirs, but has either of you seen my father? My mother has not seen him in a while, and she is concerned."

"He is fast asleep in the gaming room, Miss McRae," Hugh said. "Shall I rouse him?"

Etáin shook her head. "No. That won't be necessary. Let him be. I was certain that he must be in there." She came closer and glanced from one man to the other. "I see here a compass, gentlemen. One of you is the needle, and one of you the north."

Jack's face remained impassive. Hugh grinned and asked, "Whatever you may mean by that, Miss McRae — which of us is which?"

"I cannot yet decide, Mr. Kenrick," Etáin said. "It is something that will become apparent — *in time*." Then she took a small step back and performed a short curtsy. She smiled an odd smile, and went back into the ballroom.

For a moment, the two men stared in silence at the closed door. Then Hugh asked, "What did she mean by that riddle?"

Jack said nothing for a moment. He was still staring at the space where Etáin had stood. "I do not know," he answered almost woodenly.

"She was not teasing us with it, I'm certain of that," Hugh essayed. "She appeared to be happy to have invented it. It is a secret riddle, which she alone will ponder."

Jack said, "Yes, perhaps that is it." He paused. "But, before tonight, I did not know her ever to speak in riddles."

The gaming room doors opened and Thomas Reisdale emerged. He nodded to the two men, then addressed Jack Frake. "I wish to speak with you, sir, if you have the time. I have written a fragment on the very matters you raised tonight, and would be honored if you could read it some time. I could bring it to Morland tomorrow."

Hugh said, "Mr. Frake, I look forward to speaking with you again." He bowed slightly to the two men. "I leave you gentlemen to your intrigues." He turned and strode to the ballroom doors.

*   *   *

Hugh Kenrick did not see Jack Frake again that night. His future neighbor disappeared. Hugh did not realize this until a few hours had passed. When he asked Ian McRae, he was told that Jack Frake had left early with Thomas Reisdale, and had already bid his family goodnight. He went to the gaming room and caught a few hours of sleep. When Otis Talbot woke him up, it was dawn, and half the guests had already departed, including the McRaes.

After breakfast at the Gramatan Inn with Arthur Stannard and Ian McRae, Otis Talbot put his signature on several pieces of paper, including a draft on Swire's Bank for the purchase of Brougham Hall. Hugh Kenrick signed his name beneath his companion's.

At one o'clock in the afternoon, the two men boarded the *Amelia*. When the sloop gained the middle of the York River, a brisk wind filled her sails and the vessel cut swiftly through the water, leaving Caxton to quickly diminish astern.

Hugh remained on deck and watched the town diminish until he could no longer distinguish it from the trees ashore. The town vanished in the haze that enveloped the entire river and the western horizon beyond.

Chapter 6: The Empty Houses

It was to an empty house that Jack Frake returned in a chilly dawn. Upon leaving the ball, he and Thomas Reisdale claimed their mounts and ventured down the dark roads beyond Enderly, guided by a three-quarter moon, to the attorney's house across Hove Creek. There he drank coffee and read some of Reisdale's "fragments," learned commentaries on a variety of political subjects, which included the British constitution and colonial charters, with copious citations of authorities as late as John Milton, John Locke, and Hugo Grotius, and as ancient as Tacitus and Cicero. They had talked for a while, speculating on the weal and bane of a British North America. Then Jack thanked his host, remounted his horse, and rode home in the darkness as dew formed on the leaves and grass, and as birds awoke to greet a sun that had not yet risen.

Morland was an empty house, emptied swiftly and completely in a handful of years. To Jack, those years seemed like a lifetime ago. The contrast between the present and past was jarring. He had difficulty reconciling the contrast. Years ago he was an indentured felon, sold to John Massie by John Ramshaw for a penny. He never learned what Captain Ramshaw had told his new master about him. Later, by the time his indenture had expired, he had become virtually a fourth son to the planter, and a special, mutual affection grew between them that did not exist between Massie and his sons. Jack supposed it was because John Massie was something of an adventurer and renegade himself, when he was a youth, the son of a smaller planter who had wooed and married the daughter of Archibald Morland, the original owner of the plantation. He later was a lieutenant in a Virginia militia company and had taken part in the capture of Louisbourg, and after that, had commanded a company of volunteers during a punitive expedition against marauding Indians in the western part of the colony.

Massie, he learned later, had developed a special arrangement with Ramshaw to import and export commodities taxed and regulated by the Crown. The illegal imports — from Portugal, the Netherlands, France, and Spain — were in turn sold to distributors and merchants in Yorktown, Williamsburg, and Fredericksburg. Massie had not forced Jack to labor in the fields with other servants whose indentures he owned, but allowed Jack to be tutored with his own children. Jack eventually became the man's scrupulous and confidential clerk.

Morland, like the other large plantations, had its own private grave-yard. Jack passed this on his way home, and paused for a moment to look down on the flat, roughly chiseled stone markers. There was John Massie, the last of the family to go, buried next to his wife, Grace. There was his oldest son, John, heir apparent to the plantation, killed in a senseless, impromptu duel outside a Williamsburg tavern after an exchange of drunken insults with a stranger from the Carolinas over each other's honesty and pedigrees.

Two of the markers rested on graves that contained no remains. The youngest and middle sons of Massie were both casualties of the Braddock disaster. William, aged sixteen, was killed outright in the first minutes of that battle; his body was never recovered. Rufus, aged nineteen, was also cut down, but was saved by Jack from the raised tomahawk of an Ottawa who rushed from cover to collect a scalp. It was in furious hand-to-hand combat with the determined Indian, and then with another who followed the first, that Jack received the scar from a war club that had nearly brained him. After felling the two Ottawas, he had managed to get Rufus to his feet and walk him to the rear of the confused and panicked column of British regulars. After pushing Rufus into the river to make his own way back across it, he ran back through the unending hail of bullets, stumbling over the growing matte of downed redcoats. He paused only once, to hold the reins of a frightened horse, whose rider, a British major, had been shot out of the saddle, so that a tall Virginian, Colonel George Washington, could mount it. He made his way back to Captain Massie and his Queen Anne militia only to find that his benefactor was wounded while leading a sally into the woods to rout the French and Indians there. Whether he was struck in the hip by a British or enemy ball, no one could say.

Half of Massie's small company of Virginians was felled, he learned later, by that same volley from British ranks, whose officers mistook the militia men for French or Indians, simply because they saw irregularly dressed men using the thicket as cover and loading and firing from kneeling positions. This method of frontier fighting was alien to the sensibilities of men trained to fight in Europe. The perception and fatal error occurred up and down the column as its officers struggled to preserve order in the ranks and their own presence of mind, more often than not losing their ranks to bullets and desertion, and then their own lives to a well-aimed ball.

Jack saw one British officer dismount and lead the remnants of his company in a bayonet charge into the surrounding thicket — the sole intel-ligent action he witnessed a regular officer take that terrible day — and begin to drive the bayonet-fearing Indians back into the forest, only to find himself alone after another British volley brought down most of the redcoats behind him. As the survivors bolted back to the column, the officer flailed away with his sword at the returning Indians, until he was surrounded and struck in the head and back by war clubs. One of the black, orange, and red painted creatures dipped down out of sight, and a moment later rose again over the bushes with a shrill, prolonged whoop, holding aloft the officer's bloody scalp and silver gorget. Jack raised his musket, fired, and placed a ball directly into the screaming, undulating mouth.

Whether the creature was an Ottawa or an Ojibwa, Jack could not tell, and from that day onward he saw no reason to make a distinction between any of the numerous tribes. And, it was the last act of respect he would ever pay a British officer.

The person who helped him carry John Massie to the rear, as other Queen Anne militiamen escorted them under fire, was another Indian, John Proudlocks, a lad only a few years younger than Jack. Proudlocks was adopted as a boy by Massie during the Louisbourg campaign and had acted as the man's valet and cook ever since. His Oneida tribe was wiped out by Mohawks, and he and a few others kept alive as slaves. Proudlocks escaped, and appeared one morning in camp before Massie's tent with some rabbits he had trapped and killed. Other militiamen had wanted to shoot him, suspecting him of being a spy for the French, but Massie stopped them. Proudlocks and Jack Frake matured together under the strict but benevolent regime of their mutual master.

In the retreat across the Monongahela River and through the forests beyond with what was left of the shamed army, Jack and Proudlocks nursed John and Rufus Massie the best they could. Rufus, hit twice in his upper torso, died en route, and was buried in a meadow somewhere near the Pennsylvania border. John Massie, back in Caxton, lived long enough to lose his last son, to see Jack marry his daughter, Jane, and then to lose her, too, to childbirth. He died in his sleep about a month after Jack and Jane's own son succumbed to what Mrs. Rittles, the midwife and wet nurse, called "the chills."

Jack Frake looked down on the markers of Jane Frake and their one-month-old son, Augustus, and wondered how his life might have been different, had they lived. He sat in his saddle for a long time, contemplating the imponderable. The years between the passing of so many he had been close to and the present were subsequently filled with a ruthless determination to make the plantation pay for itself — as a means of trying to forget.

After a while, he looked up when the first full ray of the sunrise filtered through the trees and touched his forehead. For a reason he could not explain to himself, he felt that some new phase of his life was about to begin. By the time he stabled his mount and stepped inside his house, he was smiling in amusement at the thought that it might have something to do with Hugh Kenrick. The younger man had impressed him; that is, surprised him with his agreement with the sentiments he had expressed in the gaming room; had pleased him with the ease with which Kenrick had made his acquaintance; had given him some strange hope of friendship. He had been dubbed a solitary man ever since he was brought to Caxton, and a near-hermit ever since the deaths of his wife and father-in-law. Well, he thought, solitary men are solitary only because they have not met their companions in character.

Yes, he admitted to himself; he was impressed by Hugh Kenrick. So had been Etáin McRae. "You are very much like him," she had said.

He tried to imagine Hugh Kenrick as a rival for her affections, and ultimately for her hand; as a neighbor; perhaps as a political ally. He chuckled to himself as he lay down in bed to take a short nap — on any other day, he would have been awake and busy for an hour by now — when he realized that Hugh Kenrick was occupying his thoughts and concerns almost as much as had Halley's comet and Wolfe's victory in Quebec. When the man returned to take possession of Brougham Hall, what difference would the newcomer make in the lives of the people here, in the life of Caxton itself?

A few hours later Jack rose and had a breakfast prepared for him by Mary Beck, the cook, an older woman whose indenture John Massie had bought but who stayed on years after its expiration. "How was the ball, sir?" she asked him in the sunlit breakfast room.

"Fancy enough and fine, Mary," said Jack.

"Pardon me for sayin' so, sir," she said as she set his meal before him, "but you ought to attend those things more often. You look bright and cheery this morning, more than usual, if I might make the observation."

"Thank you, Mary. I even feel brighter and cheerier than usual."

"You spoke with Miss McRae, I'm betting."

"Yes. She enchanted the company."

Mary Beck stood for a moment, holding an empty tray, before leaving the room. "Pardon me again for the observation, sir, but you looked darkly there for a moment, when I mentioned the young lady. All I can say is, you'd better pick the apple before it's poached. Miss McRae is fillin' out in all sorts of ways, and other gentlemen, bein' men half the likes of you, can't help notice it, too, and that devil of a father of hers might make other arrangements before you stakes your claim."

"That's not likely, Mary," Jack said. "I've got things in hand. Please, don't concern yourself."

Mary Beck broke off her scrutiny, turned, and walked to the door. "I'm just lookin' after your natural interests, that's all, sir," she threw over her shoulder.

Jack wondered for a moment what about himself had emboldened the usually reticent woman to volunteer her comments. All he was able to conclude was that attending the ball at Enderly had noticeably altered his demeanor.

After breakfast, he went to the stable, saddled another horse, and rode out to inspect the progress of the corn and barley harvests. He stopped at the tobacco barns first, though, and saw that the prizing was nearly finished. Six Negro men were busy at the weighted levers that pressed the cured leaves into the hogsheads. Though they were slaves, he paid them laborers' wages for the work. He had convinced John Massie, even before the Braddock expedition, to begin selling his slaves, when he could, to Quakers in the west and north, who in turn freed them as Virginians could by law not. Massie had detested the institution and did not need much persuasion. "If you pay a man to perform a task," Jack had told him years ago, "then you may depend on one of two things: he will perform it, or botch it. Then you are free to retain him, or dismiss him. A slave, who has no stake in the task done or undone, will perform it only in an approximate manner, just enough to avoid punishment. And then, unless you choose to resort to the whip, you are as bonded to him as he is to you."

John Massie's eyes had lit up in comprehension. "You make a point that's eluded me, Jack," he said. "By your reasoning, we slave-owners are as much enslaved by the practice as are the slaves."

"And no amount of kindness to a slave will lessen the evil, sir," Jack continued. "Kindness is an affection one shows a prize pig, or a resourceful dog. Kindness is a kind of slavery, too, if it is practiced by men who ought to think better of themselves. It is mistaken for humaneness."

The six slaves were the last slaves at Morland. They were the last, because they were the best and hardest working. They were as devoted to Jack as they had been to John Massie. They did not wish to be sold. Mouse, the oldest of them, told him once, "Sir, you try to get us a new master, we run away. You put irons on us to hold our feet, we stop work. You are a good man, and treat us so. Leave it alone." Mouse and his five companions each had the freedom of Caxton and the county; each carried a safe conduct pass to deter arrest by slave patrols and bounty hunters.

Mouse and his companions behaved like freedmen and took their freedom for granted. They could do anything but vote and own property. They were content with the purgatory of their liberty. Jack, for his part, both needed them and hated his need of them.

The tobacco crops — as well as all of Morland's other crops — were raised by tenants, whose little wood-frame cottages ringed the Morland plantation. The tenants were not actually tenants, but employees. Jack paid them a small retainer, and then percentages from the profits of the harvests. Each tenant was responsible for a certain amount of acreage and the crops on them, once the seeds were planted. There were six Morland tenants, three of them indentured servants left over from John Massie's day: George Passmore, Caleb Threap, and Timothy Bigelow. Isaac Zimmerman and James and Dorothy Moffet were originally employed by John Massie, Moffet as an overseer. As the slaves were sold off, first by Massie, then by Jack, the need for an overseer diminished, then vanished. Jack retained the overlooker, William Hurry, who saw to it that crops were properly cared for, harvested, and stored. His business agent, Obedience Robins, oversaw the details of the sale of all the crops. Robins also filled the position of steward for Morland, ensuring that especially the main house was stocked with necessities.

Then there was John Proudlocks. Jack had persuaded him to become a tenant in charge of the livestock, swine and fowl, and to help the other tenants when they needed extra hands in the fields. For years, and even now, Proudlocks was the closest thing to a friend Jack had since coming to Caxton. He could not pronounce the long string of incompatible consonants and vowels that was Proudlocks's Oneidan name. John Massie had simply named the boy after himself. Later, the boy appended a surname of his own invention, inspired by the portrait of Archibald Morland that still hung in the main house's library. "John Who is Proud of His Locks" was eventually shortened to John Proudlocks. He was a tall, slim man now with black hair that fell in curled rivulets over his shoulders. He wore English clothes, except for shoes, which his feet could not tolerate. In their stead, he wore moccasins, which he made himself.

When they were still boys, Jack, who hated ignorance, took it upon himself to teach Proudlocks how to read, write, cipher, and speak English. Proudlocks, who hated his ignorance of the white men of whom he stood in awe, was a diligent pupil. One day, after a lesson in simple mathematics, Jack asked him why he had surrendered to their benefactor.

Proudlocks did not answer immediately. It was only hours later, after they had both finished their chores and sat together, in the late afternoon, in the room used by the resident tutor to school the Massie children, that he spoke.

"You people," he began, as though no time had passed, "you people, you see things we do not. We Oneidas, and Mohawks, and Senecas, all the tribes, we...look at ground only and today only all our lives. You people, you look at sky and beyond and tomorrow." He paused. "We always had wind, and wood, and water, but no Iroquois ever built boat to sail beyond edge of earth." The boy paused again, not certain that his words expressed what he wanted to say. "You people, there is some magic about you...but it is not magic. I feel it is good magic, do not fear it. It explains much about you, but I cannot explain *it*. It brought you here over the water, and spelled death for all old ways...the looking-at-ground ways. This is why Iroquois and other nations fear you, hate you, make war. You people...you are like shamans who despise worshippers and believers and their chants and foolish ceremonies, sweep to side old ways and people with feeble arms and hands in lazy little heads, and claim earth as no Iroquois could, not shaman or warrior or chief, and make it your servant. You are men like us, like the Iroquois. You are born, you live, you die. But there is some magic about you. I wish to learn this magic of yours, so it is magic no more, and then I look at sky and beyond and tomorrow."

But you do now, Jack said with a wordless smile to the expectant, bronze-hued face. He was answered a moment later by Proudlocks's own smile, one of self-knowledge heavy with the quiet, contented dignity that accompanies such a smile.

Jack could only imagine the hell that John Proudlocks had endured, before wandering into John Massie's militia camp, to cling to that vision of himself and of the possible, living among people indifferent to their own ignorance and hostile to anything that demanded abandonment of it and all the rituals, customs, and brutality that symbolized that ignorance. In terms of Jack's own moral endurance, in terms of physical hardship and the concerted efforts to degrade him, the hell that Proudlocks had endured made his own trials seem petty and mundane by comparison, without diminishing their importance or his own self-respect. An ineluctable sense of justice moved him to grant Proudlocks a species of esteem he had once reserved for Augustus Skelly and Redmagne. Proudlocks sensed this special regard, and reciprocated in his own unobtrusive way.

Jack remembered that day well, for something that Proudlocks had said inspired him to take the boy to his room and show him a gift that Captain Ramshaw had given him on one of his visits to Morland. It was a pair of Italian-made mariner's pocket globes, tucked securely inside a sturdy oak box. One was celestial, the other terrestrial. They were of painted marble, with intricate images, letters, and numbers cut into the stone. Jack pointed out the oceans, Virginia, England, and France. "There are no edges on the earth," he said. "Only horizons." Then he told Proudlocks to hold out his palms, and dropped the globes into them. "There," he said. "Now you hold the sky in one hand, and the earth in the other. Like the ship captain who uses them, you can go anywhere, and by studying them, can know where you have been, where you are, and where you are going. All your yesterdays and tomorrows." He paused. "No more looking-at-ground and today only."

Proudlocks's eyes were ablaze with fascination and comprehension. Glancing from one globe to another, he grinned fiercely. "Knowledge not magic," he said. "Put on paper, in books, written in smooth, cold stone. In numbers, in words. And pictures." He paused. "Pictures made from numbers and words here." He looked up at Jack. "Earth this form? Round? No Englishman saw Virginia from sky, and made picture?"

Jack shook his head. "Nor England," he said. "Nor any of the continents."

Proudlocks looked doubtful. "Sky not round?" he asked, hefting the celestial globe.

"No. The earth sits in the sky, and travels around the sun. The stars on the globe represent what we can see from down here, on the earth. If the stars on the stone match what he sees in the night sky, a captain can know his position — provided he calculates his latitude and longitude, or his numbers."

Proudlocks balanced both globes. "Understand. Knowledge not magic." He brought up the terrestrial globe and tapped his forehead with it. "Knowledge find home here. Must fill head. Secrets not secrets. Open to any man with busy hands in mind."

It occurred to Jack only later that night, as he tossed for a time in his bed, that he must have looked much like Proudlocks that day, when Parson Parmley showed him the maps so long ago. He smiled at the benign irony of it. He wondered if the parson had derived the same pleasure as he had, from seeing a mind awaken to a larger universe, without and within.

But knowledge of the world was only one element of what Proudlocks had deemed "magic." Another element was missing, one taken for granted by both of them. He agreed with Proudlocks that his "magic" explained much, but he, too, was unable to identify and explain the unnamed element. It was knowledge, too — but of what?

*   *   *

It was midmorning by the time Jack neared Proudlocks's shack on the edge of a field. The fowl and swine were kept here in special pens, while the cattle were allowed to roam free in fenced-off pastures beyond the crop fields. Under Proudlocks's care, the guinea hens, muscovy ducks, turkeys and chickens had increased in numbers to the point that Morland could sell the birds to other freeholds and to the taverns and still have plenty left over for its own tables. The guinea hens and turkeys were let loose in the tobacco fields during the growing season to combat the hornworms that could infest the leaves and eat their way to the stalks. "The birds are more efficient than men for worming and grubbing," said Proudlocks once. "Men look under each leaf, hoping not to find something to pluck and crush. My hens and turkeys are hungry, and hope to find a meal under each leaf. It is only the top leaves they cannot reach. We should order some ostriches from London."

Proudlocks was a vociferous reader now, regularly borrowing books from the Morland library with titles that ranged from history to science to agricultural treatises. Jack often thought that his friend was more widely read than he.

He found Proudlocks in one of the pens, in the midst of scores of birds, pouring water into their troughs. The bronze face looked up. "Greetings, Jack," he said. He was the only person at Morland who addressed Jack Frake by his first name.

"Greetings, John," Jack said.

Proudlocks put down his pail and came to the fence. "You returned early from the ball. I heard you pass by this morning."

"Yes. I stopped at Mr. Reisdale's for a while."

"I saw the fireworks. Watched them from the roof of the coop." Proudlocks laughed. "And, I caught the fox."

"The one that carried off your prize guinea two nights ago?"

"That one. He was not expecting me to be out and waiting in so black a night."

Jack smiled. "Good. Moses and Henry are going into the woods in the afternoon to pick out wood for more grain hogsheads. Would you go with them to cut it and haul it back?" Moses Topham was Morland's carpenter, Henry Dakin its cooper.

"Yes." Proudlocks frowned. "Heard one of Swart's people ran away last night."

"Who?"

"Champion."

Champion Smith was Brougham Hall's master blacksmith — and a slave. "How did you hear?" Jack asked.

"Bristol crossed over to see his wife and daughter at Mr. Otway's place." Bristol, another slave, was the blacksmith's apprentice. "Stopped here to trade news. Said they all heard there was to be a new master. Also, Champion got into a fight with the others. Bristol didn't say about what."

Jack grimaced. "Swart will advertise for him when he returns — if he returns — and offer two or three pounds reward, which he won't need to pay. The gentleman who is buying Brougham Hall this morning will pay it, if Champion is caught and returned."

"He carries no pass," remarked Proudlocks. "It is true, then?"

Jack nodded. "I spoke with Mr. Kenrick last night. But, I don't think Swart's people need fear him."

They talked about what else needed to be done on the plantation to prepare for the coming winter. "I'll be joining Henry and Moses in the woods. Have supper with me tonight. Miss Beck is preparing one of her potpies that you like so much, and plum pudding. Then we could have a game of chess."

Proudlocks agreed, and Jack rode off to see the other tenants about the day's chores.

Chapter 7: The Empty Houses

In February of 1759, Handel died, and was interred in Westminster Abbey. William Pitt the "Younger" was born in May. In Bohemia, Haydn completed his first symphony. In Salzburg, Austria, Leopold Mozart was preparing his three-year-old son, Wolfgang, for a tour of the courts of Europe the next year. An English dilettante undertook to translate French physiocrat François Quesnay's *Tableau Économique*, published the year before; it was the first attempt to analyze an entire economy.

In Geneva, his latest residence-in-exile, Voltaire completed *Candide*, and broke with Rousseau over the latter's public attack on an article by Jean d'Alembert in the *Encyclopédie* that extolled the theater, which was banned in Geneva. In Rome, Pope Clement XIII put the *Encyclopédie* on the Index of prohibited books and decreed that all Catholics who did not have their copies of it burned by a priest ran the risk of excommunication. The French government, bowing to pressure from the clergy and conservatives in all strata of society, revoked the *Encyclopédie*'s printing license, but retained the services of its director of book production, Chrétien-Guillaume de Lamoignon de Malesherbes, who found a loophole in the law and arranged to have the great work published in Paris under a Swiss imprint. He also alerted Denis Diderot to planned raids by the authorities, and found places to hide new pages of the *Encyclopédie* until the danger passed, often in the basement of his own house.

Samuel Johnson published that year *Rasselas, or the Prince of Abissinia*, his first major work since completing the *Dictionary*. David Garrick produced at Drury Lane his *Harlequin's Invasion*, a patriotic stage piece about a foiled French invasion of England, for which William Boyce composed the score for "Hearts of Oak."

Adam Smith, dean of faculty at the University of Glasgow, published *The Theory of Moral Sentiments*, the subject of which was heavily influenced by David Hume's *Treatise of Human Nature*. A copy of the latter work was confiscated from Smith years before when he was a Snell scholar at Balliol College at Oxford; it had been deemed heretical and atheistic. Hume, now a close friend of Smith's, was busy publishing the quartos of his *History of England*, a work which Thomas Jefferson decades later would fault for being partial to royal tyranny. Among Smith's other Glasgow friends were Joseph Black, a professor of anatomy who discovered carbon dioxide and latent heat; young James Watt, who would patent the first high-pressure steam engine; and many merchants and entrepreneurs from whose congenial contact Smith would be partly inspired to begin taking notes for what would become *The Wealth of Nations*. And Benjamin Franklin, in London representing the Pennsylvania legislature, was collaborating on a book that would urge Britain to expel the French from North America by annexing Canada, arguing that an unrestrained, growing colonial population would be a boon to British manufactures. Franklin's book was an early critique of the dominant mercantilist theory of trade, whose premise of static wealth was a major contributing factor to most of the century's wars.

Frederick the Great, who six years earlier had broken with Voltaire, suffered one of his bitterest defeats at the hands of the Austrians and Russians at Kunersdorf, near Frankfurt. So distraught was the warrior king by the rout, that he deliberately exposed himself to enemy fire, begging fruitlessly of every bullet that flew his way to strike him down. He was ungently removed from the field by his loyal subordinates.

That same August, at Minden, near Hanover, field marshal Prince Ferdinand, Duke of Brunswick and an ally of Frederick, with a smaller army nearly destroyed the French army that threatened to capture George the Second's principality — nearly, but for the funk of Lord George Sackville, British commander of a cavalry detachment, who repeatedly ignored Ferdinand's orders to rout the fleeing French cavalry. For this impudent conduct, described by a fellow officer as "frightened trauma," a delicate euphemism for cowardice, Sackville was court-martialed and cashiered in disgrace from the British army. A witness to his "trauma" was an aide-de-camp on Ferdinand's staff, Lord Charles Brome, a 21-year-old officer of the Grenadier Guards, who later became the second Earl Cornwallis. Sackville, after sedulously inveigling his way back into politics, was some fifteen years later, as Lord Germain, appointed by Frederick Lord North to be Secretary of State for the Colonies, in which capacity he would deal firmly with his enemies from afar.

And John Harrison, a clockmaker and a commoner, in this year completed the construction of his fourth marine chronometer. The scheduled sea trials of the third were delayed by a combination of the war and the meddling interference of envious royally appointed astronomers.

*   *   *

Hugh Kenrick had also observed Halley's Comet.

But while Jack Frake wondered half-seriously whether it was a har-

binger or an omen of the future, to Hugh, studying the bright streak in the
night sky through the smoke of Philadelphia's chimneys, it was a salutary
punctuation mark for his past.

It marked his decision to remain in America for a few more years. Two
events influenced his decision: the worsening of relations between his
father and uncle to the point that his seniors now rarely spoke to each
other; and Reverdy Brune's engagement and marriage to Alex McDougal.

It began with a letter from his friend, Roger Tallmadge, who reported
that his older brother Francis was killed at Hastenbeck. Seconded from the
Duke of Cumberland's Own Regiment of Horse to serve as a courier on the
Duke's staff during the campaign to protect Hanover, Francis, carrying
orders from the Duke to his Hanoverian allies during the heaviest fighting,
rode into the path of an errant French cannon ball and was picked neatly
and fatally from his galloping horse. Stung by the humiliating and unnecessary capitulation of Cumberland and his brother's seemingly wasted
death, Roger persuaded his equally bitter father to try and purchase him a
commission in the same regiment. This proved impossible. Roger ended up
as an ensign in the Grenadier Guards.

In the course of his correspondence, Roger alluded both to the feuding
between Hugh's father and uncle, and to the frequent exchanges of visits
between the Brunes and the McDougals. He did not feel it his place to spec-
ulate or give Hugh details. His careful allusions were discreetly worded
warnings.

The details were supplied in gently couched missives from Hugh's parents and from Reverdy herself. The widening rift between his father and
uncle unfolded as slowly and inexorably as did his loss of Reverdy.

"Your uncle and I do not much speak to each other, except on unavoidable business," wrote his father during Hugh's first year in Philadelphia.
"Our servants are kept trim and busy in the carrying of notes between Milgram House and your uncle. Often they pass each other on the road. By the
bye, I have decided not to erect a new place for us. It could be done, for our
interests in the Portland quarries would give us an advantage. But Milgram
House, your mother and I have concluded, will do until such time as we can
return to the seat of Danvers."

Months later, Garnet Kenrick wrote his son: "Your uncle Basil had
some guests down from London last week, among them that fulsome fellow
we encountered some years ago, Sir Henoch Pannell, who was accompanied by his fribblous creature of a wife, Chloe. Sir Henoch, I have heard it
said, now controls a bloc of votes in the Commons, and he and your uncle
seem to be forging some kind of unholy alliance. I do not worry about the
longevity of such a pact; devils prefer to work alone, and one can only sur-

mise that two such objectionable persons would not long be able to tolerate each other. I was obliged to sell to Sir Henoch a small number of shares in the bank, in exchange for his silence on your last London escapade. Your uncle arranged this, having fixed in his noodle the possibility that if His Majesty heard of it, his legal counselors could find a way to annul our patent on Danvers."

Effney Kenrick wrote her son: "Mrs. Tallmadge reports to me that the Brunes have been receiving the McDougals with 'suspicious frequency.' We had the Brunes over to Milgram for a Michaelmas supper once after your departure, but they have since begged to excuse themselves from our subsequent invitations in every instance, pleading prior social commitments, or illness."

Reverdy wrote Hugh: "Thank you for the description of Philadelphia and of the quaint environs in which you have been ensconced. It sounds like lovely but rude country. Is it true what I have read here, that the Quaker women there must go about in public with veils over their faces, and that the authorities there allow Indians to roast Presbyterian captives alive in the square and say prayers of thanks after their repast?"

The undertone of flippancy eluded letter-hungry Hugh, who was usually sensitive to literary turns and twists. He said in an amusing but instructive letter:

"The Quaker women here are pious and intelligent, often outspoken, very resourceful, and dress as plainly as their men. They do not wear veils. At times, however, their bonnets are so large and umberous that their features are in shadow, and one must peer into their depths to properly ascertain the age and phiz of the speaker, and to hear her muffled words. You have been reading low magazine accounts of the Indians. Most of them are at sixes-and-sevens and have been pacified by the preachful emissaries of various denominations. They are so stunned and stupefied by the arrival of so much civilization that they remind me of our own country folk when they learn that a manor and its adjacent lands are to be enclosed. The assembly here tries to assuage them with settlements and charity. They have little notion of property, and cannot fathom wheels. They are doomed. The only cannibals I have heard of are the western tribes, who are often engaged by the French to extinguish our settlements beyond the mountains.

"When Fort William Henry fell to Montcalm, hundreds of these beasts violated the terms of the surrender and descended upon our soldiers and the militia men, who carried muskets but no powder and ball. They were to be escorted by the French to another British fort, but neither the Canadians nor the French regulars moved to protect them. The Indians beheaded or scalped the wounded in the fort's hospital, then butchered the camp-followers — mostly women and children — in a similar fashion, and finally turned on the men, taking their clothes and useless weapons and often their lives. Montcalm and his officers are reported to have intervened, but quit the effort because it was too risky as the beasts were drunk on rum and blood. Montcalm bought most of the hostages back, and saw that they were safely escorted to Fort Edward. Many of the Englishmen, however, were kept by the savages, and were forced to porter the rum and gunpowder Montcalm had paid the savages, then were tortured and made meals of on the trek back to Canada. The last one was flayed alive and boiled in Montreal and consumed there. This I have from a French deserter who has settled in Philadelphia and established a tannery.

"The forests beyond the settled regions must be salted with the bones and skulls of many who journeyed here to escape the wars, conditions, and persecutions in England and on the Continent. An expedition through these dark woods must follow morbid trails and come upon sad instances of families and farms come to grief. It is, I suppose, difficult enough to tame this wilderness and try to wrest a living from it, and to be on guard against hazards such as panthers, bears, wolves, and snakes. It must be more difficult to take precautions against human predators, whose notion of manhood is the number of scalps they can lift from especially women and children. However, whether they are Christianized or savage, the Indians are doomed by their manner of living and customs, which encourage neither industry nor measurable increases of their numbers...."

Hugh wrote Reverdy many such letters, eagerly composed to share with her the wisdom and knowledge he was acquiring. Their unintended consequence was to cause her to reconsider his value to her. For a year or so, there was no hint of the McDougals in her letters to Hugh; her letters could have been penned by an acquaintance or a stranger.

Then, at the beginning of his second year at the Academy of Philadelphia, he received a long apologia from her explaining her engagement to Alex McDougal.

"You are a man," she said in one part of the letter, "in whom any discriminating woman could count dozens of reasons to love him. But these reasons can only be docketed like goods on a merchantman. They are worthy and commendable reasons, but a cargo of virtues cannot inspire love of its owner. Love springs from the inscrutable but feckful heart, it cannot be analyzed or measured or subjected to rational scrutiny, not without causing it to wither and die. Love can only be felt or observed, never judged or justified. I have tried to love you in the manner you expect me to, and cannot. I have imagined loving you in that manner, and have come to know that I have not the strength to sustain that mode without regarding it in time as an unfair, cruel trial that would exhaust my endurance...."

This was the only section of Reverdy's rambling letter that Hugh could make sense of. He read it over and over, unbelieving of its meaning, but eventually being convinced of it.

He sat still at the desk in the room he occupied in Otis Talbot's house, not moving for a long time, holding a letter in his hands he could no longer read. It was such a mortal, unexpected blow that he was in a numbed stupor, unconscious of time and sound and light. As the growing dusk claimed the corners of his room, it seemed also to claim his soul. He felt that Reverdy had died, and that he would soon follow her.

Then he felt an inquiring hand on his shoulder, and turned with a start to find Mrs. Talbot looking down at him, a candle in her other hand.

"Excuse me, Hugh," she said, "but I have been knocking on your door for the longest time to inform you that supper is ready.... Good gracious, Mr. Kenrick!" she exclaimed, bringing the candle closer to his face. "Are you ill?"

"No," said Hugh. "No, I am not ill." He paused. "I shan't be joining you and Mr. Talbot for supper. Please convey my excuses."

Mrs. Talbot glanced at the letter that was still clutched in one of Hugh's hands. "Oh...I see...." She frowned. "Dire news from home, is it? I hope not."

Hugh shook his head. "From home? No, Mrs. Talbot. Not from home."

"Well," said the woman, unsure of what to say or do, "I'll have Rachel fetch up a plate of something for you later...if you gain an appetite." Then she turned, left the room, and closed the door gently behind her.

A kind of fever possessed Hugh's mind for weeks, tossing him from mood to mood. For a while, he was uncharacteristically morose and reticent. This mood was deepened when he received a letter from his mother, who wrote:

"Reverdy seems to have been persuaded by Mrs. Brune of the knottish dilemma posed by a match between you and her. Mrs. Tallmadge, who has been kind enough to take up the spy for me, reports that Mrs. Brune exhibits an angry blush when the subject of your London affairs is broached. Apparently the woman now views you with the same abhorrence she would express had she found you out to be a member of the Mad Monks club of Sir Francis Dashwood's, and could no more imagine her daughter marrying you than she could Lord Chesterfield or that rake Mr. Wilkes. We have not consorted with the Brunes for months, and Mrs. Tallmadge has not the indelicacy to query Reverdy herself, and so I cannot report to you what may be the girl's views on this unfortunate matter."

Hugh eventually roused himself from despondency to a furious, almost uncontrollable bitterness. This new state of mind was exacerbated by a letter from his father, who wrote:

"Your uncle has been insisting that I order you home so that you may challenge Mr. McDougal for Miss Brune's hand. I do not order you so, not to spite your uncle, but because it is a matter of your own choice. I believe you are wise enough to see that this is not an issue of honor. In your uncle's view, you would be redeemed somewhat in his estimate were you to risk your life by acting out some silly duel.

"But in this affair, Mr. McDougal is near blameless. *Viva voce*, Mr. McDougal is a most inoffensive and obliging person who sports the prunella of arid constancy, and is liberal to a fault. Neither Miss Brune nor her mother will have difficulty managing and moulding him. I suspect he was pushed into Miss Brune's attentions and affections by his father, just as she was to Mr. McDougal's by her mother. The alliance of him and Miss Brune is taken by your uncle as a personal affront authored by Squire Brune, chiefly because it scotches an opportunity to acquire an interest in the Brunes' holdings, which a marriage of you and the lady would naturally have given our family. I once conveyed to you my thoughts on such a union, and they have not changed.

"One thought, however, which neither I nor your mother expressed at the time, because you could have easily contradicted us with your authority on the matter, was that we had the mutual impression that Miss Brune unwillingly nurtured a curious fear of you. Forgive me for saying it, but perhaps she did not need to be convinced by her mother of the truth of Mr. Addison's dictum, that 'there is no glory in making a man a slave who has not naturally a passion for liberty.' Because such a 'glory' was manifestly impossible through you, the illusion of it could be achieved in the person of Mr. McDougal by means of his effortless complaisancy, conscientious respectability, and conjugal contentment. Please do not be angry with me or your mother for having had these doubts about your lady. Our vantage is that if she is now more disposed to settle in matrimony for a clipped shilling over a gold guinea, perhaps she has spared you both the misery of a disagreeable denouement as husband and wife...."

Hugh was able to lose himself, at times, in the demands of his studies and in his work in Otis Talbot's office on the Philadelphia waterfront. But the madness would well up in him unbidden, and distract him from his work at the Academy and in the partnership. The simplest tasks would then require a special, dumbfounded effort to perform, as though he were an illiterate street hawker who had never learned to read or cipher or think beyond the next day. His schoolwork and merchant's duties thus became only temporary refuges from the storm of his emotions.

It was only when the twin conflagrations of anger and pain had sub-
sided that he was able to reflect calmly on Reverdy. The anger was reduced
to the residue of indifference, the pain to an ash of regret. The regret was
that her courage to love him had failed. He still loved the idea of Reverdy,
but accepted the fact that what he had been in love with did not exist in
her. The actual person of her began to diminish in his mind. This in turn
transmuted into the indifference. He wrote his parents, assuring them that
"the man of reason had fought a duel with the man of blind passion, and
vanquished him." He did not reply directly to his father's remarks about
Reverdy. He respected his father's perspective and conceded that there was
some substance to his allegations. And, a suspicion of the truth of them sat
in the back of his mind; perhaps in all those years, Reverdy had seen him,
but ultimately concluded that what she saw, could not be conquered or
tamed. Perhaps she had rejected him for the same reasons his uncle hated
him, and instead of subjecting him to invective and malice, wrote him a
kind letter of forgiving apology.

He reached the point, at last, when he regained his objectivity, and was
able to write Reverdy a cordial note of congratulations, cold in its formality,
dismissive in its brevity, and brutal in its justice:

"Mr. McDougal is, I do not doubt, deserving of your love, as you must
be of his. You both will always be what each of you expects the other to be.
I feel obliged, however, to caution you that in future, you will find that love
can be subjected to a most private and honest rational scrutiny. Perhaps, by
that time, nature will be kind to you, and, having followed its own inexorable course, rendered you insensible to the weight and wisdom of its just
and dutiful verdict...."

One thought did not occur to Hugh throughout his emotional turmoil:
He never once compared himself to or with Alex McDougal. His self-respect
was so secure in his character that his rival was virtually nonexistent, except
as an incidental, secondary measure, as an afterthought, as a pathetic, diffi-
cult-to-remember foil. He neither hated the man, nor despised him. Nor
envied him — now that he knew the reasons for Reverdy's decision.

*   *   *

Reverdy's decision led Hugh to the realization that not only was there
no pressing reason for him to return home after he graduated from the
Academy, but that he did not wish to. At least, not for a while. He felt
strangely at home. A few months after sending his last letter to Reverdy on
the *Sparrowhawk*, he resumed the routine of a life divided between the
Academy and the business of Talbot and Spicer. As his second and final

year at the school neared an end, an idea grew in his mind. He wrote his father about his desire to stay in Philadelphia longer than had been planned, and broached the idea of purchasing a plantation, which he would manage and own in the family's name.

"There is now nothing in England that requires my immediate presence. A plantation here, intelligently managed, would help buttress the family fortune. The papers here carry many notices of these places for sale, either in whole or in part. I know that our *Ariadne* and Mr. Worley's *Busy* call regularly in Virginia, which is where the best tobacco plantations are to be found. Managing such an enterprise here would better prepare me for managing our own lands, once I return to Danvers. Not least important to me, it would be something of my own...."

Garnet Kenrick said:

"I not only think your idea a good one, for all the reasons you cite, but your continued sojourn so far away from our affections may help to alleviate relations between your uncle and me. If you notice any property for sale that suits your fancy, I would gladly underwrite its purchase, provided the price was reasonable and our own vessels could be guaranteed a portion of its trade. I would also insist that Mr. Talbot, who has some knowledge of the planting business there, appraise any property. In separate correspondence I have sent him a letter appointing him my proxy in such a transaction, together with a draft on Formby, Pursehouse and Swire in the amount of five thousand pounds. I have given Mr. Talbot other instructions concerning this matter.... Your mother, Alice, and I all earnestly hope that, though your endeavors are ambitious, you mark some time for a visit here, once this dreadful war is concluded...."

                              *   *   *

Once he and Otis Talbot returned to Philadelphia from Caxton, Hugh found a letter waiting for him from Roger Tallmadge, in which his friend regaled him with the details of the battle of Minden:

"...The French horse were confounded by the sudden and steady advance of our grenadiers and regulars, with the Hanoverian troops behind us. We would march boldly, yet with admirable calmness, toward the cavalry, then stop to fire volleys by platoon, emptying more and more saddles as we went. This we did many times. Some of their dragoons tried to engage us and check our progress, and their hot fire brought down many of our men. But we were not to be deterred. The senior ensign before me was felled by a dragoon's ball that struck his head. He was Ensign Michael Ramsey, of Croton-Abbas, Devon. I suppose he was dead before he went down, still clutching the King's Colours. Before I could think to do it, because it was my duty, I paused in my stride to pick up the Colours, then raised them high for all our men to see, and found myself in front of our company. We advanced and fired twice again, and I must have sweated a gallon of salt, for I was now a fair target and the bullets sang past me all the while to smack into the cloth of our conspicuous Colours or some brave but unfortunate fellows behind me.

"Finally, the French horse, seeing that they had lost their momentum, and perhaps fearing that we would any moment charge with bayonets fixed to our muzzles as they milled about in the disorder we caused in their ranks, removed themselves from the contest in great confusion. Our colonels ordered us to halt, to allow our own horse to sweep in and pursue the French. But, to our amazement and consternation, Lord Sackville's men, although drawn up for just such an action, did not act, and sat immobile at the far end of our lines, thus permitting the French horse to retire without further abuse. Some say that Sackville did this to spite Prince Brunswick, whom he constantly criticized and quarreled with bitterly; others whisper incontinent skittishness. Brunswick was furious, and swore that he would take up the matter with our George and see Sackville punished and ousted.

"For my courage, I have been brevetted a lieutenant, and now wear a gorget.... The Duke is determined that the French shall not traipse through Hanover, nor roam through Germany unmolested. He is an able commander, bolder and wiser than was Cumberland. The French know that if they can capture and hold Hanover, they could treat separately with our sovereign and deny King Frederick an army in the west and Mr. Pitt's money aid, and leave Prussia open to French mischief. We shall remain under Brunswick's command for the duration.... I was granted leave to visit Francis's grave near Hastenbeck. He was not a loving brother, and tormented me no end, but I nevertheless felt sorrow for him, and pray that my conduct has balanced his loss. He did not survive his gallantry, and I thank God I have survived mine....

"At the Marquis of Granby's suggestion (he is the ranking British officer here), we junior officers were feted at a victory supper by an aide-de-camp, Lord Charles Brome, who was shortly after the fight promoted captain in the 85th Regiment, and has since returned to London. He studied at the military academy in Turin, and is a lively, keen fellow who reminds me somewhat of you in age and manner, and also because he, too, will someday become an earl...."

Roger went on in his letter to describe German towns and culture, and the rigors of camp life. Hugh envied his friend a little; in a way, Roger was on a kind of Continental tour, something Hugh had not had a chance to experience himself. He smiled when he read Roger's postscript:

"I remembered what you told me that day we went shooting, and have been practicing with a firelock I borrow from one of our grenadiers. I can now load and fire it four times in a minute, almost as quickly as a Prussian. My fellow officers are either amused or scandalized, and chide me for the diversion. But, I tell them that I may some day see service in the colonies, and the skill may be an opportune one to have there...."

*   *   *

In between packing his possessions and arranging with Otis Talbot to have most of them follow him to Caxton on another vessel, Hugh wrote his last letters in Philadelphia to his parents and Roger Tallmadge. A quiet excitement grew in him now, one rooted in many causes: a determination to begin anew; the prospect of making something his own; a break with a painful part of his past. The neglected state of Brougham Hall sat in his mind like an island of virgin land waiting to be tamed, cultivated, civilized, and made prosperous. If the place had had any repute before Amos Swart's ownership of it, Hugh was resolved to surpass it.

A letter arrived two weeks after Hugh's return to Philadelphia, cosigned by Arthur Stannard and Ian McRae, stating that the purchase of Brougham Hall was registered with the court of Queen Anne County and that all fees, charges, taxes, and tithes were paid, and that Hugh could invest himself in the main house at his pleasure. It also informed him that Amos Swart had returned from his other properties and was informed of the purchase, and removed from Brougham Hall together with what movable possessions he could lay legal claim to.

"This nasty man made such a disgraceful scene," wrote Mr. Stannard, "that Mr. McRae and I were obliged to request the assistance of Sheriff Tippet, who posted a constable in the main house to ensure that Mr. Swart did not depart with anything from the inventory or do damage to what remained. Mr. McRae and I, together with Mr. Tippet and a few other citizens, were present to escort Mr. Swart forever from the property. We rode with him as far as the Hove Creek bridge, and bid him *adieu* as his wagon clattered across it."

In his letter to his father, Hugh described Brougham Hall and Caxton, then dwelt on a number of ideas that would guarantee the plantation's solvency:

"...Many merchants here in Philadelphia defy the law and contrive to be paid in Crown specie for the goods they manage to sell to factors in the various outports of Britain. If they did not subvert the law, they would be in a bad way and little could be accomplished in the way of trade between the mother country and these colonies. There is such a shortage of coin here that a needlessly complex system has grown up of barter, tobacco notes, colonial paper, and foreign coin, all fixed to the value of sterling; and the merchant farmer, artisan, mechanic, or planter who can pay for necessities with hard money has an advantage over his perhaps more prosperous-looking brother in trade, whose prosperity is in fact owned by a distant creditor. Mr. Talbot is one of the former, I am happy to say, and his credit and solvency are as solid as the Portland Bill. Now, although many Virginia planters live in a more gorgeous style and manner than do a great many landowners in England, it is at the price of continual indebtedness to their London agents. I do not propose to put Meum Hall in such a precarious circumstance, and herein suggest that the value of the tobacco and other material Captains Eales and Rowland take out on the Ariadne and Mr. Worley's Busy be reimbursed in part with coin, British or foreign, it matters not which...."

Following a discussion of other means of ensuring success, Hugh added, "Of course, the foregoing methods are in direct contravention to the ruinous wisdom of the Board of Trade and Parliament. At the moment, Father, my only advice to these powers is that the Crown acquire an interest in a silver or gold mine in Mexico or Alto Peru. God knows it makes war on the Spanish for more specious reasons than that. If it were not for Lord Anson and his treasure-gathering prowess, in what penurious state would the Crown be this year? But, I believe that we would both agree that, whatever our Mint's policies or shortcomings, I should receive credit in your books for five hogsheads of tobacco, and be paid again for five, if I ship you five. I will await your reply in Virginia...."

Two days before his departure, almost a month after his return from Caxton, a mail packet arrived in Philadelphia, bringing Hugh a letter from his mother. In it she announced the marriage of Reverdy Brune and Alex McDougal by the vicar of St. Thraille's Church in Eckley, Surrey. "The banns were posted here for some time," wrote Effney Kenrick to her son, "but I spared you the news of that. I suppose the Brunes and McDougals felt that a ceremony here at St. Quarrel's would have been awkward and perhaps cheeky enough to provoke interference by your uncle...."

Hugh felt a brief pang of loss when he read the news. He could not decide whether it was a pang of disgust or regret. And the emotion passed. He put the letter away with his other correspondence in a trunk, not because of its contents, but because it was a letter from his mother.

On the following Tuesday, he boarded the brig *Tacitus*, bound for ports in Chesapeake Bay, including Yorktown and Caxton. Four days later, he stepped ashore in Caxton, and hired a cart and horse to take him to Meum Hall.

Chapter 8: The Newcomer

Hugh Kenrick was a true aristocrat. This everyone in Caxton knew before the wind and current had carried the *Amelia* a mile up the York River on the October afternoon of his departure. The news, eagerly spread by Arthur Stannard and Reverend Acland, shocked the planters, townsmen, and their families out of their post-victory ball lethargy. Reece Vishonn, once he had recovered from his amazement, began to talk with other planters about having a welcoming banquet for Hugh Kenrick. "But only after a decent interval has passed," he explained to the others over a meeting at the Gramatan Inn, his favorite "place of public retreat." "We must allow his lordship to settle into his new home." The banquet was scheduled for November at Enderly.

In the mid-November issue of the Caxton *Courier*, at the top of a back page column of advertisements and announcements, there appeared this notice:

> *The Honorable Hugh Kenrick, lately removed to this county, desires all who would deal with him and his property in future to send their regards, courtesies, business, etc., to his residence, Meum Hall, formerly Brougham Hall. He further desires that persons favor him with the address of Mister Kenrick, in private company, in public, and in correspondence. Salutations in any other form or style will not be acknowledged either by him or by his agents. — Hugh Kenrick, Esq.*

The notice in the *Courier* bewildered the planters. They could understand neither the design nor the motive behind such a request, and neither Mr. Stannard nor Mr. McRae could enlighten them much on the matter.

"Why would he wish anyone to flout the courtesies due his rank?" asked Henry Otway. "It don't make sense!"

Mr. Stannard could only shrug his shoulders. The *Courier* notice was printed three days before the scheduled banquet, to which Hugh had accepted the invitation. "I cannot say, sir," he answered. "I can tell you that his purchase of Brougham Hall was contingent on Mr. McRae and me respecting that very same *dictum*. When we enquired, he said to the effect that such courtesies have no place here, and that they were tiresome to him."

"Balderdash!" exclaimed Vishonn. He was not only disappointed and confused, but vexed; he somehow felt cheated of the opportunity to entertain a person of high station and possibly lucrative connections. "Is he ashamed of his rank? Many of his rank ought to be, but not that lad!"

Mr. Stannard shrugged again. "Who is anyone to question the wishes of a baron, sir? But, I must warn you, Mr. Vishonn: Honor his preferences, or he may never again set foot inside your house. Mr. McRae and I can vouch for the steadiness of his mind. He is a determined young man."

Jack Frake, who had heard the news about his new neighbor a day after Hugh Kenrick had sailed back to Philadelphia, also read the notice. He did not venture an opinion on the subject to anyone. He waited.

*   *   *

The leading planters of Queen Anne County, descendants of the last century's Cavalier adventurers, entrepreneurs, and settlers, inherited a presumption of aristocracy. Their reasoning was that if it had not been for the Commonwealth and Protectorate, they would have come naturally into the landed aristocracy that remained after the passing of the Cromwells and the return of the Stuarts. Many of the planters were distantly related to faraway, ennobled descendants of families that had survived the strife and turmoil of that very different age, the high points of which were the Glorious Revolution, the accession of an unambitious monarchy, and the Act of Settlement.

Yet, were they offered the chance, not one of them would have traded his status in Virginia for a baronial estate in England. In the colony, while they carried no titles, they wielded some power and influence, were allotted some prestige, and commanded much respect. Ladies and common womenfolk curtsied to them in public, merchants, artisans, and tradesmen doffed their hats to them in greeting, and humble farmers, landless dependents, and slaves made room for them on the road and in Caxton's streets. And, just as in England, first sons had uncontestable claim to all that their fathers owned, once their seniors had passed on to their final reward. Queen Anne County was Tory in attitude and tradition, Whiggish in practical politics, and comfortably complacent in a re-created English venue of the planters' yearnings and imagination.

The Caxton aristocracy — headed by Reece Vishonn, represented in the House of Burgesses by Edgar Cullis and William Granby, and in full control of the county court and church vestry — respected Jack Frake, but did not count him one of their own. They were obliged to respect him, if only because he was once a confidant of the late John Massie, and also that man's son-in-law. That he had proved himself a crop master also counted for something in their scale of approval. Also, they were grateful that he was himself a gentleman, and had retained the name of the plantation he had inherited.

And, they were relieved that he was a solitary man. It did not escape their constant notice that he did not so much avoid their company, as neither seek it, nor miss it, nor depend on it. Their encounters with him were nearly always accidental or happenstance. He was approachable by them, but did not often approach his fellow planters. He did not envy them their power, riches, or respectability. These omissions saved them the effort and obligation to value him as an ally in their common concerns. The respect Jack Frake commanded and which they granted him chafed against their gentlemanly sensibilities. A gentleman in everything but his parental lineage — they had heard stories and rumors about his Cornish background — he was too admirable to detest and openly ostracize, as they did Amos Swart. A commoner in everything but his bearing, character, and hard-won wisdom, Jack Frake could not be forgiven his criminal past. Were they certain that he had been reformed and remolded by the late John Massie, his fellow planters might have deigned to overlook Jack Frake's status as a former felon.

But they sensed that John Massie had had little to do with the character and purpose of the man who now owned Morland, that the key to Jack Frake's character and actions lay in his criminal past. They knew nothing about the Skelly gang, other than that it had been a smuggling ring eradicated by the Crown, and that Jack Frake had been a member of it. They could not reconcile the phenomena of Jack Frake and a band of cutthroats. They sensed that he was merely a felon matured, that he had never been reformed, was not reformable, and would spurn any attempt to reform him. They could not decide whether he would view such an attempt as a grave offense to his character, or dismiss it with amused contempt. Nor could they decide if the violence he could visit on any one of them with pistols or swords on a field of honor was worse than the violence he could inflict on their self-respect. They suspected that the latter was worse. So, they left him alone.

Only Reverend Albert Acland seemed to understand Jack Frake, and was unafraid to express what he truly thought of him. Attendance in his church was mandatory, and a person who neglected to regularly audit his services could be arrested and either fined, jailed, or put in the stocks. He could not recall the last time he had seen Jack Frake among the congregation. The Massie family pew stall was usually vacant on Sundays, or occupied by strangers. But the men who had it in their power to punish Jack Frake as a religious truant, would not make him answerable. The men who served as county judges and parish vestrymen were also the leading planters, on whose beneficence and largesse Stepney Parish and Reverend Acland depended. They refused to even discuss Jack Frake or the possibility of privately reprimanding him for his transgression.

Reverend Acland attributed their obstinacy to insipid favoritism; he also strongly suspected that they feared the owner of Morland. Resentment and righteous contempt festered in his mind. He was powerless to bring Jack Frake to justice. He took his revenge on the other planters by preaching frequently and insistently to them at services against pride, power, negligence, arrogance, and all the other sins which he — and they — knew they were guilty of committing. If you will not answer to me for your calculated, gross oversight, he reassured himself, I will remind you that you will someday be answerable to God. Reverend Acland was an exception to the rule among Anglican ministers in the colony. His sermons were delivered with the fervor and persuasiveness of a New Light divine.

*   *   *

Forewarned by the notice in the *Courier* and Arthur Stannard's earnest assurances, Reece Vishonn in turn impressed upon his fellow planters the importance of heeding Hugh Kenrick's wishes. The welcoming banquet, as a result, was a qualified social success — qualified only because of the grudgingly observed request, together with a formal distance that the young newcomer seemed to place between himself and his host and host's guests. Hugh Kenrick's only compliment to the company was that "Virginia planters are, as a rule, better garbed and better read than their counterparts in England, and certainly more hospitable."

Mr. Vishonn and his guests did not know what to make of Hugh Kenrick. Here was a true aristocrat who paradoxically disdained his rank, or seemed to be indifferent to it. His mien implicitly mocked their pretensions to being a colonial, disenfranchised elite, and this made his presence uncomfortable to them.

Although it was a less spectacular event than he had hoped for, Reece Vishonn felt the satisfying relief of knowing that Mr. Kenrick had no political plans and had shown no evidence of interest in usurping his position as the county's *de facto* leader.

This was subtly confirmed for the master of Enderly by Hugh Kenrick near the end of a brief speech of thanks to his host and his companions. "In conclusion, allow me to cadge a line from the unfortunate Polonius, which he addressed to King Claudius, and which will indicate my sole purpose for having come to this fair setting: 'Let me be no assistant to the state, but keep a farm and carters.'"

Before the company could answer with applause, one of the guests laughed, and rose to reply, "You may rest assured, sir, that you will encounter no manslaughtering Hamlets here. Swords there are aplenty, but nary an arras!"

Only then did the rest of the company fully grasp the meaning of Hugh Kenrick's words and applaud. He bowed slightly to the speaker. "Thank you, Mr. Granby, for a worthy riposte. Rest assured that I am not the hiding kind, neither of myself, nor of my designs."

"What do you make of him?" Vishonn asked Ralph Cullis after Hugh Kenrick and most of the guests had departed. The banquet had been a mid-afternoon dinner, and now the sun was beginning to touch the western horizon. The host, Cullis, and Reverend Acland sat together in Vishonn's spacious study with glasses of claret.

"He is an amiable fellow, sir," said Cullis. "Charming to a fault, wise ahead of his years, earnest, thoughtful, already a lodestone of distaff spec-ulation — I have heard my daughter Eleanor remark that he is the most eli-gible bachelor in these parts — excepting, perhaps, your son James," added the planter, referring to his host's son. "But, he is remote of deportment. I could not help but think, throughout the affair here, that he was merely humoring us."

Vishonn frowned in disagreement. "Not my impression, sir! I would say that he is shy, and had his property on his mind. He confided in me that today the rest of his things from Philadelphia had only just arrived." He paused. "I would say that he is a brave and enterprising fellow to undertake such a sticky problem as Brougham Hall. He did not show it, but I sensed a little fear in him concerning the project. He knows it will be no mean feat to return old Covington's place to its former glory." Vishonn turned to Rev-erend Acland. "And you, sir? What do you say?"

"It remains to be seen whether Mr. Kenrick is a Polonius or a Hamlet, sir," said the clergyman. "I did not engage him much in conversation — he is skillful at not speaking with persons with whom he does not wish to speak — but observed his commerce with you others. He is too young to be so gravely melancholy." Acland smiled in expectation of appreciation by the two other men of his allusion to the "melancholy Dane."

But Ralph Cullis merely stared blankly at him, while Vishonn scoffed. "*Melancholy??* Gads, sirs! Forgive me for saying so, but that's a most tilted appraisal! He is a lively, spirited, strong-keeled fellow, no more melancholy than I am!" but he paused to add, "However, you seem convinced of your observation, Mr. Acland. Why?"

The clergyman shrugged once. "Perhaps he has come here to expiate some great sin, or to absent himself from the sins of others. My friends and brothers of the cloth in England have some intelligence about his family. It is not complete, but it indicates a stormy household, in which *Mr.* Kenrick has been as much sinned against, as has sinned." Reverend Acland paused to sip his claret. "The truth of one or the other will emerge only after he has been among us for some time. He strikes me as a man who is struggling to quell some racking torment. I would be flattered if he came to me for spiritual consolation or advice, but he has not yet crossed the threshold of our church."

Whatever that torment may be, sir, thought Reece Vishonn, I earnestly hope that it is nothing into which you may sink your righteous teeth.

Ralph Cullis toyed with the temptation to remark on the slim odds of Hugh Kenrick being lashed or fined by the sheriff for nonattendance, but thought better of it and settled for clearing his throat.

Reverend Acland departed shortly after this exchange to take advantage of the waning daylight. Vishonn and Cullis pondered Hugh Kenrick's marriage prospects, but only briefly, for all the planters but Henry Otway had eligible daughters, and an unspoken rivalry among the families had ensued to win the prestige of claiming a baron for a son-in-law and a baroness for a daughter. The two gentlemen also ventured speculation about Hugh Kenrick joining their Freemason's lodge. They concluded that they could not predict how he might reply to an invitation. Finally, as Ralph Cullis prepared to leave, he asked his host the question that was on their minds all day: "I wonder what Mr. Frake will make of him, and he of Mr. Frake?"

Reece Vishonn barked sharply once in a laugh. "Of this I'm certain, Mr. Cullis," he answered. "They will either find themselves to be brothers in spirit, or they will be two wild boars, and we shall be witnesses to a savage brawl!"

Chapter 9: The Master

The household staff of Meum Hall, fearing their new master and anxious for their futures, contrived to be as unobtrusive as shadows in his presence. Hugh, absorbed for the first few weeks of his residence in familiarizing himself with the property, was aware of his staff only as a series of bodies hastening at his beck, call, and command. He was a fascinated prisoner of the engrossing greed of ownership, and did not notice much else around him.

Rupert Beecroft, the business agent who doubled as steward, was the most worried. He and most of the household were holdovers from Covington Brougham's days. Under Amos Swart's dilatory, slovenly, and often abusive management, Beecroft and his colleagues had grown accustomed to taking what they thought was their due from an unjust master. Their larceny and studied pilferage was motivated partly by necessity, and partly from a vengeful loyalty to the memory of Covington Brougham. Beecroft, to protect himself and the staff, became adept at juggling Brougham Hall's account books, able to hide actual income, costs, and inventory from an employer who was rarely alert to the discrepancies in the plantation's balances, debits, and credits.

William Settle, the overlooker who also acted as steward, was responsible for the physical maintenance of the property and for seeing that tasks were accomplished on time. Under Beecroft's blind eye, he had managed to siphon off about ten percent of the value of Swart's annual crop, which value went into the purchase of land in York County.

The housekeeper, Ann Vere, originally came to Brougham Hall as an indentured servant, and helped to raise Feliśe, Covington's daughter, from an infant. She had come to treat the girl as her own daughter. She had never forgiven Swart for the girl's death years ago. It was she who had secretly suggested to Sheriff Tippet that Feliśe Swart was smothered that tragic night with a pillow, and that Swart, in a calculated ruse to establish his innocence, slept at the side of his dead wife until a servant failed to wake her the next morning.

Fiona Chance, the cook, another former indenture, regularly sold meat and vegetables from Brougham Hall's stocks and gardens to Caxton's ordinaries, taverns, and shipmasters, and pocketed the proceeds.

Radulphus Spears was brought to Brougham Hall as an indentured tutor for hire to other planters' families. Swart had demoted him to servant and valet. Spears became deft in channeling chest loads of plate, cutlery, and bric-a-brac into the markets and shops of nearby towns.

Spears performed another service in memory of the Brougham family. Once there had been over five hundred volumes in Covington Brougham's library; only three hundred and fifty remained. Some fifty of the missing volumes were used over the years as kindling by Swart. The other missing hundred had found their way, thanks to their steady removal by Spears, onto the shelves of gentlemen's libraries in a dozen Virginia counties. Spears, a learned man, respected books; they paid him better and more often than did his master.

Amos Swart, as a rule unshaven, bellicose, cruel, and half-sober, did not miss the things he either placed no value on, or had no knowledge of. Beecroft and his charges maintained a united front of implicit deference and efficiency. Proportionately, however, they gained more from contemptuous dishonesty in the furtive liquidation of the estate than had their master. Swart's staff was the commendable envy of many planters. Other planters suspected why so many worthy people continued in the employ of such an unworthy man. But neither the envious nor the suspicious among them ever communicated their thoughts to Amos Swart.

The staff's wariness of Hugh Kenrick was based, initially, on fear of his unknown character, coupled with the knowledge of his elite pedigree. This fear diminished, after a time, once they realized that their young master was not callous, arbitrary, whimsical, or given to drink or brutality. A new fear quickened their movements: that their larceny would be found out. Hugh Kenrick, they discovered, was a just man, as liberal with his compliments as with his criticisms and condemnations.

"Mr. Beecroft," he said one evening to the business agent after spending half a day examining the account books, "henceforth you will keep neater and more legible ledgers. For example, I could not, at first, distinguish your 'ones' from your 'sevens,' until I had recalculated some of your sums. And, many important entries were smudged and unreadable. Please refrain from touching new entries until they have dried. I noticed also that too many of those entries were inked over the ghosts of pencil entries. That untidy habit will cease."

Mr. Beecroft nodded. "Yes, sir."

Hugh rose from the business agent's desk and went to the door. He paused long enough to turn and add, "And, Mr. Beecroft, please tell the others this, and mark it well: It will stop, or I shall find replacements, and you and they shall find themselves in Mr. Tippet's jail." He held the agent's glance for a moment to convey the unmistakable meaning of his words.

The agent pursed his lips, blinked once, and said, "Yes, sir."

Hugh opened the door and left.

"Mrs. Vere, you will dust the books in the study once a month. With the exception of the ones I brought with me, their tops are thick with dust, and teeming with insects, alive and dead."

"Yes, sir."

"I found a plant growing in the mud that has accumulated in the corner of one of the bed chambers. And enough dirt has collected beneath the wainscoting in the central hall that it could spawn a row of beets. It must all be removed. Find a small rug in Mr. Rittles's shop in town, or in Mr. McRae's, and place it outside the main door. Instruct everyone who comes to that door to wipe their shoes on it before they enter. The floors must be swept and kept clean."

"Yes, sir."

"Mr. Spears, you will help Mrs. Vere remove the mattress from my bed chamber, then have it burned. Not all of Mr. Swart's small companions departed with him. Replace it with one from one of the other chambers. If I fail to rise at five in the morning, you will see that I do, unless otherwise instructed. I take coffee in the mornings, and tea at dinner. I dress myself. You will simply see that my public garb is regularly laundered."

"Yes, sir."

"The inventory of books in the library is useless. You will draw up a new one, and maintain it, for I expect to add more volumes in future."

"Yes, sir."

"Miss Chance, you will henceforth wash all meat, vegetables, and fruit in a tub of boiled water, making sure that the water is then only tepid, before preparing anything for consumption at my table. Yesterday at supper I encountered some foreign matter on my plate. I could not identify it. The tub water in turn must not be consumed or reused, but taken out to freshen the gardens. Here is a list of my likes and dislikes."

"Yes, sir."

"Mr. Settle, you will have constructed a shed in which to deposit manure and other compost a suitable distance from any habitation. The collection of this fertilizer, I have observed, is irregular and haphazard, and thus a waste of time. I want it collected every other day. You will also have collected all the quahog shells that litter the place, and have them ground to dust and added to the compost, for plowing into the soil when necessary. I have read that these shells are good nourishment for the soil."

"Yes, sir."

Hugh and the overlooker rode together around the plantation. It was a crisp, late November afternoon. They stopped to watch the slaves uproot and gather the bare tobacco stalks into piles. "Mr. Settle, what is the most worrisome concern for any planter?"

"Watering the fields, sir," answered the overlooker. "Rain, or lack of it."

"Yes. And that problem will be solved. This property will not depend for its sustenance on the whims of the weather. The solution to it lies somewhere here."

"Yes, sir," answered Settle. "The prizing of the hogsheads is nearly done, sir. There are six 'heads of nearly nine hundred fifty pounds each, and one of a thousand. Shall I have your mark put on them, or Mr. Swart's?" Each planter branded his tobacco hogsheads with his own unique mark, which was sometimes a figure, but more often his initials.

"Mr. Swart's," said Hugh. "I am not responsible for their contents. Next year's crop will bear my initials. The capital letters 'H' and 'K,' with the 'K' formed on the right down stroke of the 'H.'" After a moment, he added, more as an afterthought to himself, "My initials, perhaps set in the silhouette of an ascending sparrowhawk." He urged his mount forward, and Mr. Settle followed. Hugh said, "These stalks, Mr. Settle: have them chopped into lengths of one inch or so, and add them to the compost. There are nutrients in them that are otherwise wasted."

The overlooker frowned. "We usually burn the stalks, sir, and plough in the ashes."

"No more. We will experiment with unburned stalks for a few seasons. I believe they will make a difference." Hugh asked, "Has this place ever sold produce to the town?"

"Not since Mr. Brougham's time, sir," the overlooker said too quickly, trying to keep knowledge of Fiona Chance's secret trade with Caxton's taverns from his words.

"I see," remarked Hugh. He stopped his mount to survey a cleared field. The overseer, John Ockhyser, could be seen in the distance, standing on a tree stump, a fowling piece cradled in his arms, watching some slaves clear away corn stalks. Hugh said, "I noted in Mr. Beecroft's records that Mr. Ockhyser was hired after Mr. Brougham's passing. He is, in fact, the sole one of you who did not know Mr. Brougham."

"That is true, sir."

"What is he like?"

"Able, sir. The boys heed him."

Hugh rode on without further comment. They came to the end of the estate, near Hove Creek, and paused in a stand of bamboo trees that covered a wide patch of flat ground. "Who owns the other side of the creek, Mr. Settle?"

"No one, sir. No one owns either bank of the creek, from beginning to end. That was arranged years ago, before my employ, when all these properties were being surveyed and laid out. It's to prevent disputes over water rights. The creek is little used, sir. If we need extra water, we go to the river."

"Has no one ever damned the creek, or built a mill on it?"

"No, sir. Not even Mr. Vishonn or the others. There's not enough water or force in it to run a mill."

Hugh studied the creek for a while, and observed how, from his side of it, his property gradually inclined. He sat in his saddle for a long while, thinking.

He read the records of the staff and obtained from Mr. Settle the slaves' records. The tenures of all the indentures had expired years ago. The slaves were second and third generation adults, all but two born at Brougham Hall. Two field hands were purchased by Brougham from another planter in Gloucester, for forty pounds each. Amos Swart, he saw, had inherited forty slaves; four had died during his residence, while six had "run away" and were never returned or brought back for a £10 bounty, the advertisement for which Hugh found in the records, as well.

Hugh summoned John Ockhyser to his library that evening. Ockhyser was a tall, burly, grubby man who carried a pistol and a rolled-up whip in his belt. He was, to Hugh's knowledge, the only man in Caxton who sported a beard, a tangled mat in which Hugh noticed some tiny things crawling. Hugh did not like the looks or manner of the man, and did not bid him to sit down. He asked, "What are your duties here, Mr. Ockhyser?"

Ockhyser blinked once in surprise. "Why, to see that the Negroes get done what Mr. Settle says need doing."

"How do you accomplish that?"

Ockhyser shrugged. "By being there to remind them what'll happen if they don't get it done." The overseer paused. "They need watchin', Mr. Kenrick. All the time."

"I'm certain they do." Hugh nodded to the pistol and whip. "How often do you use your tools, Mr. Ockhyser?"

"Now and then, sir, if they earn it, and when I get permission from Mr. Swart, or you, sir."

"Have you any other trade?"

"I tried farming for a while, up river, after I left off sailing. Was a bosun's mate for years. But the farm didn't work out. Mr. Swart put a notice in the newspapers and I saw it and he hired me."

"I will address these people tomorrow afternoon, Mr. Ockhyser, in their quarters, before dinner. You will accompany me."

Ockhyser frowned. "Tomorrow's Sunday, sir, their day off. A preacher comes and talks to them in their quarters, sometimes."

"That's as may be. Come here at one of the clock. You may leave."

"Yes, sir." Ockhyser scrutinized Hugh for a moment. "You're not afeared of them, are you, Mr. Kenrick?"

"No, Mr. Ockhyser, I am not. At least, not for the reason *you* might be." Hugh smiled pointedly, but the overseer did not seem to grasp the allusion. "That is all, Mr. Ockhyser. I will meet you in front of this house at one of the clock. Be punctual."

"Yes, sir."

Hugh had put off addressing the slaves until last, chiefly because he did not know what to say to them. He felt no guilt for having bought them; they were regarded as property and had come with the plantation, like its tools, outbuildings, and livestock. Legally, he owned the slaves; in his mind, he did not. He felt that he owed them something more than assurances that he would not abuse them.

That Sunday afternoon Hugh stood on a rock in front of about thirty curious, upturned black and brown faces in the slave quarter. Beyond the group was a long, weatherworn wooden barracks that was home for most of the unmarried men. Another, smaller shack housed the women and the few children. In a round pit nearby brooded a low fire, over which were suspended from an iron pole some copper and iron pots of soups and stews.

Ockhyser stood to one side of Hugh, slightly behind him, a pipe in one hand and his loaded fowling piece in another. He wore a wide brim felt hat that shaded his eyes from the bright afternoon sun. Hugh turned to him and asked for his whip. The overseer hesitated for a moment, then reluctantly took it from his belt and handed it to his employer. Hugh held it at rest in front of him, the fingers of both hands wrapped tightly around the raw, greasy grip. Ockhyser, noting his employer's stance, looked hopeful and permitted himself a smile.

Hugh looked at each of the adult faces gazing up at him, and tried to imagine that each of them was a Glorious Swain. Then he spoke. "I am Hugh Kenrick, owner of this place. It was once called Brougham Hall. I have renamed it Meum Hall. I own this place, but, before God and nature, I do not own any of you, although the laws of this colony, and of England, contradict both nature and my knowledge."

He paused for a moment. "I have as little to say to you, at this time, as you have to me. So, I shall be brief and say what is most on my mind. You may speak yours afterward, if you wish. I am not permitted to manumit a single one of you without the sanction of a bill having passed the House in Williamsburg and made law. And it is more likely that I would win a wager on which one of a dozen raindrops would first course down a window pane, than it is that such a bill would secure the mutual assent of the House, the Governor's Council, and the Governor himself. So, I must find another way of retaining your services as freed men. Until then, you shall at least be paid like them, in coin or in kind, according to your skills and abilities."

Hugh held the dumbstruck faces for a moment, then raised the whip in one hand and said, "This is not my way." Then he tossed it disdainfully into the fire in the pit.

The pipe dropped from Ockhyser's mouth. The overseer took a step forward to rescue the whip and to protest, but thought better of it and said nothing. The slaves began to whisper among themselves. Some of their faces were incredulous, others uncomprehending. An adolescent boy crept up to the fire and stared into it. The whip had caught fire instantly, and was now an unraveling coil of flame. The boy frowned and stared up at Hugh.

One of the men spoke. "You mean to free us, Master Kenrick?"

"In time," said Hugh, "when I have found a means that penalizes neither you nor me."

Another man asked, "You want us to work off what you paid for us, like the white slaves do, Master Kenrick?"

Hugh shook his head. "No. You all repaid your original owner's cost to him ten- or twenty-fold, long ago. If your appraised value was part of the amount I paid to purchase this place, then that is a cost I am willing to absorb."

One of the women stepped forward and the crowd became silent. She said, "You are a very Christian man, Master Kenrick, to say you will free us." There was an unmistakable irony in her words, one that verged on scorn.

Hugh studied the woman for a moment, then asked, "What is your name, madam?"

Many of the men, and all of the women, laughed when they heard this style of address. The laughter was directed at the woman, not at Hugh. The woman scowled at the crowd, then turned and answered, "My name is Dilch, Master Kenrick."

Hugh smiled, then said, "Well, Dilch, I am not certain I am very Christian. But I do know that your free services are neither free of cost nor practical." He paused. "Were you in my position, and I in yours, could you ever be certain that I rendered the value of the service you thought was due you from me?"

After a moment of thought, the woman said, "We can't know what we would think, Master Kenrick. Free services is just as cloudy as free words. If you don't need to pay for something, there ain't nothin' you can truly and rightly expect it to give you back. Could be your body and soul, or twixt them, or nothin' at all."

The frank honesty of Dilch's words was punctuated by the ominous silence of the crowd of slaves. They had never heard one of their number speak in such a manner to any slave owner, nor to any other white person. The crowd stood braced for an angry retort from the elegant young man, who, they had heard, came from a family of princes.

Hugh smiled again in genuine appreciation of the woman's reply. "Ably put, Miss Dilch," he said. "My point exactly."

The crowd gasped. Dilch was considered the wisest and strongest woman in the quarter, wise in her common sense, strong in her character. Few of the men were willing to argue with her, and none of the women. She had even corrected Ockhyser, and had been cursed and punched by him for the impudence. Her right cheek bore a scar from the barrel of the overseer's pistol. Ockhyser hated her because, even though she terrified the other slaves with her "mouth" — as he called her talent for arguing — the others implicitly supported her whenever necessary. She had an indomitable will that refused to submit to anything but brutality or the threat of it. The overseer had always wanted to whip her to within a few weary pants of death, but she had never given him an excuse to use the hide on her. He had spent that urge on many of the others.

The crowd watched Dilch now, waiting to see what she would do or say next. And it gasped again when, after taking a short moment to consider Hugh's words, she nodded once to him and stepped back in among them. Ockhyser glanced up at Hugh with almost superstitious awe, then remembered where he was and shifted the fowling piece from one hand to another. The slaves looked repeatedly from Hugh to Dilch, unable to decide which was the greater marvel: Dilch, or the new master.

Hugh continued. "Beginning tomorrow, Mr. Beecroft will keep a record of what each of you is paid, and for what. For the time being, women and field hands will be paid a shilling a month, artisans such as smiths and carpenters and the like, two shillings. One of you men will be selected to be an apprentice overseer, and work with Mr. Ockhyser here. This man will be paid three shillings, and assume equal responsibility and authority."

Ockhyser's face contorted first into a flash of disbelief, then, when he knew that Hugh meant it, a mask of pure hatred. He spat on the ground.

Hugh heard rather than saw the action, and turned to look down at the overseer. The crowd of slaves became quiet. Hugh said, turning back to the slaves, "That is all. Enjoy your day of rest." He stepped down from the rock and strode out of the yard. "Mr. Ockhyser, unless you prefer to remain with your charges, you will accompany me."

The overseer rushed to obey, more from anger than from fear. He did not wait for his employer to speak. "You're courtin' trouble, sir! And you'd no right to burn my whip, not in front of *them*! I won't be able to run them now! Nobody will! And I don't need no damned apprentice!"

Hugh did not turn to face the man, but walked on. "I've never met a tradesman who needed an overseer, Mr. Ockhyser. Apprentices, perhaps, need an iron hand to keep them on a profitable course, but a man who is free to hire out his services or skills, is his own overseer."

"That's just fancy talk!" scoffed Ockhyser. "You give them money, you'll spoil them! They won't work any harder!"

"I'm not a gambling man, sir, but would you care to make a wager on that likelihood?"

"They're not like us! They got a different attitude! God made them different. The only thing that makes them behave is fear!"

Hugh chuckled. "You are either a disciple of Mr. Hobbes — or his inspiration," he remarked. Then he shrugged. "Can you blame them for their 'attitude,' sir? And, please, Mr. Ockhyser, do not be so presumptuous as to include me in your society."

Ockhyser spat on the ground.

Hugh stopped and turned so suddenly that the overseer nearly collided with him. Ockhyser jerked to a stop and stepped back awkwardly. There was a look on his employer's face that the overseer had seen only in water-front taverns before fights occurred.

Hugh said, "If you wish to stay on here, Mr. Ockhyser, you will cease watering my property with your education. You will neither contradict me nor question the wisdom of my decisions. You will oversee the work of these people through an intermediary, and merely observe and report. Those are my conditions. If you cannot accept them, then I cannot retain you."

"I won't," growled Ockhyser. "You can't make a man work like that! It ain't heard of! I'll tell the others in the mansion-house what you're up to!"

"They already know, sir. You came with Mr. Swart, and they will be happy to see you follow him." Hugh turned and walked on. "You must be off this property today, Mr. Ockhyser. If you have not left by sunset, I shall send someone for Sheriff Tippet. You may collect your final wages from Mr. Beecroft."

Ockhyser shouted after him, "You won't turn your back on them so fancy like you do me!"

Hugh stopped again, faced Ockhyser, and waited. The overseer tried to stare down the man who was fifteen years his junior, but his insolence withered under Hugh's imperious and unmoving glance. Quite against his intention, but wholly consistent with his character, the young man's glance made him feel small, mean, and merely nasty. Ockhyser grunted once, then turned and strode in the direction of his quarters.

The incident did not go unnoticed by two groups of interested spectators: the slaves in the yard, and the household staff, who watched from the windows of the great house.

Three hours later, Mr. Beecroft entered the library and asked Hugh for a moment of his time.

Hugh put aside a book he was reading. "Yes, Mr. Beecroft?"

"Mr. Ockhyser has been paid his last wages, sir. Six pounds and expenses. He has vacated the staff house, and left on his own horse."

"Did he trouble you?"

"No, sir. Mr. Settle and Mr. Spears were present whilst I paid him, and they saw him to the gate."

"Very well. Ask Mr. Settle to post a few men at the tobacco barns and corn barns. Mr. Ockhyser may feel inclined to return and bid us farewell with his matches."

"Yes, sir." Beecroft hesitated, then went on. "He was the devil gone to seed, sir, and we are all glad to be rid of him, but...."

"Go on, Mr. Beecroft. Speak your mind."

"Well, sir, are you certain it's wise to treat the Negroes so...well...charitably?" The business agent paused. "We are all wondering about it, sir."

"It is not charity that moves me, Mr. Beecroft," Hugh said. "It is an alliance of practical wisdom and unspoiled revulsion for the custom that constrains Mr. Ockhyser's former charges."

Mr. Beecroft mulled over this reply for a moment, but did not comment in answer to it. Instead, he asked, "Will you replace him, sir?"

"Mr. Ockhyser? Yes, with one of them. Have you a recommendation?"

"Pompey, sir. He is the senior of the field hands, and the others listen to him. If you ask him, Mr. Settle will be of that opinion, too."

"Good. I shall interview him myself tomorrow." Hugh frowned. "Who is the minister that comes to preach to them?"

"Reverend Acland, sir. He visits all the quarters hereabouts, after regular services. Some of the Negroes even attend his services in the church. He has baptized and instructed nearly all those who wish it." Beecroft smiled. "A most vigorous parson, sir. Not like most clergymen one observes, who are content to collect their salaries and compose slumberous sermons."

"I see." Hugh gestured to a chair near his desk. Beecroft parted the tails of his coat and sat down. "How well do you know our people, Beecroft? Their domestic situations, their characters, and so forth?"

"Sir?" The business agent looked genuinely perplexed.

Hugh chuckled. "Come now, Beecroft. They are not mere silhouettes of us," he explained. "They have minds, and emotions, and desires, and inner turmoils, as much as any king or commoner."

"Oh," said Beecroft. Then he dutifully answered all of Hugh's questions, and imparted to his employer a more intimate knowledge of the affairs and personal lives of the slaves than he realized he had. An hour later, he concluded, "And Bristol, a smith, has a wife and daughter over at Mr. Otway's. And Pompey is squiring a girl over at Mr. Vishonn's."

"And Dilch?"

Beecroft shook his head. "Never married, and has no suitors that I know of." He paused, and added in a lower voice, "It's been said that she refuses to risk bringing any children into, well, her condition."

Hugh looked thoughtful. "Do you see, Beecroft? They are not so different from ourselves, except that their lives are submerged in a netherworld."

The next morning, after interviewing the astounded Pompey and telling him to report to Mr. Settle for assignments, Hugh rode into town with a list he had obtained from the overlooker of all the slaves' names. He called on Wendel Barret and placed an order for forty safe conduct passes, one for each of the slaves, each pass to bear the slave's printed name, specifying no particular purpose, and carrying no date. Ten passes were to leave the name space blank. A week later the passes were ready. Hugh signed them, then visited the slave quarter again, this time alone, after most of the men had returned from their labors in the fields. He called out to each person and handed him a pass, and advised everyone that a pass was not to be abused, or it would be taken back.

When he entered the stark, almost bare wooden hut that Dilch shared with her mother, Jemma, and other women, and gave them their passes, he involuntarily paused to bestow on Dilch a smile of respect.

Dilch mumbled some words of thanks. She was in her midforties, short, wiry, of studied movement, with a face hardened into a permanent, almost noble frown by years of care, travail, and obstinate certitude. As she accepted the pass from Hugh, her eyes as much as asked him: What trick are you playing on us? They as much as said to him: You can buy and sell our lives, but you can't buy our souls or affections, not with a shilling or a piece of printed paper.

Hugh might have been stung by the ingratitude he saw in the woman's eyes, had he not understood her proud, unyielding suspicions. But he was neither hurt nor offended, and Dilch saw no trace of guilt or atonement in his face or manner. She regarded herself as a good judge of men, white and black. She was secretly in wonder of Hugh, though she would admit it to neither herself nor to anyone else. Hugh defied all her past criteria of assessment. She could not decide whether to praise him or despise him; praise meant acknowledgment of his actions, actions she despised for his having the power to take. Hugh was the first man in many years who troubled the quietude and dignity of Dilch's soul.

*   *   *

A month passed, and Hugh established his authority at Meum Hall. He entered the lives of everyone who lived on the decaying enterprise, and breathed new life into them as well as into the property. He was on the minds of many men and women in Caxton; his actions were the subject of speculation and appraisal in the town's shops, on the waterfront, in the supper rooms of the planters. Word had spread like lightning of his intention to free his slaves. No one could say how he could ever accomplish it. Most of the other planters casually assured themselves and each other that he could not.

Hugh would sit in the evenings, in his library, reading, thinking, or planning, unaware of the fact that he was being observed and appraised. Often he would pick up his brass top and anchor his thoughts to the whirling dervish that spun atop a pile of papers. His hands were now large and strong enough that he could launch it with his thumb and forefinger without the aid of the cord. And he would smile contentedly in the knowledge that the boy who had once played with that top would recognize himself as a man, and approve of him, just as he recognized and approved of his memory of that boy.

Chapter 10: The Host

Late one Saturday morning in mid-December, Jack Frake rode to Meum Hall, and was told by Mrs. Vere that her employer was somewhere in the fields. He rode out again and espied his neighbor on the western-most edge, near the worm fence that divided the property from Henry Otway's plantation.

Hugh was sitting on a log studying a spread of brown weeds. He heard the jingle of reins and turned. He smiled in recognition of Jack Frake, then gestured to the weeds. "The soil here is so scurvied that even wild weeds take on the color of dead bark." He reached out and snapped one of the weed stalks in two, then tossed it away. "I've not seen its like anywhere else."

"It will take years for this soil to recover," remarked Jack. "Let it lie fallow for a few seasons, then plough and manure it for a few more. With care, it will come back to life."

"Yes," Hugh said. "But first I'll plant some turnips in a part of it, and clover and sainfoin in another, just to see which works faster. Red clover, I have heard, is best for that purpose."

Jack stood in his stirrups to better survey the weeds. "Five hundred hills of tobacco," he said. "Or a thousand of corn, never to be grown for a while. Swart reduced this soil to little better than sand."

Hugh rose and faced his visitor. "To what do I owe your presence, Mr. Frake?"

Jack smiled. "Friendly curiosity, Mr. Kenrick." He paused. "You've got the planters and the town talking about your intentions."

"Concerning the slaves? Yes, it's true." Hugh was dressed in a shirt, a short wool jacket, trousers, and a straw hat. He reached down, picked up a field bottle, and took a drink from it.

"How?" asked Jack.

Hugh shrugged. "When I have coined the means, I shall make no secret of it," he said. He stooped again to drop the bottle into a cloth bag, then slung the bag over his shoulder. "Come, walk me back to the house. I've finished assessing the fields today. Been out here since dawn, and I'm famished. You will join me for dinner."

Jack grinned and looked away. "Yes, *milord* Danvers," he remarked half-humorously.

Hugh glanced up at his neighbor. "No more of that, Mr. Frake. Not even in jest."

"Not that it's a custom I would fall into, sir, but — why not?"

"Because I shall get enough of that when I return home someday," Hugh said. "But, for a few years, at least, I shall be a whole man. Here."

Jack turned his mount around and started back again. Hugh walked beside him. "When do you expect to return to England?"

Hugh sighed. "When my uncle has died, and my father assumes the title and claims the seat in Lords. The patent allows it. Then it will be my turn to manage the estate. It is many times larger than Meum Hall. What I learn here will greatly ease that responsibility."

Jack studied his companion for a moment. "Will you want to return?"

"Very likely not."

They walked together in silence for a while. Then Jack said, "Ockhyser has signed on with a slaver that called on Yorktown last week. The *Dorothea*."

"Good riddance," remarked Hugh. "And, please, Mr. Frake, no more queries about the slaves or Mr. Ockhyser. Mr. Vishonn and some of the others practically invited themselves over for a visit after dinner today. They, too, are curious. Stay and listen to how I plan to enlighten them."

"Thank you, sir. I will." Jack paused. "Your property looks improved, and your people, free and unfree, even seem to step livelier. Mr. Vishonn and the others will notice that, but will probably ascribe the difference to the fair weather."

*   *   *

"You are right, sir," said Hugh. "The correct form could have been either *mea* or *meus*. However, I wished to make a statement, and not merely append an inert name to a stationary object. Thus *meum* — 'It is my hall, my place.' Do you see? It is quite as correct as your instances, but has the virtue of being assertive and memorable."

Thomas Reisdale grinned and dismissed the subject with a movement of his hand. "I cannot argue with that explanation, sir. You have a penchant for nonpareil reasoning."

Seven men sat around the supper table, which was bare except for glasses, several bottles of claret, and a silver epergne whose branching bowls were piled with dry sweetmeats. Reisdale had arrived in the company of Reece Vishonn, Ralph Cullis, and Ira Granby. Arthur Stannard came shortly afterward, uncertain of his reception. Hugh had welcomed him, too.

Until now, the conversation had flitted around mundane subjects: the shortage of skilled labor and the exorbitant rates being charged by itinerant and usually careless artisans; the expected surge in trade once the war was concluded, especially in tobacco, shingles, and lumber; the unimaginable possibilities of western settlement and exploitation, now that France's influence on the continent had been all but eradicated; and bills and matters being debated in the House of Burgesses.

Then Reece Vishonn too casually broached the subject that was on the visitors' minds. "Do you think it was wise to dismiss your overseer, sir?"

Hugh had changed into a clean silk shirt and breeches, but had not bothered to don a coat or waistcoat. His visitors were slightly scandalized by this mode of receiving guests, but assumed that this was a new style in England. Hugh frowned and said, "Yes, I do, sir. He accomplished but a nullity, and was costly in that regard. Retaining him in that capacity was as silly as paying a man to watch cattle graze. He had no other arts to offer me."

Mr. Cullis asked, "But...suppose there is discontent among your people, sir. Who would dispel it, or oppose it?"

Hugh scoffed. "If Mr. Ockhyser and his ilk were meant to be the sole check on the fire and brimstone of revolt, Mr. Cullis, you would have had a taste of hell long ago. You misconstrue the farrago. Most of the slaves I've encountered here and in the north are inured to the numb palsy of their servitude, just as their owners are resigned to their being sentient engines of toil and obedience." He shook his head, and added, "Just as their owners are inured to liberal servitude under the Crown." He shook his head again. "It is a mutual bondage that both parties find themselves in, sir, and one that someday will be severed only with great difficulty."

Jack Frake, who sat in a corner of the long table and took little part in the talk, looked up from lighting his pipe and studied his host with new interest.

Vishonn queried, "Do you refer to the Crown, or the slaves, sir?"

"Both, in truth," Hugh said.

After a moment of silence, Ira Granby remarked, "What a novel construction."

Arthur Stannard ventured, "I have not heard the problem put in such terms before. Not even in Williamsburg. About the slaves, I mean."

Reece Vishonn looked thoughtful, then said, "Indeed, it is a bondage, Mr. Kenrick, for us as well as the poor souls, as you say. But, there is no correcting it. There is no other economical means of raising our crops but with slaves, especially tobacco."

"Most of the planters here wish to stop the importation of Negroes," added Granby, "especially the West Indies type, who are, as a rule, refractory curmudgeons. But the Board of Trade and the Privy Council disallow every direct duty our House lays on the gentlemen who bring them in."

Reisdale said, "The only tax London will permit is the *ad valorem* the House impose on slaves brought in from neighboring colonies, and that is paid by the buyer, not the seller. This trade does not greatly affect the business of the slave merchants, so it does not greatly worry them."

"There is talk in the capital of repealing the ten percent passed some five years ago," mused Granby. "Again, that is a purchaser's levy, not a merchant's."

Vishonn chuckled. "And that talk, sir, has arisen not long after the Governor gave his assent to a twenty percent *ad valorem* on neighborly slaves proposed by the House. In April, it was! What confusion!" exclaimed the planter, waving his hands in the air. "And what is more, we are obliged to tithe each slave as though he were a real person!"

Arthur Stannard said, "No slaves have even been imported here these past three years, not to my knowledge. There are many planters here who would like to see that stoppage made permanent, but I fear that at war's end, slavers will be auctioning fresh loads of Negroes, from Norfolk to Richmond town."

Hugh listened patiently to this outburst of complaints with an expression of near-indifference. Had the light of the supper room been truer, his guests might have imagined that his eyes expressed contempt.

When he thought they were finished, he glanced briefly at Jack Frake, then smiled and said, "Gentlemen, it is quite a congeries of conundrums that weighs you down. It calls for consummate contumacy."

Thomas Reisdale, after a scoffing grunt, remarked, "You are in a gay, alliterative mood, sir!"

Hugh shrugged. "Some tragedies can be amusing, sir. Taking together the Crown's venal means of trade, by which we are all captive traders, the Crown's encouragement and sanction of slavery, the confiscatory method of payment for imported goods, the eight and one-third pence per pound duty on tobacco we send to England — well, all in all, I must concur with Mr. Frake here, that in the Crown's jackdaw eye, we are but glorified factotums."

Reece Vishonn opened his mouth to answer, but Hugh raised his hand and continued. "Allow me to ask you this question, sirs: Why do you not chafe under such circumstances? Oh, you *do* chafe — I have just heard some vigorous scratching — but is it any more than an annoying itch? By God, sirs, there is not one among you who would fail to challenge a sharper to a duel if you discovered that he had bilked you out of a fortune at cribbage! Yet, you allow the Crown to fit you into the bilboes of restraint and constant debt. We know what is the Crown's advantage. What is yours? A near monopoly on the tobacco trade, and the occasional generosity of the drawback scheme, by which you are credited with the eight and one-third pence per pound if your tobacco is fortunate enough to be bought for trans-shipment to the Continent. For those dubious sops, you are expected to be grateful for your thralldom of debt and enforced dependency."

Ralph Cullis began to speak, but, again, Hugh raised his hand, and continued. "Of course, you would rather have the liberty of choosing your own buyers, of demanding hard coin in payment, of shipping on French or Spanish or Dutch vessels, whose carriage would be infinitely cheaper, and of paying no duty at all." He grinned slyly. "Do not tell me otherwise, sirs. I have worked both ends of this business, and speak from personal observation." He paused. "I will tell you that I am ashamed of my country, for the fraudulence it practices on its most industrious sons!"

No one said anything for a while. All the men but Jack Frake sat staring at Hugh in astonishment. Jack also stared at him, but with pleased amazement. Only Ira Granby seemed to be contemplating a reply. At length, he said, "Well, sir...we have English law, through which we may strive to correct those...disparities."

Hugh cocked his head. "Only insofar as the law recognizes your existence as an Englishman, Mr. Granby. And so far as that law allows, here in Virginia, or anywhere else in the colonies, you are a political bastard who may be tolerated, and perhaps even coddled and cajoled, so long as you do not complain, or become too familiar, or presumptuous about your legitimacy."

Granby's face turned red, while Vishonn's turned ashen. Both men were gathering the courage to rise and leave, but were stopped when Thomas Reisdale commented, "This is true."

Vishonn pursed his lips, then said, "You paint a hopeless picture, sir. But I do not believe our situation is as desperate as you depict."

"As you wish," answered Hugh.

Arthur Stannard said, "If I did not know you better, Mr. Kenrick, I would be tempted to believe that you are recommending a gross flouting of the laws."

"The Crown regularly flouts your liberties, Mr. Stannard, and thus some portion of our excellent constitution, yours less so than those of our companions here." Hugh shook his head once. "No, sir. I do not advocate anarchy. I am recommending at least an admission of what Mr. Granby has called 'disparities.' Someday the Privy Council and the king's ministers may find the resolve and rationale to disallow *all* our liberties."

Reece Vishonn sighed, and glanced at Hugh with a pitying look. "What dark and insinuating sontiments to harbor in the Empire's brightest year, sir! You see devilish designs all about you, while we practical men observe only the natural course of things. Oh, yes, I concede that there exists some unfairness in our ancient arrangements with the mother country, and that some men in London overreach their mandate. But there is little that cannot be resolved between practical men!" He laughed. "Consider the business of empire, sir! What a farrago *that* must be! I don't envy the fellows charged with its management. And, I honestly doubt that, should I sit on the Privy Council or the Board of Trade, I could do much better or otherwise myself! The Crown, you must know, must think and behave in extraordinary ways, for the good of the nation. *We* are that nation, sir, and I am *not* ashamed of my country, neither of England, nor of Virginia! *I* am proud to be a subject of its empire!" exclaimed the planter. "Proud, and grateful to boot!"

Ralph Cullis leaned forward and said, "And, consider this question, Mr. Kenrick: How many Frenchmen have the liberty to compose addresses to King Louis, or the opportunity to send memorials to his *parlement*?"

"Very few, Mr. Granby," Hugh said. "I cannot even remember when the last *parlement* sat. But, an absence of liberty in one nation is not to be measured against the incremental loss of it in another."

"Speaking of France," Reisdale said tentatively, "and of empires. Recently a friend and correspondent of mine in London sent me a transcript of an address to the Sorbonne in Paris, by a prior of that institution, some ten years ago. Oh, what is its title now? Yes, I remember! *Tableau philosophique des progrés successifs de l'sprit humain.* The fellow's name? Yes, Turgot. Anne-Robert-Jacques Turgot."

Vishonn chuckled. "Are you going to assault us with more French wisdom, Mr. Reisdale? I must declare, you are a veritable repository of obscure erudition!"

"Obscure erudition has often trounced conventional wisdom, sir," said the attorney with a smile. "To a London lighterman, Sir Newton's natural observations may comprise a compendium of arcane learning, but *that* erudition will affect that fellow's life nonetheless."

"Well, sir, what did this cleric say that you're so eager for us to hear?"

Reisdale paused to relight his pipe. "Well, the title explains itself. The address was a literal hymn to our age — at least to its accumulation of wisdom. One remark in it stands out in my mind, and always will. Mr. Kenrick's dark but frank sentiments lured it from its hiding place. It has a bearing on his imagined devilish designs — and also what Mr. Frake here spoke to us about at the ball."

Vishonn, Granby, and Cullis all glanced at Jack. Vishonn said, "Sir, you are strangely quiet, by the bye. Have you nothing to say?"

Jack smiled serenely and looked briefly at Hugh. "My neighbor and host speaks for me, Mr. Vishonn, and very ably."

Hugh nodded in acknowledgment.

"You are in agreement with his sentiments?"

"Had I his talent for speech, I might have expressed them in the same manner."

"Don't doubt your talent for that, sir," said Vishonn with humor. "It seems that Caxton now has two fellows who are comfortable with teasing treason." He turned to Reisdale. "Well, sir, what did this Frenchman say that you wish us to hear?"

"He said — and it is a remarkable simile," prefaced the attorney, "'Colonies are like fruit, which clings to the tree only until it is ripe. By becoming self-sufficient, they do what Carthage did, what America will sometime do.'"

Granby frowned. "Do what, sir?"

"Why, fall from the tree, sir," Reisdale said.

Ralph Cullis groaned, as if in pain. Reece Vishonn's face contorted in incredulity. Ira Granby made a contemptuous, spitting sound. "What rot!" he muttered.

Vishonn chuckled again. "What fantastic ideas come from a most unlikely venue!" he remarked. "A bureaucrat advocating *that*! And a Papist priest, no less! Well, we are not self-sufficient, so we cannot fall."

Hugh looked thoughtful. "I must read this Frenchman's address some time, Mr. Reisdale."

"I would gladly lend you the transcript, sir."

"I must disagree with him, however, at least on that one point." Hugh reached over and moved the silver epergne closer, and demonstrated his words by touching parts of the serving dish. "I see our empire as a human and political manifestation of this piece of table furniture — the colonies, these tiers made of the best crystal, the crystal of English science and enter-prise and arts, holding all the fruits of our nation, fixed firmly to the silver trunk of English law refined and made clear and just." He paused. "Abbé Turgot neglected to mention that ripened fruit will also shrivel or putrefy, whether it has been picked, poached, or has fallen. It is not a perfect simile, which should precisely match the object of allusion in cause, consequence, and condition."

"Well, sir!" exclaimed Vishonn happily, "at last you say something with which I can agree!" He reached across the table and took a few candied dates from the epergne. "But, good lord, sir — you are a worrisome fellow!" He popped a date into his mouth and chewed it noisily.

Granby and Cullis also smiled in relief and made similar remarks.

"I concede that," Reisdale said. "But, nonetheless, Abbé Turgot's point is novel, and, well, shall we say...revolutionary?"

"True," said Hugh. "And I hope that the simile is his only failing. I look forward to perusing his address." He then abruptly steered the conversation away from politics to plantation matters. He rose after a while and invited his guests on a tour of the grounds around the house, and pointed out what repairs and improvements he was having made. Reece Vishonn and the others complimented him on the condition of the estate, and reminisced about their past visits to Brougham Hall, which once rivaled Enderly in the town's social life.

At last the planters took their leave, thanking Hugh from their saddles for his hospitality and inviting him to call on them in the near future.

*   *   *

"See?" said Reece Vishonn when he was certain they were out of earshot along the main road that led from the house. "I told you that the chap was no recusant. Not a bit of one."

"He's a fly fellow, though," said Ralph Cullis, "*and* threapish, as well. I'd wager he could talk Reverend Acland down from his pulpit and convince him to write love notes to Monsieur Voltaire!"

Ira Granby chuckled as they rode past a harvested tobacco field. "Keeping this place up will mellow his views," he said. "In a few years, he may even begin to sound like you, sir," he added, glancing at Vishonn.

"Perhaps," said the senior planter. "You are likely right. His views and ardor need topping, just as our tobacco does. They *will* be topped, I am sure of it. Don't you doubt it, either, gentlemen. He'll advertise soon enough for a new overseer, or come to us requesting a loan of one of ours."

Cullis said, after a pensive hum, "*I* say that he remains worrisome — and disturbing. If he put his mind and ardor to it, he could rile the other planters and growers here. Even the townsfolk."

Vishonn turned in his saddle with a perplexed frown. "On *what* occasion, sir?" he asked. "Over *what* matter?"

"A political occasion," answered Cullis. "I believe there is some truth in what he and Mr. Frake have said recently. When the war is over, I believe we will witness more politicking here than any man would wish to endure." He paused. "I don't know over what matters...but I fear it all the same."

Thomas Reisdale, who rode alongside Arthur Stannard in the rear, said, "Disturbance is not always a thing to be feared or avoided, sirs. It has the bracing effect of reminding one that what one takes for granted, such as our liberties, may be taken away, as surely as water sinks into sand."

Vishonn laughed. "Is that another of your Gallic sweetmeats, Mr. Reisdale?"

"No, sir," said the attorney. "It is a morsel of English wisdom. Or Virginian, if you prefer, and I am its author."

"I quite appreciated Mr. Kenrick's simile of the epergne," remarked Stannard. "So much so, that I intend to write my firm in London about it. There are men in the Commons who may be able to employ it to good effect — should the occasion ever arise. Though I am less certain than is Mr. Cullis that it ever will."

"Strictly speaking, Mr. Stannard," Reisdale said, "it was an analogy that our host demonstrated. And an excellent one, too. Your men in the Commons may be able to put it over all the gentlemen there — should the occasion call for it."

"'Put it over,' sir?" queried Stannard, a little offended. "Why, you are ascribing what sounds like dishonest oratory to a man you have not even heard speak."

"Sharp persuasion it may be, sir — depending on the intent of the speaker and the honesty of the gentlemen of the Commons. The analogy, you see, is not perfect, either. I don't much like the idea of being plucked like a confection from a bowl by the Crown, though many in the Commons may find that idea both attractive and expedient." His four companions turned to look at Reisdale. "Beware, sirs!" he added with a smile. "Castor and Pollux are among us now! Or, if you prefer, Cato and Cicero!"

Reece Vishonn sighed and turned to face the front. He exclaimed, "God spare us the company of scholars and lawyers!"

Chapter 11: The Olympians

Aﬂer the first breathless astonishment of discovering all that one has in common with another, comes the mutual, happy knowledge that the commonalities overshadow the multitude of differences, and that the former render the latter irrelevant, for they have a deeper, more vigorous foundation for friendship than have happenstance, coincidence, or accident. Such a friendship becomes an inviolate continuum. When it is born, the world seems a saner, cleaner, and more welcoming place. The wearisome, aching partner of loneliness is instantly abandoned and forgotten. Virtues, aspirations, and experiences mesh hungrily and effortlessly for the discoverers, and become the fast norms by which all other friendships are judged. Other men, together with their society and concerns, become intrusive, almost amusing annoyances, to be endured with a civility that defines their beginning and end. Warming affection and genuine graciousness are reserved for those who mirror one's soul.

To be reciprocated in this manner is a rare, priceless reward for all the tests and pains of isolation one has known in the past. Distant, elusive *oughts* abruptly become palpable *is's*. One then feels a right to laugh in recollection of those who dream without contributing any personal substance to their professed visions — provided one remembers to think of them.

Reece Vishonn was alert enough to sense the commonalities shared by Jack Frake and Hugh Kenrick, but insensible to their common roots.

* * *

Hugh Kenrick and Jack Frake stood in the yard in front of the house and watched the planters amble on horseback down the main road. The winter sun was beginning its rapid descent in the west, and chilling breezes from the north swept off the York River and whipped around the corners of the outbuildings.

Jack glanced at Hugh. "They must be relieved, now that they know that you don't plan to put Caxton to the torch, Mr. Kenrick," he remarked. "They half expect me to."

Hugh smiled in amusement. "They frighten easily, Mr. Frake, and are consoled too quickly. It will take some extraordinary event or speech to enrage them."

Jack nodded once. "The peril we see is not quite real to them."

Hugh sighed. "They are comfortable in their dependency. Complacency has dulled their sensibilities, as much as would a monteith of rum."

"I am afraid that the peril must first come beating down their doors, before they can believe it exists, and grasp that they won't be exempt from its depredations." Jack paused in thought. "Until they do believe it, they won't be whole men — and we will be the town's moonrakers."

Hugh smiled again, and folded his arms against the chill. "Moonrakers! Are we the cause of their uneasiness, Mr. Frake? Or is it the Crown?"

"Both, I imagine," Jack said. "We are, because we are not in awe of the Crown. The Crown is, because we remind them that it does not stand in awe of their liberties."

"If we are to ever have an enduring empire, it must be founded on a polity that does."

"Not the Crown?"

Hugh shook his head. "Not the *Crown* itself." He paused. "It is time that men advanced beyond kings and crowns and ancient privileges."

This time Jack smiled. "I am certain that your ideal empire is not feasible, Mr. Kenrick. I mind very much the notion of my being some placeman's handy confection. If Parliament could ever be persuaded of the value and wisdom of your arrangement, it would be only because its members and their constituencies saw in it a means to satisfy their appetites for colonial sweetmeats. To heed reason, these men must see something in it to gain for themselves — at our expense. Then, of course, it would not be reason they heeded, but a...circumspect, dissembling expediency." Jack shook his head. "If there is little prospect of political gain, they will never sanction your empire of reason."

Hugh grinned in appreciation. "A 'circumspect, dissembling expediency,'" he repeated. "An excellent way of naming what may well be the best of their good intentions. Why, it is the companion of our neighbors' stubborn disbelief — a circumspect, dissembling delusion!" He shrugged lightly. "Then the solution is to somehow wrest the power from the placemen and Parliament and boards and councils to pluck us from the epergne of empire, and to find a means to deny it to them and their ilk for all time. It is an engineering task, one that has maddened many a fine mind." He smiled again, and bowed slightly to Jack. "You may very likely be the one to make that enraging speech, Mr. Frake."

"Or you," Jack said.

Hugh gestured to the house. "Will you stay to supper? We have much to talk about, aside from our parliamentary division."

"I was about to ask you to supper."

"You're here, and I insist."

*   *   *

"Wonder," noted a contemporary of Samuel Johnson, "is involuntary praise." Supper passed, and then midnight. Astonishment erased all sense of time in the two young men, and astonishment itself gave way to wonder. Each man wished to understand why the other was so much like himself. Their conversation over tea, supper, and spirits, a conversation composed of a constant exchange of episodes, incidents, and adventures, silently wove the fabric of a bond for which friendship was merely the hem, and their politics the seam. They were able to speak of themselves without boasting, without vanity, without the necessity or compulsion to surpass each other in courage, accomplishment, or supremacy.

"I defied a press gang...."

"I defied a mob at Charing Cross...."

"I joined a smuggling gang...."

"I was admitted into the company of freethinkers...."

"I lost my friends to the Crown and corrupted law...."

"I lost my friends to the same pair...."

"I watched my friend's book burn at the gallows...."

"My uncle burned my books, or tossed them into the Thames...."

"I helped my two best friends die on the gallows, to end their agony...."

"I watched my friends perish at sea, and another die on the pillory...."

"I remember seeing fireworks in London, and wishing I could stay there for the balance of my life...."

"I remember the fireworks at the celebration of the last peace, and thinking that I belonged in London, that metropolis of possibilities...."

"Skelly's last words to me were 'This Briton will never be a slave'...."

"I neglected to bow to the Duke of Cumberland, and would not apologize...."

"Your words may have condemned your friends at the King's Bench...."

"But *you* copied out *Hyperborea*, and I envy you that crime...."

Each man privately appreciated, in mounting stages, that the other had lived just as unique and glorious a life as had he himself. Each understood that the glory was a consequence, not a cause or a quest. But neither did they abjure this species of pride in their self-estimations, nor deny its presence in each other. Their divergent politics, within the span of a few hours, ebbed in importance to the role of a half-remembered pretext, smothered by tales of tragedy and heroism. Each was certain that the other's politics was not the product of serendipitous book-learning or of a vacuous, illiterate meanness, but the expression of some unconquered element in his character. The words spoken by each of them were glittering, tantalizing clues to what moved them, and these words, each man dimly sensed, were faint overtures to the words each of them had vowed to find some day: Jack, in dedication to the memory of two hanged outlaws; Hugh, in dedication to the memory of a dying man who had ordered him to live.

"I remember Ranelagh Gardens, and the bookshops, and the Pool of London," sighed Hugh at one point, as he gazed wistfully in the flames of the library fireplace.

"I remember Ranelagh, too," Jack said, "and St. Paul's, and the theater Redmagne and I went to, and the incredible energy of the city." He paused. "And Westminster Bridge, a white gash of stone arcing from bank to bank. It was the first thing I noticed."

Hugh smiled. "My father wrote me that a new bridge is to be thrown across the Thames, at Blackfriars. Our quarry may win a contract to provide some of the stone."

Jack frowned. "I'll never cross it or Westminster. If I ever returned to England, I would risk sharing the fate of my friends."

Hugh nodded. "And if I returned, I do believe that my uncle would try to have me assassinated. I must wait until he is...gone."

Jack rose from his chair to study a framed picture on one of the walls. It was Hugh's sketch of the members of the Society of the Pippin. "So," he remarked, "that was Glorious Swain?"

"Yes," Hugh said. "My elder brother — in spirit and mind, at least."

Jack glanced at his host. "I thought that of Redmagne, too." He shook his head in amazement. "Both of them, unexpected discoveries. You rescued yours, and mine rescued me. We have so many things in common — sorrows, triumphs, places, our kinds of friends...." He laughed, and added, "And Captain Ramshaw and the *Sparrowhawk*. I came here on it as a felon, you as an exile."

Hugh studied his guest for a moment. "As an exile," he mused. "How true." He paused. "And, we seem to have common enemies. It was Henoch Pannell who captured you, and ensured that your friends were executed in Falmouth, was it not?"

"Yes," Jack said with new interest. "What of him?"

"He is now a member for Canovan. I have sparred with him, too. All in all, an unwholesome man. He is no friend of the colonies."

"I wouldn't think he would be." Jack frowned and sat down again. "Canovan? That was Skelly's old London borough." He shook his head.

"So, he's looted that, too. Well, Parliament is the right place for him."

Hugh picked up a silver coffee pot and gestured with it. Jack shook his head. Hugh poured himself another cup. "He is plumb, plump, and wily, thanks to an opportune marriage, good eating, and consorting with his ilk in the Commons. My uncle has drawn him into an alliance with Crispin Hillier, our own member, for the express purpose of controlling votes for keeping the colonies dependent, in addition to whatever other villainy the Commons wishes to visit on England. If any man is capable of persuading Parliament to team the colonies in a common yoke, it is he. Sir Henoch is an effective speaker." Then Hugh laughed. "No, no! Forgive me for overestimating him! I am certain there are better speakers than he for the job."

Jack packed another pipe and lit it. "Tell me how you came to encounter him."

Hugh told him about the Bucklad House concert, his exchange with the M.P. outside St. Stephens, and the supper with his uncle.

Hours later, they talked about *Hyperborea*. Hugh held one of the two duodecimo volumes of the novel, and asked, "Was Romney Marsh, or Redmagne, anything like his hero, Drury Trantham?"

Jack looked pleasantly puzzled. "You know.... That question never before occurred to me. But, yes, he was much like his hero. Like him in many ways. Or rather, Trantham was much like Redmagne, but projected onto a more ideal and lively and fast-moving canvas."

"Yes," remarked Hugh. "But Redmagne's own canvas is no less heroic or elevating than Drury Trantham's." He paused and stared into the darkness of one of the room's corners. Their exchange had triggered the sudden memory of a moment he had experienced in Ranelagh Gardens, when he saw his own life as a series of canvases, lit by the light of innumerable fireworks. He looked noble, solemn, and joyous at the same time.

Jack, surprised by his host's abrupt silence, studied the face of his new friend, and saw these things. He thought: Your company is invigorating, Mr. Kenrick. You have caused me to remember painful, urgent, pressing things. But, somehow, your company lessens the sting of those memories. You are, somehow, a justification for all that I am and have done, apart from everything I am and have done.

They both heard a noise at the library door and turned to see it open. A figure in a nightgown, carrying a candle, took a hesitant step inside. It was Spears, Hugh's valet. Hugh asked, "What is it, Spears? What are you doing up at this hour? Is something amiss?"

Spears frowned. "Pardon me, sir," he said, nodding to the window, "but it is your rising time."

Jack and Hugh glanced out the window, and noticed the gray-black of the predawn light beyond it. Throughout the night, they had heard the ticking and chimes of the floor clock, but paid them no more attention than they had the crickets and tree frogs.

Jack Frake stayed long enough for breakfast, then mounted his horse for the ride back to Morland. In one of his saddlebags was a leather portfolio that contained many of his host's essays and Pippin addresses, in addition to what few addresses Hugh was able to salvage from Glorious Swain's garret in London years ago.

"Good day, to you, Mr. Kenrick," said Jack, touching the edge of his hat.

"Be seeing you, Mr. Frake," Hugh said.

They did not bid each other goodbye. Jack Frake rode home at a trot, while Hugh Kenrick went back inside the great house and climbed the steps to his bedchamber, stopping only to instruct Spears to wake him in three hours.

Chapter 12: The Governor

"Lately," said the gentleman, "I have been so befuddled by the demands of this office that this morning I consulted Dr. Johnson's definition of Governor. Four of the five meanings he gives may, in ideal circumstances, be applied to my duties. But, in fact, I can neither steer a supreme direction, nor wield much authority, nor exercise my delegated power. I am neither pilot, nor regulator, nor manager." The gentleman paused and leaned forward. "Dr. Johnson might have added a sixth definition of Governor, sir," he added. "Something witty, on the order of his definition of oats. Exempli gratia, 'A Punchinello who presumes to act for his absentee master.'"

"Dr. Johnson's *Dictionary* is without peer. Yet, there are in it many definitions that could have benefited from less wit and more precision."

"I cannot but agree with you, sir. In my quieter moments, I have annotated and enlarged on many of his entries, if not corrected them in part or in whole." The gentleman shook his head and chuckled. "I am afraid that I have spoiled my copy of his opus! It is cluttered with my own emendatory marginalia!"

"Then it must be some relief to you that he hasn't the power to hurl acerbic thunderbolts across the ocean in retaliation, your honor. I have it our reigning critic does not brook criticism."

"Oh, no," said the gentleman, shaking his head. "I don't believe he would be so vindictive. I have heard that he is quite generous in regard to his own fallibility. He would very likely welcome correction." He sighed. "Would that their lordships on the Board of Trade and the Privy Council were less offended and more lenient, in respect to my actions. They are not so friendly to enlightenment." He paused and noticed his visitor's empty glass. "Will you have another bumper of Armagnac, sir?"

Hugh Kenrick nodded and volunteered, as his host rose to fill his long-stemmed glass with Armagnac from a crystal decanter, "A Punchinello, your honor? I believe you underestimate the esteem in which many persons here hold you. I have heard little else but praise for your character and conduct."

*   *   *

It was inevitable that Francis Fauquier, Esquire, Lieutenant-Governor of Virginia, would be informed of the permanent presence in the colony of a member of nobility. His secretary did not pass on to him all the letters addressed to his honor, but among those he did were several on the subject of Hugh Kenrick, Baron of Danvers. The Governor, finding the mental time to be curious about why such a person would refrain from announcing himself, instructed his secretary to compose for his signature an invitation to the newcomer to present himself at the Palace in Williamsburg so that His Majesty's representative could at least pay his own courtesies. Many of the things said about the young man were profusely complimentary, while other statements made about him were quite disturbing. The Governor wished to judge for himself.

Fauquier, aged fifty-seven, an Anglicized Huguenot, was a Fellow of the Royal Society and a former director of the South Sea Company. His father had been a colleague of Isaac Newton's at the Royal Mint and a director of the Bank of England. The Lieutenant-Governor arrived in June 1758 to assume his post. No one knew for certain why he was appointed. He was a friend of the Spanish-raiding George Anson, now First Lord of the Admiralty; it was said by some that he had lost his inherited fortune to the navigator over a game of cards and that the appointment was a means of escaping his creditors. Others assumed that it was a combination of factors: his friendship with George Montagu Dunk, the third Earl of Halifax and president of the Board of Trade; his popular pamphlet, published in 1755, on the ways and means of funding the new war and reducing the national debt; and his knowledge of commercial practices and law, all contributing to his name's being put on the list of candidates for colonial Governorships.

He was a short man, with dark, avid eyes set in an oval face. A widow's peak atop a broad forehead complemented a long nose. He was the most polished and urbane Governor the Crown had ever imposed on the Council and the House of Burgesses: widely read on many diverse subjects, able to read and write Latin and French; a musician; dabbler in science and economics, gracious; a consummate conversationalist; wickedly deft at cards; well-meaning; and increasingly torn between his duty to the Crown and a growing fondness for Virginia.

The burgesses liked and trusted him, chiefly because, outside of the purchase of two parcels of land in Williamsburg, he did not, as had his predecessors, evince the least interest in acquiring large tracts of uninhabited wilderness in the west; this absence of avarice lent substance to his sincerity, honesty, and devotion to his duties. The Council, composed largely of the wealthiest planters and landowners in the colony, and which acted as his advisory board, as a senate, and as the supreme court of the colony, liked him because he seemed to be what all twelve of them wished to be: independently wealthy and well-connected in the maze of colonial and imperial influence.

Hugh Kenrick received the Lieutenant-Governor's invitation in late January 1760, and cursed silently when he read the brief missive. At the bottom were Fauquier's signature and embossed imprint of the Great Seal of the colony. It was not an invitation he could ignore. He instructed Mr. Beecroft to compose a reply for his signature, stating that he would call on the Palace some time in February, before the next session of the General Assembly. In mid-February, he donned a heavy coat, secured a traveling bag to his saddle, and rode off through a light snowfall to the Hove Creek bridge and the road to Williamsburg.

Williamsburg was a larger town than was Caxton, and as neatly laid out. The sparse buildings of the College of William and Mary stood at one end of the Duke of Gloucester Street, the imposing, square-cornered Capitol at the other. In between these points, on both sides of the wide boulevard, stood a few dozen houses with their gardens, and shops, taverns and hostelries.

Hugh had followed the road from Caxton that let out near the college's grounds, and he soon found himself on the boulevard. The hooves of his mount thumped leisurely on the street's frozen mud as he made his way in the direction of the Capitol almost a mile away. He nodded or touched his hat in reply to the curious glances of some men and women who paused to watch him ride by.

Unlike Caxton, Williamsburg was a sleepy town, this capital of the richest and most populous of Great Britain's colonies — a port that might have been, but for its dead-center location on high ground between two great rivers. But Hugh sensed that it was now girding itself for the opening of the General Assembly next month. Then there would be court days in the county courthouse, the arrival of plaintiffs and defendants and their attorneys, of farmers and artisans and entertainers, of planters and merchants to see that their bills were introduced and read in the House by their burgesses, of busy men who came to settle debts and acquire new ones, of idle gentlemen who came to be diverted by the theater, by other men's daughters, by horse racing, card games, cock-fighting, and amusing company.

Drays and carts were pulled up before many of the shops and taverns, and men were unloading from them everything from bolts of cloth to sides of beef. Smoke gushed from the chimney of a smithy, and he heard the persistent, purposeful hammering of metal from that enterprise. He passed a cumbersome wagon laden with raw lumber, pulled by a team of oxen. From one of the houses he heard someone practicing on a violin, and from another a woman singing "Pretty Little Horses," a lullaby his mother had sung to him long ago. Many of the shops and taverns sported modest signboards that winked at him as they rocked in the cold wind; they reminded him of the Strand in London. He rode as far as the Capitol, just to see the place that mattered so much in Virginia. He cocked his head in appreciation of its size and the simplicity of its lines; it was as grand an edifice as any in Philadelphia.

Also grand, he thought, was the Governor's Palace midway down the boulevard, at the end of a long park. After arranging for a room at Raleigh Tavern and a stall for his mount, he walked the distance to the Palace. At the great iron gates, he presented his letter from Fauquier to a black footman, who in turn presented it to the housekeeper. This worthy man, when he read the letter, bid the unexpected but special guest to wait in a parlor to the right of the foyer. But Hugh declined, choosing to wait instead in the spacious, marble-floored hall.

The wheel of muskets fixed to the hall's ceiling startled him. And everywhere he looked, he saw arms: pistols, swords, sabers, halberds, pikes, and more muskets, all arranged on the walls in some ominous effort at decoration. Directly opposite the entrance, above the arched portal that led to the inner sanctums of the Palace, were three half-furled banners: the Virginia Regimental, the Great Union, and the King's Colors — crossed on polished mahogany staves, draped over a drum. The foyer alone, he concluded, was more impressive, and perhaps more intentionally intimidating, than was the whole of St. Stephen's Chapel that was the House of Commons. When a secretary rushed in to escort him upstairs to the Governor's office, Hugh inquired about the purpose of the arms.

"The Palace, you see, milord," said the man, "is an extension of the magazine that is just up the way. There has never been enough room to store all the weapons owned by the colony, and I suppose it was judged convenient by past Governors to house them here, too. And, aside from their utilitarian presence, they serve a symbolic purpose, which is to remind his honor's visitors and petitioners of his favors of the power and majesty of the Crown."

Hugh knew little about Francis Fauquier's career in Virginia, other than that he had assented to the tobacco act of a year and a half ago, the riders of which had become a liability to him. One of his first official vetoes, however, was of the removal of the colony's scalp bounty law during the same session of the General Assembly. Queen Anne County's major planters praised him, the middle planters did not fully trust him, while Jack Frake and Thomas Reisdale predicted that Fauquier would probably be the last popular Governor of the colony. "He cannot placate the burgesses and London, too," was Reisdale's comment one evening.

Hugh repressed a grin when the secretary showed him into the Governor's office. Not only was Fauquier a foot shorter than he, but his friendly, almost puppyish manner contradicted and made ludicrous the Palace's array of decorative armament. In the course of their initial cordialities, Hugh tactfully but firmly corrected the Governor. "My preferred manner of address, your honor, is *sir*," he said. "It saves me the bother of unnecessary protocol, and others the effort of undue humility." He then offered his hand to the Governor, something a titled aristocrat in those times would never have done for a commoner. Francis Fauquier was but an accomplished and respected commoner.

The Governor was momentarily startled, but smiled and timidly shook the proffered hand. He waved Hugh to an armchair of crimson silk damask and plopped down on a similar chair opposite him. In between them was a massive desk piled high with papers and books. "So," he had said, "it is true...what some persons have written to me about you." A servant knocked on the door then and came in with a tray of spirits and glasses.

*   *   *

Lieutenant-Governor Fauquier replenished his own glass with Armagnac, then set down the decanter. He said, "Thank you...sir. And, I am not unaware of that praise. However, the persons who praise me do not reside in London. All the burgesses and the whole Council know my instructions. Even these parsimonious parsons who bedevil me. If I followed the Board of Trade's instructions to the letter, sir, I should become little better than a tyrant. Then I would merit the opposite of praise. My instructions leave me meager room for discretion and judgment. The originals I brought with me have been so amended, abridged, and supplemented, that I cannot be blamed for not knowing any more what they are. I expect more of that, and more than one rebuke from their lordships on the Board and the Privy Council."

Fauquier made an anguished face. "But, if I am to lend some congeniality to the governing of this place, I cannot but employ my discretion and judgment, qualities I had presumed were responsible for my commission."

He paused to sip his Armagnac, then put down the glass and gestured with his hands. "From Punchinello, I assume the guise of Jason in ancient Greece, caught between the man-eating monster Scylla — that being the Board — and the whirlpool of the Charybdis — that being the unending difficulties and concerns associated with this colony." Fauquier rose suddenly and paced nervously before his desk. "If it is not the Cherokees who need presents and wooing, it is the Creeks, or some other amorphous 'nation' of barbarians. If it is not settlers on the frontier raiding Indians, it is the Indians raiding the settlers. If it is not the burgesses pressing me for assent to their laws, it is the clergy hounding me for their veto. If it is not the dearth of specie, it is the cascades of unsecured paper money. If it is not having money enough to raise an effective militia for the frontier, it is not enough men to fill the militia when the money has been voted. Creditors and debtors inveigh against each other. Tobacco prices are too high or too low. London's merchants trade accusations of fraud and sharp practice with the planters. Oh, sir!" sighed Fauquier, sitting down again. "I could go on, but I fear I should distress you, too!"

Before Hugh could reply, the Governor leaned forward and wagged a finger. "Virginian lives and money purchased the forks of the Ohio at Pittsburg, but Pennsylvanians hope to claim them with no risk of men or money, and they are reluctant to take any action against the savages who imperil their own western frontier. Lastly, I thought — together with the Council and the burgesses — that we had finished with the Cherokees in the Carolinas and west of here, and that Governor Lyttleton's treaty with them would hold, at least until the French war is concluded. But, not surprisingly, French agents among the tribes are stirring them up again. If it pleases you, sir," added the Governor in a near whisper, and also because he could not forget that his visitor was of the aristocracy, "that bit of information may not leave this room. The House must be officially apprised of the situation."

Hugh nodded.

Fauquier sat back in his chair, seemingly exhausted from his tirade. "I have been here only some two years, sir, yet I sometimes believe that the Governorship of Bedlam Hospital in London would be less aggrieving and troublesome."

Hugh smiled in brief sympathy. "You have described to me your Charybdis, your honor. How does the Scylla worry you?"

Fauquier's prominent eyebrows went up. "The Board? They wish me to work miracles, but ignore the fact that I lack the magic. They expect bounteous loaves and fishes, and a supine waiter to supply and serve them. For two thousand pounds per annum. No man could perform to their satisfaction for ten, or twenty! Look at Virginia, sir! It is half the area of France! Do the Board and the Privy Council actually believe that the most populous colony will do their bidding forever, without question or reservation, at its own cost?"

Hugh shook his head. "I do not think it is a matter of what they believe, your honor. Belief is immaterial to them. It is a matter of what they *want*."

Fauquier grunted in agreement. "The people here are accustomed to governing themselves, for better or for worse, in many matters, and London did not much interfere. Until very recently, the colony's and the Board's interests were amicably meshed. Now, though, it seems that the Board and the Privy Council have expunged the word *reciprocity* from their own dictionary!"

Hugh remarked, "As you imply, your honor, the situation is sown with future conflict and tragedy." He paused to finish the contents of his glass, then ventured, "The people here — and I now count myself as one of them — may be accustomed to governing themselves, but they should not be surprised if the Board and the Privy Council frown upon their actions and laws, and act to constrain a presumptuous colony. It is not so novel a notion. Are not the prisoners of Newgate and the Fleet obliged to pay their own turnkeys?"

The Governor's face abruptly turned stern, and he studied his visitor for a moment. His expression was now that of a man in command. "What are your thoughts on the Indians, sir?"

Hugh considered his answer for a moment, then said, "They are nature's orphans, your honor, and our society is an irresistible force. It matters not how frequently they assault the western settlers. They are doomed — or, rather, their preferred mode of living is doomed, and if they do not abandon it, they themselves will be doomed. They wish to hunt and roam about in the wilderness without the benefit of ownership, patent, or industry. They wish to trade with us, but reserve the option of making war if the trade is not to their liking. They have little or no notion of rights, liberty, or property. Their view of the world extends not much farther than the range of a shot arrow. They depend on the lottery of fortune, error, oversight, or our benevolence to preserve their mode of living." Hugh waved a hand in dismissal. "I would no more treat with them than seek a peace with the sea's natural predators, for they are of a fickle, unpredictable mien. They sense the mortal threat to their precarious state of savagery, and they know well that our society will not be contained east of the Alleghenies, regardless of the Crown's assurances, and that they will be driven farther and farther west."

Hugh saw reluctant concession in the Governor's expression. He went on. "If the Crown must devise a policy, your honor, the most honest one might be to issue a proclamation to the Indians: Join us, mingle with us, or perish — and if perish, then by a provoked sword. Discard your bear grease and scalping knives, and discover Locke and Diderot and Newton. For we shall not remove ourselves, and you have no other alternative but to remove yourselves clear to the Pacific Ocean, or suffer a violent, sad, and certain demise."

Fauquier frowned, then exclaimed, "By God, sir! You are a flinty man!"

Hugh shrugged. "I have as little compassion for their predicament, your honor, as I might have for that of a Thames coal heaver, who, chancing upon a means to leave his brutal employment and improve his condition, spurns it because it would require effort and cogitation; and, eschewing reason, tosses it back into the river, allowing his mental caducity to choose his future, which is to lug coal for pittance for the balance of his short and ekish life."

Fauquier seemed to nod in agreement, and said, "But if we do treat with them, honor requires that we observe the terms, especially if they confound the claims and patents of land made by speculators here."

Hugh shook his head. "There is a snare in such honor. On one hand, it would oblige us to extinguish, if not our ambitions, then ourselves in order to protect barbarism and wilderness. On the other, it would be a disservice to the Indians to assure them a continued life of ignorance and abject poverty. If compassion is to be the moral measure of our treaties with them, I believe my policy would be the most merciful. It would not permit broken promises, because no promises would be made. The parties would be spared a *folie à deux*: on the Indians' part, the fragile delusion that their chosen state of living was guaranteed; on the Crown's part, the disgrace of failing to honor terms it had no power — indeed, no motive — to enforce."

Fauquier thought to himself: "Sir, if there were a vacancy on my Council, I should immediately nominate you to fill it." Aloud, he said, "You seem to have given much thought to our vermilion brethren, sir. What have you to say about the sable race?"

Hugh knew by the Governor's expectant look not only that his views on slavery had been communicated to Fauquier by one or more persons in Caxton, but that his answer would reach sympathetic ears. "That the trade in those people be abolished, and that they be manumitted and instructed in the arts of living as free subjects." He paused. "It is a simpler, grosser wrong we discuss, your honor, requiring a simpler solution."

Fauquier glanced out his window, and saw that the snowfall had stopped. He rose suddenly and said, "Come, sir. If you don't mind it, take a turn with me through the garden. When it's in bloom, it is quite as pretty as any in England."

As they strolled through the frigid, snow-dusted garden in the rear of the Palace, the pair talked of many things: of London, music, the theater, and other missed amenities offered by the faraway metropolis. Fauquier was an accomplished violinist, and promised to invite Hugh to the Palace the next time he planned to play with other musicians in the town and legislature.

As they came near the end of their circuit, the Governor remarked with a sigh, "I could talk with you the rest of the day and into the night, sir, and introduce you to my wife, Catherine, and my son, William. However, some members of the Council are coming over soon, and I am afraid their business shall fill the rest of my day. Are you staying in town?"

"For one night only, your honor. I have a room at the Raleigh."

Fauquier said with a chuckle, "Well, I have heard some good things about that place — and some bad." He patted Hugh's arm. "You must come again, sir, and soon. I shall make the time to show you more of the Palace." He paused as they mounted the steps that led back inside the mansion. "I must apologize for having regaled you with the adventures of my office. But those burdens and duties remind me of Galba's advice to Licinius Piso, whom he named his successor as emperor of Rome. 'You are going to rule over men who can endure neither complete slavery nor complete liberty.' I often wish the Board of Trade had appended that *consilium* to my instructions."

Hugh smiled and said, "Perhaps the Board was wise not to, your honor, because its members recalled the fate of Galba and Piso. But, about Galba, I believe Tacitus commented that he was, 'in the judgment of all, capable of ruling, if he had not ruled.' So, I do not think the Board is at all influenced by the lessons to be found in Tacitus's chronicles of political folly."

Fauquier studied his companion. "You are a daring yet compelling young man, sir. I do not believe the word *moderation* is much exercised in your thoughts." His eyes narrowed in mischievous challenge. "How do you propose to free a single slave, when that action depends not only on the approval of the House and my Council, but, ultimately, on my assent?"

Hugh only smiled again. "That remains to be seen, your honor. Perhaps I shall not require your assent or any governing body's approval."

The Governor hummed in doubt at Hugh's reticence. "Why do you oppose the institution, sir?"

"Among my reasons are purely selfish ones, your honor," Hugh said. "When I look at a man, I do not wish to be troubled by pity for him or by the injustice of his involuntary station. When a man looks at me, I do not wish it to be with deferential envy, honey-masked hate, or obsequious fear." Again, he smiled in answer to Fauquier's startled expression, and added, "Aristotle may have been in error concerning the movement of the earth and sun, but he was entirely correct about the expectations and norms of a virtuous man."

"So," queried the Governor, "I should not expect to hear word of you declaiming from the benches of the House chamber on whether a slave ought to be counted as real estate, and so eligible for the payment of a portion of his owner's quit-rents, or treated as personal property?"

Hugh shook his head. "I would sooner take up conjugal residence with an addled slattern, your honor, than suborn my mind by concocting such petty, irrelevant distinctions."

Fauquier permitted himself a single, short laugh. "I fear, good sir, that there are not so many addled slatterns who would long tolerate you. Even ignorance and inelegance have their limits. I mean that as a compliment, of course." He paused to reach for his silver pocket watch. "And, I fear, I must go. The Council members must have already arrived and be pacing worriedly upstairs." Hugh opened one of the double doors, and they went inside. "I'll see you to the foyer, sir," said the Governor as they walked down a hallway. "In regard to your bold intentions, however...far be it from me to oppose miracles, should you manage to accomplish one. No more than that can I say."

In the foyer, a footman brought out Hugh's greatcoat, which he had left in the care of the housekeeper. Fauquier waited until he had donned it, then, after some hesitation, held out his hand. "Thank you for your call and your diverting and invigorating conversation, *Mr.* Kenrick. I do hope that we have many more hours of such talk, in less hurried circumstances."

Hugh clasped the Governor's hand and shook it. "As well, I, your honor. Thank you for your time, and I look forward to the pleasure of listening to you play Vivaldi." With a slight nod of his head, Hugh turned and strode casually out the door that was held open for him by the footman.

*   *   *

As he conferred with the Councilmen for the rest of the afternoon on a number of matters likely to be discussed by the burgesses during the next General Assembly, Francis Fauquier had difficulty sustaining in his mind the reality of Hugh Kenrick. The Councilmen were the kinds of men he dealt with daily, and occasionally he caught himself comparing them with the young man, and imagined the comparison in terms of meringue pies and cannon balls. He would chuckle involuntarily then, and these cautious, well-heeled, timid men would pause and glance at him, and he would shake his head and gesture to one of the gentleman to continue making his point.

He had been communicated many of the particulars of Hugh Kenrick's background and family, but it was only after the young man's departure that the Governor remembered that he had forgotten to enquire about the family and especially about the allegations, so palpable was that person's

presence. He was more than a little disturbed by this lapse in his usual dili-
gence. He wondered also what it was about Hugh Kenrick that made him
confess so much to him.

The reality of the Councilmen, however, triumphed in the end. The
details of his gubernatorial duties, together with the absolute necessity of
appeasing the powers in London, sapped the strength of the Governor's
mind to retain the reality of his visitor. Later, though, in his most private
moments, and at the oddest times, the image and hard reality of Hugh Kenrick would flash through his thoughts. It would gladden him, when it
occurred, if he happened upon some unanswerable idea, principle, or eloquence while reading a political tract in his library. Or, it would shame him,
when it occurred, if he was laboring to compose the draft of a report to the
Board of Trade, and he found himself writing such things as, "In explaining
my latest actions, I hope to receive the approbation of my royal Master,
which is the height of my Ambition. His gracious acceptance of my poor
service will be an additional Spur to me to merit it in the future. His
Majesty's approval will always cause my humble Gratitude...."

The worlds occupied by the two kinds of men were irreconcilable, and
Francis Fauquier, loyal servant of the Crown, knew that he owed his station and future to the one and not to the other. Beyond this conclusion, he
was unable to go. That the two worlds must eventually conflict and war
was an unfathomable projection beyond his ken. He would never understand why he failed to govern Virginia to anyone's satisfaction.

Hugh Kenrick, sitting alone that evening in his room at the Raleigh
Tavern, reflected on his visit to the Palace that day and on his time with the
Governor. Although it was a near-obligation, the visit had been a pleasant
chore. He had even come close to liking the man, allowing himself to hope
that the echo of comprehension and agreement he saw in the man in
response to his words was evidence of some power and willingness to think
and act on those words. But Hugh was certain that it was only an echo. In
private, the Governor could think and speak and act as a private man. In
his public capacity, he was duty-bound to be a symbol of the Crown, and
the private man vanished.

He also marveled over how much the Governor was an Englishman,
and how much, now, he himself was not.

Chapter 13: The Freeman

On his way back to Caxton the next afternoon, on the road near the College's pastures, Hugh was startled to encounter Jack Frake, who was on horseback, and John Proudlocks, who drove a horse and cart, coming in the opposite direction for Williamsburg. He smiled and tipped his hat. "Good afternoon, gentlemen. What brings you here?"

"Necessities not carried in Mr. Rittles's store," Jack said. After a pause, he asked, "How is the Governor?"

Hugh frowned. "How could you know I've seen him?"

Jack laughed. "Everyone in Caxton seems to know that you were summoned to the Palace." He paused again. "And many of our neighbors will be disappointed that you do not return chastised. Have you been?"

Hugh shrugged and shook his head. "No, not in the least. And, I was not summoned. I was invited. The Governor and I had a very illuminating conversation."

"What do you think of him?"

"He means well, and will mean well for the duration of his tenure here. But I do not expect his good intentions to prevail over his duty to the Crown, for which I sensed he has a genuine but unreasoning affection. He is one man among many to whom it will never occur that there can be no feasible arrangement between the Crown's present purposes and our own. He is neither a knave nor a fool. I found myself wishing that he had stayed in London, and made a career of writing papers on natural phenomena for the Royal Society. Or being a director of my father's bank," Hugh added with a chuckle. "However, I fear he will attempt to establish a sly balance of the Board of Trade's desires and Virginia's needs. He must ultimately fail."

Jack cocked his head. "I've heard that about him, Mr. Kenrick. But if he took the side of Virginia with obvious conviction, he must know that he would be recalled in a wink, and probably suffer the fate of Admiral Byng, and be executed outside the offices of the Board."

"As a traitor and a rebel," remarked Hugh.

Jack nodded. "Well," he said, "if you are right about him, we can be grateful that his good intentions will purchase us time to gather, order, and refine our wits."

"And if you are right about the Crown's ends, we will need those wits."

The two men regarded each other with studied certitude. After a moment, Hugh asked, "What makes us so sure that we will need those refined wits, Mr. Frake?"

Jack grinned. "Perhaps it is because we know we are both ascending Mount Olympus — but from opposite sides. We are not made to be kept on plains."

Hugh smiled in reply. He knew that his neighbor could have answered in that manner only if he had finished reading the Pippin essays he had loaned to him.

"Had the Governor anything to say about your slaves?" asked Jack.

Hugh said, "He challenged me to work a miracle. Well, he shall soon have one. And if he learns of it in the same manner that he learned of me, he will marvel about it, but not oppose it."

Jack chuckled. "I, too, will marvel about it." He paused. "Mr. Reisdale has proposed that you, he, and I form a kind of Attic society, and meet regularly to discuss matters close to our hearts and minds."

"A wonderful idea, Mr. Frake. We must discuss the idea when you return." Hugh touched his hat, nodded to both Jack and Proudlocks, and rode on.

As Jack and Proudlocks continued into Williamsburg, Proudlocks remarked, "You are friends with him, but spoke in riddles. You must explain these riddles to me, Jack."

Jack did so as they rode up Duke of Gloucester Street. When he was finished, Proudlocks observed, "So, there are clouds gathering on the other side of the globe, and they will rain trouble."

"Much trouble, John," Jack said. "And anger, and heartbreak."

*   *   *

"Business will take me in early March to Londontown, on the South River, across from Annapolis, in Maryland. At your convenience, if you will contrive to be there, we may meet and make the transaction which you propose in your letter of January 10th. I shall bring all the necessary papers; you may bring a little money (no Virginia paper, please), and a list of all the items. Enquire after my vessel, the *Prudence*, a brig owned by my brother and me, for that is where I plan to make my billet. I would send the papers to you, but your signature is needed on them to prove a sale, both here and in your dominion. Also, I am reluctant to trust such papers to the vagaries of His Majesty's post (even though Mr. Franklin has mightily improved it), and I would lief make this a very personal matter. Mr. Talbot sends his regards and bids you write him....Your respectful servant, Novus Easley."

When he returned to Meum Hall late that afternoon, Hugh found mail on his library desk, left there by Mr. Beecroft. Among the letters was one he tore open immediately, because he recognized the hurried handwriting in the address. Novus Easley was a Philadelphia merchant and a Quaker, who, with his brother, Israel, imported and exported a variety of commodities. The brothers were also active in the insurance business. Otis Talbot had known them for years, and the Easleys were frequent supper guests at the Talbot home during Hugh's residence.

There was also a letter from Talbot advising him that he expected the *Busy* and the *Ariadne* to call on Philadelphia in late March, and asking Hugh to inform him if he wished either of them to call on Caxton.

Hugh rang for Spears, and told him to have Mrs. Vere prepare some tea and cold cuts. "Who went to the *Courier* for the mail, Spears?"

"Mr. Beecroft, sir. The *Belfast* docked at Yorktown shortly after you left for Williamsburg, and a post-rider came late yesterday noon. He told me that the *Belfast* will stay at Yorktown until tomorrow or the next day, loading some things it will take to Norfolk, and then return to Philadelphia after a stop at Hampton."

"Ask him if the post-rider is still in town here."

Spears went on his errand. Hugh sat down and drafted two brief letters, one to Mr. Easley, the other to Talbot. The valet reappeared with a tray holding a tea service and a plate of cold cuts. "Mr. Beecroft informs me that the post-rider crossed the river to Rosewell, sir, and will circuit up to De la Ware Town, thence round to Williamsburg, delivering and receiving letters in those parts."

"Then you must ride to Yorktown with some letters for the *Belfast*, when I am finished with them. Saddle a horse, and come back here in thirty minutes."

After Spears was dispatched with the letters and money to pay for their postage, Hugh opened his "diary of ideas" and recorded from memory his conversation with Lieutenant-Governor Fauquier.

*   *   *

In a move to raise the quality and value of the tobacco leaving Maryland's shores, and to put the product on a par with Virginia's, the assembly of that proprietary colony in 1747 enacted a law that reduced the number of tobacco inspection ports. The purpose of the act was to eliminate "trash" tobacco from its exports. It bolstered the fortunes of some river and Bay towns in that colony, and condemned others to a swift or slow demise.

Londontown, at the time a bustling, prosperous commercial center comparable to Norfolk, was absent from the list of official inspection ports.

Whether it was deemed guilty of having sent more than its share of "trash" to Britain, or was the victim of political maneuvering for the composition of the final, shortened list, is a matter of speculation. Londontown was abruptly denied its livelihood. No longer could planters transport their hogsheads to the town's warehouses for inspection and loading onto vessels bound for Britain; the warehouses became, less and less, storage for transshipment to other Maryland ports. Ship captains and masters grew less willing to anchor at Londontown to load on other agricultural exports, such as wheat and corn, and so the producers of those commodities were obliged to take their harvests to where the ships docked. English and Scottish factors closed their shops and extended no more credit. Fewer and fewer British manufactures came through the town. The warehouses became the spacious abodes for pigeons, rats, bats and other vermin, the wharves and piers rotted from disuse and neglect, and the taverns, shops, and houses became starved for reasons to exist.

What saved Londontown from the instant fate of many other excised towns was its location on the main road between Philadelphia, Annapolis, and Williamsburg. One or two ferry services across the South River and the Bay still thrived, and a handful of enterprises catered to travelers between those points.

Hugh told no one the purpose of his trip to Londontown, except that it concerned business. On the first of March, after giving instructions to William Settle for tasks to be completed while he was gone, he packed a pair of saddlebags and rode from Meum Hall to Yorktown.

Among his instructions was the branding of his tobacco hogsheads. All planters had devised marks, usually their initials, that would distinguish their hogsheads from others for easy identification by warehousemen and agents both in the colonies and in England. On a visit to Morland Hall, Hugh had seen Jack Frake's brand, which was the silhouette outline of a diving sparrowhawk containing his initials. Hugh handed Settle a sketch of his own mark, which was an ascending sparrowhawk containing his initials, *HK*, for Primus, the chief blacksmith, to fashion.

From Yorktown Hugh and his mount were ferried across the York to Tindall's Point. Four days later, after crossing the Rappahannock, Potomac, and Patuxent Rivers, he arrived late in the morning in Londontown on the South River.

He was immediately struck by the dilapidated condition of the town. There were many houses, shops, and other buildings on its checkerboard of streets — many more than in Williamsburg — but almost every one of them was boarded up or looked abandoned. Here and there he saw crews of men tearing down structures, but met few other people. Weeds and locust tree saplings grew in the foundations of buildings vanished years ago. A thin layer of snow on most of the near-deserted town's unheated roofs looked to him like a shroud that nature had prepared for the place's passing.

Hugh found the *Prudence* moored at a pier. Once he was onboard and had exchanged greetings with Novus Easley, he asked for an explanation for what he had seen.

"'Tis the evil that men do, if they have a dollop of power, Mr. Kenrick," said Easley, who then explained the act passed by the Maryland legislature. "The law assuredly abolished one kind of trash, and created another," he concluded, waving a hand vaguely at the town beyond the captain's cabin that he occupied.

Novus Easley was in his late forties, stocky, energetic, and married. He was noted for the fineness of his plain clothes and the frankness of his speech. He offered Hugh a glass of rum to warm himself, but Hugh declined. Easley asked why. It was Hugh's turn to explain the custom of the Society of the Pippin.

"What a noble abstinence!" exclaimed the Quaker. "Brandy, then?"

Hugh nodded. Easley handed him a glass of brandy. "You must, of course, plan on staying the night, young sir, after your journey. There is an extra billet down the way. I don't recommend either of the surviving taverns in town. There used to be a dozen of them. The chaps who are left will charge you for a banquet but serve you army rations."

Hugh was seated in a chair opposite Easley's desk. He frowned and asked, "What business could bring *you* here, sir?"

"I am here to purchase what I may from ship chandlers and the like, from their dusty stores. Cables, log and leadlines, sewing and boltrope twine, compasses, glasses, sailcloth, anchors, ballast shovels, sail duck...whatever is needed to complete or repair a vessel. There is a rope-walk here for all sorts of cables, cordage, and rigging. Owned by the Blevins family for nigh fifty years. I have bought it and its stock, and will have it taken down and freighted to Philadelphia." The Quaker paused to sip the mug of coffee a crewman had brought him shortly before Hugh's arrival. "I have also come for brick. There is some fine brick here — plain and glazed — going to waste in these sad, empty houses, which were built by men with a vain eye on eternity. Do not misconstrue me, sir. You have seen my home in Philadelphia, and know that I love vanity. But when other men have a mere iota of say in the disposition of one's property, there can be no such thing as eternity. Much of the brick I shall take away will go into the construction of homes for my children, when they are married and anxious to leave mine, good riddance all around!"

Hugh asked, "Are you buying on credit?"

Easley shook his head. "Credit? Banish that foul word, sir! No! With lovely, cold specie! And not a day too soon for the folks I purchase from. Mr. Steward, who owns the shipyard on the West River just south of here, has been presumptuously lax, and has not snagged all that may be had here. The owners and heirs of all this sorry property have only been waiting for opportune persons to come by and relieve them of their former livelihoods." The Quaker grinned. "If you on your way here passed by men busy in destruction, they are my men, some of them locals, others I brought with me."

"How will you dispose of all the naval stores?"

"I know a man, who knows a man, who knows a man who will want these things. You know that this is a large part of my business, to know others' lacks and wants. Such a prospect is possible in a town like Philadelphia." Easley paused. "And, I know certain men in my assembly. Do you know any in Williamsburg?"

"Two burgesses for my own county, and Governor Fauquier, whose acquaintance I have recently made."

The Quaker looked genuinely impressed. "Are you on good terms with *him*?"

Hugh nodded. He told Easley what he and the Governor had talked about, and ended, "He assured me, too, that he would not oppose a miracle, should I accomplish one."

"The miracle meaning your proposed transaction with me?"

"Yes."

Easley hummed in doubt. "Perhaps if he knew you better, you would not be on such good terms with him."

"He is an earnest man of piecemeal convictions. I do not believe he will grant himself the time to examine them so closely that he would see that no concordance is possible among them."

Easley shook his head. "Oh, no, sir. They must be in concordance, my good friend, in some habit of way, for otherwise he would go mad. Perhaps you meant that it is a harmonious *unity* of convictions that he lacks."

Hugh laughed and threw up his hands. Novus Easley laughed in triumph. He had provided Hugh some intellectual company during his two years in Philadelphia.

After an early dinner aboard the *Prudence*, Easley took his guest on a tour of Londontown to show him what he had purchased and planned to purchase, including the ropewalk, the chandlers' warehouses, the brick, timber, and shingles of three houses, a tavern, and a church. "I have not been so fortunate in window glass," he remarked to Hugh as they strode along the main street. "That has either been broken or removed. The ferrymaster here, Mr. Brown, is the most likely culprit for its removal. You will have noticed a new place being constructed on the hill yonder. It is to be his home and a tavern for travelers. It will remain when the others are gone."

"You will need to order glass from England."

"Oh…not necessarily," Easley said. "I know a man in Philadelphia whose business outwardly is hemp, but who has retained the talented services of some Swiss fellows who make glass. My brother and I provided him with the secret capital to do that business. It has paid us very nicely."

Hugh frowned in mock disapproval. "That is illegal, Mr. Easley. All glass must come from England, and be cut to size by glaziers here. Or, used as sent."

"Perhaps it is illegal, Mr. Kenrick, but it is less costly. Many homes and shops in your former residence boast windows that cost a mere tenth of English glass. Do not misconstrue me. I am as patriotic as you are."

The two men talked well into the evening and over supper.

In his cabin, Easley reached for a portfolio on his desk and removed some papers from it. "Well," he said, "let us complete our business, young sir. Have you the list I requested?"

Hugh went to his saddlebags in the corner, retrieved a sheet of paper, and handed it to Easley. The Quaker pursed his lips as he read down the list. With feigned concern, he remarked, "This will be a very costly trade, Mr. Kenrick. Have you a shilling?"

"A purse full, sir."

"One only will be needed. After all, we must be truthful, if asked, when we assert that money changed hands." Easley chuckled. "My signature comes cheaply, when I am asked to endorse another man's freedom."

Hugh handed Easley a shilling, which the man dropped into his frock coat pocket without a glance. He rose and went to the cabin door, which he opened to call out, "Mr. Norris, you are needed here!" He returned to his desk and said, "My best clerk has accompanied me."

When Norris came in, Easley handed him the portfolio. "Here is the task we discussed before we departed." He introduced Hugh to the clerk. Then Norris turned to Easley and asked, "At what price, sir?"

"Oh, forty pounds per item ought to be right." Easley glanced at Hugh for agreement. Hugh nodded.

Norris smiled. "Yes, sir. Forty pounds per. The documents will be ready in the morning." He nodded to his employer and Hugh, and left the cabin.

Easley gave a short, triumphant laugh. "If anyone in your parts has a mind to contest the authenticity or legality of our business, sir, it will be only at some expense to himself or to the public revenues."

*   *   *

Hugh bid Novus Easley goodbye the next afternoon and rode out of Londontown. In one saddlebag now were a copy of a bill of sale to Novus Easley for thirty slaves by Baron Garnet Kenrick, nominal owner of them and Meum Hall, signed by his proxy, Otis Talbot, for forty pounds sterling per slave; a deed of manumission signed by Easley and witnessed by his brother, Israel, naming all the slaves of Meum Hall; a copy of a Pennsylvania slave-purchase tax receipt, with the expertly forged signature of a Crown tax collector and bribable acquaintance of Mr. Easley; copies of letters from him to Baron Kenrick and Hugh, advising them of his intention of manumission; and thirty preprinted certificates of manumission, signed by Easley, for the freed slaves to carry, their names to be filled in the blank spaces by Hugh himself.

Hugh journeyed back to Meum Hall, at once glad that the thing was done, and fearful of the possible consequences. He did not try to reassure himself that the slaves would stay in his employ out of gratitude or for any other reason, nor did he contemplate his problems if they did not stay. He was determined to own Meum Hall without any of the real or moral encumbrances other men took for granted as the price for living their own lives.

After a day's rest at Meum Hall, he advised his staff of the action, then went alone into the slave quarter, called its residents together, and told them what had been done. He concluded, "If you wish to remain here, it will be as employed tenants of the property. If you wish to leave, you may. At the risk of contradicting myself, as I am no longer your master, I grant you a day of rest and reflection tomorrow that you may contemplate your immediate futures." He paused and addressed Dilch, who stood in front of the crowd. "Miss Dilch, I know you can read. I saw your Bible in your quarters. It would be appropriate if you did this." He walked up to her and handed her the thirty certificates. "The law in the colony cannot contest your freedom now. If it does, it will need to answer to me."

The woman took the bundle of certificates and read the one on top. She saw her name elegantly inscribed in one blank space between printed words, and tomorrow's date filling another space. Hugh saw some emotion in her face, but could not decipher it. He inclined his head, then turned and left the slave quarter.

*   *   *

Without any encouragement or assistance from Hugh, word of the manumission spread throughout Caxton and the county. It was his former slaves who helped to spread it from plantation to plantation. Some of the men that night slipped into the slave quarters of Enderly, Granby Hall, Morland, and a few of the smaller freeholds to break the news to other slaves and show them their certificates.

On the afternoon of the next day, as a steady rain washed away the snow, Jack Frake and Thomas Reisdale arrived at Meum Hall. They asked their host if it was true. Hugh showed them the documents. Reisdale examined them. He closed the portfolio in which they were contained and said, "It's a true bill."

That evening, two of the former slaves disappeared into the darkness, carrying only bundles of their belongings and their certificates. Three came to the great house to inform Hugh that they had decided to leave and try their chances in the north. Hugh wished them well, and gave each of them a small sack of shillings and pence.

On the morning of the next day, Primus and Dilch arrived at the great house. Primus presented to Hugh the iron brand he had fashioned to mark Hugh's hogsheads, and said that he had decided to stay. Dilch spoke next. "Speakin' for all the rest of us that's left, we will stay...*Mister* Kenrick. There's this war goin' on, and we hear things are unsettled all about, so we'll stay until things quiet down."

As the pair left Hugh's library, they turned to glance at their former master. In their eyes Hugh saw hesitancy and embarrassment; he knew that they wanted to thank him, and that they knew also that it was a thanks which neither they nor anyone else should ever have needed to offer another man. He saw gratitude in their eyes, and he merely nodded in acknowledgment of the words he knew they could not speak.

That afternoon, Sheriff Cabal Tippet arrived at Meum Hall, accompanied by Reece Vishonn and several other planters, including William Granby and Edgar Cullis, recently returned from the adjourned session of the General Assembly. Thomas Reisdale accompanied them. These men also wished to know if it was true. Again, Hugh produced his documents. Sheriff Tippet examined them, and blinked when he saw the signatures of the parties. He shook his head and handed the papers over to Reece Vishonn. The planter exclaimed, "I know this Easley fellow! That is, I sold some bar-iron to him. The damned fool!"

Hugh merely smiled. "Which I believe he had made into lampposts to light some of Philadelphia's streets."

Sheriff Tippet addressed the two burgesses. "Sirs, you may worry over the precedent here, but as this business transpired beyond the county's and the colony's jurisdiction, and was transacted by a man of means and a peer of the realm...well, I don't think it can be pursued to any purpose, except at the expense of your reputation and pride."

Thomas Reisdale added with a slight, self-effacing smile, "The legality of this transaction may be disputed very likely over a course of years, and to the benefit only of numerous lawyers."

William Granby remarked, "Mr. Cullis and I will consider writing a bill to prohibit this kind of carelessness, to be read at the next session."

Hugh said, "And Mr. Reisdale will study it for its constitutionality. If any suits are brought against me on this matter, he will represent me in any and all proceedings."

Sheriff Tippet laughed. "Mr. Reisdale?" He glanced at the two uncomfortable burgesses. "Sirs, you would do better tangling with a French privateer!"

Reisdale nodded in acknowledgment of the compliment. "Thank you, sir."

The party soon left Meum Hall. That was the end of the matter. Hugh half expected a deputy of Attorney General Peyton Randolph, or an emissary of the Lieutenant-Governor's office to call and demand to examine the documents. But no one from Williamsburg either wrote or came.

Later in the month, Hugh rode out to the cooper's shed and watched Primus brand the first hogshead that would hold his first crop of tobacco in the fall. He smiled as the hot iron burned into the wood, and, when the brand was removed, he saw *HK* in the silhouette of a soaring sparrowhawk.

Meum Hall was now truly his own.

Chapter 14: The Rivals

Jack Frake's assessment of Lieutenant-Governor Fauquier was only partly correct. Two other men, far higher up in the Crown political structure, were also to purchase the colonials time to gather, order, and refine their wits: William Pitt, and George the Third. In a seemingly endless contest for power that matched the Seven Years' War in animosity, Pitt and the king both began to lose their own wits.

In October 1760, George the Second, aged seventy-seven, died, and was succeeded by his grandson, George William Frederick, or George the Third. George, aged twenty-two, claimed in his first speech that he "gloried in the name of Britain." His immediate agenda — though some historians aver that it was more an obsession than a considered policy — was to recoup the powers of the monarchy, which since his great-grandfather's time had been checked or absorbed by the Whigs. George wished to be a "Patriot King," and actually govern the nation and establish supremacy over a Parliament undivided by petty factions and smoldering jealousies. To aid him in this quest, he brought in his long-time mentor, tutor, and confidant, John Stuart, the third Earl of Bute, former Secretary of State for the Northern Department.

Bute was a disciple of the late Henry St. John, Viscount Bolingbroke, who in a series of essays propounded a Tory interpretation of good government and patriot kings. Bute also had political ambitions, but knew in the secrecy of his heart that he had not the wit or stamina to immerse himself in contemporary party politics and emerge from the struggle the better. His only chance in politics was to have the trust and backing of a king who meant to rule a unified and grateful nation.

But the combined political intelligence of Bute and George the Third was not equal to their ambition, which was opposed by that of a patriotic minister, William Pitt. This man's intelligence was equal to his purposes, which were, on one hand, the reduction of France to the status of Portugal, so that it no longer posed a threat to England's commercial and maritime hegemony; and, on the other, the reconciliation of imperial power with constitutional liberty.

Naturally, George disliked Pitt. Here was this mere commoner behaving himself like a patriot king, and having credited to his name an immense popularity, a string of victories over the French, and the efficacy of his policies. Also, Pitt was so overbearing and demanding that even Henry Pelham, Duke of Newcastle and First Lord of the Treasury, alternately feared and despised him. If George was truly to govern, in addition to authoring a peace and ending forever his grandfather's detested "German business" — the alliance with Frederick of Prussia against France, Austria, and Russia — Pitt must somehow be removed, or at least neutralized. But not before the Great Commoner had laid the foundations of an agreeable peace with the French. George therefore intrigued with Bute to rid the government of the man whose actions and policies were to hand the king an empire greater than ancient Rome's. They were, on this point, bright enough to know that the man who could accomplish this Herculean task was not one who would tolerate the designs on that empire of a man who was merely born into his royal station.

If George the Third had been brighter — his mental acumen was certainly not greater than either his father's or grandfather's — and had given the Secretary of State free rein to conduct the war and foreign policy, events in the American colonies might have been postponed for another generation. For while Pitt agreed with others that the colonies were beholden to the Crown, he also would deny Parliament's right to govern or legislate for them in any matter beyond the regulation of trade. It was, after all, a secure mercantilist empire that he was fighting for. His policies had already won him respect in the colonies. He recalled incompetent generals, and ordered that colonial officers be treated and promoted on a par with regulars. As an effective champion of the colonists' rights as Englishmen under the Constitution, he might have purchased the empire in North America a greater longevity.

But this was not to be. Neither George the Third, nor Bute, nor the Secretary's colleagues in government, nor many in Lords and the Commons, could tolerate, much less wish to emulate, a man who could say such things as, "I am sure I can save this country, and nobody else can," and "Three millions of people so dead to all the feelings of liberty as voluntarily to submit to be slaves would have been fit instruments to make slaves of the rest." He denied Parliament's right, but Parliament exercised it nonetheless. Men envied his determination and eloquence, but failed to see that Pitt was the apotheosis of that other national anthem, and as did the man himself, dismissed all hints of contradiction both in the policies and the anthem.

George the Third had, by 1762, experienced the first of many bouts with his porphyritic madness. Pitt, too, was afflicted with a recurring illness. He alternated between long periods of lucidity and longer periods of morbid melancholia. He possessed a temper and a flare for verbally abusing friend and foe alike. His malady caused him to be absent from some of the most crucial moments of his nation's history, when his presence might have made a difference.

Pitt was not what Bolingbroke, via Lord Bute, warned George against. He was not among "the prostitutes who set themselves for sale," not one of the "locusts who devour the land." He did not seek the services of "spies, parasites, and sycophants," and in fact despised them as much as did George. He was not to be counted among "swarms of little, noisome, nameless insects" that "hum and buzz in every corner of the court," and would wave them away with the same distaste and impatience as his king. George the Third, anxious to be Bolingbroke's model Patriot King, however, was convinced that Pitt was all these things and more, simply because the man did not fit into his vision of himself as a God-sent pilot of the nation. He ascribed Pitt's malignity to party politics. He wished to rule a united nation, and to lead it and Parliament down the path of honor. A virtuous king, after all, would cast off such an intemperate, impertinent minister, and banish him forever from politics.

Pitt, friendless on the throne and in the Privy Council, was now isolated. Having learned that Spain planned to declare war on England through a "family compact" of the two Bourbon dynasties that ruled it and France, Pitt demanded that the king do the logical thing and declare war on Spain first before it could put its army and navy in working order. The king and Council refused. Pitt resigned in answer in October, 1761, stating, "I will be *responsible* for nothing that I do not *direct*." His most ardent enemies on the Council regarded his words as presumptuous self-flattery and even near-treasonous.

George and Bute were successful in their aim. What George got in Pitt's stead, however, was a succession of ministers and counselors who were not so easily remolded, and that became a small, transient swarm of noisome, nameless insects. It is not apparent from the record that he was ever able to discern the difference between them and his chronic nemesis, William Pitt.

In a dispute over supporting Frederick of Prussia's claims against Austria, Newcastle, who wanted to continue the Prussian subsidies, in May of 1762 resigned from the Treasury. Bute immediately replaced him — with himself. Unofficially, it was a contest over who, Newcastle or the king with Bute, was going to control patronage and preferments. Fortunately for Frederick, Empress Elizabeth of Russia died in January, and her successor, Peter the Third, a maniacal admirer of Frederick, abruptly took Russia out of the continental coalition and even put his army at Frederick's service. The Prussian king a little later received probably false intelligence that Bute was secretly negotiating with Austria to force him to make hitherto impossible concessions. Rightly or wrongly, it was Frederick who coined the epithet "perfidious Albion."

George the Third and Bute inherited the fruits of Pitt's war policies, but nearly gave the bowl away. By the terms of the Treaty of Paris, signed in February, 1763, France was restored most of the sugar- and molasses-producing West Indies islands it had lost to British naval action; Gorèe, its principal slave collection port on the west coast of Africa; and the right to maintain unfortified trading posts in India. There was some controversy in Parliament and the newspapers over which conquest was more important: Canada, or the islands. Bute and his negotiators bowed to British sugar interests in Jamaica, who feared that more British sugar on the market would create a glut and drive down prices. The strategic value of the French islands was considered, and dismissed. Spain, trounced by Britain with humiliating swiftness, ceded Florida to Britain in return for keeping Cuba, but won from France the right to occupy the west bank of the Mississippi River, the better to block any British moves against its Mexican silver mines. This was more or less a French bribe to persuade Charles the Third of Spain to agree to the treaty. Britain was ceded the east bank, and retained its conquests of Grenada, Senegal, and Canada, and secured a near-monopoly on fishing waters off the coast of Newfoundland.

The man who maneuvered a triumphant Britain into accepting these terms was the French secretary of state, Étienne-François, duc de Choiseul, who was so relieved at news of Pitt's engineered ouster that he remarked that he would rather have been sentenced to slavery on a galley than deal with him again. Shrewder and more adept at diplomacy than either Bute or his negotiators, and certain that the victors were in haste to end the war, Choiseul cajoled from them terms which a year before he would not have dared propose without risking having them thrown back in his face. As the ink dried on the Treaty of Paris, he immediately began planning the resurrection of the shattered French navy.

Pitt, in the Commons, excoriated Bute and the treaty terms being debated by a committee of the whole House, to no avail. In those times, the best means the Crown had for removing or silencing an implacable or obstinate political enemy, other than dismissal, was to elevate him to a peerage, or award him a pension, or both. Pitt, on leaving office, was given a £3,000 a year pension and a barony of Chatham for his wife, Hester. Years later, as part of an inducement by a desperate George the Third to form a new government in the wake of Rockingham's collapse, Pitt was offered the earldom of Chatham.

There was, however, a catch to this glittering reward. Aside from souring an adulatory public, Pitt's acceptance of the earldom effectively removed him from the Commons, where he had the most influence. A seasoned politician would have first weighed the advantages and disadvantages of such an offer. In his career, he had often enough witnessed the consequences. But by this time, his mental malady was growing more and more pronounced, and perhaps he did not believe that a bestowed peerage would much hamper his ability to persuade men to be reasonable and pursue more practical, less tyrannical policies. He was wrong.

Peter the Third, endowed with fewer wits than was George, after a five-month reign was perfunctorily assassinated with the knowledge and probable connivance of his vastly more intelligent wife, Catherine, who would later be accorded the appellation "the Great." In the West, weak, venal men with short-ranged minds and shadowy motives could rise to power. In feudal Russia, they were rarely tolerated and rarely survived. Catherine the Second was as autocratic as any of her predecessors. After abandoning a recodification of Russian law *à la* Montesquieu, she expanded serfdom, raised taxes, and took part in the first three partitions of Poland.

Samuel Johnson, lionized now as the literary giant of Augustan England, was in July of 1762 offered an annual pension of £300 by Lord Bute. Johnson had derided a *pensioner* in his *Dictionary* as "a state hireling paid by a stipend to obey his master." After polling his friends concerning the propriety of accepting Bute's offer, and being assured by Bute himself that no obligations would be pressed on him, he agreed to it with gushing gratitude. Later in his career, though, a master appears to have requested a favor — or two. Johnson authored a series of pamphlets for the government on Crown issues, none of them memorable. Among them was one that was a bitter, sneering attack on American revolutionaries.

*   *   *

The depth, scope, and perspicuity of Hugh Kenrick's essays made Jack Frake inexplicably sleepless. One night, while his neighbor was journeying to Londontown, he rose, went down to his own library, found an unused ledger book, and sat down to record his own thoughts and what he could remember had been said to him by Augustus Skelly and Redmagne. For a reason he understood well enough, Hugh's observations had evoked the spirit of those men. A vault of stored-up wisdom imparted to him by them now demanded expression. At first, he had to dredge the past for the context of those memories. But after he put the first few recollected statements on paper, they spewed forth so rapidly that he could barely keep the point of his quill wet with ink.

Two memories in particular glowed in his mind. The first was of the lecture Skelly had given him in the caves after he was sworn into the gang.

"Chains are a more honest form of slavery than the bogus liberty enjoyed by most of our countrymen…. We will submit to chains, but we will none of us submit to their paper and ink parents!" Jack wrote it all down, as much of it as he could remember. "Most of those who join me discover something about themselves, and in themselves — something roused by more than mere disobedience, but which learns to glory in its unfettered state…. I've not been able to say what it is. Perhaps, you will, some day…." His own reply to Skelly that day came to him effortlessly and seemed to guide the motions of his hand as he wrote it down: "Even though we are chained by our outlawry, we are free men, more free than ordinary folk."

The second memory was of Redmagne's remarks in the caves after he had completed *Hyperborea*: "Oh! Wild imagination! Suppose our colonies in America did such a thing? Can you imagine them nullifying their numbing bondage? Revoking their oath of loyalty to the king? Not petitioning *him* for protection from Parliament? What an outlandish miracle that would be! Perhaps too far-fetched! The parable of the loaves and fishes is much more credible a tale!" Jack heard all the words spoken by Redmagne on that occasion, and they were put on paper. "…*My* Hyperboreans are something like the Houyhnhnms, only much pleasanter to know…. They live on an island in the frigid climes, but their greatness warms the earth and makes it habitable…."

When he reread these thoughts in the chilly air of his library, Jack sighed in sadness for their inadequacy. Yet, he did not gainsay Redmagne and Skelly for anything they had said or believed. They had lived the truth of their statements as closely and honestly as they knew. In the scheme of things, that meant living in outlawry. And when they stood on the gallows in Falmouth that last day, their entire beings were embraced by the calming angel of moral certitude.

In the scheme of things, thought Jack…meaning that they had not been willing to hold piecemeal convictions — that was what Hugh had once called the mode — as were their fellow men, not to live and watch some malign power corrupt themselves and everything about them, absorbing and dissolving their convictions one by one, until it engulfed and consumed everything — but to remove themselves completely from all contact and compromise with the phenomenon. To remain cleanly and proudly whole, in body and mind.

John Ramshaw, on one of his visits to Morland years ago, had asked him why he thought Skelly and Redmagne had not tried to escape the night the army began to encircle the Marvel caves.

After a moment of reflection, Jack answered, "I think there comes a time in such a man's life when he refuses to run or hide, when he tells his pursuers, 'Stalk me no more. You will die here, or I. I assert my right to live without you or what you represent.'" Jack paused. "I think they both had reached that apex in their lives then, when defiance is no longer profound enough an action, but transfigures into revolt, or a supreme kind of assertion…. And at that point, one must be finally satisfied with the way one has conducted one's life, satisfied in some summary way that demands a final, summary action, and the prospect of death or imprisonment no longer frightens or taunts one."

The captain of the *Sparrowhawk* puffed thoughtfully on his pipe and studied his young protégé for a moment. "You have given the matter some close attention, I see."

"It intrigued me for some time, John, as it did you. As I grew older, I understood it better, and understood it enough that I could find the words for it. It ceased to be a paradox."

"A paradox? Rather, it seems a dilemma that confronts tired men."

"A dilemma? No, not a dilemma. Not for long. Any man possessed of trimmed sails and an unwormed keel is capable of it. My friends were capable of it, as was I. Yes. I have given it close attention. But I cannot predict the time when I will undertake that risk. And that risk, John, I can assure you will not come from tiredness, nor will it necessarily guarantee death or defeat."

Sitting alone now in his library, Jack paused again to reread what he had recorded. There were three instances when Skelly had bequeathed to him the honorable task of understanding what moved men to such heights. The third time was from the Falmouth gallows, when the man looked directly at him and paraphrased the last words of an anthem: "This Briton will never be a slave." He understood, but had yet to find the words. That they existed and could be found, he was certain.

And now there was another man who had glimpsed those heights, and who called them "Olympus": Hugh Kenrick. Jack was certain, too, that his new friend was moved by the same quest. He packed and lit a pipe, and sat back to rest from his labors. He was pleased with this rivalry.

Chapter 15: The Conduit

Two factors beyond their control and powers of prediction governed the prosperity and happiness of the planters and farmers: the market, and the weather. The rains of 1760 seemed to portend a bright, undisturbed future for the planters of Queen Anne County. Tobacco, rye, barley, corn and even hemp were harvested that year in bounteous quantities, with little spoilage or waste. Commerce between Britain and her colonies, and between the colonies themselves, boomed and was not much affected by the war at sea. Tobacco, lumber, and raw materials for Britain's infant industrial economy were traded for credit; lumber and foodstuffs were traded with the West Indies for sugar, molasses, and French spices. Arthur Stannard, the English agent, happily dispatched vessels groaning with hundreds of hogsheads of tobacco to London and the custody of Weddle, Umphlett and Company, and just as happily extended credit on their sales to large and small planters alike. Ian McRae, representing Sutherland and Bain of Glasgow, extended little credit, but bought most of his customers' hogsheads outright in exchange for farm implements, cloth, and household goods from his warehouse. He did a particularly good business that year in salt, for he had made special arrangements with entrepreneurs on the Eastern Shore who boiled sea water and collected bundles of salt, which were loaded onto coastal vessels and sent to Caxton. "Salt for the cellar, sir, or salt for the cattle? Refined, or by the gross?" were questions he asked several times a day of his customers.

In the next year, the rains would not come, except in brief, miserly showers that would moisten only leaves and the surface of topsoil. Then the sun would reappear and burn off the moisture, drying and often browning the unnourished leaves and baking the soil back to dust or dry, cracked clay. Masses of dark, heavy clouds would form over the county, only to drift away to favor other counties with steady downpours. The York River, too, taunted planters and farmers, for it never fell, fed as it was by faraway rivers and streams and buttressed by the sea level of the great Bay into which it flowed.

The plantations and freeholds of most property owners were too vast to water by conventional means, which was to organize brigades of slaves, tenants, and itinerant laborers to lug water bucket by bucket from the river, although some ambitious planters and farmers resorted to this inefficient expediency for lack of any other alternatives.

At balls, suppers, and in the course of occasional visits, Hugh had listened to other planters' tales of woe and tribulation caused by past droughts. Poor crops, late plantings and harvests, and insect pests that seemed always to accompany every dry spell and ravage especially the tobacco, all meant short credit on bad terms, postponed improvements, a tightening of budgets and spending, and ulcerous tempers.

The only planter who did not complain of past droughts and had no tales of woe to tell, was Jack Frake. He showed Hugh how he dealt with such weather. He had had built by his coopers several oversize hogsheads — four of them — and on the top of each was a hole in which to pour water. At the side of each was a tap. These four enormous barrels were each filled with about a hundred of gallons of river water as they sat in a wagon, which was then hauled up to and through his fields by a team of oxen. Jack's tenants would then fill buckets from the taps and water each tobacco or cornstalk, usually twice. Hugh marveled at the idea, and was also astonished that no other planter emulated his neighbor's practice.

Jack told him the winter before the drought, "Otway's place is crowded by a little inlet, from which he's built a narrow, shallow canal. It's about a quarter mile long and comes right up to his main field. His people get their water that way, when necessary, and also fish in it."

"And Mr. Vishonn, and the others?"

Jack shrugged. "They wait out the weather." He paused, then asked, "What will you do, come a drought?"

"I have an idea." Hugh smiled, then asked, "How often do you water your hills that way?"

"During a drought? Twice a week. We haven't had to take water to the fields for two years now. But we're due for another dry season. They happen regularly."

The idea was born in Hugh's mind the day he first toured the plantation. His first crops of tobacco, rye, and barley — his own crops, not those of Amos Swart, not those sown, tended and harvested by slaves — were large, almost as large as Jack Frake's, even though he had set aside over fifty acres of exhausted soil to lie fallow. He had donned the rough shirt and trousers of his black tenants and sweated alongside them in all the stages of field work. His hands became calloused from wielding shovels and hoes, and grimy with dirt and oily with the remains of countless destructive hornworms he plucked from underneath tobacco leaves. And at the end of each day in the fields, the spaces beneath his fingernails were caked with green from suckering hundreds of tobacco hills, when he would need to pinch off young bottom shoots on each stalk so that they did not deprive the broader, more mature leaves above of water and nourishment. The tips of his fingers grew brown, and when he held them to his nose, he could smell the tobacco. This made him happy.

And at the end of each day that first summer and fall, he would discard his shirt and shoes and plunge from Meum Hall's pier into the cool river water. He would rest against one of the posts, close his eyes, and let the current cleanse him of the dirt and sweat.

He knew that Primus, Dilch, Bristol and the other former slaves talked about his presence among them in the fields, but he never learned what was said. William Settle, his overlooker and steward, expressed his objection to it in the guise of curiosity. "One hand more or less, sir, won't make a difference. Besides, that is work you are paying them to do."

Hugh knew the purpose of Settle's query. He answered, "They are my fields, Mr. Settle, and I shall work in them when I please. And I know of no better means to grasp the nature of the work and what is demanded of the fields and the men and women who tend them. More planters should taste the labor. Perhaps they would appreciate what they get for free."

That winter, for weeks on end, Hugh embarked on the first stage of his idea to combat drought. He could be found in the bare tobacco and cornfields, digging small holes and examining handfuls of soil — and making notes with a pencil in a little ledger book. He could be seen riding into the bamboo forest near Hove Creek on the south end of the property, measuring the height and breadth of the plants — and making notes. For a week he traversed the whole length of the arable fields with a plumb bob and an adjustable tripod, stopping every few yards — to make notes. Mr. Beecroft and Mrs. Vere, when they came into his library on errands, would see his desk covered with papers containing strange drawings and multitudes of odd numbers. Mr. Settle could hold his genuine curiosity no longer, and one afternoon, as he and his employer were discussing how much lumber would be needed to build extra tenements for the men, he remarked, "Mrs. Vere seems to believe that you are practicing witchcraft, sir. She can make no sense of the drawings she has seen on your desk."

Hugh laughed. "Witchcraft? If she could read as well as she keeps house, she would know I do not practice witchcraft. Come into the library and I'll show you. I've about finished with the plans."

Hugh opened a large leather portfolio and revealed those plans. "We no longer wait on the weather, Mr. Settle. I refuse to be at the mercy of insentient nature." He waited a moment to allow the overlooker to flip through the many pages of notes and drawings, then said, "At London Bridge there is a great machine that can collect, pump, and raise nearly one hundred thirty thousand gallons of water an hour. This water is transported by conduit to a water tower, and raised to a height of one hundred and twenty feet. From the tower the water flows into mains beneath the streets and into the lead pipes of any house on that side of the Thames that pays a fifteen-pound or more rate. Windridge Court, my family's London home, has running water. Houses paying a lower rate avail themselves of neighborhood pumps from the mains."

Mr. Settle did not know what the drawings before him had to do with this astonishing information. His expression said so.

Hugh went on to explain his idea of creating a conduit of bamboo to carry water to the fields. "From Hove Creek, to the well of this house. The gradual elevation of this property from the river to the creek lends itself perfectly. There are countless bamboo stems of the right diameter and length, many two inches by five feet. We would have enough for three conduits, but I first wish to demonstrate the efficacy of just one. The ends can be connected and sealed with tar and rest on stands on the ground. Each stand must be carefully tailored to accommodate the height of the ground it sits on in order to create a straight and trim line in the conduit. At intervals we will put plugs and tap holes from which to draw water into buckets. The end of the conduit near the house will be fitted with another tap, and when we wish to empty the conduit, it will be either near the house well or into the well itself."

The overlooker studied the drawings again and blinked. "But, sir: What will pull the water?"

"Gravity, of course, Mr. Settle."

"And how will water enter the conduit?"

Hugh hunted through the papers for and found another drawing. "In Hove Creek we will build a platform, and on top of that, a collection tub that will empty into the conduit. I have studied the possibility of putting a dam at that point that could work with a water wheel with buckets, but the creek is too small and would not produce enough force to turn a wheel. But two men working with buckets for an hour or so would be able to fill the conduit."

Hugh grinned when he saw comprehension, then appreciation, change his overlooker's expression. "That is not all," he added. "Allow me a question: Why do we welcome long rains? Because they sink deeply enough in the soil to be drawn up by the roots. Watering the hills during a drought accomplishes little. Here is what I have in mind." He found another drawing, of a funnel from whose spout protruded the stem of a plug. "Henceforth, every tobacco plant, when necessary, must be watered with a funnel, which can be pressed into the bottom of a hill as far as its rim. The plug here will prevent soil from blocking the nose. After removing the plug, a bucket of water is poured into the funnel. The water will be absorbed by the soil around and beneath the roots. It will take more time, this method, but fewer stalks will be lost by it. We will want about a dozen of these funnels, made of tin or lead. Mr. Rittles and Mr. McRae both carry them in their stores. The plugs can be fashioned by Primus or Bristol."

Hugh searched for and found a larger drawing, one that was a complete plan of the conduit. "And here is a wonderful aspect, Mr. Settle. Come winter, all its sections can be marked, together with the stands, and the conduit taken apart and stored away from the fields to allow for spring ploughing, and also to prevent water from freezing in the bamboo and cracking it. If in the next year we conclude that another drought is upon us, the conduit can be speedily reassembled." He moved a caressing hand in the air over the drawing. "Iron pipe would be ideal, of course, and easier to work with, but I would need to order it from England and I fear the cost would be prohibitive."

"We could not hope to see it for a year," remarked Settle. "Mr. Vishonn has iron to sell, " he suggested.

Hugh shook his head. "Mr. Vishonn would charge me nearly as much as I would pay to have the pipe imported. And, you are right, imported pipe would arrive too late." He paused. "Well, now that we have entered an idle period, time and effort must be invested in making the parts of the conduit and platform. I have marked the bamboo we need from the forest. Have some men go in and cut it. Have it stacked at the cooperage. Here is a plan for the creek platform. Anchor its posts with brick. It must be sturdy enough to tolerate a busy man standing on one of its cross beams. The second man will hand him buckets to pour into the collection tub. As for the conduit, it presents another tricky task."

Hugh reached down and held up a three-foot length of bamboo. He turned it around so that the overlooker could see down its length. "Do you see the diaphragm, the black disk there? Holes must be bored through these, large enough to allow passage of water, but not so large that they would weaken the bamboo. These diaphragms will help keep the bamboo from collapsing. So, a special awl must be fashioned or adapted that will allow us to gouge a hole. It took me about an hour to make this one hole with one of Miss Chance's kitchen knives."

Settle took the bamboo and examined it, then glanced at his employer. "Yes," he said, "this idea, and the funnels, may save us much labor."

"And the crops," Hugh said.

"Mr. Frake's hogsheads carry about a hundred gallons of water each, sir. With this conduit, we could have hundreds more without the effort."

The overlooker shook his head in amazement. "Yes, sir. I'll get the men cutting the bamboo tomorrow." Then he looked puzzled. "But, sir, why not just do what Mr. Otway has done: dig a canal from Hove Creek? It would be much simpler way to water the fields."

Hugh shook his head. "I have located boulders beneath the fields that are perhaps half the size of this house, Mr. Settle. They divide the fields almost precisely in half, running in a line from Hove Creek nearly to the house here. They could not be removed or broken apart, not with all the powder in the Williamsburg magazine, nor by an army of sappers. The conduit will parallel those boulders the entire length."

Throughout that winter, the conduit took shape, length by length, closely supervised by its confident creator. In the cooperage, Hugh experimented with sections of it, linking the ends together with pitch or tar, perfecting the stands on which the conduit would rest, making drawings of taps, designing a wooden lock valve for the well-end of the conduit.

His obsession with the idea was contagious. Primus and Bristol, the two senior black tenants, began offering suggestions and making improvements, as did Mr. Settle. Primus, a tall bull of a man, was especially intrigued by the conduit. He asked Hugh why the lock valve was so important.

"Because it must allow no leaks at that end," Hugh said. "Also, when water is first being flushed into the conduit, the valve must be open, or otherwise the water will be stopped somewhere in the conduit by air, which would have no place to vent and could burst the bamboo. That is why I also want little holes drilled at intervals on top of the conduit, just to ensure there is no stoppage."

When not working on the conduit, Hugh was occupied with other demands of the plantation. Rye and barley were sown, and new tobacco seeds planted in seedbeds in the woods and carefully covered with straw. All the fields were ploughed and reploughed and generously manured. Into the soil also went the dust of ground quahog shells. Hugh himself took a shovel and hoe and leveled the uneven parts of the conduit's future route, which bisected the tobacco field. The *Busy* called on Meum Hall that winter, bringing supplies he had ordered from England and Philadelphia, in addition to books and newspapers, plus letters from his father and Otis Talbot. And money, his first payment for the tobacco and crops he had shipped out the year before. When the *Busy* sailed back down the York, it carried the balance of Hugh's tobacco hogsheads and wool from the fall shearings.

*   *   *

Hugh met once a month with Jack Frake and Thomas Reisdale to discuss actions and proposals during the current session of the House of Burgesses, together with news they read in the Caxton *Courier* and other colonial newspapers. He exchanged visits with Ian McRae and his family, and occasionally attended winter balls hosted by the other planters. He wrote letters to his family in England, and sent them sketches of Meum Hall. Garnet Kenrick wrote to his enterprising son: "Your uncle has secured the loyalty of Henoch Pannell and his coterie of *seats* in the Commons, and I fear is emerging from a life of lethargy and indolence and embarking upon the most active period of his life. I fear it, because it can mean little else but mischief."

Jack Frake told Hugh about his efforts to record the things said by Augustus Skelly and Redmagne, and allowed him to read the ledger book. "They were truly remarkable men," Hugh said when he had finished. "They would have been fast friends of the Pippins. And, yet, who remembers them, but you, Mr. Frake?"

"Some remnants of our gang still work in Cornwall," said Jack.

Hugh sat for a while, thinking. Then he asked, "Do you still remember their appearances?"

"Of Skelly and Redmagne? Vividly."

"I have an idea. As I have done portraits of my own mentors, perhaps you could have portraits of your own. You must describe them to me. I will begin with a head and all its features, and then together we will refine the features until we arrive at each of their likenesses."

Jack studied his guest for a moment, then asked, "Why would you be willing to do that for me?"

"Because it is the Christmas season, and we have had little to exchange in goodwill these twelve festive days but our hospitality and some fine French liquor. Such men deserve a permanent record. And, I am curious to know what your mentors looked like." He paused. "Perhaps, someday, when *Hyperborea* is free to live outside the caves, Redmagne's likeness will appear in a new edition of that marvelous book."

Jack poured himself another glass of wine. "All good reasons, Mr. Kenrick. But the driving one is your curiosity."

Hugh merely smiled in acknowledgment.

Two weeks later, the pencil sketches of Skelly and Redmagne were completed, and Jack instructed his cooper to make frames for them. The portraits now hung on a wall opposite his desk in his library.

They could not help it, but the talk between the three members of Jack's "Attic" society always returned to politics. The three men were certain that grave political crises lay ahead for all the colonies. Reisdale was certain of it because of his vast, scholarly readings in "ancient republics" and "arcadian" and modern constitutions.

One evening he said, "The problem has always resulted in one or another political mode. Ideal republics — or republics that promoted prosperity and happiness in all realms of human endeavor — have without exception degenerated into one or the other despotism: an oligarchy, or democracy. Rule of the privileged few over the many, or rule of the privileged many over the few — which in time sired another oligarchy, one more ruthless and absolute than its predecessor. The two phenomena are intimately linked and married by their natures. The ideal republics themselves sire the ensuing and inevitable phenomena because they lack something, something that is merely implied but then neglected or even suppressed, or is overlooked. Mr. Locke I cannot but help suspect nearly identified that principle. He performed a feat of great intelligence, assembling the scattered pieces of a political puzzle and correctly putting them in their right places. But for all the love I have for his work, he leaves me hungry for an answer to that paradox. I am certain that the cycle of these troubling phenomena can be broken, but I am at a loss to say by what."

Jack Frake and Hugh Kenrick were also aware of this lack in all their political readings, but not in themselves. Their certainty of coming crises lay in the senses they had of themselves. They were both what they assumed other men ought to be, and were aware of that species of egoism, too. For them the political crises they were certain would come would be mere consequences of another kind of crisis, one driven by a force that was more invasive and corrupting than a new law or tax.

"Whatever that may be," said Hugh that evening in Jack's library in reply to Reisdale's remarks, "that lack, once discovered and expounded, will serve to choose an empire of reason that protects a man's life, liberty, and property. Its temporal form exists for him, not he for it."

Jack shook his head. "Whatever that may be," he said, "it must aid in the dissolution of the existing empire, and we will begin anew."

"I say that once the empire is threatened with ruin," countered Hugh, "the powers in London will see reason and defer to it."

"I say that once the empire is threatened with ruin, they will attempt to disown reason and resort to force, fraud, and transparent chicanery. Reason is a path they dare not tread, neither the lords, nor the men in the Commons, nor the merchants. It is a straight line, reason — as straight as the conduit you are creating, Mr. Kenrick — and its logic is compelling and intolerant of expedience. Oh, they will see reason, and they may even follow it for a distance. But once they see where it is leading them, they will renounce it, as they must."

"Where would it lead them, Mr. Frake?" asked Reisdale.

"Yes," Hugh said. "What do you think they would see that would frighten them?"

"Revolution in England. Or at least some radical reformation in her politics." Jack paused. "Here? It would lead to independence."

Hugh frowned. "Why do you believe they must renounce reason?"

"Because it will not give them what they want, which is a continent of glorified factotums, made passive and submissive by chains of paper and ink, chains of a thousand links and taxes."

Reisdale also frowned. He studied his host, who smiled at the attorney's scrutiny, as though daring him to question the truth. Reisdale asked, "Why are you so certain that what you say will occur, must occur?"

"Because I am waiting for the rest of you to allow your honesty to govern your thoughts. When you do, you will think as I do, clear down to your bones. You will say, 'Virginia is my country, and the Crown will violate her no more.'"

"Yes," Hugh said, who also studied Jack with new wonder. "Virginia is our country. But — the solution is to deny Parliament the power to make enslaving laws, to deny them the right and opportunity to produce so much paper and ink." He shook his head. "Independence? I do not see any or all of the colonies severing their bonds with England. Nor can I imagine them independent of her. They are as contentious with and envious of one another as are the nations of Europe. They would neither last as sovereign nations nor tolerate each other without the foundation of English law."

Reisdale nodded in agreement, then said, "Mr. Frake, you speak of us as though we were a conquered people. We are not. We are Britons."

"No, we are not a conquered people, sir," Jack said. "But I fear that the Crown, casting about for a monied means to keep and sustain its empire, will begin to treat us as one."

*   *   *

By the beginning of April, the conduit was completed and assembled. This slender, artificial thing was of the earth, yet at the same time in defiance of it. Almost a mile in length, it sat empty and untested, a brownish-green straight line that shot through the brown of the fields, no wider than the palm of a man's hand, running from Hove Creek to the fringes of the outbuildings near the great house of Meum Hall. It rested a foot and a half off the ground in the snug grooves of a hundred flat, oaken stands that were secured with brick. Scores of taps, each carefully sealed with tar, punctuated either side of the conduit.

In Hove Creek stood a short tower, half brick, half trimmed oak, topped by an open wooden tub, at the bottom of which was fixed the mouth of the conduit. At the other end were a wooden lock valve and an extension of the conduit that was connected to the base of the main well of the great house. What water was not used on the crops, Hugh had decided, would replenish the well.

Hugh rode up and down the length of the conduit, searching for oversights and inspecting the workmanship. At Hove Creek he sat on his mount and looked down the whole length. He could see it curve imperceptibly until the far end disappeared from his sight. He had lived with the idea for a year and a half, and the reality of the conduit still caused a thrill of pride to stiffen his back. Questions teased his mind: Would it bear the weight of hundreds of gallons of water? Would the force of the rushing water cause leaks or breakages? He had thought of every little detail and taken every precaution. He was certain that none of these things would happen.

On that April morning, the sky was dark with storm clouds. It had rained only the night before, and the earth was soft and smelled rich with life. The corn was planted, and the hills prepared to receive thousands of transplanted tobacco shoots from the seedbeds in May. His workers had been hoeing those hills, getting rid of the weeds that would compete for water and nourishment with the tobacco. Hugh watched them begin to drift away from their work back to the tenements and shelter from the approaching storm.

Thunder rumbled over Hugh's head, and rolled to the west. He glanced up at the sky as though it had expressed jealousy. He laughed once, and doffed his hat at the imagined personification. As heavy drops of rain began to fall, he rode unhurriedly back to Meum Hall the whole length of the conduit.

In the last week of April, when it had not rained in three weeks and men's footsteps kicked up little swirls of dust in the ground, Hugh ordered the conduit opened. Two men worked at the platform in Hove Creek, pouring bucket after five-gallon bucket into the collection tub. Mr. Beecroft, notebook and pencil in hand, stood nearby on the bank, counting the bucketsful so that, once the water reached the well-end, the exact capacity of the conduit could be known. Several men stood at points along the length of the conduit holding makeshift flags, ready to relay a signal to the tub men to stop once the conduit was full. Groups of laborers milled around the line, their buckets and funnels stacked in the field. Many kneeled at the conduit, pressing their ears to the vent holes, listening for the sound of water. Everyone at Meum Hall felt a subdued excitement, for not only were they anxious about the conduit, but they knew that its success today meant the end of a generations-old routine of caring for the tobacco, which was to carry water over great distances to coax struggling seedlings to grow. The transplanting of those young plants from the seedbeds would begin tomorrow, the first of May.

William Settle stood with Primus and Bristol at the end of the conduit. Bristol held a signal flag. The lock valve at the well was open. Hugh's original idea of a screw valve proved to be beyond the capabilities of the materials available to the cooperage. He redesigned the valve, incorporating an iron disk that could be turned on an iron ring and locked into place with a wood pin behind the external turning wheel. The valve could be opened or closed in stages by means of carved cogs. When he had to abandon the screw valve, Hugh spent three days working out the problem of a new valve; it had taken nearly two weeks of patient labor at the forge to perfect it.

Hugh remained apart from the others, hands locked behind his back, watching and waiting.

A quarter of an hour later, Primus exclaimed, "Look!"

But Hugh had already seen some laborers in the distance gesturing excitedly at the conduit and laughing. The water was flowing. It reached the well-end fifteen minutes later with a muffled gurgle and gushed into the well. Hugh nodded to Bristol, who instantly signaled the command to the tub men to stop. Hugh went to the well and peered into it to watch the water exploding from the bamboo, then a few minutes later knelt before the valve to close it.

This was a more crucial test for the conduit than its ability to carry water; it must endure the gradual stoppage of the water and stand without bursting or springing leaks from the new pressure. Hugh grasped the handles of the wheel and closed the valve slowly, cog by cog, his hearing focused on the rush of water into the well. When he heard only a trickle, he gave the wheel one last turn. The trickle diminished to an erratic drip. He waited a moment. The dripping ceased. Then he let the lock pin fall into a ring and tapped it securely into place with a hammer. He glanced up to see Settle and Primus watching him. Both men smiled at him in congratulations. Hugh nodded once, then rose and strode to where he could look up the length of the conduit. Laborers stood near it, waiting. Hugh said, "Mr. Bristol, signal them to open the taps."

Bristol obeyed and waved his flag in another prearranged signal. Men knelt down all along the conduit and positioned their buckets directly beneath the taps. Hugh could see the man closest to him, over a hundred yards away, jerk the lever of the converted ale keg tap forward. After a moment, the man rose, brandished the bucket, and with a broad grin tilted the bucket over. Water splashed to the ground.

Only then did Hugh permit himself to smile.

With Settle and Primus, he walked up the line, stopping now and then to demonstrate to laborers how to use the funnels properly to water the hills of the young corn stalks. He met Mr. Beecroft halfway. The business agent reported that the men had poured four hundred and sixty gallons into the tub before they were signaled to stop. "Very good, Mr. Beecroft," said Hugh. "That is over my calculations by fourteen gallons."

"Well done, sir," said Beecroft, gesturing to the conduit. "It is an oddity, this conduit, but it will do the work. We won't lack for water ever again, I would venture."

"Thank you, Mr. Beecroft," Hugh said. "You are right. But we are merely emulating the aqueducts of the Romans."

Later in the day, just before the light began to slide into dusk, and when the laborers had finished their work and returned to their quarters, Hugh, driven by restlessness, wandered out of the great house and past the out-buildings to the well-end. He stopped when he saw the sun's last rays shine on the whole length of the conduit. For a brief moment, the brownish-green of the bamboo was turned into an almost incandescent white. An inner glow lit up inside him then, one that did not change the set of his mouth. At that moment, he felt prouder of what he had accomplished today than of anything he had ever done in the past. The glowing streak that vanished into the darkening trees beyond was fused with the living, headlong impetus of his soul, mind, and being. He raised a hand in the air and closed his fingers around the vision. *Mine*, he thought, *and through it, all the earth.*

The sunset's rays faded then. The vision flickered away, first to silver, then to brownish-green. But the vision never faded in the man who was Hugh Kenrick.

He heard the jingle of a bridle, and turned to see Jack Frake on his horse on the other side of the conduit. He was leaned forward, resting an elbow on the pommel of his saddle, studying him with a kind of distant intensity. Hugh saw in his eyes that he knew what he had been thinking and feeling. He remembered that his arm was still raised, and lowered it in a simple confession of the moment.

Behind Jack was John Proudlocks, also mounted. The man dropped from his saddle, took a few steps closer to the conduit, and stooped to brush a reverent hand over the bamboo. He glanced once at Hugh, then up at his employer. He said, in a matter-of-fact tone, "I once called this kind of thing magic. Just as you have, Jack, Mr. Kenrick here has proven that it is not. It is there," he said, slapping the top of the conduit once with his palm, then pointing to his forehead. "But first, it must be here."

Hugh laughed, not at Proudlocks, but from joy in discovering another man who understood such a thing. "It can begin nowhere else, Mr. Proud-locks."

"Nowhere else," echoed Proudlocks.

Jack sat up in his saddle. He knew what his neighbor had been working on all winter and spring, but until now had doubted the practicality of the conduit. He said, without breaking the moment, "We heard about it. We came to see for ourselves." He did not need to say more. He nodded to Hugh in apology and concession, a simple, happy action that ennobled him and raised him in the estimation of his friend and neighbor.

Chapter 16: The Riddle

Once she had a single, irreplaceable hero, and a certain future with him.

Now there were two heroes, and the future was a clouded uncertainty. It was an unparalleled circumstance for a young girl to find herself in, ominous and dangerous. Yet, it thrilled her, and caused her to hold her head up with pride. She thought she was equal to the danger, and worthy of the rivalry that was sure to ensue.

Ian McRae left the education of Etáin to his wife. It was simple logic to him: he loved Madeline, was proud of her, and reasoned that she was best qualified to produce an admirable daughter. He gladly paid for Etáin's books, music lessons, and occasional tutor. Although he did not always approve of what Etáin learned from her mother, he also reasoned that if such knowledge did his wife no harm, it could hardly tarnish Etáin's reputation or moral character, nor diminish the prospects of an agreeable marriage of his daughter to a respectable gentleman. The occasional, fleeting comparison of her with the daughters of the planters engendered a disapproval that lasted the length of a breakfast. Besides, it was an understanding between the couple that Etáin was being prepared and educated to become the wife of Jack Frake. This assumption was also subscribed to by Etáin, who needed little persuasion concerning the desirability, suitability, and success of such a match.

Ian McRae was placidly oblivious to the danger. Madeline McRae was too aware of it. She spoke briefly with her daughter about the matter, once she was certain that Etáin's head was being turned by Hugh Kenrick. "But, *Maman*, they are both perfect. There are no faults in either of them to balance against their virtues. They are somehow identical, but each possesses his own *élan*."

A colonial girl, whatever her rank, station, or status, was raised to be one of two things: an ornament of her future husband; or his working partner, if her intended spouse was a farmer, merchant, artisan, or in one of the "professions," such as law or medicine, preferably a deferring, nearly invisible partner whose partnership was limited to assuming the management of the household she married into. She was educated up to a certain point, enough to enable her to be witty and conversant in a superficial manner on unimportant matters; philosophy, politics, and most other serious subjects were considered beyond her ken or proper interest. The rules that governed her range of knowledge and action were as painfully restrictive as the hidden stays that bound the bodice of her gown. This was the norm which few women had the skill or courage to flout without inviting the dire consequences of social ostracism and spousal rebuke. Obliged to disguise or suppress their minds, many colonial women, consigned to the great houses of their planter husbands, found outlets of expression in poetry, diaries, or in anonymous or pen-named letters in newspapers.

Madeline McRae frowned on such a fate. Her daughter, she decided, was not going to become an animated doll. She wished Etáin to be grounded as thoroughly as possible in the ways of the world. She introduced Etáin to reading matter not normally allowed in the hands of other "educated" girls: histories of Rome and Greece; Cato's letters in the *London* and *British Journals*; volumes of *The Spectator*; English and French poetry, plays, and essays; and newspapers and magazines not intended for delicate, impressionable eyes. Under her direction, Etáin McRae began to assume the perspective of a woman of the world, without losing her innocence. Moreover, with the arrival of Hugh Kenrick, Etáin began to assume the persona of a Greek mortal who attracted the combative attentions of two gods. It was a development Madeline McRae could not have foreseen.

It caused her brief consternation, until she better understood that Hugh was more like Jack than unlike. Her fears were allayed, and her suspicions confirmed, on the occasion of a visit which she, her husband, and Etáin made to Meum Hall one fall afternoon, the first of many visits. Among all the titles of the books in Hugh's library, she espied a copy of *Hyperborea*. Madeline McRae had read it, as had Millicent Morley. She gave Etáin the late governess's copy when her daughter was seven. "It is quite pagan in its sentiments," she told the girl then, "more pagan than Plutarch. I recommend it. Study the character of Circe, the heroine, and how she views men. Be her some day, that is, learn to want an Apollo."

Etáin read *Hyperborea*, and was hopelessly drawn into its universe. No other work of literature could coax her out of it; no other work would she admit into it. And as she grew older, the novel became a litmus test for many men and events in the real world. And she reached a point of maturity when the test of the literal against the real transfigured into simply a test of the spirit of Drury Trantham's world against that of the real world.

Once, only Jack Frake passed that test, in terms of the man to be worshipped and to be gladly owned by. Then, without warning, came the glorious interloper, Hugh Kenrick. Madeline McRae was more aware of the difference his presence would make than was Etáin. She was dismayed, and happy for Etáin, at the same time. She envied her daughter the dilemma she would face in the future.

Etáin McRae was not popular with the other girls of Caxton. Nor did their parents approve of their associating with the daughter of a Scottish factor. Still, the other girls were drawn to her by a fascination with the fact that she had won Jack Frake without even trying. The future match was a paradox they wished to understand. They were raised to be seen, not often heard, and then only with cultivated coyness, affected modesty, and muted intelligence, and trained to be distant and aloof where men and especially suitors were concerned. Once, at a ball, Etáin had listened to other girls gossip or boast about the men who sought their company with discreet, unspoken intentions of eventual engagement and marriage. She asked, with some incredulousness in her words, "Does not one of you hope to marry a hero?"

Selina Granby, some years older than Etáin, laughed and said, "A hero? Of course, Etáin — provided he owns ten thousand acres, a handsome annuity from the consols, and has a friend on the Board of Trade!"

"But not a man who could be a man without having or needing those things?"

"You poor dear!" exclaimed Eleanor Cullis. "Such a man is a fiction! A fable! The true measure of a man's worthiness is his fortune and respectability. Also, he must be of good character and good family. How secure is he in the world? That is the question every girl must answer before considering any other."

"Can he dance, and show a good calf?" chimed in Annyce Vishonn. "Are his manners above reproach? Are his vices moderate and discreet? These are only a few of the many questions a girl must ponder before she may tolerate a man's attentions."

"And *intentions*," giggled Eleanor Cullis.

Etáin felt sorry for these girls. Also, she felt a twinge of contempt for them. She did not believe that their indifference to heroes had much to do with their not having read *Hyperborea*.

She had little trouble conforming to the crucial criterion of maidenhood of being distant and aloof. No young man ever called on her at home, but not a few managed to steal a moment alone with her at balls and other social gatherings. They, for their part, were tutored to regard an eligible young lady as something of a saint, and to come to her humbly and with profuse bows, uttering flourishing blandishments and verbose protestations of affection. She would discourage timid men who mumbled their words with statements such as, "Speak up, good sir! Or are you so dumb with wisdom that you do not know where to begin?" She would offend flattering, presumptuous young dandies with replies such as, "But, sir, your arguments are Sisyphean. Some day they may roll back down and crush you!" Such young men would conclude that Etáin, as a wife, would be either a nagging shrew, or a troublesome threat, and with relief they would forget whatever designs they had had on her. To Etáin, these men were as forgettable as one of Reverend Acland's Sunday sermons, and would flit from her memory soon after taking their leave.

For a long time, there was only Jack Frake. They had never kissed, never touched hands, not even when they were alone, except briefly during a country-dance. A bond existed between Etáin and Jack. He wanted a completed, mature woman, and wanted her to progress to that point without his influence and constant presence. He was willing to wait for her to accomplish that. Etáin understood this, and knew that she was not yet his equal, neither in spirit nor in knowledge, nor in some intangible form whose identity eluded her. When they met, in public or in private, they spoke to each other as though they had been married for years. Their bond was the foundation of an intimacy and familiarity that was real and alive in all possible expressions but one.

There was a time when the bond did not exist. Etáin was too young to do anything but note Jack's marriage to Jane Massie, too young to appreciate his loss when she and the infant boy died. Jack never spoke of them. Now that she was a near-woman, she respected his reticence. One thing that she admired about him was his capacity for overcoming the most crushing events in his life — imprisonment, indenture, the death of people close to him, and war — yet he would emerge from them unscathed, indestructible, unchanged, and somehow stronger. His initial stoicism would surrender to an irresistible charm.

Hugh Kenrick had that same capacity. Once, when she and her parents had supper at Meum Hall, she had seen the sketched head of a comely young woman on the wall of his library. She did not ask him about it, but he noticed her studying it. "That was her," he said, as though she had inquired. "Reverdy."

"Why do you keep it?" she had asked.

"Because I cannot forget what I thought she was, but was not." He paused. "It is a fair likeness of her."

Etáin noted the absence of bitterness in his words. He could have been speaking now of a distant relative, or of a mere acquaintance.

The histories of both men were common knowledge in Caxton, discussed in secretive, oblique terms when the subject of Jack Frake or Hugh Kenrick arose in company, and when the subjects were not present. Their characters instilled whispered caution among those critical of their pasts. Many young men harbored a repressed envy of Jack and Hugh, but, wishing to appear respectable and upright, publicly frowned on their histories. And many young women, even married ones, developed unacknowledged fantasies of being wooed and conquered by either of the two men, attracted by a vitality lacking in their *beaux* or husbands. Their own disapproval of Jack and Hugh was caused by an equally repressed knowledge that, to those two men, they were fundamentally invisible. They were women scorned by courteous indifference.

Madeline McRae was one of Jack's and Hugh's few defenders. "An absence of scandal in a man's life," she remarked once at a supper party at Granby Hall, "is evidence that he is incapable of passion." She was replying to a cryptic exchange by other guests at the table about Jack and Hugh and their disreputable pasts. "Here are two men for whom scandal is a ribbon of honor. You will concede there is a difference between scandal and disgrace. But it is exhilarating to see them bring passion to everything they do. You ought to thank fortune that two such scandalous men choose to live among you."

The table was quiet for a moment as the host, hostess, and guests absorbed this tactful reproach. Then Damaris Granby ventured, "As food for conversation, Mrs. McRae?"

"No, my dear," said Madeline McRae. "Either man would serve as a *beau-idéal* of Virginia manhood, worthy of emulation by this colony's sons, and of admiration by its daughters."

"I see little distinction between scandal and disgrace," said Ira Granby, coming to his wife's defense. "Disgrace is bred by scandalous behavior. A scandal, after all, is but a failed passion — say, for outlawry, or for insulting a king's son and associating with probable regicides — failed because it is frustrated and checked by lawful moral decency." He scoffed. "It is no wonder to me that they are *here*, and not in the mother country."

Madeline McRae shrugged her shoulders. "More to the shame and loss of the mother country, sir," she retorted, "that they belong here, and not *there*."

Ian McRae, seeing that the conversation was becoming heated, spoke up. Not addressing his wife, but the rest of the table, he said, "Do not contradict wisdom, good people. You will only embarrass yourselves, and what a scandal *that* would be!"

Etáin, too, knew the histories of Jack and Hugh. For her, their scandals were acts of heroism, as thrilling as the adventures of Drury Trantham in *Hyperborea*. She shared with them some special approach to life. She was certain of this; it was felt by her as an emotion, yet she knew that its root was a knowledge whose words eluded her. There was Jack, who had risen and grown and triumphed in spite of a society that had repeatedly knocked him down. He was a living, incurious contradiction of that society. There was Hugh, who had rebelled against that same society, yet who seemed to be a purified symbol of it.

"He is like so much of our music," she told her mother one day. "Aspiring to an elevated, blameless, logical glory amidst so much pettiness, artifice, and silly distraction."

"And Jack, your intended?" asked her mother.

"He, too, is like that music. He would be a barbarian, or a Turk, but for his dedication to reason."

"One might say that about Mr. Kenrick," reminded the mother.

"Perhaps," Etáin said. Her brow creased in thought. "But for Hugh, reason and all its children are pedestalled gods to whom he has pledged undying love and allegiance. For Jack, the love and allegiance come from somewhere inside him."

Etáin had seen Jack and Hugh together many times. She thought that they should have been antagonists. Yet, they acted like brothers. Moreover — and this observation perplexed her more than anything else about them — she saw no rivalry between them for her. It was as though they were waiting for her to make a decision. But she could not yet decide on her own role in the riddle. On one hand, she was Circe, the temporal seductress of mortal men; on the other, she was Athena, who had the power to dispense a final justice on them.

One of them was the needle, and one of them the north.

* * *

And one of them was right, and the other wrong — about England. Both men were certain of it. This was the nature of their rivalry. Yet, for the moment, even this did not much concern them. Nothing else divided them but England. Not even Etáin McRae.

Jack Frake had grown in love with her over a period of years. This did not mean, however, that he had not noticed other women. But all other women had disappointed him. Some telling things in their words or behavior smothered any interest he may have shown in them. Moreover, in a time when courtship demanded that a man be humble and self-depre-cating to a woman whose special esteem he labored to win, Jack could not force himself to observe the ritual; he could not be what he was not. It required a dishonesty and charade that revolted every fiber of his being; he did not tolerate it in anyone, least of all in himself. Although he was nei-ther boastful nor vain, he could see no reason why he should wear the domino of humility. In a society whose leitmotif was largely a masquerade of manners, he was artless by choice.

This was one reason why he loved Etáin; the capacity for falsehood, intrigue, and mannered modesty did not seem to exist in her, just as it did not exist in himself. She loved him, he was certain, though she had never said so. He fully expected her to say so, when she was ready, when her pride and perspective matched his own. When she was certain.

Hugh Kenrick, unaware of the depth of the problem he posed for Etáin, was only preparing to fall in love with her. Like Jack, he saw a girl-woman who was steadily progressing toward full womanhood. He, too, was willing to wait until she revealed her permanent, self-molded character. He watched her grow, in the years after his arrival in Caxton, with the same fascination with which he had noted the progress of his mother's portrait long ago through the careful, selective strokes of Emery Westcott.

Unlike Jack, he had been wounded in the most painful way a woman could contrive to hurt a man: by rejecting him for his virtues. A woman scorned might seek vengeance to salve her injured pride. A man so scorned may also seek an impossible justice. Or, he may simply shut himself off from feminine company until his pride regains its senses and stature. There was now no other woman Hugh cared to contemplate, except from a wistful distance. He saw crude traces of Reverdy Brune in all but Etáin. He did not doubt that a woman such as Selina Granby, regarded as the most beautiful in Caxton, would in time become a mature, responsible woman, once the realties of adulthood imposed themselves on her. But, to him, an adulthood without passion was as deadening as a childhood without vision or hope. He could imagine such a life, but it was never quite real to him. He could observe it in others, but it did not concern him.

As with Jack, the discriminating milieu of loneliness moved Hugh to raise the stakes of solitude, not from a wish to spare himself the sapping drudgery of a conventional, passionless marriage, but rather to gamble on the existence of a just goddess. Like Jack's, his core being was attuned solely to the enrapturing company of a scintillating paragon, to a woman who was indivisibly and alluringly noble.

Chapter 17: The Hiatus

Early in 1763, the Caxton *Courier* published the marriage banns of three engaged couples: of James Vishonn and Selina Granby; of William Granby and Eleanor Cullis; and of Morris Otway and Annyce Vishonn. The nuptials would have been performed that spring in separate ceremonies in the homes of the brides' or grooms' parents, but Reece Vishonn persuaded all the concerned parties to agree to a triple wedding at Enderly, officiated by Reverend Acland for a special fee. His private reason was that since two of the children were his own, they would have been married in his home anyway.

The unusual event also gave him an excuse to combine it with a special ball to mark the Treaty of Paris, signed in February and officially announced by Lieutenant-Governor Fauquier at the opening of the new session of the General Assembly in mid-May. Word of the treaty had reached Caxton in late April from ship captains fresh from London. Once the planter had the idea of a wedding-ball, he wasted little time getting out word of it. Soon after, rumor reached him that the Governor himself might even attend, arriving in his resplendent gilt coach-and-six. The possibility sent Reece Vishonn and his wife, Barbara, into joyous if subdued hysteria. Fauquier did not come, though the general disappointment in this was lessened by the attendance of three of his Council members, who reported that the Governor was "overly pressed with the business of his office."

Jack Frake attended the affair. Reece Vishonn kept a nervous though discreet eye on him the whole time, afraid that he might engage the Council members in "provocative politics." Jack reassured his host at one point after the wedding ceremony, "Have no fear, sir. For the moment, I have said all I need to say about the consequences of the peace."

"Are you convinced now that the empire is secure?" asked Vishonn.

Jack shook his head. "Quite the opposite, sir. I am certain that its management will prove to be a challenge to the skills of liberal men, who must either be replaced by *petit* tyrants, or become themselves tyrants."

Reece Vishonn glanced around, hoping that no one else in the crowded ballroom had heard this. Then he sighed. "Really, sir, a little faith in your fellow men might greatly contribute to your happiness." He added, "I mean no insult, sir, but speak in the role of a friend and fellow planter."

"None taken, sir," said Jack with a smile. "However, I must point out that what you and the others fear, has already begun. The empire is not secure. No doubt you have read Mr. James Otis's remarks in the *Gazette* concerning the constitutionality of writs of assistance. Mr. Otis lost that case in Boston, but the words were spoken and are a matter of record. Then, there is the matter of the uprising of the Indians on the far frontier, led by this chief, Pontiac. If I wish the empire any success, it is that His Majesty's troops can extinguish it. That is the extent of my faith in my fellow men."

"That is only a rumor, sir," Vishonn said. "There has been nothing in the *Courier* or the *Gazette* about an uprising." He paused for a moment to think. "But, if it is true, what of it?"

Jack shrugged. "Will a military problem be employed, in time, in the solution of a political one?"

Vishonn scoffed. "I am not aware that there is a political problem, Mr. Frake. But, I do agree with you about solving the Indian one. If I did not know any better, I would say that you were a personal advisor to Lord Amherst on how to best deal with the savages. You *and* Mr. Kenrick, so I've heard." The planter leaned closer to Jack and said in a near whisper, "I've also heard that Fauquier has nearly convinced Lord Amherst to visit Virginia to see for himself what a tidy state he has put it in. Sir Jeffery *is* our true Governor, after all. He is so close to the colony, but has been overly pressed himself with his duties as commander-in-chief and Governor-General."

"And you would plan another ball," said Jack, "should he decide to accept Governor Fauquier's invitation?"

"Without question, sir," chuckled Vishonn. He glanced around again. "Well, there is my wife, waving to me with another problem. Please, enjoy yourself, sir. And thank you for expressing your good wishes to my son and daughter." Reece Vishonn rushed away.

The McRaes were there, as was Etáin with her harp, and as were the Kenny brothers and almost enough guest musicians from Williamsburg that, together, they nearly composed an orchestra. Jack spent most of his time with Etáin and her parents.

In the placid interval between Quebec and the avalanche of events that was to overtake Virginia and the colonies, Caxton had recovered from, and reconciled itself to, such local disturbances as the manumission of Hugh Kenrick's slaves; Jack's decision to free his remaining slaves, over their protests, using the same "Quaker" ruse; Hugh's conduit, which attracted the curiosity of some planters beyond Queen Anne County after Wendel Barret ran a description of it in the *Courier*; Reece Vishonn's attempt to duplicate the conduit on his own land with iron pipe, without success; and

the defeated bill, introduced in the House of Burgesses by Edgar Cullis and
William Granby, to impose an eleven-pence per pipe levy on imported
molasses and a three-pence per pound levy on West Indian spices, over and
above what was already imposed by Crown customs collectors, for the purpose of establishing and administering a Virginia-controlled maritime
piloting service on all the colony's bays and rivers.

There had also been some controversy over the proposal by the
vestrymen of Stepney Parish to approve Hugh's offer to make available
from his brickyard the materials to create walkways along the shop fronts
on Queen Anne Street, in exchange for a six-year abatement of parish
tithes for Meum Hall. Hugh had hired an itinerant brickmaker, Henry
Zouch, to repair the disused kiln on his property, with the ultimate goal of
making and selling bricks to the rest of the county. Substandard or mar-
ginal bricks could be used, he explained to Vishonn and the other
vestrymen, to lay down walkways. "Think of the advantages, sirs," he told
them. "The proprietors would have cleaner floors, you would have cleaner
boots, and the town could boast of an amenity lacking even in Williamsburg. The mud and dust that we accept as an unavoidable nuisance, could
be baked into sturdy, durable rectangles on which to tread with a confident
foot." The matter sat unresolved on the vestrymen's official agenda; the
twelve notables were evenly divided on the practicality of the idea.

At the wedding-ball, one Council member enquired after this remarkable young man, Hugh Kenrick, who eschewed his title, who introduced the
novel ideas, who had freed his slaves. Reece Vishonn had wanted to introduce Hugh to the man — he was quite as proud of having such as person
as his neighbor as he was of Enderly — but the master of Meum Hall was
not in Caxton for the festive occasion.

Hugh Kenrick was aboard the merchantman *Roilance*, bound for
England.

*   *   *

In April, Hugh received a letter from his father, who wrote: "I have
ventured into a realm I once disdained and swore never to soil my hands
in: politics. I will say no more on this subject. The details can be wrung
from me by you only in person. Your mother and I hope that you are suffi-
ciently intrigued by this teasing revelation that you will think of favoring
us with a visit, if only to satisfy your probable astonishment. My son, you
have been away for five years! Must we remind you of the last time we saw
you, when we waved worried farewells to you in Weymouth Harbor, and
you to us from the deck of the *Sparrowhawk*? Our last sight of you was a

speck of white sail on the horizon, as it carried you to Plymouth and beyond. I would undertake such a voyage myself to see you and the property — your sketches of it that you sent us are themselves intriguing — but I do not trust your uncle enough to absent myself from Danvers or London for so long a period of time. I will say this much, though: Your uncle is one of the reasons I have purchased a seat in the Commons...."

Hugh was doubly astonished by his father's news, and by the years. After a moment, while he sat holding the letter, the significance of all those years became weightier in his mind than the news of his father entering politics. Until he read that sentence, it had not seemed so long a time to him. Those years had been filled with the action of his new life, and they were no more important to him than if they were chalked strokes on a piece of slate. He reminded himself many times over those years that he should go home on a visit, but the reminder became a mere mental habit that receded further and further to the back of his consciousness, driven there by the immediate concerns of a vigorous, headlong life.

He had frowned, and read on: "Matters between your uncle and me have grown so acerbic that we can no longer share Windridge Court. Our staff are also in bitter conflict with your Uncle Basil's. We have therefore taken a long lease on a gracious house in Chelsea called Cricklegate from a merchant of Mr. Worley's kind acquaintance. It was designed by Mr. Robert Adam, and comes well-appointed. It is on Paradise Row, close by to Cheyne Walk, not far from the river. We have arranged for your sister Alice to attend a ladies' academy at nearby Gough House, run by a Mrs. Pemberton, the widow of an East India Company merchant....

"There has been some progress on the new Blackfriars bridge. The first arches are completed, and our Portland quarry has supplied a goodly tonnage of stone for it. They are only just now planning to fill up the Fleet Canal to make a new avenue of it. I cannot, however, help but draw similarities between the bridge and the political situation. The road of peace has begun, but all I see before us is a chasm gusting with the winds of uncertainty, anger, and avarice....

"By the time you read this, Parliament will have adjourned until November. Lord Bute is not expected to remain at Treasury for long; that is, most hope that he will have surrendered the seals of office before the next session of this Parliament. He is disliked and opposed for a number of reasons, not least of which is the treaty he has concluded with France. Although it and the peace preliminaries were violently debated in both Houses, some aver that he overcame the opposition with base trafficking in bluster and favors to secure enough votes for approval, so that the treaty could receive the king's assent. This favorite of His Majesty is nonetheless so detested that even Sir Charles Pratt, who is His Majesty's counsel and a member of the Privy Council (and lord justice of the Common Pleas — he is a man to watch!), is one of many who are whispering the notion that the French minister Choiseul paid Lord Bute handsomely for 'delivering' the treaty. Lord Bute has not one supporter on the Council, excepting the king himself, who must weep in secret in his closet over the difficulties encountered by his mentor and friend.

"Adding to Lord Bute's universal unpopularity is his commitment to the proposed cider tax. The western counties have already promised wholesale civil disobedience if it is made law, even though their representatives may vote for it. Perhaps the sole person in the kingdom who might express some gratitude for Lord Bute's tenure is Dr. Samuel Johnson, who, as you must have read in the colonial newspapers, was awarded a pension last year by Lord Bute from the king's secret service fund. Dr. Johnson must have gulleted a full tankard of his own pride to have accepted the emolument. It was a pension, tendered by a Scot no less, and only he can know which he claimed to have abhorred more. Well, even a court jester may retire with some dignity, but some men of great lights and accomplishment, it seems, exhibit an unbecoming humility that ranks them beneath the most craven fool, a humility, I believe, founded on duplicity...."

"But once Lord Bute is gone, and a new government is formed, the great question that will occupy everyone's minds and labors will be how this nation is going to pay for its victories...."

There were other matters and subjects reported in Garnet Kenrick's letter. "Mr. Worley has disposed of the tobacco you sent. M. Edouard-César Bric, a commercial agent who purchases for Dutch and Danish interests as well as for the French Farmers-General, has remarked that your leaf is among the best quality he has ever seen, and hopes to purchase more. He intimated to Mr. Worley that he may even venture to the colonies to appraise their trading situations. The French seem to be as eager to get back to business as the English."

His father also discussed some business concerning the *Ariadne* and the *Busy*, but returned to politics again. "Lord Edgremont is ailing and not expected to survive the year.... Henry Fox was created Lord Holland, Baron of Foley.... The Marquis of Rockingham, young though he is, is proving to be ever as much adept as his late father in politics. He appears to be inactive in these matters, but is quietly assembling a party of allied seats in the Commons. He nearly beat me to the seat I have purchased.... I was proven wrong about the partnership of your uncle and Sir Hennoch Pannell. They work well together, it seems, Sir Hennoch being the glove, and your uncle the hand...."

Garnet Kenrick ended his letter with another plea: "Your mother, Alice, and I wish most earnestly that you will come, for we are aching to see the man who has reported to us in his letters his many triumphs in Virginia. Perish the thought that his Herculean labors have so cost him such affections for us that he must think twice about presenting himself before proud and happy parents after so long a sojourn.... We are going to Cricklegate in June, so you must address your correspondence there, or perhaps appear on our doorstep...."

The letter dropped from Hugh's hand. In that instant he decided to visit England for a while. There were some plantation matters he wanted to see to first over the next few weeks. And after he arranged with Mr. Settle and Mr. Beecroft how to manage Meum Hall while he was gone, he could leave with an easier mind. He drew forth a sheet of paper, picked up a quill, and wrote a reply to his father, briefly stating his intention to sail for England in early May.

He told Jack Frake: "My father intimates that things are aboil in the government, and that once Bute is gone, Parliament and the ministry that succeeds him will begin to ponder the war debts and the costs and means of keeping Mr. Pitt's gains — or rather what is left of them."

Jack looked thoughtful for a moment. "What does your father fear that he has taken up politics?"

"My Uncle Basil, I suppose," said Hugh. "He has spoken in Lords for the status quo, or for more of it, as has Sir Hennoch in the Commons, my father writes, arguing for the same. But if my father is so uneasy that he has invested time and money for the privilege of being heard in the Commons, my uncle cannot be the sole reason, on whom he would not spend a penny for spite."

"Perhaps he has our perspective on things," suggested Jack.

Hugh shook his head. "No. He is a wonderful and honest man, but his acumen is only a little better than is Governor Fauquier's." He saw the amused, perplexed look on Jack's face, and went on to explain. "That is, he will agree upon reflection on the rightness or wrongness of certain matters, but, without prodding, rarely delve to the core of them." He paused to smile. "That is an affectionate criticism."

Jack thought: I almost envy you for having a father to criticize. Instead, he nodded, and said, "When you return, you will undoubtedly bring with you news that our Attic society can discuss."

"I expect that I shall be brimming with news," laughed Hugh.

Their group had grown from three to seven regular members, and now met once a month in a reserved room at the King's Arms Tavern. Steven Safford, the establishment's owner, was also a participant. Like Jack, he was a veteran of the Braddock debacle, and shared the planter's views on politics, and also the same worries and doubts. He was a tall, thin man in his forties with sandy-blond hair and a forbidding, ascetic face. For years he had remained aloof from Caxton's social and political life, rarely volunteering his opinion on anything. His reputation for solitude was nearly as notorious as Jack's.

One of his doubts had been of Hugh Kenrick's value to Jack as a friend, until Jack accompanied Hugh one evening to the King's Arms for supper and speculation. And, like Jack, Safford was won over to Hugh by his informed positions, his dedication to work, and a certain genuine quality in his character that belied his aristocratic background and bearing. He was astounded, after their formal introduction and hours of talk, that an aristocrat could be so likable and more than sympathetic with colonial views.

"I shall also bring newspapers, and magazines, and perhaps even a copy of the *North Briton*," Hugh said. Then his face brightened. "Perhaps my father was alluding to that paper and its author, John Wilkes, who is a member for Aylesbury. His paper constantly attacks Lord Bute and the government, my father writes, and he mentioned in a past letter that last November a general warrant was drawn up to arrest Mr. Wilkes and the printers of his paper on vague charges of libel, but it was withdrawn. I wonder if that matter has been revived."

He stood with his hands locked together behind his back at Jack's library window, gazing thoughtfully out at the York River. Today it was a calm, still blue, broken now and then by a lone whitecap. The forests and fields far across the river were a spread of brown tinged with the green of spring.

Jack, seated in an armchair near his desk, asked, "Why would they be arrested? Aside from speaking their minds, Mr. Wilkes is a member of Parliament. Are not members privileged against arrest, as our burgesses are here?"

Hugh shook his head without turning around. "Not if they've been charged with treason, or murder, or breaching the peace. Near to treason is libeling members of the government, with intent to sedition." Hugh paused, then turned to face Jack. "Of course, if one libels the king's ministers, by implication one libels the king, and suggests that he is not fit to occupy the throne and ought to be removed from it. That was the nub of the charges against the Pippins years ago." He picked up a glass of brandy from the windowsill and finished it. Putting down the glass, he said, "If only Englishmen could divest themselves of that *corpus mysticum*, that tenacious, unreasoning aura of awe that envelops the subject of *kings*, they could make so much progress in their own liberties. And ours." He paused again. "You have read my paper on that *corpus mysticum*, so I needn't dwell on the subject."

Jack nodded. "Does your father share your views on it?"

"No," Hugh said. "His mind, too, stalls on that subject, and loses verve, and purpose. But his is not an exclusively English fault. So many learned colonials are similarly affected."

Jack rose and refilled Hugh's glass from a decanter, and then his own. "We colonials," he said as he put down the decanter, "sooner than most Englishmen, will be pressed to choose between that *corpus mysticum* and our liberties."

Hugh nodded once. "But only after first grasping that there can be no lasting agreement between them. They must learn that there is no such thing as a good king, only an unambitious one who confers an illusory stability."

Jack smiled and touched Hugh's glass with his own. "A toast then to the Skelly gang, my friend, and to the Pippins, and to ourselves, as their rightful heirs."

Hugh grinned. "And to all men of like mind — and God damn the king!"

When they finished downing their drinks, Jack said, "I will have some letters to friends in England ready by the time you leave. Will you carry them over and post them?"

"As many as you wish," said Hugh. "I will spend at least six weeks there. Is there anyone you would wish me to see and speak to?"

Jack shook his head. "No. I would say Captain Ramshaw, but he must be at sea by now. Very likely your ships will pass each other."

When Hugh returned to Meum Hall, he went to his own library, took down an atlas of English maps, and turned the pages to Dorset. There were almost a dozen boroughs in the county, including Onyxcombe, which his family had controlled for generations, and whose political boundaries enclosed the village of Danvers and the Kenrick estate. The other Dorset boroughs, such as Poole, Corfe Castle, Lyme Regis, and Weymouth, ranged in type of franchise from scot and lot to householder to freeman.

Onyxcombe, however, was the only burgage; the Kenrick family was its major freeholder, owning nearly all the land and buildings in the borough, except for the Brune and Tallmadge estates, and so held the solitary vote. Onyxcombe was anomalous again in that it was one of the few boroughs in the entire country that returned a single representative to the Commons; most others sent two. The Kenrick family had never tried to influence the elections in Poole, the borough nearest to Onyxcombe, nor attempted to usurp the control which the merchants there had over the port. Poole was the homeport of the *Busy,* the *Nimble*, and the *Ariadne*. All three vessels also regularly called on it to unship Newfoundland fish, Carolina rice, Virginia corn, and New England timber, as well as Continental cargoes. His father was all too pleased with the corporation of Poole, and had amicable ties to many of the freemen-merchants who retained the franchise.

As he studied the maps, Hugh wondered which borough his father had acquired control over. And whichever it was, he also tried to imagine his father rising in the Commons to address its tightly packed audience. For all that he found admirable in his father, he did not think he could number among his virtues a gift for public speaking. After a while, Hugh closed the atlas. It was fruitless to try to surmise the details of his father's new career.

Chapter 18: The Journey Home

A round of bon voyage suppers was held in Hugh's honor in the weeks before his departure. At the home of the McRaes, he promised he would bring Etáin some new sheet music; her mother, French newspapers; and her father, new pattern books, catalogues, and copies of *Gentleman's Magazine*. At Enderly, he assured Reece Vishonn that he would return with some new agricultural books the planter had read about, and wished the man's children, James and Annyce, the best happiness for their weddings.

Jack Frake gave a farewell supper at the King's Arms the night before Hugh was to board a sloop that would take him to Philadelphia. Here, too, he made a list of things that other men requested. The most unusual request came from John Proudlocks, who expressed curiosity about the subjects he heard his employer and others discuss with a seriousness that intrigued him.

"Would you bring me a copy of the British constitution, Mr. Kenrick?" he asked. "A tattered copy, not a new one. I can only afford what is called a 'second-hand' copy."

Everyone seated around the wide table glanced at the Indian. One man suppressed a snort, another a giggle. Hugh threw a reproving look at them. Jack turned wordlessly to Hugh, and waited to hear how he would answer the request.

Hugh said, "You could not afford a copy of our constitution, sir, tattered or new, for one does not exist. Mr. Reisdale can vouch for this. It is, you see, a great pile of precedents and decisions, not all of them reasonable, accumulated over centuries, and collected in a hundred tomes. Our constitution is the common law, which is everywhere around you, like the air." He paused when he saw the disappointment on Proudlocks's face. "Our constitution excludes much of Parliament's mischief, which is also everywhere about you."

"Like the vapors of smoldering horse dung," remarked Reisdale.

The men all laughed. Hugh said, "I will, however, try to find a digest of our constitution's salient points. Also, my father writes that an eminent jurist has given a clear presentation of it in a series of lectures at Oxford University, and has published them in a book. I happen to want a copy of it myself."

"Which jurist, sir?" asked Reisdale.

"William Blackstone, of the Middle Temple, I believe."

"I am not acquainted with him. *I* would be interested in reading what he has to say."

Hugh asked Proudlocks, "What is *your* interest in the subject, sir?"

The man looked thoughtful for a moment, then said, "I have heard much babble about it lately among you gentlemen. Some say this constitution is in trouble, that its protection will be denied us. Others say it will cause us trouble, because it will allow the Crown to possess us. I wish to know how this can be." He paused. "I wish to judge for myself."

"A wise policy, sir," said Hugh. He beamed, and glanced briefly at Jack, who sat next to Proudlocks. He was happy that his friend could make such a friend. Then he rose and exclaimed, gesturing to Proudlocks, "Gentlemen! *Hic de nihilo crevit homo!* — He is a self-made man!"

"Hear, hear!" seconded Reisdale. He was echoed by others around the table.

Proudlocks seemed to blush at the compliment paid him, but grinned in grateful acknowledgment.

Jack tentatively raised his glass of port to Hugh. "If you have a family coat-of-arms or crest, my friend, you ought to discard its motto and adopt that one."

"Though first substituting *ego* for *hic*," added Reisdale.

"I will think on that suggestion," remarked Hugh. "Gentlemen, I am happy to have you as company. While I am away, I shall miss you all."

"As we shall you," said Steven Safford. "You are one of us, now."

Jack Frake rose to propose a toast. Looking at Hugh, he said, "Long live Lady Liberty."

Hugh took up his own glass and raised it in answer. "And to the memory of those who knew her, and to those who know her today."

*   *   *

The next morning, Hugh reviewed his instructions to William Settle for managing Meum Hall.

"How long do you plan to stay, sir?" asked the overlooker.

"At least six weeks. Probably longer. It would not be worth going if the stay were shorter than the voyage. I hope to return by September. I doubt that I could bear a longer absence from this place."

He gave last instructions to the housekeeper, Mrs. Vere, and to Beecroft, then visited the tenants' quarter and said goodbye to its residents. His trunks were loaded onto a cart, and Spears, the valet, drove him down to Caxton's waterfront.

It was a dry, crisp morning. At the pier, waiting for him, were Jack Frake, John Proudlocks, Thomas Reisdale, and the McRaes. They came aboard with Hugh to talk until the sloop was ready to embark. It was the *Amherst*, formerly the *Nancy*, renamed in honor of the British general who had secured the surrender of Montreal and thus closed Canada to the French.

The *Amherst* took Hugh to Philadelphia, where he stayed with Otis Talbot while waiting for the *Roilance* to take him to England.

As the *Roilance*, driven by a good westerly wind, plunged through the whitecaps toward England, Hugh stood at the stern and watched the continent shrink to a thin, dark line on the bobbing horizon. He felt that he was leaving home, a place he had made his own, a place that gave him the same experience as *Hyperborea*. "You are one of us, now," said Steven Safford at the supper. He had not attached any special importance to the remark when he first heard it. Now it recurred to him for a reason he understood too well, prompted by the sight of the tenuous, receding vision in the west. For the first time, a question formed in his mind, and it caused him a poignant sadness, because he knew that it would require an answer: Could he still call England home?

Then the line in the west disappeared beneath the waves, and, once again, he was surrounded by mere ocean. He turned to lean against the rail, and looked up at the pennants snapping in the breeze above the full sails. He saw one crewman climb the web-like rigging, intent on some task, oblivious to the wind that whipped his jacket. But Hugh imagined he saw a man ascending Mount Olympus.

Chapter 19: The Homecoming

"I boast a constituency of one — your father." Sir Dogmael Jones grinned and indicated Baron Garnet Kenrick with a brief gesture of his hand.

Hugh Kenrick glanced from the serjeant-at-law to his father, who sat at his desk, placidly watching him for his reaction. Hugh frowned, then also grinned, though not in amusement. He asked Jones, "For which borough?"

"Swansditch, milord," answered Jones. The barrister grinned again. In his grin were a hint of self-effacement and a touch of contempt for the whole business. He began pacing back and forth, and spoke as though he were lecturing law students at the Inns of Court. "Swansditch is a dreary, cankerous collection of tenements, warehouses, and odoriferous alleys that clings to the eastern fringe of Southwark like an incurable lesion. It is on the Thames, some distance downriver from London Bridge, and is nearly always gripped in a smoky mist or fog. In area, it is not much greater than the Covent Garden market, roughly one hundred paces by one hundred. The place once served the same purpose as Smithfield; cattle, sheep, and horses were driven to it from Surrey and Kent for sale. I suppose there were once swans and a ditch or canal there that would account for the name. The ditch has become a kind of boulevard, if only for the profusion of evil-looking weeds and crippled poplars that line its sides. It was, they say, filled in with rubble from the Great Fire, and since then with naval debris, silt, offal, and the carcasses of innumerable, luckless livestock. As to the swans, if any ever domiciled there, they have long past anyone's memory fled to more salubrious climes. Among the living, there are perhaps a dozen or two souls who are the borough's constant inhabitants, though they have not the vote. They are mostly employed in the warehouses, or by the borough's only solvent enterprise, a carriage-maker's works that neighbors Southwark.

"Swansditch, like Onyxcombe, is the odd borough that sends but a single member to the Commons. A Mr. Robert Ingoldsby, a factor of leather and linen goods and a career contractor for the Army, held this seat for nigh on twenty years, until he unexpectedly expired last Michaelmas from a surfeit of wrong mutton. His own warehouse and works were situated in Southwark. There are many men like the late Mr. Ingoldsby in the Commons, contractors, and merchants, and bankers who come to life on the benches only when a bill for economy threatens to abridge their incomes or

appointments. They do not go to the Commons to acquire fortunes; fortunes they already have. They are there to preserve them, or for the prestige, or to justify their idleness. If a contract or preferment happens to come
their way...well, and why not? They vote this way or that not in hopes of
earning Crown *lucre* from a grateful administration or from colleagues, but
from purblind loyalty to foibles or friends, or from eclectic inclinations governed by the quality of their dinners or of the day.

"But, I digress. To continue: Mr. Worley, of Worley and Sons, your
family's agents here, had had some business with Mr. Ingoldsby, and alerted
your father to his demise. Your father subsequently purchased the tenements and the leases on the other properties from his widow for a sum that
has allowed her to retire comfortably and indefinitely to Bath to take its
waters for her rheumatism and its society for her widowhood. Too late did
an agent of the Marquis of Rockingham approach the dear lady with an
offer to purchase; the money was paid, and the transfer of ownership registered with the courts a week before he essayed an interest. Mrs. Ingoldsby
was rather put out by the late offer, as she undoubtedly could have gotten
more from the Marquis, but the deal was done. Proprietorship of the tenements and leases secures for your father not only the income from the properties, but the vote for him to nominate and elect the candidate — and
therefore the seat. I am certain you know how these things work.

"One qualification for a person to claim a seat in the Commons, of
course, is that he own landed property of some kind. Your father was kind
enough to loan to me, at least on paper, the price of some indifferent pasturage in Wandsworth." The barrister paused to shrug. "It little mattered
to me what I owned, only that it would permit me a place on the benches.
So, I was duly chosen by his lordship in a by-election the duration of a
whore's wink, after all other formalities were observed." Jones chuckled. "I
journeyed to Swansditch out of curiosity, and to introduce myself to its
inhabitants. Some of the sober ones were not aware that a change in repre-
sentation had occurred. Others were not even cognizant of the fact that the
borough had ever been represented." He sighed. "A remarkably dormant
constituency, Swansditch.

"In conclusion, milord, it is from this rotting, decrepit pedestal that I
shall speak in the Commons." The barrister bowed slightly, then resumed
his seat in an armchair, took up a glass from a little table by it, and finished
his Madeira. "Or," he added, "should I fail miserably to rise in time to
attract the Speaker's finger, it will be a mere roost, from which I may at
least audit the warblings of ambitious fools, the querulous misgivings of the
cautious, and the trembling confusions of the timid."

The two older men waited for Hugh to respond. This time, Hugh rose from his chair, paced for a moment or two in thought, then turned and, glancing at both his father and the barrister, asked, "Why?"

"To begin with," answered his father, "I cannot sit by and watch the country drift so aimlessly. Not any more. It is a corrupt system, our Parliament, but we shall attempt to either overcome the corruption, or make it work for us...for liberty." Garnet Kenrick paused. "You know that I become a lump of coal when I am expected to speak before any audience larger than can sit at a long table. Sir Dogmael here will become my voice." He smiled at the barrister. "He has had much practice at it."

Jones said, "Why do I wish to sit in the Commons, that great colosseum of cowards, caitiffs, and compromisers? To begin with — Mr. John Wilkes."

*   *   *

Steady westerly winds over an untroubled ocean, together with fair weather and smart seamanship, allowed the *Roilance* to cross from Philadelphia to Portsmouth, England, in six weeks. From Portsmouth Hugh took a coastal packet to Dover; from Dover an inn coach to Canterbury; from Canterbury another coach to an inn yard near Charing Cross in London. There he hired a hackney to take him and his luggage up the Thames to Chelsea, and finally to the doorstep of Cricklegate on Paradise Row. It was on a warm, cloudless mid-June afternoon that he raised the brass knocker on the door, let it fall once, and braced himself for the reception he was certain to receive.

The maid who opened the door recognized him with open-mouthed surprise, and blurted, "Master Hugh!" Her exclamation was loud enough to be heard in the rest of the house, and was followed by a joyous shout from somewhere inside. His parents rushed into the foyer. They paused in pleased shock at sight of the tall, tanned, strapping young man standing in the doorway, the young man who was their son. They hurtled forward to embrace him.

After a moment, Garnet Kenrick grasped his son's shoulders and held him away at arm's length. "Look at him, Effney! My God, the colonies have done well by him! You've grown a few inches, Hugh, and you're almost as dark as an Arab!"

Effney Kenrick wiped the tears from her cheeks and laughed. "Yes, Garnet, look at him!" She poked her son playfully on his arm and chest with delicate fingers. "I would pity the boxer put in the ring with our Hugh! Why, he is worthy of a statue!"

"A statue!" exclaimed the Baron. "No, not quite. Perhaps a portrait. Yes! We shall have one commissioned of you during your stay!"

Hugh was as happy to reunite with his parents as they were with him. An energy of animating joy overcame his exhaustion from the voyage home and the journey from Portsmouth. At one point, he asked, "But, where is Alice?"

"She is at the academy," answered his mother. "Bridgette will fetch her later in the afternoon." Bridgette, who was his former governess, was now his little sister's. The woman stood in the background with Owen Runcorn, the family's *major domo*, watching the reunion.

Hugh raised a hand and touched the silver that had appeared in his father's dark hair. "You, sir," he said with jesting fondness, "are beginning to acquire more wisdom."

Garnet Kenrick chuckled. "Your mother predicts that, in a few years, it will be so white, I will not need to wear a wig. Not that I often do."

Hugh turned to Effney Kenrick, saw the admiring worship in her eyes for him, and embraced her. "But you, mother, are as beautiful as ever!"

She returned the embrace. "My magnificent son!"

Hugh espied Runcorn and Bridgette over his mother's head. He disengaged, went to them, and shook the former valet's hand before the man could protest. Runcorn blinked at the gesture, and blinked again when Hugh bussed a startled, blushing Bridgette on the cheek.

Then a man stepped into the foyer from a room that adjoined it. He was a lean, elegantly dressed man with more silver in his hair than had Garnet Kenrick, tied in back with a plain ribbon. A pockmarked face and intense black eyes, however, made him look feral and dangerous. Under one arm he held his hat, in the other hand a silver-knobbed, silver-tipped mahogany cane.

Hugh frowned in surprise and the effort of recognition. "Mr. Jones...?"

Sir Dogmael Jones, barrister, serjeant-at-law at the King's Bench, reader of law at the Serjeants' Inn, and now a bencher or manager of that Inn, nodded in greeting. "*Sir* Dogmael Jones," he said, "though *mister* will suffice, milord."

Hugh went to him and offered his hand in greeting. Jones glanced once at it, smiled, then shifted his cane to his other hand so that he could clasp the one offered him. As he shook it, he said, "Welcome home, milord Danvers. Your apparent excellent health and vigorous presence of mind substantiates what your father has told me about you, which is that you have met with much success in Virginia."

"Thank you, sir," said Hugh. He studied for a moment the man who had defended his friends in court years ago. "You, too, are looking much wiser."

Jones grinned. "Wiser — and bolder. As are you, milord." He put on his hat, and turned to address Garnet Kenrick. "Milord, I shall take my leave now. I will not intrude upon this occasion."

The Baron shook his head. "No, sir. Stay. We have a spare room."

Jones shook his head in turn. "Thank you, milord, but, no. I have business I should see to in the City. My protégé there needs counseling on how to present to his students the matter of public places and the laws that govern them. I shall return on the morrow, if that is convenient."

"Convenient, and necessary, sir," said the Baron.

Dogmael Jones performed a series of brief bows to the Kenricks, followed Runcorn to the front door, and left the house. Hugh glanced at his father in silent inquiry.

The Baron said, "It will be explained on the morrow, when he returns. No more about it until then. For the moment, we must make amends for your long but profitable absence."

"You must tell us more about Meum Hall, and Caxton, and Virginia," said Effney Kenrick.

Hugh laughed. "Fewer people live in Caxton than in Chelsea. You could very likely fit them all inside this house."

*   *   *

Wilkes and liberty. They were to become the slogan, battle cry, and excuse for an extraordinary movement in politics and lamentable excesses by mobs of men who could neither read, nor vote, nor much think.

The Treaty of Paris, signed in February, 1763, signaled a succession of events that was not to end for twenty years. The blood and treasure expended by Great Britain to acquire an empire, would now be spent on preserving it. How, the lords and ministers of the Crown knew not. Not yet. With the coming of peace, matters submerged by the pressures and exigencies of the Seven Years' War abruptly bobbed to the surface. In England, the recessional allowed the Crown's servants to ponder the vexingly delicate problem of how to pay for, govern, and profit from the empire. In the colonies, the hiatus permitted their more thoughtful and inquisitive subjects to more closely examine their relationship with the Crown and their true place in the empire.

Following soon in the *Roilance*'s wake were mail packets and merchantmen from the colonies bearing news of a dire event, an event as troubling as the news their captains, passengers, and crews read in the taverns and coffeehouses of Plymouth, Falmouth, Portsmouth, and Dover. The Treaty immediately birthed these events as overtures to everything else: an Indian uprising on the western frontiers, and a Crown rebellion against the

British constitution, aided and abetted by Parliament. The uprising, led by Ottawa chief Pontiac, served eventually to provide the Crown with some rationale for more tightly policing and more efficiently exploiting the colonies. The rebellion, sanctioned by First Lord of the Treasury George Grenville and Crown attorneys, prepared the government and Parliament for steps to be taken against fellow citizens, both at home and abroad. Englishmen suddenly found themselves assaulted by terrifying, painted, merciless savages on one hand, and by pale Oxford alumni and gentlemen lawyers on the Privy Council on the other, in both instances for the sake of upholding a status quo.

The Treaty obliged the French to leave North America, and their departure created a vacuum that was filled by the stern, unyielding policies of British Governor-General and commander-in-chief of North America Sir Jeffrey Amherst, Knight of the Bath. Unlike the French, Amherst refused to patronize the Indians. And when they struck, neither did he wish to employ the colonial militia to check them, for he despised colonial fighting prowess. The Indians, accustomed to being consulted by the generous French, and advised by their agents that the English victory would mean an end to their freedom to roam the forests and rivers at will, bridled at the unresponsiveness of the British. Pontiac persuaded several western tribes to make war on the settlers and British outposts. By May of 1763 every outpost had fallen to their attacks but Detroit and Fort Pitt, which were besieged. Settlers and soldiers alike were butchered indiscriminately, or captured and subjected to torture and grisly death. It was a blind, desperate strike against the new power, against a force which neither side fully comprehended, intended to thwart the inexorable progress of a vigorous culture as it advanced westward. It was doomed to fail, and did, three years later.

In London, the Treaty was the subject of provocative commentary in private conversation and in political publications, most notably *The North Briton*, founded in June of 1762 and entirely subsidized by an Opposition lord who, like the majority of London and Liverpool merchants, was angry with the surrender by Lord Bute's negotiators of Guadeloupe and other British conquests. *The North Briton* was begun as an answer to Tobias Smollet's *The Briton*, a weekly paper whose aim was to justify and explain Bute's policies. The scathing, immoderate attacks of *The North Briton* contributed to Bute's eventual downfall. Its principal editor and contributor, John Wilkes, member for Aylesbury, was a master of innuendo, insinuation, and circumlocution, and said in the paper what he dared not say from his seat in the Commons. He assailed not only the peace arranged by Lord Bute and John Russell, the Duke of Bedford, and the means by which that peace was arrived at and approved in the Commons, but Bute himself, his assumed intimate relationship with George the Third's mother, the Princess Dowager, and the motives and characters of anyone associated with the "court party."

One inviolable tradition of the status quo was never to take the sovereign to task for his policies, actions, or behavior. The king, after all, could do no wrong. Worse still was to suggest, no matter how tactfully, that the king was a liar, a fool, or the dupe of his ministers. In the eyes of the courts and the Act of Settlement, to flout this tradition was to invite the grave charge of seditious libel.

Having accomplished their purpose, which was Bute's resignation and the formation of a new administration under Grenville, Lord Temple — who was the new First Lord's younger brother — and Wilkes were about to cease publication of *The North Briton* when George the Third, in an address to Parliament, endorsed the terms of the Treaty. A few days later, in April, 1763, Number Forty-five of the paper opined, among other things, that

> ...*The Minister's speech of last Tuesday is not to be paralleled in the annals of this country. I am in doubt whether the imposition is greater on the Sovereign, or on the nation....*

Friends and enemies alike of Wilkes knew that the man in doubt was doubtless John Wilkes, who explained that "the King's Speech has always been considered as the speech of the Minister." By the standards of the day, this was as venomous a shot at the king as could be imagined. The "Minister" spoke for the king, by the king's leave. Ergo, to doubt the sincerity of the one's words was to sully the character of the other. Parliament regularly approved the king's addresses to that body, and composed humble counter-addresses of thanks to him. To have a member of that body subject the king to such criticism was intolerable, his subtle disclaimers notwithstanding.

Parliament had adjourned until November, but the offense could not be allowed to stand unnoticed and unpunished. Three days after the appearance of Number Forty-five, the Secretaries of State for the Northern and Southern Departments, Lords Egremont and Halifax, jointly signed a general warrant for the "arrest of the authors, printers, and publishers of a seditious and treasonable paper," *The North Briton*. No one person was named in the warrant, nor was the specific act of sedition or treason described or identified. The Crown simply wanted to lay hands on Wilkes, then decide at its leisure which charges and action could be credibly and lawfully brought against him that would still his infuriating pen.

By the time Hugh Kenrick arrived in England, the initial round of the conflict was over. Wilkes was arrested, interrogated by the Secretaries of State, and committed to the Tower — but not before the king's messengers succumbed to his charm and inadvertently allowed him to destroy the original manuscript of Number Forty-five, and therewith evidence of his authorship of it. He later secured a writ of *habeas corpus* from Chief Justice Charles Pratt in the Court of Common Pleas, and after two appearances in that court at Westminster Hall was released by Pratt and other judges who upheld his privileged, protected status as a member of the Commons. Wilkes's attorney had also claimed wrongful commitment to the Tower and questioned the legality of the general warrant, but these arguments were dismissed. That summer, the triumphant Wilkes and the arrested printers filed suits for damages against the Secretaries of State and the Treasury's solicitor.

Forgotten by nearly all in the legal and political pandemonium that extraordinary spring and summer was the Treaty of Paris.

* * *

"John Wilkes?" asked Hugh. He turned to his father. "You mentioned him briefly in one of your last letters. What has he done?"

Garnet Kenrick chuckled. "What hasn't he done?" The Baron searched through some papers on his desk and pulled out a newspaper, then handed it to his son over the desk. It was a copy of *The North Briton*, Number Forty-five.

Hugh returned to his chair and read the opening paragraphs on the front sheet of the multipage broadside. He grimaced in doubt, then frowned. He said to Jones, "This is a lesser transgression than what the Pippins were charged with and tried for, Mr. Jones. It is subtle and cutting, to be sure, but I fail to see why the king would take so much offense at it."

Jones shrugged. "All true, milord. But the difference is that he is in the Commons, while the Pippins were not. Fundamentally, though, the circumstances do not differ. As the persecution of the Society of the Pippin was a premeditated, arranged affair, achieved in concert with the King's Bench, so was this action. The government have been wanting to silence him for over a year, ever since Lord Bute's accession to the throne — if you will allow me the libel."

"In my home, it is allowed," remarked Garnet Kenrick with a smile.

Hugh put the paper back on his father's desk. "And what has happened to Mr. Wilkes?"

The Baron and the barrister took turns retelling each episode of the sequence of events.

When they were finished, Hugh asked, "And the affair is past?"

"Oh, no, milord," said Jones, with a shake of the head. "They have not done with him, not by a whim. Certainly the House will make Mr. Wilkes one of the first orders of the day when it reconvenes in November. His words will be taken down, and if he wishes to remain a member, the House will require him to beg its pardon — on his knees, no less. Not only did he tweak the king's nose with relative impunity, but very likely he will win his suit against Egremont and Halifax. He cannot be allowed the satisfaction of victory. It would embolden others to emulate him and essay their own breaches of the royal peace. Half a dozen members are eager to make him a premier order of business."

"Had he no champions in the Opposition?"

Garnet Kenrick shrugged, then sighed. "The man is disliked by his allies," he said. "Mr. Pitt, Lord Rockingham, even Lord Temple, were reluctant to defend him publicly. It was Temple who subsidized the paper, and who has parted ways with his brother, Grenville — much as your uncle and I have parted ways. One irony among others is that it was Grenville who helped to promote Mr. Wilkes's career and material gains, not to mention arranged his candidacy for Aylesbury with Mr. Pitt — who, incidentally, is Grenville's brother-in-law."

"I have met this squinting, cross-eyed wretch, milord," said Jones. "I paid him a call when he was committed to the Tower. He is the most odious rallying point for liberty one could have the misfortune to encounter. But for his attire, manners, and ready wit, you would take him for a career beggar, or a mad creature released on bad advice from the confines of Bedlam Hospital. He inveigled his way into the profitable acquaintanceship of his patrons, married his money, and more or less purchased his seat for Aylesbury for some seven thousand pounds from that borough's householders. His dissolute past is legend. Poets and men of letters are as much dazzled by his company as are ladies of commerce, some of whom were present in his well-appointed cell when I called. He can revel in any society. I can imagine him seducing the intellects of the likes of Dr. Johnson and that exalted gossip, Horace Walpole. He is ambitious and capable, and has a certain appeal to the working populace. I have heard that he is planning to publish all forty-five numbers of *The North Briton* in a single volume, in addition to some questionable parody of Mr. Pope's *Essay on Man*, together with other scurvy prose." Jones waved a hand once. "But — he is in the right. I would not choose him for constant company, but I admire his audacity." He paused. "Mr. Pitt and other cold friends of Mr. Wilkes? Well, it is easy to champion a virtuous hero, but much less so a grasping, disreputable rogue. It so happens, however, that it is a rogue who has done a hero's feat, which in this case is to say what needed to be said in the face of certain official reprisal."

Hugh asked, "Do you think he will apologize to the House?"

"No," said Jones without hesitation. "In which case, the House most certainly will vote to censure him in some way. Failing that, perhaps the ministerial party among the members will conjure up some other means of ridding their pristine persons of his presence. More likely, though, Mr. Wilkes will hand them the means with the collected *North Briton*. He is determined to speak freely without fear of recrimination. Rogue or hero, that is what every man ought to strive for as an unassailable liberty. That is why I say they are not done with him."

Hugh smiled, and glanced from Jones to his father and back again. He shook his head once and laughed. "I cannot explain it, but you two seem to complement each other. Your association pleases me more than I can say."

The two older men laughed in appreciation and gratitude.

Just then, Alice, fourteen years old, burst into the study to announce dinner. She was a pretty, sandy-haired girl, vivacious and gracile. It also pleased Hugh that she had not forgotten him, and their reunion yesterday afternoon had been as happy as that of the parents and son. In a spontaneous display of affection, she wrapped her arms around Hugh's neck and kissed him on the cheek, then conferred the same feeling for her father, and finally, to Hugh's bemused shock, for Dogmael Jones, whom she addressed as "Uncle."

Chapter 20: The Member for Swansditch

"Sir Dogmael and I struck up a long and fruitful correspondence after your departure, Hugh," Garnet Kenrick said from the head of the dinner table. "Very soon we found that we agreed on so many matters that we felt we should meet. He became a regular guest at Milgram House, and now here at Cricklegate. We enjoy his company, and he ours. I did not know that a lawyer could be so likable."

Jones chuckled as he passed a plate of beef to Effney Kenrick. "And I did not know that a baron's company could be so agreeable."

"All in all," continued the Baron, "our friendship — and it is that as much as it is an alliance — was propinquitous. At about the time that we were both expressing concern over the heat generated by Mr. Wilkes's statements, Mr. Ingoldsby went to his final reward. Mr. Worley informed me of it, and I instantly tendered Mr. Jones the idea of his replacing him, provided I moved quickly enough to purchase the seat. He had in the past alluded to a wish to enter politics. However, he lacked the means and the friends who could put him up. I had the means, and a qualified wish to be heard, but lacked both the skill to speak on my feet and the desire to address so many heads. Also, until then, there were no boroughs open to purchase. Your uncle retains control of Onyxcombe and Mr. Hillier. And there you are: Swansditch."

Jones leaned forward and remarked to Hugh across the table, "Your father often addresses and refers to me as 'Mr. Jones.' It is out of respect for my knighthood. That way, you see, he secures two friends in the guise of one."

Everyone at the table laughed, including Alice. Garnet Kenrick waved a fork at the barrister. "There, Hugh, is the reason I want him to speak for us in the Commons. There are few men who could match his quick oratory."

Hugh studied the barrister for a moment. "Aside from Mr. Wilkes, sir, why do you wish to sit in the Commons?"

"I have many reasons, milord," answered Jones. "First, I wish to see the debates — which in the past I was obliged to pay a crown to audit from the gallery — reported to the public. The public have a right to know what is said and by whom, since it is their pockets and how they may be best emptied that are the subjects of so many debates. Further, I for one am tired of second-guessing the coy, allusive reportage that appears in our newspapers. It is an ancient complaint, mine. Both Houses wish to keep their proceedings sunk in the murky waters of privilege, tradition, and unaccountability. Half my career in the courts has consisted of defending printers and writers who dare drain that swamp of secrecy, or who at least part the cloak of scum floating on top to see what lies beneath. Beginning with the next session, I intend to raise the matter as often as I can entice an ally to second the motion. I fully expect my motion to be ignored or opposed. But I shall persist. I shall bedevil them."

The barrister paused to take a sip of wine. "Then, I wish to push for a change in the statutes, so that every man may say that the king can do wrong, without risking persecution with general warrants, without fear of suits for libel for having made an honest or truthful observation, without provoking a summons to attend the Commons or Lords to be excoriated, humiliated, or bullied. And, I shall speak against general warrants and attainders, those legal pistols of royal and ministerial scamps." Jones returned Hugh's attentive study of him. "Mr. Wilkes is the wedge with which our privileged burglars may apply the rum lay and crack open the door to our liberties. From him, they may progress up the ladder of honor and repute, until they can prosecute and harry a man of the highest virtue, and call him criminal with impunity. I am certain you see the relevance, milord. If this is what the ministers and Parliament are wont to do to one of their own, what might they be moved to commit on the rest of the nation, or even on the colonies, in the name of an unbreached peace and national tranquility? Your father and I agree on this, as well, that the whole *North Briton* affair portends an assault on English liberties no less bellicose than if a Stuart proposed to exercise his scepter, or his messenger his mace, on our backs and heads!"

"Bravo!" exclaimed Effney Kenrick.

Her husband said quietly, "Hear, hear!" and raised his glass in salute to the barrister.

Hugh smiled at them. "You will honor the House with such sentiments, sir, and rouse it to action with your passion."

Jones nodded once in acknowledgment. "Thank you, milord." He chuckled once, then added, "Let us hope that the action is not a call to have a general warrant served on me." He paused to smile in the expression of a solemn penance. "It is only justice that, having failed to secure the acquittal of your friends the Pippins, I become one myself."

"You honor their memory with such dedication, sir," said Hugh. He glanced at his father, and indicated Jones with a movement of his head. "It was well worth the voyage home, if only to hear this man speak."

"I expected you to say that, Hugh, sooner or later, knowing the importance you place on well-strung words."

The table was quiet for a while, except for the sounds of silverware on porcelain plates and the soft ringing of glass. Then Hugh asked the barrister, "How do you find the Commons, Mr. Jones?"

Jones dabbed his mouth with his napkin and shrugged. "I took my seat near the end of the last session, I confess not without some trepidation. You know that I am not easily cowed. My anxiety was based, not on shyness, but on fear of what I should find. I called attention neither to my positions nor to myself. My purpose was to take stock of my future arena of combat. As I grew more familiar with the rules and runagates of that cyclopean raree show, my anxiety waxed to contempt. Now, there are nearly six hundred members in the Commons — and thank God for lassitude that only half that number deign to attend on a regular basis, for otherwise we should all suffocate in that chamber, or crush ourselves to death, in a repetition of the Black Hole in Calcutta! Well, perhaps a tiny fraction of that body can grasp reason, and require only plain common sense garbed in the raiment of eloquence.

"Most of the others are Calibans who require merely harmonious sounds strung together, peppered here with an ounce of anger, and spiced there with a humorous quip, to hold their attention, whether or not a speaker conveys any meaning." Jones paused to smile with mischief. "I crib liberally from that lancet of rhetoric, Earl Chesterfield, whom I chanced to overhear one evening discoursing on the same subject to his company at Ranelagh, in the next private compartment."

Jones paused to take a sip of wine, then continued. "As to individual members, most of them, upon being engaged in conversation, succumb to the vanity of importance and will emit an aura of influence, and pose as persons intimately connected to the pilots of policy. They will tell you, whether or not you have ventured the least curiosity, that they regret they are not at liberty to divulge any information on the question before the House, or to violate the confidence of their ghostly compatriots. They would have you believe that they know something about what is to happen, when in fact they are as ignorant as you are of the intentions, ploys, and purposes of the pilots. As their own noggins are swayed by tricked-up folderol, they assume that you, too, swoon before airy influence, or are a rival vessel of awful intrigue."

Jones sighed and shook his head. "Nevertheless, when I am called on to speak, all my persuasion shall shine silver. I shall stand and face the clock on the gallery above the Chair, and with half-closed eyes, imagine that I am addressing an assembly of Solons."

"As a paladin of liberty," said the Baron, smiling with pride at the barrister, "as the new Fierabras, undaunted by the number of his foes, unbaptized by the perjurious deceit of Crown sinecures, towering over the heads of the trolls of complacency and circuitous virtue!"

Jones laughed. "I have yet to make my maiden speech, milord," he said. "I beg you to wait until I have had an opportunity to wield my cane in the House and have earned that appellation. But, I thank you for the encouragement." Then he added wryly, "And you claim an absence of eloquence! Do not blame me if I cadge your table talk."

"'A paladin of liberty,'" mused Hugh, glancing from his father to Jones. "I like that. I have every confidence that you will earn the title, sir." He paused. "Tell me, though: Have you solved the riddle of public places?" he asked, referring to their first meeting at Serjeants' Inn years ago.

Jones shook his head. "I should have expected that you would not forget that, milord," he said. "No, not quite. I am taking notes for a book on that aspect of property and law. And I am certain I will contradict some of Mr. Blackstone's meditations on property and speech. His Toryism at times skews his honesty and objectivity."

Hugh remembered the list of things he was asked to find and take back to Caxton. "Blackstone! Yes! You must help me find a digest of the constitution, sir. Has he published anything of his Oxford lectures?"

"Yes, milord. *An Analysis of the Laws of England.* It is addressed to students. But, I have heard that he is compiling an elaborate commentary on the laws." Jones paused with a sour frown. "Mr. Blackstone is a member for Hindon, and has been made solicitor-general to Queen Charlotte."

"Then I must find several copies of his *Analysis* for friends in Virginia." Hugh went on to describe his friends in Caxton and their interest in the constitution.

The company listened with fascination to his description of Jack Frake, John Proudlocks, and other men who were his neighbors. At length, Jones remarked, "They are wise to want to know more about the intricacies of the laws, milord. They may have reason, some day, to adopt and amend them — as their own."

The dinner talk progressed, over coffee and cake smothered in marmalade of orange, from law to another current controversy, which was the dubious authenticity of *Fingal*, a collection of Scottish epic poetry by the third-century warrior Ossian, published earlier in the year by a scholar, James Macpherson. The prose was generally thought to be a hoax by many critics and other scholars, who suspected that Macpherson was the true author.

Jones said, with a shrug of dismissal, "If this barbarian Conan and his chronicler Ossian actually existed, then some mention of them would have been made by one ancient historian or another. But I have not encountered these names in any of the standard Roman accounts of the conquest of this island."

Hugh asked, "Why would a person invest so much labor to perpetrate a literary fraud?"

"To give himself and his ancestors a glorious past, himself alone a fellowless reputation among scholars, and a princely income. But Mr. Macpherson's crime is not fundamentally dissimilar from the fanciful cogitations I hear voiced in the clubs and taverns that neighbor Westminster Yard. There are many in Parliament who wish that body to rule the colonies in the stead and name of the king." The barrister paused, then added, "Not that the colonies would fare much better from His Majesty's gentle ministrations."

"Have you met Sir Henoch Pannell?" Hugh remembered encountering the member for Canovan in the Yard, and listening to his speech in the Commons.

Jones scoffed and nodded. "That one? Oh, yes. I have met him. He is noted for his Parthian shots, or barbs flung over his shoulder as he departs the scene of verbal combat."

*   *   *

The days and weeks passed for Hugh with a kind of luxuriant, unhurried ease. He spent much of the time with his parents and sister, on excursions by boat up the Thames to Hampton Court, during evenings at Ranelagh Gardens just a short carriage ride down the Thames from Chelsea, and in the warm, landscaped garden of Cricklegate. Often he went to London with his father to see Mr. Worley at Lion Key on business, and to the bank of Formby, Pursehouse & Swire, in which the Baron was a major partner, and to the Royal Exchange to meet with other merchants and traders. There were concerts, and theater, and art galleries to attend, and bookstores and print shops to scour for volumes and pictures to take back to Virginia.

"Have you heard from Reverdy?" his mother asked him as they strolled together along Cheyne Walk one afternoon late in June.

"No," Hugh said. "Not since her last letter. Have you?"

"No. The Brunes and we no longer exchange visits. And we were strangers to the McDougals."

Hugh felt his mother's probing scrutiny, and looked down at her. "It is past, Mother. Do not concern yourself."

"Do you...think of her?"

"At times," Hugh said. "Almost as often as I think of the moon. Her decision no longer pains me. If that was the depth of her courage, we could not have long endured each other. I have accepted that."

Effney Kenrick's hand was linked to her son's arm, which she squeezed once in relieved affirmation. "Have you met any ladies in Caxton?"

"Many," Hugh said. "But the only one who stands out is the daughter of a Scottish trader. She is a lovely girl. She plays the harp. Spoken for, though, by my friend, Jack. I must find some fresh music for her."

"We exchange visits with the Tallmadges," said the Baroness, "when we are in Danvers and they are here. I suppose you know that Roger's regiment was reduced, and he is on home service now."

"Yes, as an instructor of mathematics at Woolwich for the engineers and artillery officers." Woolwich was the Royal Military Academy, far down river near Deptford. "Would you mind it much if I went down and spent a few days with him? He is a fully commissioned lieutenant now, but there is a chance he may be appointed secretary to a diplomatic mission to Copenhagen next month."

Effney Kenrick laughed. "I would mind it very much, Hugh, and so would your father, but at least you won't be a thousand leagues away."

After a while, Hugh asked, "Has there been any word of poor Hulton? The last I heard from him, his regiment was being sent to the Isle of Wight for marshalling."

"No," sighed his mother. "I am afraid he has quite vanished on us."

On another day, Hugh and his father went on horseback on an excursion to Wandsworth, "to see Mr. Jones's indifferent pasturage," explained the Baron. From Chelsea they rode to the toll bridge at the villages of Fulham and Pultney, then east through the countryside. On both their saddles were holsters with pistols loaded with double-shot. There had been a rash of robberies by highwaymen of travelers in the area. On the way, they talked of politics, of Dogmael Jones, of the family, of the goods brought in by the family-owned merchantmen the *Busy*, the *Nimble*, and the *Ariadne*. And of Basil Kenrick, the Earl of Danvers, Garnet Kenrick's brother.

"How does he feel about your seat in the Commons?" Hugh asked his father.

Garnet Kenrick rolled his shoulders. "Frankly, Hugh, I don't know. We do not communicate much any more on family or any other matters, except when I send him copies of the accounts and the monies owed him from the estate. I don't know who feeds his malice more: You, or I for having put you out of his reach."

"It troubles me that any man could nurture hatred for so long a time."

"I have the sense now that his malice has lost even a particular object. Your uncle has become merely a nasty, malicious man. I am as glad as you must be to be away from him."

They rode on in silence for a while. When they neared the little collection of farmhouses that was the "seat" of Dogmael Jones's pasturage, Garnet Kenrick cleared his throat and said, "Not many winters ago, Hugh, in Danvers, you told me that you wanted to be something." The Baron paused to smile at the look of astonishment on his son's face. "No, I have not forgotten that day, not that one, nor many others. Well, you have become something, as surely as if God had fashioned you with his own hands. But — the hands were your own. When you first arrived last month, and I saw you standing in the foyer, I saw, not just my son, but a planter, and a full man, and the future — a future so thrilling and inevitable that I am reluctant to imagine it." He chuckled to himself. "I believe I told you that you were going to be a baron, and then an earl. But even then, I knew that my answer was not enough, that it was poor consolation to you, and I galloped away from the knowledge, quite certain that you were right."

After a moment, Hugh looked at his father. "You should not worry, Father. I will not stop loving you and Mother. You will not lose me."

Garnet Kenrick nodded in acknowledgment, and then looked away. "In all your letters to me and your mother, I sensed an air of liberty, one that you could not have discovered and enjoyed here, for all the advantages of your station. That is why I will say now that *you* are the chief reason I have ventured into politics. To protect you, to speak in your name through Mr. Jones, to somehow introduce here what you have known there, in Virginia. For myself, it is both a means of atonement for the neglect I am guilty of, and a means of asserting myself."

Hugh shook his head in genuine bewilderment. "I cannot think of anything for which you should atone, Father, least of all neglect. The notion is absurd."

The Baron cleared his throat again. "Not so absurd, Hugh. Much of our fortune in the past came from illicit trade. There was a smuggling gang in Dorset known as the Lobster Pots. I had close connections with them for years, long before you were born. Your mother does not even know of them. The *Busy* and the *Nimble* for years dealt with them. Your education and time in London were largely paid for with the proceeds from that furtive association."

"I see." Hugh studied his father for a moment, then looked away. After a while, he shrugged. "Well, many of the most prosperous merchants in the colonies have a hand in smuggling. As well as many merchants here. If it were not for the navigation laws and taxes and regulations, they would trade openly. They would prefer to." He paused. "Mr. Talbot keeps separate account books for that trade. So do many of his colleagues, up and down the seaboard, in all the colonies."

"I know," confessed the Baron. "But, we profited from injustice, Hugh. No more, though. At about the time I became a partner in the bank, I broke our association with the Lobster Pots." He glanced at his son with a new wonder. "I had expected you to be offended by the knowledge."

"I am not," Hugh said. "I have observed that such a gross injustice can sire two kinds of cunning: insensible or pragmatic, and rebellious or defiant. In time, however, if the injustice continues, they must ultimately oppose each other. Or, the rebellious and defiant become corrupted and wish the injustice to be perpetuated."

The Baron shook his head. "Please, Hugh, do not make any distinctions for my sake. Although your uncle and I may be counted in the first instance."

Hugh was quiet for a while. Then he said, "But, I must make a distinction, sir. I see now that *I* am not the sole reason why relations between you and Uncle Basil have become so evil. You are a good man, and I am proud to claim you as a father. Do not deny it. You would offend me with a contrary pretence."

Garnet Kenrick fell back behind his son, slowing his mount a little with the reins. He did not wish his son to see the emotion on his face. He said, after they had ridden some distance, "One reason why I sent you away, Hugh, was that your uncle threatened to inform you of the Lobster Pots."

Hugh turned and faced his father with a challenging smile. "If you are ever of a mind to enter that business again, Father, write me in Caxton, and together we shall defy both him and the Crown."

While a great burden was lifted from Garnet Kenrick's mind, his son's words caused him a tinge of sadness, for in them was a hint of the future he was reluctant to contemplate. And, the notion flitted through his mind that it was his son's character and welfare that had redeemed him.

*   *   *

Once the novelty of his homecoming had passed, Hugh could not resist the temptation to revisit his old haunts. He journeyed to London alone, and wandered through the city he knew so well and missed. On the Strand, the Ram's Head Tavern had replaced the Fruit Wench. He went inside and back to the partitioned private room where the Society of the Pippin had held its meetings. On Quiller Alley, under the shadow of St. Paul's Cathedral, he stood across the street and gazed up at the garret atop the tenement where Glorious Swain had lived. He strode through Charing Cross, past the equestrian statue of Charles the First, and by the pillory, now vacant, on which he had defied a mob and Glorious Swain had died. He walked to Windridge Court, and saw by the busyness of the stable hands and coachmen in the courtyard that his uncle the Earl was in residence.

On his way back to the Strand, he encountered Alden Curle, once his uncle's valet and now the *major domo* of Windridge Court and the family seat in Danvers, returning from an errand. The man did not recognize him and rudely brushed by him.

Hugh turned and tapped him once on the shoulder with his cane. Curle stopped to face him with an indignant, superior expression. Hugh said, "I have not forgotten your role in Mr. Hulton's dismissal, Mr. Curle."

The servant gasped and stared at him in growing, stupid recognition. He attempted to reply, but could only sputter unfinished words. The parcel he carried, something bulky wrapped in paper and string, slipped from his hand to the ground with a muted shatter of glass or porcelain. Curle's glance darted down and he gasped again.

Hugh asked, "How is my uncle, Mr. Curle?"

The man blinked once and managed to stammer, "He is...fine... milord." He glanced again at the parcel that lay at his feet, then back up at Hugh. "May...I inform his lordship that you enquired after his health...?" he asked tentatively.

"You may, at the risk of your own," Hugh said. He studied the frightened, trembling man for a moment, then abruptly frowned, turned, and walked away. Although he felt nothing but contempt for the man, he suddenly realized that Curle was no longer worthy of any expression of that appraisal.

One afternoon he went to the city with letters he had written to Jack Frake, Etáin McRae, and Thomas Reisdale to give to Mr. Worley to put on the first colonial vessel to clear the Pool of London, then walked to Serjeants' Inn to meet with Dogmael Jones. They talked politics and law over dinner, and then Jones took him to the reading room in the Middle Temple where the Pippins were tried years ago.

Jones raised his silver-tipped cane and swept it in a gesture to the chamber. "The place has a special significance for me, milord," he said. "Here is where your friends were condemned to their fates, where I met my worst defeat, and where I began to follow a course that led me, ultimately, to a seat in the Commons." He faced Hugh. "I might have followed another course and fruitlessly quenched my anger and despair in bottled spirits of progressively cheaper quality, but for a brief visit by you. For that little obtrusion, I am both grateful and in your debt."

Hugh smiled at the barrister. "You may call me *sir*, or *mister*, Mr. Jones."

Jones nodded in acknowledgment.

They spent the rest of the day visiting bookshops. Hugh found several copies of Blackstone's *Analysis of the Laws of England*, while Jones recommended other learned disquisitions on the law and government by Samuel Puffendorf, Hugo Grotius, Robert Molesworth, and Emeric de Vattal. "The literature of liberty is vast, Mr. Kenrick," remarked Jones as they carried Hugh's purchases in a hackney to Lion Key and Mr. Worley's warehouse, "as you undoubtedly know. Some of it is tedious, some of it is wrong-headed, and much of it peg-legged by its premises. But when it is right, it is glorious." Hugh put his purchases in a special crate that Benjamin Worley had set aside for things his former protégé was taking back to Virginia with him. "When the Crown runs out its entire array of legal guns against Wilkes or a Pippin, the gun ports of liberty should snap open in answer, one after another, to reveal the primed barrels of Mr. Locke, Mr. Sidney, Mr. Harrington, and that whole potent armament of enlightenment. The order of fire should be commanded by a master gunner, such as Sir Charles Pratt — he has not had a last word on the matter of general warrants — and the vessel captained by Aristotle."

Hugh laughed. "I wish I could be in the gallery of the Commons when you make your maiden speech, Mr. Jones."

"I will send you transcripts of all my perorations."

That evening the pair went to the Mitre Tavern for a light supper. The place reminded Hugh of the Fruit Wench. It consisted of a large front room with many tables and the bar, and a number of partitioned "rooms" in the rear that were occupied by private parties. "I come here often," said Jones as he lit a pipe. "The patrons are a more homogenous and convivial sort, given to weightier conversation than the raucous commentary on the mundane and grosser aspects of life that one usually encounters in most other establishments. However, I do not as a rule participate in such conversation. I merely enjoy its proximity, of being in the company of men who bring some spark to their speculations. It reassures me that I dwell in a society not completely dominated by dolts, priests, and politicians."

They sat at a table next to one of the partitioned sections, more to be able to hear each other speak in the hubbub than from fear of being overheard. Jones regaled his companion with anecdotes about the Commons. His remarks were humorous and condemnatory at the same time. Hugh felt invigorated by the man's vitality and outspokenness. At one point in their conversation, the barrister declaimed against a schedule of things he would work for the repeal of, ending with the king's civil list and secret service fund. "Nothing more encourages the preservation of a tepid, suffocating status quo than rewarding members for having helped perpetuate it. A vested and stubbornly inert personal interest is then acquired by them in such genteel corruption. They come to regard this lawful subornation as practical wisdom and entitling propriety."

Hugh shook his head, not in denial of Jones's points, but in frustration. "But, sir, do you truly believe that a corrupt Parliament can be a vehicle of reform for liberty? That body must first be thoroughly purged. Its members must be put above bribery by the government, private interests, and by those for whom oppression and slavery are ideal states of polity. It must be reformed to eschew all purposes but that of preserving liberty. The Commons, and even Lords, while they no longer are the servants of the Crown, instead must be bribed to accomplish the same *quid pro quo*. By your own account, many stalwart members of the Opposition regularly cross the floor upon being granted places by their enemies in the government."

Jones frowned in thought, then cocked his head once in concession. "It is a harsh conundrum that you pose, sir, and I have not the answer to it. It must be solved by a sage, or by general disgust. My own disgust has not yet made me sagacious enough to solve it."

They were aware of a lively discussion taking place in the private room beyond the thin partition. At that moment, a voice in that quarter bellowed loudly and distinctly enough for them to hear, "...If the abuse be enormous, nature will rise up, and claiming her original rights, overturn a corrupt political system!"

Both Hugh and Jones were startled by the words. Hugh remarked, "You were right about this place, Mr. Jones. I have not heard that sentiment even in Virginia."

Jones chuckled and asked, "Overturn? Or sever all ties to it?" He shook his head. "I recognize that voice. It is Dr. Johnson's. He and his friends come here oftener than do I. I have gained a greater understanding of my enemies by discreetly auditing his numerous and disjunctive pearls of thought, from this very table."

"He spoke a truth, though," remarked Hugh.

"So he did," said Jones, "about that, and many other matters. But for how long will his pension permit him to speak his own mind, to proclaim errors of his own judgment, as well as truths?"

Chapter 21: The Voyage Home

Like any holiday crammed with endless leisure and cherished company, Hugh's stay in England passed with a swiftness that caught him by surprise in late August. As September came nearer, his parents and sister began to regard him with expectant, wistful longing. With an odd melancholy of reluctance and anticipation, he found himself making brief, conscientious preparations for his voyage back to Virginia. He regretted neither having come, nor having to leave.

His only true disappointment was having to settle for a single afternoon with his friend, Roger Tallmadge, before the younger man departed the next day with a commercial envoy to Denmark, "to discuss the levies on our goods taken there, and other matters," explained the lieutenant, "among them, the price of Baltic timber that Danish brokers sell to our Navy. The Admiralty think their fees are too high. As his secretary, I shall aid Mr. Everett in drafting reports of his negotiations to their lordships. A fine irony it is," he remarked as they strolled along a path, "that an Army officer should be selected to assist an emissary of the Navy in his spelling and pointing."

Lieutenant Roger Tallmadge conducted Hugh on a tour of the Woolwich artillery park and the practice range where gunnery officers, under his watchful and impartial eye, applied what they learned from classroom lectures.

Hugh chuckled and said, "Irony or no, Roger, you have done well for yourself. I would never have imagined it, but a military life seems to agree with you. You look splendid. Now we are both something."

Roger grinned and stopped in his tracks. He bowed in acknowledgment of the compliment. Today, in honor of his guest, he was in the full dress uniform of a junior officer of the Grenadier Guards, from which he was detached to be an instructor at the Academy. The silver epaulettes on his scarlet coat flashed in the sun, as did the silver gorget at his throat. An immaculate red sash divided his spotless white breeches and waistcoat, and the black, polished, knee-length gaiters made him look taller. One hand rested on the pommel of the sword at his side; the other reached up and briefly doffed a silver-traced tricorn in a personal salute. "To hear those words from you, sir, means more to me than you might imagine — *elder brother*."

His friend's last words startled Hugh, and caused him to remember the man to whom he had addressed the same words, on a pillory at Charing Cross, long ago, followed by an almost effortless recollection of the comradely badinage between him and Roger as boys in Danvers, when he had granted Roger the privilege of being his younger brother. The associations startled him, and pleased him. He smiled and inclined his head.

They walked on. "Well," Hugh said, "you *do* look splendid. I'll wager you attract the attentions of many worthy ladies."

Roger laughed. "And many more *unworthy*," he said. "Whether in a tavern or a ballroom, if one is not trying to cadge a shilling from me for her rent, another is trying to wheedle me out of my half-pay for the price of a Fleet marriage, and I'm certain you know the ignominious fate of those intemperate unions." He paused to sigh. "Women can be so…mercenary, I needn't tell you. I sometimes believe that they are more predatory than are men."

Hugh glanced at Roger. His friend had campaigned with the British army that was attached to Prince Ferdinand, and had seen action at Bergen, Warburg, and Minden, yet he saw no scars on him. His words, however, were evidence of another kind of wound. "Who was she?" asked Hugh.

Roger's mouth creased in bitterness and he shook his head. "No one you knew, Hugh. I will spare you the details. I am trying to forget them myself." This time, he glanced at Hugh. "Do you hear from Reverdy?"

Hugh shook his head in turn. "No. Nor she from me."

"I see her now and then, when we both happen to be visiting our families in Danvers. I do not speak to her. I cannot forgive her for her treatment of you."

Hugh's reply was brief but brittle. "Do not trouble yourself about it, Roger," he said. "I don't." And then his anger was gone.

Roger led him to the end of a line of cannon. The range was empty and quiet, except for the sound of crickets and faraway crows. "I make my 'cadets' form their own crews, so that they can know what to expect from the crews they will command," he said. "Most of these officers resent that, at first, but I have received letters of appreciation from some." He nodded with pride to another of his innovations, a line of "straw men" in the distance that represented an enemy formation. "I had a deuced time persuading the school to put that up," he explained, "and of convincing them of my reasoning. The purpose of artillery being, chiefly, to prompt opposing troops to abandon their ranks and so skew a formation, and thus thwart a commanding officer's tactics, intentions, and effective fire, I introduced the notion of scoring against an officer in training for smashing a bundle of straw, and in his favor for dropping a cannon ball in front of it and missing. Knocking a man down is the task of the firelock, that of a field gun of instilling in him the frightening prospect of being rearranged beyond the arts of surgery. A musket ball, at least, can be removed from him, provided it does not cause instant or certain death. A six- or eight-pound ball, however, will simply remove the man, and perhaps the man behind him, and continue on its terrifying way until its force is spent. And, firing a cannon ball expends almost as much powder as a regimental volley. But, every soldier knows the terror of a cannon ball, and fears the thing, and acts accordingly, whether he is English, French, Austrian, or Prussian. He will dart from the path of a bounding, hurtling orb of iron, no matter how many lashes on his bare back his sergeant has promised if he breaks ranks." Roger swept a finger over the long, distant row of straw men. "One day, though, some fiendish mind will perfect the fuse and fashion exploding cannon balls, and that will be the end of infantry tactics, and even fortifications, at least as we know them. And, I fear that our army will be the last to appreciate that advance."

Hugh studied his friend with admiration. The boy who had needed his protection and guidance was now a mature man, self-confident, certain of his capabilities and worth, and unafraid. Hugh was unaccountably proud of the way Roger had turned out. He said, "If you ever tire of the Army, Roger — or, if it tires of you — see my father. You might find the merchant's business interesting. Mr. Worley would welcome the help. Then, there is Swire's bank. I am sure that if you can calculate the arcs and distances of flying eight-pound balls, you can master interest rates and percentiles. I'll speak with my father about it before I leave."

"Thank you, Hugh," said Roger. "I don't expect either party to tire of the other, not in the foreseeable future, at least. But, I will keep your suggestions in mind." He paused, then grinned. "Still the elder brother, looking out for me?"

Hugh laughed, and shrugged. "If you were a spendthrift, or one of those presumptuous fops I saw at the school back there who are your brother officers, no, I would have disowned you. But, I still feel like a brother to you, though I confess I also feel somewhat helpless, because I can no longer tell you what to do."

Roger touched his friend's arm, and with the gesture added, "And, I can now load and fire six volleys in a minute."

The officer checked two mounts from the Woolwich stables, and the men rode down to Greenwich for supper in a tavern. "At dusk, we must part," said Roger as they followed the road. "I must finish stuffing my kit this evening, and see to some school business. Tomorrow I take a packet to Great Yarmouth to await Mr. Everett and his party. From there, we sail to Copenhagen. I was informed that the mission will last perhaps three months. And you?"

"I will depart later this month, or early next, on the first vessel available. I hope to be in Virginia by late October." Hugh paused. "Three months, versus the three years we may not meet again."

"Who knows?" said Roger. "When my secretary's task is completed, I will be asked to continue on at Woolwich. In the meantime, I could enquire about a posting to the colonies."

Over their supper in Greenwich, they talked of their pasts, presents, and futures. And when they had made their final toasts to each other with glasses of ale, they rode back to Woolwich in the dusk. Hugh reclaimed his own mount from the stables, and leaned from the saddle to shake his friend's hand. "Be well, Roger," he said. "Write to me about Copenhagen and your duties there. Perhaps you will find a Danish beauty, and bring her back as a bride."

Roger touched his hat in another salute. "Calm seas, Hugh, and a prosperous voyage. Be sure to write, so I'll know that you're safely home. Send your letters to my parents in Danvers. They will ensure that I get them, wherever the Army next posts me."

With a touch of his own hat, Hugh pulled on the reins to turn his mount around, then trotted away. When he reached the Thames again near Greenwich, he turned west for the ferry that would take him back across the river.

*　　*　　*

Emery Westcott, the portrait artist commissioned years ago by the Kenricks to do the entire family, was brought in again to render Hugh for his parents. Hugh reciprocated by commissioning him to paint a group of his parents, sister, and principal servants in a domestic tableau. "The walls of my supper room are quite bare," he told his mother. "Mr. Westcott's skills will allow me to be with you and this household every evening. Besides," he added in a mock confidential tone, "this picture will also allow me to show you off to my friends."

Effney Kenrick smiled a sad smile. "I'm so happy that you have friends there, Hugh."

"Friends I have, Mother, and they are as close and fiery as Mr. Jones."

Westcott completed both his tasks a week before Hugh was to leave for the Pool of London to await the clearance of a colonies-bound merchantman.

And when the week was past, the whole family rode to Mr. Worley's offices at Lion Key. The agent had found Hugh a cabin on the family's own *Busy*, which sat at anchor and in moorings at the Key and would be piloted back down the Thames the next morning.

The farewells were as emotional and wrenching as they were on the Weymouth dock five years earlier. Alice sobbed, Effney Kenrick cried, and the Baron managed to be nervously stolid. But this time they were able to board the vessel and see Hugh's cabin, his home for perhaps the next two months, and the family was together until the early evening. The captain of the *Busy*, Thomas Rowland, had them in his own quarters for supper.

Hugh accompanied his family back down the gang-board to the Key wharf. Waiting for them there was Sir Dogmael Jones, who had been expected earlier. The barrister greeted the Baron and his family, and apologized for his lateness. He waited again while Hugh escorted the family to their chaise and gave them his last consoling assurances, then said, "I come to wish you *bon voyage*, sir, and to present you with a token of my esteem." He gestured to the vessel with a leather satchel he was carrying. "May we talk in your cabin?"

In that confined space near the captain's quarters, Jones laid the satchel on the cabin table. "In my new career, sir, I have found it necessary to cultivate some familiarity with men of all kinds of professions, particularly those in the lairs of power and other Crown venues. Most of these placemen naturally assume that I am cooking them for favors, when in fact I seek only intelligence." He scoffed. "It is no more revolting a pastime than frequenting the company of common rogues, who differ from the placemen only in a want of manners, the crudity of their garb, and an absence of fine, cunning discretion."

He paused to tap the satchel once with his cane. "*This* required the application of not a little mental stealth and some expenditure of guineas. Your father will be similarly honored tomorrow. I ask you not to peruse the contents until you are well out to sea, preferably in midocean. If you read them now, or even when our island is but a smudge on the horizon, you may very well resolve to remain here. But, I assure you, Mr. Kenrick, that the contents will be of greater value to you in Virginia. It is there that they can make a difference." He studied his attentive host. "I have a second request: that you do not divulge the contents of this parcel to any officer of the Crown, be he parson, Governor, or customs man." He paused again. "Have I your concession on these points, sir?"

Hugh nodded, mystified by Jones's caution, but ready to give his word. "You have, sir."

"Good," said Jones with a sigh of relief. "Forgive me the ominous pre-
amble, but I promise that you will not regret having heeded my advice."

"And, I will heed it, Mr. Jones." Hugh indicated a bottle of claret, a gift
from Captain Rowland. It stood next to the satchel. "Will you join me in a
glass, sir?"

Jones nodded. Hugh found two glasses and poured the claret. Jones
said, "Pray do not allow the contents to sour the memory of your visit. That
is not my intention or hope. If they do, I offer my apologies. But, after your
perusal, I urge you to adopt a view of greater breadth than that of the sentiments you will read. That is the only answer to perfidy."

Hugh could only smile in answer. He handed the barrister a glass, then
raised his own. "To your health, sir."

Jones's stern, guarded expression softened a little. "And, to your health,
sir." He touched Hugh's glass with his own. "And, long live Lady Liberty."

*   *   *

An uneventful three weeks at sea passed before Hugh remembered
Jones's satchel, which he had secured in one of his bureau drawers. Until
now, his mind had been occupied with memories of his visit, and with some
speculation prompted by Jones's remark about "a view of greater breadth."
A notebook lay open before him on the cabin table, and an inkstand, and a
hand holding a quill that paused at the end of a sentence. A squat hurricane
lamp with a stubby candle swayed over his head, suspended from a chain,
and cast moving shadows in time with the swaying and creaking of the
ship.

Hugh favored metaphysical speculation, at the expense of episte-
mology. Indeed, there was no term yet for the latter field of philosophical
inquiry, though this did not prevent men from inquiring into the question
of how men perceived what they were certain existed. Hugh had written,
with some uncertainty, three pages of observations on Jones's remark.

"The picture is broader, or grander, than most men can see. I have with
some modest success sketched that vista for others, to convey it and the
importance of seeing it, as others have done for me. But most men must
begin with small things and progress to the larger, and have their natural
relevance demonstrated, often tediously. And I suppose that Mr. Frake and
I and a few others see it in the beginning, and do not relinquish it, and so
see it daily, much as we see our own faces in a looking glass. Perhaps all
men see it in the beginning of their lives, but, fearing its demands, or caring
more for a mess of banal vices, or settling for a slothful torpor, cannot or
will not retain it. The picture is rooted in some appraisal of oneself, and

projects outward to create a realm of one's actions, actual and contemplated. We think in that direction, from the minutiae to the grand, and become sovereign of it all. We attempt to persuade other men to see it, to think in that manner, men who are habituated to seeing but a small frame of things. They are more numerous, who care not to bother with the task. Who, then, when power and liberty are in contest, is at the disadvantage: We, or they?"

Hugh sighed in frustration, for he was exploring a subject unfamiliar to him, and was not certain that he had made observations on Jones's remark, or had gone beyond it. But the thought of Jones caused him to remember the satchel. He grimaced, closed the notebook, and put it aside. He leaned over, opened the bureau drawer, and took out the mysterious bundle. He untied the string that bound the rough leather satchel, and removed a small pile of papers. On top was a short letter from Jones, dated the day before the *Busy* left the Pool of London:

"My dear sir:
Appended to this missive are copies of drafted documents procured by me a few days ago from a pair of compliant gentleman clerks in the Treasury and the Board of Trade — procured, I might add, for a fee, for a sumptuous repast at the Bear Inn, for the cost of a trifling amusement or two — for a bribe. They are not the authors of these documents, but merely the copyists of the secretaries of those trusting worthies. The documents are in my own hand, as I could not trust the task of copying to another person without risking the same betrayal. The ministry seem to be preparing a proclamation to appear over His Majesty's seal and signature, and they have not yet settled on its wording.

You see, most first ministers have only a vague idea or notion of what policies they should adopt. Lords Grenville and Hillsborough (Halifax vacated the Board presidency this summer, you may have read) and their coterie are like their predecessors, disposed to whatever policy will cause them the least grief in the Commons and in audience at St. James's Palace. The task of dressing those policies with the particulars of means and ends is assigned to lesser men. In this instance, the task fell to Mr. Pownall, secretary to the Board, and Mr. Morgann, Lord Shelburne's private secretary (Shelburne was offered the Board presidency, but declined). Mr. Morgann, author of one of these documents, is a gentleman of advanced tastes, worthy of Dr. Johnson's company. I have heard that he is an authority on Mr. Shakespeare, and writes profusely on his dramas. Given the tone and thrust of his own proposals here, I should put it out that he would canonize Iago as an icon of politick virtue, except then I would betray my venal clerk friends in the Treasury and the Board, and so close the door to future acquisitions of this nature...."

Hugh finished the letter, then picked up the first document. He read it, and then the second.

From somewhere on the deck above came the rhythmic clopping of sailors dancing to the tune of a hornpipe. Across the passageway, in another cabin, two men, Captain Rowland's bursar and first mate, were engaged in a friendly argument over a game of chess. A sudden, stiff breeze filled the *Busy*'s sails, and the vessel lurched forward with a muted groan.

Hugh heard none of these things. He was rereading the documents for a third time. His face was ashen in sustained shock, his eyes narrowed in an alliance of rage, contempt, and self-control.

After a while, as the ship's bells marked the night watch, he tossed the documents down and leaned forward on his elbows, his face in his hands, two fingers pressing shut his eyes. He realized now that a great picture, accurate to the smallest detail and encompassing a wide purpose, was not inherently benign. He knew that this redefined the conflict, from one over the minutiae and particulars of mutually inimical vistas, to one of philosophy.

Chapter 22: The Bellwether

At about the time that Hugh was reading the purloined documents, Alden Curle was being interrogated by Basil Kenrick, the Earl of Danvers, concerning a missing Italian vase, which the Earl had purchased in a shop on the Strand and had sent Curle to collect. The vase was to have been placed on the fireplace mantel of one of the rooms formerly occupied by the Earl's brother, who no longer resided at Windridge Court. The Earl had instructed his staff to close many of those rooms, and to turn some into guest rooms. He had recently inspected the rearranged and refurnished guests rooms, and noted the absence of the vase.

Curle now stood before his master's desk in the study, trying to suppress trembling panic, his mind racing to screw up the courage to concoct a credible web of lies that would explain the missing vase, whose value was nearly half his annual wages. He had thrown the parcel with the broken pieces into the Thames after his encounter with Hugh Kenrick.

"I met your nephew, milord, on my way back with the vase. I did not think you wanted to hear of my encounter."

Basil Kenrick knew that his nephew was in town, that he had stayed with his brother's family in Chelsea, and that he had returned to Virginia some weeks ago. "And...?" prompted the Earl.

"He is a frightening creature, milord, if you will forgive me for saying so," said Curle. "More than ever before! He is a...man. He...he beat me with his cane, and knocked the vase from my hands! Were it not for passersby, I believe he would have drawn his sword and run me through!"

The Earl squinted, and shrugged vaguely. "Did he accost you with words, Curle? His tongue, as I remember, is every bit as wounding as a point of steel."

Curle tried to disguise a gulp. "No, milord. He did not. But, he did ask after your health."

The Earl grunted in surprise. "What did you tell him?"

"That you were in fine health, milord," said the *major domo*, confident now that he had covered the truth and found a thread of deception to follow. "But, I could not help but think he would have been overjoyed to hear a report that you were ill, milord, or in a bad state."

Basil Kenrick studied his servant for a moment. His dagger-like scrutiny caused the man to avert his glance and bow his head.

The Earl chuckled. "Now you are lying, Curle," he said. "A dollop of truth mixed with falsehood is always a poor shield. I know my nephew. He was being civil, and I do not believe he beat you with his cane or broke the vase." He paused. "Why did you not inform me of this meeting, as it was your duty to?"

Curle could only gulp again, and this time did not try to disguise the action. He ventured, "I...I was afraid that the well-known displeasure of his lordship with his nephew would be...turned on his humble servant, milord. I beg forgiveness for the presumption."

"That's better, Curle," said Basil Kenrick. "You know as well as I do that he can be civil to a fault. And further, that he would not expend the effort to accost a worm. That energy he conserves for dueling with dukes, and marquesses, and mobs." He sighed and shook his head. Secretly, he was pleased with the man's attempt at deception. "You were wrong to fear my wrath, Curle. You offend me with the presumption. For that, and for having lied to me, the price of the vase must be deducted from your honorarium — unless you can produce that sum today."

The base, exquisitely decorated with painted scenes of the ruins of the Roman Forum, and inset with gold filigree, had cost six guineas. Curle mumbled, "No, milord, I cannot."

The Earl shrugged again. "Very well. You may go."

With a bow of relief and gratitude, Alden Curle left the study. The deducted wages would cause him some inconvenience, but no hardship. There were valuable objects of art and the Earl's cast-off clothing stored in the cellar, items missing from the house inventory, and which Curle was certain the Earl had forgotten about and which he could easily dispose of in London's street markets to cover the penalty.

The rebuke worried him more than did the difference the penalty would make in his purse. He was consoled, however, by the knowledge that the Earl would never dismiss him. Just as he knew that he could never last in the employ of an honest, just man, he knew that the Earl had no use for an honest servant. His master needed an obsequious, discreet servant who could repeat, without having to be instructed to, his own lies and falsehoods and shams with nary a blink of an eye or a twitch of the cheek. He knew that, in the Earl's eyes, this was his chief asset in the household. Curle's only regret was that his art disintegrated in the presence of the Earl himself.

*   *   *

The evening of that same day, the Earl entertained supper guests at Windridge Court, among them Bevil Grainger, Viscount of Wooten and

Clarence, retired Master of the Rolls, King's Bench; Sir Henoch Pannell, member for Canovan, a "pocket borough" tucked within the confines of London and the county of Middlesex, themselves boroughs; Crispin Hillier, member for Onyxcombe, Dorset; Sir Fulke Treverlyn, an attorney and member for Old Boothby, Cheshire; and Captain James Holets, member for Essex, Oakhead Abbas, company commander in the Foo Guards. There were others, for a total of fourteen male guests, all members of the Commons, too, except for the Earl and the viscount, who sat in Lords.

It was unusual for the Earl to entertain guests; and more so the number of them this evening. But Crispin Hillier had suggested to him that it would be a practical gesture that would serve to cement the bloc of votes the party represented in the Commons, or rather that the Earl controlled there. Also, the occasion would give the Earl the opportunity to meet the members of his bloc and to appraise their interests and loyalties. The supper was treated by the guests as a kind of celebration for the formation of a strong and vocal force in the Commons, and by the Earl, as an exercise in annoying but necessary drollery.

Basil Kenrick, at the head of the table, flanked by Viscount Wooten and Crispin Hillier, set the tone of the supper party. He announced, as the guests sat at the long, resplendently set table, waiting for the first course, a development in the ministry. He rose and said, "I have it on good authority that the Treasury is near to completing a memorial to the Privy Council. It will state its recommendations concerning the matter of a more stringent collection of duties and levies from the colonies. Further, I have it on good authority from a person on the Council that the Council will refine the memorial to include other North American colonies for an Order in Council to be enacted with His Majesty's approval. Both the memorial and Order are undoubtedly overtures to a royal proclamation by His Majesty himself, whose own and rightful purpose is to contain and regulate the colonies in a more masterful manner than heretofore exerted. His Majesty's proclamation will be published in a few weeks, before the next session of Parliament convenes."

All the guests, except for Hillier and Pannell, stared at their host, amazed, speechless, and delighted. It was not news to either Pannell or Hillier; the Earl had informed them earlier, before the other guests had arrived. Pannell looked smug and all-knowing; Hillier was taciturn. The Earl glanced up at the portrait of his father, Guy Kenrick, the fourteenth Earl of Danvers. For the first time ever, the dour, haughty visage seemed to regard him with approval. He smiled at the stupid faces down the length of the table, and added, "Your task, sirs, is to persuade your House to complement His Majesty's wishes with actions commensurate with his patri-

otic spirit, actions that will ensure the political and material solvency and
security of the Crown, of this nation, and of the empire."

"Hear, hear!" said Crispin Hillier quietly. Other guests seconded him.

Henoch Pannell grinned broadly, and addressed the table at large. He
had invested a great deal of time and energy putting the bloc together,
working with Hillier. He felt he had a right to second the Earl's motion in
his own way. "In a word, milord and my many sirs," he ventured, "His
Majesty intends to lock the colonies in their stables, and lunge them at the
Crown's pleasure. A more proper and just patriotism than that, I cannot
imagine!"

By the third course, Viscount Wooten cleared his throat and said, "Lord
Danvers, Sir Henoch there tells me that your brother has secured a seat in
the House. For Swansditch, I believe. Now, I knew the man who will sit for
him. He defended some libelers in a trial of mine some years ago, and
nearly libeled me in the bargain! He is a violent, rash, outspoken man,
much like this Mr. Wilkes. A most troubling and troublesome chap. What
could your brother be thinking by endorsing such a fellow?"

Basil Kenrick grimaced and shook his head in dismissal of the subject.
"He is opposing me out of spite, Lord Wooten. That is all there is to it. I
have not worried myself much about it." He turned to Crispin Hillier and
nodded.

Hillier smiled. "Troublesome, Lord Wooten? I doubt that. He is but one
man. He may be ignored at no risk. Sir Henoch and I have made his
acquaintance, and judge him to be in unmovable opposition to our party.
He may ally himself on particular matters, such as Mr. Wilkes, or against
the land and cider taxes, but he is essentially hostile to the Crown. That
stance will not only govern the character of his seat and career in the
House, but alienate the affections of his natural friends there."

Sir Henoch laughed and added, "His greatest enemies, Lord Wooten,
will not be our worthy people, but the cowards who would like to agree
with him but haven't the bottom. Mr. Hillier is correct in his assessment of
Sir Dogmael Jones. He will find himself alone. Upon my word, Lord
Wooten, you needn't trouble yourself about him. Against him, or anyone
else who questions the wisdom of the Crown, I have taken great pains to
ensure that there are no see-sawing whifflers in *our* party!"

Chapter 23: The Autumn

T he crew and passengers of any vessel making its way up the York
River in late October could see, on either bank, tentative slashes of
brilliant orange, red, and yellow in the leaves of the trees, or little
bursts of flame in the green that would spread and engulf everything by the
end of November.

The wide river was busier now than at any other time of the year, for
this was the apex of the planters' season, a time when harvested crops were
prepared for shipment across the ocean and along the seaboard to other
colonies. Merchantmen, brigs, and sloops plied up and down the waterway,
on their way back to Chesapeake Bay's ports, or upriver to load, by derrick,
lighter, and sling cargoes of tobacco, corn, lumber, and iron. Vessels sat
anchored at wooden and earthen piers and docks, sails furled and rigging
slack, their gang-boards springing and straining under the hustle of slaves
and crews who descended into cargo holds as they labored to take on casks,
hogsheads, sacks, crates, and bundles, or reappeared with them to pile them
on the piers.

Flatboats, pontoons, cutters, and yawls, weighed down with barrels of
tobacco and other crops, hugged the waters close to the banks, their farmer
or planter crews rowing cautiously and warily between shoals and hidden
sand banks, intent on safely reaching a waterfront and the ships and warehouses that awaited them. At both Yorktown and Caxton, new and old vessels, near completion or under repair, sat in stocks, and the air was filled
with the sounds of hammers, saws, and axes at work. Some larger sea-draft
vessels lay careened on their sides; workmen trod over the exposed keels
with pots of fire and smoke to burn out worms and dislodge barnacles.
Beyond the waterfronts, in the brown crop fields, smoke and fire could be
seen, too, as slaves and field-hands cleared the land of stumps, weeds, and
chaff, the residue of the last harvest.

The manual labor was moved by the mental. Outside Caxton's tobacco
warehouse, hogsheads were being pried open, their contents inspected and
weighed, then reprized, weighed again, and branded. Richard Ivy and his
clerks rushed hectically on these chores between the warehouse, scales, and
office, with planters, factors, and agents in tow, filling in crop notes,
arguing with men whose crops were condemned as trash, issuing transfer
notes to the more numerous small planters who brought in loose, unprized

tobacco in bundles or "hands," and giving hasty instructions to the over-seer who commanded the slaves who took apart, then rehooped and renailed the hogsheads of the bigger planters.

Jack Frake stepped outside of Ivy's office and tucked his crop notes securely inside a pocket of his coat. All twelve of his hogsheads had passed inspection, and were branded beneath his diving sparrowhawk device with the town name, tare, and net weight, then rolled to another part of the brick warehouse.

Quite by chance, they were put next to the eleven that bore the device of an ascending sparrowhawk, the mark of Meum Hall. For some reason, this pleased him. His own hogsheads would be taken on by John Ramshaw's *Sparrowhawk*, due to arrive any day now, once it came back downriver from loading crops and pig-iron at De la Ware Town, or West Point, as the place at the head of the York River was beginning to be called. He would give Captain Ramshaw his crop notes in exchange for a sack or chest of coins. These would be mostly silver, with some gold and copper, most of them Spanish, some of them Portuguese, few of them English. Ramshaw in turn would exchange the notes for other commodities, either here or at Yorktown or Hampton downriver.

He had been here since sunrise. Half of his hogsheads were brought down from Morland by wagon and oxen team, half by cutter from his own pier. With him were William Hurry, his overlooker and steward, and John Proudlocks, a tenant, and six men from the plantation. He had sent them back with those conveyances, for he wanted to relax and have a late dinner at the King's Arms Tavern up on Queen Anne Street above the waterfront.

As he strode through the noisy, bustling port, several small planters he knew looked hopefully at him on their way to Ivy's office. They carried sacks of cured tobacco, which, if they passed Ivy's scrutiny, would net these planters "transfer" notes, which in turn they could use as money or sell to other planters for cash or par value. Their tobacco, "dull leaf" oronoco or stemmed sweetscented, would be added to a common, unprized stockpile, for it was prohibited from exportation, first by Parliament in 1698, then by the House of Burgesses in 1730, to reduce the smuggling that cut into Crown revenues. Reece Vishonn and other "bashaw" planters here made a business of buying those transfer notes, then used them to draw from the common stockpile to either complete the prizing of their own hogsheads, or to prize now ones. By law, tobacco could be exported only in those hogsheads or casks. The product was as much a captive as were its producers.

Jack merely nodded to the men, or exchanged brief greetings with them. He might have done business with them, except that he had no use for the tobacco they grew. "Dull leaf" was favored in the French market and bought in London by agents of the Farmers-General, the French government tobacco monopoly, and constituted most of the colonial crop. He himself grew "bright oronoco," or "bright leaf," which was favored by Dutch, Spanish, German, and Scandinavian buyers. Morland was one of the few York River plantations that grew bright leaf. Much more of it was grown on the James River. Richard Ivy, the inspector, had grown it on the James as a plantation manager, and swore that Morland leaf was "every bit as good as the best" bright leaf he had seen on that other great river's plantations. But neither Ivy nor Reece Vishonn nor any other Caxton planters voiced their curiosity about how Jack was able to find regular buyers for his bright leaf and profit from its sale, when the prices they got for their own dull leaf and stemmed sweetscented were so dependent on the capricious shrewdness of French agents, economic conditions in the British Isles, and the whims of the Board of Trade.

The "how" was something neither Jack nor Captain Ramshaw was ever going to divulge. Ramshaw was able to dispose of the bright leaf on the isle of Guernsey, on Dutch and Scandinavian vessels. The redoubtable captain kept in his employ a man, listed in his crew as a shipwright, who was an expert forger of cockets, dockets, manifests, and bills of lading, in addition to the handwriting and signatures of virtually every customs man in any colonial or British port, including Richard Ivy. His concealed cabin on the *Sparrowhawk* contained a small printing press and was stocked with all the grades and types of commercial and official paper needed. The paperwork and documents that detailed the vessel's cargoes, and whether or not their duties had been paid or exempted, after the *Sparrowhawk* set sail for England, or cleared London or one of the outports, were as impeccably correct and in order as those inspected by naval officers in colonial ports and by customsmen at the destinations, but rarely were they the same original paperwork and documents.

The practice dated from the days of the Skelly gang in Cornwall, when the gang rendezvoused in galley boats with the *Sparrowhawk* offshore on moonless nights, or sailed its own vessel, the *Hasty Hart*, to Guernsey to pick up a cargo Ramshaw left there. Neither Jack nor Ramshaw nor any of the captain's other "customers" saw any reason to change the forgery practice. It helped them to keep more of what they had earned, to profit from their efforts while others moaned about the Crown's impositions.

Jack had never even confided it to Hugh Kenrick, who he knew suspected him of some smuggling ruse but had never presumed to inquire about it. His friend's own dull leaf hogsheads were reserved for the *Busy* or the *Ariadne*, whichever merchantman arrived first in Caxton. These, he knew, would go to the Pool of London, or to one of the outports, Bristol or

Liverpool, where Worley & Sons had corresponding agents. Jack in turn presumed that Hugh's wealthy family and loyal agent had established their own devious arrangements to reduce the burden of the duties on their imports from the colonies and Europe, and to flout the strictures of the navigation laws and foil the Crown's mandate to collect a levy on, as Hugh himself had once put it, "every bead of sweat, every ounce of effort, every grain of value" that rode on British vessels.

Jack reached the top of the rise. He paused to take a seegar from inside his coat, struck a match, and lit it. He preferred the pipe, but at moments of celebration like this one, he would smoke a rolled, compact leaf of his own crop. Mouse, his chief field-hand and expert "prizer," rolled them himself by the dozen. Jack allowed him to roll the seegars for sale to his other tenants and in town.

He turned to survey the waterfront. This was his favorite time of the year to enjoy the little port, when it was most alive, as it concluded one year's work and prepared for the next. Two merchantmen were moored to the larger earthen piers, both frigate-sized, the *Atlantic Conveyor* and the *Peregrine*, out of Jamaica and Boston respectively, taking on grain, pork, and beef, besides dozens of manufactured wares that came from Queen Anne county, including barrel staves, shingles, tallow, and finished candles. A third vessel, the *Pericles*, out of Halifax, rode at anchor in the river, waiting to berth once one of the others pushed off back down the York. It was already laden with pelts and hemp, and had stopped here to take on whatever else would fill the empty space in her hold. A dozen smaller vessels, belonging to farmers and small planters, were tied to a shorter pier — ketches, yawls, and even converted jolly boats — and men were occupied unloading their cargoes or loading supplies they had purchased in town with their crop or transfer notes.

In the King's Arms Tavern, crowded now with planters, crewmen from the merchantmen, and visitors from Williamsburg and Yorktown, Jack ordered his dinner, and sat down with a tankard of ale, and while he waited, talked with William Settle, Meum Hall's overlooker. They spoke for a while about a growing season that had given them balanced spells of rain and sunshine, enough of each so that all their crops had flourished without needing extra care. Settle had erected his employer's conduit in the spring, per Hugh Kenrick's instructions, but took it back down when the false start of a dry season was washed away by the second of the season's weekly rains.

"You know," said Settle to Jack Frake, "I was thinking of leaving Brougham Hall, even before Mr. Kenrick bought the place, and building up my own land. But Mr. Kenrick's made a difference. I like him, he's a bookish man, you know, but not afraid of getting dirt under his nails, and now I won't think of leaving. With Mr. Swart all we had was just so much glop and grief, but since Mr. Kenrick came, we're growing gold, gold you can hear rustle when it's hanging in the barns when the breezes cure it and it's being prized into a hogshead, and everyone's proud of it. We're just like your place, Mr. Frake, and I can't think how it could be run better."

Jack smiled. "Mr. Kenrick has made a great difference here, Mr. Settle. And he will continue to make one."

Settle frowned, bemused. "I used to think you would, Mr. Frake."

Jack shook his head. "I have, sir, and I'm not finished yet."

Just as Jack was finishing his dinner, John Proudlocks returned with a saddled horse from the Morland stables for his employer to ride back on, and also with the news that a merchantman was on the river, headed for Caxton.

The trio left the tavern, mounted their horses, and rode to the rise over the waterfront. They could see a vessel about a mile away, beating slowly up the York, the pilot's skiff trailing behind on a line beneath the red ensign, bobbing in the wake. Both Jack and Settle could recognize from a distance most of the merchantmen that called on Caxton. They glanced at each other.

"It's the *Busy*," said Settle. "Mr. Kenrick may be on it."

"It's the *Busy*, all right," agreed Jack. "If he is, I wonder what news he'll bring."

Chapter 24: The News

"The British colonies are to be regarded in no other light but as subservient to the commerce of their mother country. Colonists are merely factors for the purposes of trade, and in all considerations concerning the colonies, this must always be the prevailing idea. The Crown, through its appointed Governors and officers, should, in conformance with this idea, exert every act of sovereignty in each province, with the summary effect of rendering the colonies relative and subservient to the commerce of Great Britain, which was the end of their establishment."

Thomas Reisdale scoffed and dropped the page. He had read the words out loud, as if by doing so, the meaning of the words would acquire more reality. He already believed them, but voicing them seemed to add to them a certain potency. "They were *not*, sirs!" he exclaimed to the unseen author. "They were established as refuges from this brand of callidity!" The attorney glanced at Jack Frake, who had already read the pages. "Well, sir, you were remarkably prescient. He even uses your own language! 'Merely factors,' indeed!"

Jack Frake, seated at a table used by Hugh Kenrick as a worktable when his study desk was too cluttered, puffed on his pipe. He said, "I could not have penned the notion better myself."

Reisdale picked up another page. "Listen to this, sirs! What audacity! 'Under the pretence of regulating the Indian trade, a very straight line should be drawn on the back of the provinces and the country behind that line thrown, for the present, under the dominion of the Indians and the Indians be everywhere encouraged to support their own sovereignty.'" The attorney scoffed again, and tossed down the page. "Why, if Parliament weaves laws around this gentleman's 'prevailing idea,' one couldn't even escape west from His Majesty's clutches! This fellow proposes granting the savages leave to 'support their sovereignty,' which means, in effect, that settlers could be butchered by them at will, and could not appeal to the army for protection — not unless they wished to be fined and punished by the Crown!"

Reisdale was as angry as anyone had ever seen him. "Think of it, sirs! A string of army posts, all down the Mississippi, from Montreal to New Orleans, just as he proposes, each post a link in a chain that would imprison us all! To the north, Canada, and an army! To the south, the Floridas, and an army! To the west, protected barbarism!"

Jack sat forward, tapped out his pipe in a copper bowl, then wrapped his hands around a tankard of ale. "That could not be the end of it, sir. That chain of iron and steel and warclubs can only be meant to better dress us in the paper and ink chains of more regulation and taxation. To keep us close at hand."

"Those," Hugh Kenrick said, pointing from his desk to the pile of pages on a table near Reisdale's elbow, "are very damning documents."

The three men were in his study at Meum Hall. It had taken him some days to recover from the voyage, and then to deal with the greetings of the planters, and to distribute the things he had brought back from England. The first thing he did, after setting foot on the pier of the Caxton waterfront, was to visit the tobacco warehouse, knowing that his hogsheads should have been prized, inspected, and cleared by now. And seeing them there calmed his mind. At Meum Hall, he inspected the fields, the house, the account books, and listened to Mr. Settle, Mr. Beecroft, and the rest of the staff report on the course and climax of Meum Hall's growing season.

Sitting in the back of his mind all the while, however, was the knowledge he had gained from Dogmael Jones's documents, and the problem of how best to share that knowledge with those he thought should have it.

He said now, "These documents, sirs, must be kept in confidence. Their contents must not be revealed to anyone else. You have read his note to me. It is imperative that you do not communicate any of this to friends, and especially not to our burgesses. Our friends and burgesses have already heard what these documents say. You, Mr. Frake, have said it. And I have suspected it."

He paused. "Now, Virginia has two agents in London, Mr. Edward Montagu, who acts for the Assembly, and Mr. James Abercromby, who acts for the Council. I do not know how active these men are in their capacities, nor whether or not they would be friends or enemies of the sentiments expressed in these documents."

Reisdale said, "Any objections or agreements they might have would be put before the Privy Council, or the Treasury, or the Board of Trade. I don't believe their mandate extends to venturing to influence Parliament, except through members they happen to know. It may need to, in future."

"True," said Hugh. "In any event, these documents constitute something they should have acquired on their own initiative. And, perhaps they have. But I should not rely on them. Mr. Jones can give us advance warning of the Crown's intentions, but only if his ability to do so is not jeopardized. That is why I ask that you keep this information to yourselves." He smiled in memory of Dogmael Jones's question aboard the *Busy*. "Have I your concession on this point, sirs?"

Jack Frake and Thomas Reisdale nodded. Jack said, "Your Mr. Jones sounds like a man who ought to settle here, Hugh. You wrote to me about him from London in such glowing terms, but these," he said, pointing with his pipe stem at the pages, "are proof that he is a man of substance."

Hugh shook his head. "He loves his country, Jack. But, more than that, he is obsessed with the justice that may be had in it, and, from our own perspective, from it."

Jack studied his host for a moment. He smiled and said, "You have just uttered a troubling distinction, my friend."

Reisdale cautiously remarked, "Yes, sir. To argue the point, are Virginia and Massachusetts to be regarded as England, within its natural pale? Or does more separate these states from England than a mere ocean?"

Hugh grinned in good-natured defeat. "Yes, I own I made the distinction. And it is a distinction that we must all thresh out."

Jack rose and paced for a while in thought. Then he turned to his companions and said, "You must understand that, ultimately, it can end in but one way. Mr. Jones's documents here prove it. It may take years. It will require a slow, and costly, and difficult lesson. But, it can have but one consequence." When he saw agreement in his companions' faces, he glanced out the study window at the trees that were beginning to sport color. "The long autumn of this empire is now upon us. I am certain of it."

Hugh shook his head and sat back in his chair. "No, sir. I do not think that is true. If the worst happened, it could not last. There would be reconciliation. An epergne of empire is not impossible. It is not naturally doomed." He paused to regard the pile of pages at Reisdale's elbow, then said, "As you are, my friend, I am confident in the power of reason. I do not believe that, faced with the sole alternatives of a peaceful, just empire, on the one hand, and disaster and war, on the other, the most foolish minister would not choose the former."

Jack faced his host. "That would depend on the nature of his foolishness," he said. "Mr. Morgann and his ilk and their superiors in London have proofs of the efficacy and practicality of foolishness. Recall all the statutes and laws that already regulate us, here in Virginia, and in every colony. Our salaried wards in London have had no convincing evidence that there is a limit to their own foolishness, and to that of their predecessors. *We* have certainly not given them any. So, they would not be moved to submit to reason. Oh, I admit that there are men like your father, and Mr. Jones, and some others, who see the compounding foolishness and will attempt to warn others of it."

Jack took a step near Reisdale and tapped the top page of the documents with a finger. "But I doubt that those others — the ministers and lords who will read and reflect on the sentiments expressed here, then write a proclamation for the king, and draft new laws to be introduced and passed in Parliament — I doubt they can even distinguish the differences between reason, illogic, folly, and whim. If reason were as persuasive as you believe, my friend, there would be no need for jails. Footpads, highwaymen, murderers, thieves — they would not exist. Nor would taxes and Hat Acts and navigation laws and the necessity of proving one's honesty to dishonest or indifferent drones in the customs service. *They* would not exist, either."

He turned away for a moment, as though to collect himself, but then faced Hugh again. His expression had become grim and unyielding. He took a step forward, and with a violence neither Hugh nor Reisdale had ever seen in him before, slammed a fist down on the pages on the table. "Let no one tell *me* there is an opacity of motive in these, sir! Any man claiming a mere dram of self-respect would be wounded, offended, and angered by what is said here! *I* am, I needn't tell you *that*!" His face became a mask of terrifying, stony defiance. "I am not now, nor will I ever be, except on *my own* terms, anyone's mere *factor*! I'll see Morland burned to the ground first, and I'll rot in prison, or perish in the wilds, or go under a royal bayonet, before *that* is likely to happen!"

Reisdale, startled by Jack's emotion, at that moment knew that his friend was right. Far down the course of the coming years, the conflict must end in but one way: the inevitable clash of unmutual purposes, in a contest of imperial wills. The motives, Jack's and those of the authors and ministerial auditors of the proposals, were not opaque, and must take some form of action. Reisdale, the scholar and lawyer, looked up at Jack Frake from his armchair with an awe that was braced with a twinge of admiring fear.

Hugh, also, was disturbed by Jack's outburst, and by it was convinced of the inevitability of a conflict. Too, he was convinced of the nature and strength of Jack's character, and that it was something he could count on. But he did not see the conflict as a mortal contest in which one or the other party must perish. He was as certain of this as was Jack that one or the other must.

Hugh and Jack held each other's glances for a moment, and seeing the certitude in the other, each broke off his defiance, knowing that a resolution was not yet possible. Jack sat down again. Hugh, at his desk, toyed with his brass top.

In the silence, Reisdale picked up the pages and jogged them into a neat rectangle. He cleared his throat and asked, "There is the question now of what we should tell our friends in the Attic Society. It meets in a week at Mr. Safford's place."

"Nothing," Hugh said, "but what I can report from my own observations in London, or from the blameless correspondence of my parents."

"I agree," Jack said. "Our friends will learn soon enough the Crown's intentions."

"This is true," Reisdale said. He put a hand on top of the pile of pages on his lap. "If a royal proclamation is the final expression of these recommendations, it will be read at the opening of Parliament next month. Governor Fauquier will receive a copy of it in December or January, and the *Courier* and *Gazette* will print it shortly thereafter. Then we shall all see what the Crown intends." He paused to glance at Hugh and Jack. He sensed that the tension between them had abated. He smiled and asked, "Mr. Kenrick, will you enlighten us about Mr. Wilkes and his cause? I cannot but help think that he will be Parliament's first order of business."

"You are right to think that, Mr. Reisdale," Hugh said.

Chapter 25: The Words

John Wilkes, member for Aylesbury and now dangerously popular, was indeed made the first order of business when Parliament reopened in November, to the exclusion of nearly all other business. By means of bribery and extortion of his printers, a Treasury solicitor obtained proof-copies of his carnal *Essay on Woman* and freshly printed texts of Number Forty-five of *The North Briton* for the planned collection of that publication's numbers.

The government, through its representatives in the Commons and Lords, secured resolutions that the literature was "impious" and "seditious" libel. Number Forty-five was ordered burnt at the Royal Exchange by both Houses, but a mob stoned the hangman and sheriffs assigned the task and rescued the copy from destruction — in the same month that Wilkes recovered, in the Court of Common Pleas, £1,000 from an under-secretary of state. The Commons, in January, 1764, voted 273 to 111 to expel Wilkes, thereby stripping him of the shield of Parliamentary privilege. A grand jury of the King's Bench, exploiting his unprotected status, in February cited him for his libels, and the court ordered a writ for his arrest.

But Wilkes by now had fled to France, ostensibly to see his daughter, but actually to recover from a wound he suffered in a duel with another M.P. He was declared an outlaw by the court the following November when he failed to appear to answer the charges against him. For the next few years he lived on the charity of friends in the Opposition. He would return to England a few years later, and cause a crisis greater than the one sparked by his "impious" and "seditious" libels.

In the Commons, Sir Dogmael Jones, member for Swansditch, managed to capture the attention of Speaker John Cust, who pointed to him on the second day and allowed him to make his maiden speech. Many who were ready to vote with the government on the libel question wondered, as they listened to him — and they had little difficulty hearing him, for he was a practiced orator, and his every word reached their ears over the noise in the crowded chamber — whether he, too, might someday be a candidate for expulsion.

"...And do we not glory in our rightful power to contradict the sovereign in money and other kinds of bills? Are not our actions in those instances far more cutting to his dignity than a handful of immoderate

words? Sir," said Jones, addressing as was expected of him the Speaker —
even though he meant "Gentlemen," for he wanted no cries of "Chair!
Chair!" interrupting his words — "do we not then also question a greater
portion of his wisdom? It would be fanciful folly indeed if we presume we
did not! Sir, you must allow that we do, and concede that it is most curious
that this House has never been charged with a similar offense — at least,
not since James the Second!"

Members on the government benches murmured and rustled in their
seats. Those on the Opposition benches were silent and attentive. Someone
shouted, "Hear, hear!" and Jones continued with his speech.

"As for Mr. Wilkes's satire on Mr. Pope's *Essay*," he said, "well, that it
is lascivious and obscene cannot be denied. However, the logical action
taken by able-minded men in matters of indelicate literature is not punishment of its authors, but refusal to read it. I own that *I* have read the *Essay*
at question here, and more: that I have read better! And better and worse
than this *Essay* may be had for a few shillings or pence on Duck Lane and
St. Paul's Churchyard. It was, in a word — *dull*!!"

Members on both sides of the House chuckled at this remark. Jones
waited until they were quiet again. "My questions for the House, however,
are these: Is our hold on moral conduct and propriety so weak and feeble that
we fear the *power* of such a thing? I say that its power is derived from our
sheer funk and doubtful virtue! Are we clinging to the precipice of moral sal-
vation with but one tiny finger, fearful that the slightest breeze of prurience
will send us tumbling into the fiery chasm of damnation? If we are, we ought
not to don the weighty mantle of judgment! Are we so unsure of the strength
of our moral uprightness that, in order to maintain our pretence of it, we
rush to censure a man whose words perhaps summon to our idle thoughts
memories or imaginings of the natural delights of connubial bliss?"

Many members on both sides of the House gasped open-mouthed.
Jones heard the reaction, and was glad that he had decided not to say, "the
natural delights of rogering our wives and mistresses," as he had planned
to, for those words, he knew now, would have caused an uproar and moved
some members to demand that he be censured by the Speaker. He went on,
uninterrupted, thankful that he had decided wisely. "If we are, sir, then we
are either hypocrites and liars, or so saintly and heaven-sent that we cannot
credibly account for our children!"

This elicited a greater round of laughter than before, except, of course,
among the parsons and the devout, who wished to laugh, but would not.

"But, who among us are truly offended by Mr. Wilkes's actions beyond
this chamber? And who are merely angry with him? If offended, we may
rest on the consolation that *his* character reflects on neither that of this

body, nor on our own virtues. And if one is angry with him, this troubling state does not allow us the leave, individually or corporately in concert with others similarly irked, to gag him, to fine him, imprison him, and void his right to sit in this House! Anger of that kind has moved many a highwayman to murder his victim because his victim had little to surrender — or even because he dared speak in protest of the robbery — and anger has sent many a highwayman to Tyburn Tree!"

"Foul words, sir!" shouted a member from the government side. "Insult, Chair! Insult to the House!" cried another. A confusing chorus bellowed at the Speaker, "Take down those words!" "Offense! Slander!" "Apology! Apology!" "Move to censure that fellow!"

Speaker Cust was saved the trouble of deciding what to do when several members from the Opposition benches rose and out-shouted the government benches. "Hear! Hear!" "No outrage!" "Hear him! Hear him!" "Let the honorable member speak!" He waited for the tumult to subside, then nodded once to Jones to continue.

Jones nodded in thanks, then said, "I say that Mr. Wilkes libels neither men nor women with his debauched and lecherous scribblings! I say that the charge of libel against him on that matter is bilious and unfounded, and for these reasons: For a libel to have any legal substance, it must have an object capable of responding to it, and that object must be a *person*. To my knowledge, neither of those great, idealized abstractions, Apollo and Athena, have filed a suit for libel in any court of law in this nation!" After an imperceptible pause, he added, "And no one, neither god nor mortal, can object to a libel that remains *unpublished*, as this *Essay* is! Call it what you will, sir: false, blasphemous, indecent, lewd, or gross — it remains unpublished! And if it were published, I dare the woman vain and inelegant enough to claim that *she* was its ribald inspiration!"

After another pause, Jones said, "It is my sincere hope that this House will pursue the truth, and not the man. As to Mr. Wilkes's original remarks about His Majesty, we propose to put him in a second jeopardy over that matter, and, again, over an unpublished, alleged libel. Well, His Majesty is a man. But, then, so was Adam...."

Henoch Pannell and Crispin Hillier, seated together on a tier above the Treasury bench, listened to Jones, but were not among those who protested his statements. They were taking the measure of the man and of their colleagues' reactions to him. "He is effective," remarked Pannell to his partner, "very effective. I like his style. It may be his undoing. He stabs with words, and wounds, and shames, and invites a round of stone-casting."

Hillier nodded in agreement. "Others would say that he beggars his questions. But, they are questions I believe he knows that few here would dare answer with honesty. And that gives him a pile of stones to cast, while they are armed with soft, worn pebbles. Hardly an equal contest, sir."

Pannell smiled in smug satisfaction. "Well, there you are, sir! He asks the House to elevate itself! What greater slight could one offer? He will ask himself, I'll wager, once he has absorbed the method of this House: Who among us would wish to? Against his wounding words of stone will be the emery of inertia and what he calls 'sheer funk.' Together, they will wear down his stallion spirit! Yes, sir! For each stone he casts, a hundred emery pebbles will answer!"

Sir James Parrot, sitting with his wife in the gallery that faced the Opposition benches below, looked disdainfully down at the man he had bested at the Pippin trial at the King's Bench years ago. His wife leaned closer to him and observed, "It is a wonder to me, James, that you out-argued *him* at that rascal's trial. He has almost convinced *me* to feel sorry for Mr. Wilkes!"

Her husband shook his head, and sighed with the ennui of tired wisdom. "No, my dear. He is merely an actor. A Garrick in gown. But, if I outargued him, Lord Wooten outgaveled him. However, I am afraid for our friend down there that all his speeches here will be but soliloquies spoken to an empty House. You see, he has the hobbling habit of speaking to more than just the question at hand." He nodded to the nearly four hundred closely packed members on the benches below. "He speaks over most of their hats, and beyond their breadth."

When he was finished speaking and able to sit down, Dogmael Jones felt flushed with both the effort of his fifty-minute oration and the confidence that he had said everything that needed to be said. As a member above the Treasury bench rose to reply, some members of the Opposition picked their way through the press of bodies to compliment him. He glanced up at the gallery between acknowledgments with a tentative smile for Baron Garnet Kenrick, his wife the Baroness, and their daughter, Alice. The Baron returned his smile with a nod of approval, the Baroness silently pronounced the word "Bravo!" and Alice grinned proudly at him. Jones doffed his hat in answer, and winked at Alice, then leaned on his cane to listen to his respondent across the floor.

He subsequently voted against the House resolution that branded Number Forty-five a "false, scandalous, and seditious libel," argued with other members in the Commons lobby and coffee room and in the Yard against joining Lords in condemning it to be burnt, and, in January, voted against Wilkes's expulsion. He made copies of all his speeches for future reference, and recorded from memory significant speeches delivered in the House by friend and foe. He kept his promise to Hugh Kenrick, and sent him transcriptions of his own addresses.

And, he came to the attention of Colonel Isaac Barré, member for Chipping Wycombe, a tall, swarthy man with a musket ball still lodged in one cheek, a disfigurement he received in Canada. He had been at Wolfe's side when that man died on the Plains of Abraham outside Quebec. His frightening appearance, together with his own frank oratory, made him the terror of other members and government ministers. He and Jones became friends and allies.

Jones was also noticed by other Opposition members, who were less certain than Barré that he was the kind of ally they wished to recruit.

* * *

The business postponed by Parliament in its zeal to punish Wilkes comprised an agenda of important matters. There was George the Third's Proclamation of October 7th, fraught with implications for the future of the empire. Allied to it was the national debt, now standing at £130 millions, and its annual interest of between £3 and £5 millions, and how best to reduce it. There was the fate of the land and cider taxes to consider, and other revenue issues that affected the royal and national coffers, such as a dismal harvest, which was sure to spark more food riots, and what personal allowances to vote His Majesty and his family.

More immediate matters distracted the colonies. In November, while Parliament was preoccupied with Wilkes, British astronomers and surveyors Charles Mason and Jeremiah Dixon arrived in Philadelphia, hired by the Penn and Calvert families, proprietors respectively of Pennsylvania and Maryland, to settle the boundary dispute between the two colonies. Also in that month, Pontiac and his Indian allies, frustrated in their obsession with immediate slaughter and destruction, and discouraged that the French were not going to reappear, abandoned their seven-month siege of Detroit.

This was preceded in August by the rout of an Indian army at Bushy Run in Pennsylvania, not far from where the war had begun, by Colonel Henry Bouquet, a Swiss mercenary commanding Scottish and regular troops, a victory that lifted the siege of Fort Pitt. The Indians would continue their raids on Western settlements for three more years, until a treaty ended the unequal contest. Some time after its signing, Pontiac would be murdered by an Illinois, precipitating the extinction of the Illinois by a vengeful Algonquin confederacy of tribes.

George the Third's Proclamation was read by most members of Parliament with an insouciance abetted by an ignorance of colonial conditions.

It created four new colonies and governments for them: Quebec, East and West Florida, and Grenada. It annexed the islands of St. John and Cape Breton to Nova Scotia. It provided generous grants of land to officers and enlisted men who had served with the army and remained in the colonies. It drew a boundary line along the mountains from the headwaters of all rivers flowing to the Atlantic, prohibited colonial settlement west of it, and prohibited colonial Governors and legislatures from selling or patenting land west of it without Crown approval. It reserved to the Crown the right to purchase land west of the line from the Indians. And, it expressly authorized the "use of said Indians" by Crown officers to apprehend any subject fleeing Crown law, regardless of his offense.

Bubbles of incipient rebellion against Crown arrogance by George's "loving subjects," both at home and in the colonies, went largely unnoticed by those charged with formulating and implementing the policy. There came into the hands of ministers in office, in 1762, a pamphlet containing an address delivered in the Superior Court of Massachusetts, by James Otis, a Boston attorney. It challenged the legality of writs of assistance.

These were blanket sanctions, similar in spirit and intent to general warrants, issued by courts under the authority of the king and Parliamentary law, that permitted customs officers, on mere suspicion of evasion, to search and ransack private homes and property for untaxed contraband or smuggled goods, and if found, to seize the same in lieu of paid duties, fines, and jury decisions. Otis argued that these writs were invalid because any act of Parliament or royally assented law "against the Constitution was void," and warned that the writs represented a liberty-abridging power that "cost one King of England his head and another his throne."

These words, had they been uttered in either House by a member of Parliament, would have cost him his seat in the Commons, or his title in Lords, and earned him imprisonment and a trial on the charge of treason. But they were spoken by a mere colonial lawyer in an "inferior" colonial court that subsequently demurred the issue in deference to Crown interpretation, and so they carried neither weight nor threat nor hint of unrest.

And while men in London were fulminating against Wilkes in December of 1763, and wondering whence came the unruly crowds that rallied to his support, the ministers and lords there were naturally oblivious to the address that month by another lawyer to a jury of another "inferior" court in faraway Hanover County, Virginia; very likely, too, they would have been unmoved even had the address been communicated to them.

The Privy Council had disallowed the General Assembly's Two-Penny Act of 1758, which, as an emergency economic measure, fixed the salaries of the state-appointed clergy in Virginia below the market price of tobacco

— or rather reduced the tax on a pound of sold tobacco, imposed to support the Anglican clergy, from six pence to four. These vestry-paid salaries were disbursed in the form of crop notes, transfer notes, and depreciating Virginia currency, all tied to the widening gulf in the exchange rate between Virginia paper and British sterling. The clergy not only felt cheated, but did not feel that they, God's spokesmen, should be the recipients of curt reminders from London merchants about their mounting debts.

Reverend John Camm, divinity professor at William & Mary College and pastor of York-Hampton Parish, voyaged to London on their behalf and waged a successful campaign with the Privy Council and Board of Trade to have the Act repealed, or disallowed. Reverend James Maury of Hanover, emboldened by his colleague's success, sued his parish for back pay. The Hanover County Court recognized the disallowance, and a jury was selected to determine what he was lawfully owed.

Patrick Henry, representing the parish, persuaded the jury that when "a King...degenerated into a Tyrant," he forfeited "all right to his subjects' Obedience." He asserted the right of the colony to enact its own laws, and asked the jury to "make such an example of the plaintiff, as might hereafter be a warning." His unambiguous hostility to the established Anglican Church was underscored by his reference to Maury and his colleagues as "rapacious harpies," ready to snatch food and shelter from the poor and distressed.

The jury, charged with deciding the amount of Maury's entitled back pay, awarded him the grand sum of one penny. The disallowed Act, passed by the colony's own General Assembly, was a regulatory law, which, in the mercantilist scheme of things then, was complementary to and as intrusive and pernicious as any passed by Parliament. Still, it was an act of self-governance by Virginians that was arbitrarily annulled by the Crown. The Hanover jury both obeyed the Crown, and defied it.

Some historians date the first serious articulation of revolution to Otis; others, to Henry. It is a moot point. Their words, verging on the received definition of treason, were not "shots heard 'round the world," but rather presageful alarms that stung the restive consciousness of any man accustomed to thought. They set the tone and terms for everything that was to follow.

Jack Frake and Hugh Kenrick, rebels from two distinct strata of English society, and moved by differing visions of liberty, would now become dedicated revolutionaries: one imbued with a steady, quiet certitude; the other, with an articulate, impassioned patriotism.